"Makes very clear that we have a long v of all kinds of homophobia and racism lesbian and gay as well as the black wo ful collection gives the strong feeling .... .... ...,... writers of the near future will be gay and lesbian writers of color, western and non-western as their public and private experiences are the richest to imagine. EXEMPLIFIES THE LUSH DIVERSITY OF THE QUEER WORLDS AND THE GREAT PROBLEMS DIFFERENCES STILL POSE TO THEM."

—Gert Hekma, PhD, Gay and Lesbian Studies, University of Amsterdam

"A clear articulation and analysis of the voices, identities, and subjectivities of lesbian and gay writers of color. Speaks from the cutting-edge of the discipline as they interrogate issues of borders and boundaries, postmodernism and postcolonialism, destabilized identities and plural subjectivities, and shifting centers and margins.... AN ESSENTIAL ADDITION TO THE LIBRARIES OF ALL READERS AND WRITERS IN THE FIELD."

—Bonnie Zimmerman, PhD, Professor of Women's Studies, San Diego State University

"Offers challenging considerations of a diverse body of literature representing many nationalities and cultures. . . . The young scholars represented in this book bring contemporary critical theory and lesbian/gay theory to bear on these myriad subjects. . . . CORRECTS THE NEGLECT OF SCHOLARLY CONSIDERATION OF THE IMAGINATIVE PRODUCTIONS OF QUEER PEOPLE OF COLOR and disrupts the notion of homogeneity of lesbian and gay cultural productions."

—John M. Clum, Professor of English and Professor of the Practice of Theater, Duke University

# Critical Essays:
# Gay and Lesbian Writers
# of Color

# Critical Essays: Gay and Lesbian Writers of Color

Emmanuel S. Nelson, PhD
Editor

*Critical Essays: Gay and Lesbian Writers of Color*, edited by Emmanuel S. Nelson, was simultaneously issued by The Haworth Press, Inc., under the same title, as a special issue of *Journal of Homosexuality*, Volume 26, Numbers 2/3, 1993, John P. DeCecco, Editor.

Harrington Park Press
An Imprint of
The Haworth Press, Inc.
New York · London · Norwood (Australia)

ISBN 1-56023-048-7

**Published by**

**Harrington Park Press, 10 Alice Street, Binghamton, NY 13904-1580**

**Harrington Park Press is an Imprint of the Haworth Press, Inc., 10 Alice Street, Binghamton, Ny 13904-1580 USA.**

*Critical Essays : Gay and Lesbian Writers of Color,* has also been published as *Journal of Homosexuality,* Volume 26, Numbers 2/3 1993.

The development, preparation, and publication of this work has been undertaken with great care. However, the publisher, employees, editors, and agents of The Haworth Press and all imprints of The Haworth Press, Inc., including The Haworth Medical Press and Pharmaceutical Products Press, are not responsible for any errors contained herein or for consequences that may ensue from use of materials or information contained in this work. Opinions expressed by the author(s) are not necessarily those of The Haworth Press, Inc.

The Haworth Press, Inc., 10 Alice Street, Binghamton, NY 13904-1580 USA

**Library of Congress Cataloging-in-Publication Data**

Critical essays : gay and lesbian writers of color / Emmanuel S. Nelson, editor.
    p. cm.
    "Also . . . published as Journal of homosexuality, volume 26, Numbers 2/3 1993."
    Includes bibliographical references (p.) and index.
    ISBN 1-56024-482-8 (H : acid free paper).–ISBN 1-56023-048-7 (HPP : acid free paper)
    1. Gays' writings, American–History and criticism. 2. American literature–Minority authors–History and Criticism. 3. Homosexuality and literature–United States. 4. Ethnic groups in literature. 5. Minorities in literature. 6. Lesbians in literature. 7. Gay men in literature. 8. Race in literature. I. Nelson, Emmanuel S. (Emmanuel Sampath), 1954- .
PS153.G38C75 1993
810.9'920664–dc20
                                                    93-30614
                                                      CIP

In remembrance of James Baldwin
(1924–1987)

and Audre Lorde
(1934–1992)

# INDEXING & ABSTRACTING

Contributions to this publication are selectively indexed or abstracted in print, electronic, online, or CD-ROM version(s) of the reference tools and information services listed below. This list is current as of the copyright date of this publication. See the end of this section for additional notes.

- *Abstracts in Anthropology*, Baywood Publishing Company, 26 Austin Avenue, P.O. Box 337, Amityville, NY 11701

- *Abstracts of Research in Pastoral Care & Counseling*, Loyola College, 7135 Minstrel Way, Suite 101, Columbia, MD 21045

- *Academic Abstracts/CD-ROM*, EBSCO Publishing, P.O. Box 2250 Peabody, MA 01960-7250

- *Applied Social Sciences Index & Abstracts (ASSIA)*, Bowker-Saur Limited, 60 Grosvenor Street, London W1X 9DA, England

- *Bulletin Signaletique*, INIST/CNRS-Service Gestion des Documents Primaires, 2, allee du Parc de Brabois, F-54514 Vandoeuvre-les-Nancy, Cedex, France

- *Cambridge Scientific Abstracts*, *Risk Abstracts,* Cambridge Information Group, 7200 Wisconsin Avenue, #601, Bethesda, MD 20814

- *Criminal Justice Abstracts*, Willow Tree Press, 15 Washington Street, 4th Floor, Newark, NJ 07102

- *Criminology,  Penology and Police ScienceAbstracts*, Kugler Publications, P.O. Box 11188, 1001 GD-Amstelveen, The Netherlands

- *Current Contents/Social & Behavioral Sciences*, Institute for Scientific Information, 3501 Market Street, Philadelphia, PA 19104-3302

(continued)

- *Digest of Neurology and Psychiatry*, The Institute of Living, 400 Washington Street, Hartford, CT 06106

- *Excerpta Medica/Electronic Publishing Division*, Elsevier Science Publishers, 655 Avenue of the Americas, New York, NY 10010

- *Expanded Academic Index*, Information Access Company, 362 Lakeside Drive, Forest City, CA 94404

- *Family Violence & Sexual Assault Bulletin*, Family Violence & Sexual Assault Institute, 1310 Clinic Drive, Tyler, TX 75701

- *Gay/Lesbian Periodicals Index*, Integrity Indexing, 2012 Queens Road West #1, Charlotte, NC 28207

- *Index Medicus/MEDLINE*, National Library of Medicine, 8600 Rockville Pike, Bethesda, MD 20894

- *Index to Periodical Articles Related to Law*, University of Texas, 727 East 26th Street, Austin, TX 78705

- *Inventory of Marriage and Family Literature (online and hard copy)*, National Council on Family Relations, 3989 Central Avenue NE, Suite 550, Minneapolis, MN 55421

- *Mental Health Abstracts (online through DIALOG)*, IFI/Plenum Data Company, 3202 Kirkwood Highway, Wilmington, DE 19808

- *Periodical Abstracts, Research 1*, UMI Data Courier, P.O. Box 32770, Louisville, KY 40232-2770

- *Periodical Abstracts, Research 2*, UMI Data Courier, P.O. Box 32770, Louisville, KY 40232-2770

- *Progress in Palliative Care, "abstracts section,"* University of Leeds, Oncology Information Service, Leeds LS2 9JT, United Kingdom

(continued)

- *PsychNet*, PsychNet Inc., 980 Atlantic Avenue #105, Alameda, CA 94501-1018

- *Psychological Abstracts (PsycINFO)*, American Psychological Association, P.O. Box 91600, Washington, DC 20090-1600

- *Public Affairs Information Bulletin (PAIS)*, Public Affairs Information Service Inc., 521 West 43rd Street, New York, NY 10036-4396

- *Religion Index One: Periodicals*, American Theological Library Association, 820 Church Street, 3rd Floor, Evanston, IL 60201

- *Sage Family Studies Abstracts*, Sage Publications, Inc., 2455 Teller Road, Newbury Park, CA 91320

- *Social Planning/Policy & Development Abstracts (SOPODA)*, Sociological Abstracts, Inc., P.O. Box 22206, San Diego, CA 92192-0206

- *Social Sciences Citation Index*, Institute for Scientific Information, 3501 Market Street, Philadelphia, PA 19104

- *Social Sciences Index*, The H.W. Wilson Company, 950 University Avenue, Bronx, NY 10452

- *Social Work Research & Abstracts*, National Association of Social Workers, 750 First Street NW, 8th Floor, Washington, DC 20002

- *Sociological Abstracts (SA)*, Sociological Abstracts, Inc., P.O. Box 22206, San Diego, CA 92192-0206

- *Studies on Women Abstracts,* Carfax Publishing Company, P.O. Box 25, Abingdon, Oxfordshire OX14 3UE, United Kingdom

Book reviews are selectively excerpted by the Guide to Professional Literature of the Journal of Academic Librarianship.

(continued)

# SPECIAL BIBLIOGRAPHIC NOTES

*related to indexing, abstracting, and library access services*

☐ indexing/abstracting services in this list will also cover material in the "separate" that is co-published simultaneously with Haworth's special thematic journal issue or DocuSerial. Indexing/abstracting usually covers material at the article/chapter level.

☐ monographic co-editions are intended for either non-subscribers or libraries which intend to purchase a second copy for their circulating collections.

☐ monographic co-editions are reported to all jobbers/wholesalers/approval plans. The source journal is listed as the "series" to assist the prevention of duplicate purchasing in the same manner utilized for books-in-series.

☐ to facilitate user/access services all indexing/abstracting services are encouraged to utilize the co-indexing entry note indicated at the bottom of the first page of each article/chapter/contribution.

☐ this is intended to assist a library user of any reference tool (whether print, electronic, online, or CD-ROM) to locate the monographic version if the library has purchased this version but not a subscription to the source journal.

☐ individual articles/chapters in any Haworth publication are also available through the Haworth Document Delivery Services (HDDS).

# ABOUT THE EDITOR

**Emmanuel S. Nelson, PhD**, is Associate Professor of English at the State University of New York at Cortland. Author of over two dozen articles on ethnic, post-colonial, and gay literatures, he has edited *Connections: Essays on Black Literatures* (1988), *Reworlding: The Literature of the Indian Diaspora (1992), AIDS: The Literary Response* (1992), *Bharati Mukherjee: Critical Perspectives* (1993), *Contemporary Gay American Novelists: A Bio-Bibliographical Critical Sourcebook* (1993), and *Writers of the Indian Diaspora: A Bio-Bibliographical Critical Sourcebook* (1993).

# CONTENTS

# Preface

In the fall of 1983 I was invited by a periodical to review *Literary Visions of Homosexuality*–a special theme issue of the *Journal of Homosexuality* (spring/summer 1983) that was guest edited by Stuart Kellogg. My review, in general, was a favorable one: I pointed out that it was an impressive collection of finely written essays, that many of the contributors were eminent critics, and that the volume made a significant contribution to the rapidly growing field of gay literary criticism and scholarship. But I also felt compelled to point out the white male bias of the work. Among the twelve essays in the collection, only one dealt with lesbian writing; none acknowledged even the existence of gay/lesbian writers of color. Such exclusionary practices, I concluded, raised several troubling questions about issues of race, gender, and class in gay academic scholarship as well as in the gay "community" at large.

By chance, in the summer of 1990, I met John De Cecco–the editor of the *Journal of Homosexuality*–while we were both visiting Holland. Our conversation about the special issue and my review of that issue led to a broader discussion of the various patterns of exclusion that deform white gay/lesbian social practices, representational systems, and academic discourses. During that discussion De Cecco proposed that I guest edit a special theme issue of the *Journal of Homosexuality,* and he suggested that I might–as a calculated response to the issue edited by Kellogg–focus exclusively on the imaginative work of gay/lesbian writers of color in the United States. This collection of essays, then, was conceived at least initially as a corrective to an earlier special issue of the *Journal* and, by extension, as a challenge to the marginalization and tokenization of gay men and lesbians of color in general.

But this volume is more than a mere corrective; it seeks to be disruptive as well. The twelve essays that follow my brief prefatory statement discuss the works of selected Native American, Asian

American, African American, and Latino(a) writers. Collectively, the essays offer simultaneous challenges to ethnic as well as mainstream homophobia, to straight as well as queer racism. More specifically, however, this volume is deliberately designed to interrupt and counter the dominant white gay/lesbian discourses. It disrupts, for example, the complacent notion of a unified gay/lesbian "community" by questioning the presumed unity that is thought to be generated by a shared sexual identity. It re-problematizes the categories "gay" and "lesbian" by insisting on the interacting as well as competing nature of racial, sexual, and class identities. It seeks to affirm heterogeneity by unsettling the tiresomely absurd and pathologically imperialist assumptions of white universality. Though this volume is not by any means an outcome of a separatist critical enterprise–after all, not all of the contributors to it are scholars of color–it does actively dislodge the white subject from the center of critical inquiry, and it unapologetically centralizes the gay/lesbian subject of color.

Yet I am acutely conscious of the many contradictions that this project is vulnerable to. For example, the term "people of color," though it might be a convenient signifier, has the essentializing as well as homogenizing tendency to collapse boundaries, deny differences, and conflate identities. Moreover, the various writers discussed in this volume certainly do not collectively constitute any coherent political movement; nor do they share a common ideological agenda or advocate an identical program for liberation. And although one of its declared objectives is to subvert white gay/lesbian hegemony, this volume has the potential for inscribing a new set of hierarchies and for reinscribing old patterns of exclusion: African American gay/lesbian writing, for instance, tends to dominate this collection of essays, and there is an embarrassing absence of any direct engagement with Native American gay male experience. Even my own editorial involvement with this project–given my rather ambivalent insider/outsider position as a diasporic postcolonial Indian immigrant middle-class "gay" academic who happens to be living and teaching in the United States–is not entirely unproblematic.

I am, nevertheless, convinced of the intellectual legitimacy and the political necessity of this project. Even though this volume might perpetuate on a minor scale some of the very patterns that it seeks to subvert, it does indeed succeed brilliantly in creating a resistant, counter-discursive space where we–as gay men, lesbians, and bisexuals of color–see reflections of our lives and explorations of issues critical to our survival. Differences there are among us, of course, but our shared consciousness of the many forms of exclusion and defilement that we experience in our daily lives, I believe, is sufficiently potent and significant to encourage mutual recognition, initiate honest dialogues, and forge political links among ourselves. This volume, I hope, makes at least a modest academic contribution to that practical goal.

I would like to take this opportunity to thank all of the contributors to this project; their enthusiasm and professionalism made my editorial task a thoroughly enjoyable one. Thanks also to Hubert Kennedy at the Center for Education and Research in Sexuality (CERES) for his meticulous handling of the manuscript. And a special thanks to John De Cecco for his firm commitment to this project, for his friendship, and for the many pleasant strolls along the canals of Amsterdam on leisurely summer afternoons.

*Emmanuel S. Nelson*
*SUNY College at Cortland*
*October 2, 1992*

# Surveying the Intersection:
# Pathology, Secrecy, and the Discourses
# of Racial and Sexual Identity

Marylynne Diggs, PhD (cand.)

*University of Oregon*

**SUMMARY.** "Surveying the Intersection: Pathology, Secrecy, and the Discourses of Racial and Sexual Identity" cautions against the risks of metaphorical imperialism in readings of codified gay and lesbian representation. Taking issue with Foucault's suggestion that the secret of the nineteenth century was the secret of sex, I suggest that, in nineteenth-century American culture, where African-American identity and equality were among the most controversial issues of the century, the secrets of identity were secrets of race as well. Because scientific and literary representations of pathological and/or secret, essential identities are sites of intersection in the discourses of homosexual and mixed-race identity, they should be investigated as intersections, rather than read as codifications of sexual difference.

Surveying the discourses of scientific racism, genetics, and eugenics, and doing readings of Frances E. W. Harper's *Iola Leroy* and Alice Dunbar-Nelson's "The Stones of the Village," I suggest that Harper's representation of the mulatto leader can be read as an act of resistance to the representation of the mulatto as a degenerate, hybrid

Correspondence may be addressed to the author at: Department of English, University of Oregon, Eugene, OR 97403.

[Haworth co-indexing entry note]: "Surveying the Intersection: Pathology, Secrecy, and the Discourses of Racial and Sexual Identity." Diggs, Marylynne. Co-published simultaneously in the *Journal of Homosexuality* (The Haworth Press, Inc.) Vol. 26, No. 2/3, 1993, pp. 1-19; and: *Critical Essays: Gay and Lesbian Writers of Color* (ed: Emmanuel S. Nelson) The Haworth Press, Inc., 1993, pp. 1-19. Multiple copies of this article/chapter may be purchased from The Haworth Document Delivery Center [1-800-3-HAWORTH; 9:00 a.m. - 5:00 p.m. (EST)].

*1*

species; and that in Dunbar-Nelson's story, the thematics of passing, secrecy, and the fear of detection, while having a recognizably homoerotic quality, should not be read simply as a codification of homosexual difference and panic. I conclude with a call for more work on historicizing the intersection of racial and sexual identity in the discourses of pathology and degeneration.

## I

For scholars of gay and lesbian studies interested in literature of the United States written before the Harlem Renaissance, incorporating texts by writers of color into discussions of the representation of homosexuality is fraught with many difficulties. Writing about gay or lesbian literature before the turn of the twentieth century is problematic in itself because of the controversy involved in determining when homosexuality was constructed as an identity. If we are to avoid risking historical imperialism, it is important that we not define nineteenth-century same-sex representations in twentieth-century terms. This historical imperialism is often compounded in lesbian criticism with a kind of metaphorical imperialism. As Julie Abraham suggests, the interest in codified lesbian representation and the use of lesbian as a metaphor, insofar as these approaches see narrative experimentation or figures of monstrosity or abjection as characteristically lesbian forms of representation, threaten to subsume under the sign of lesbian a variety of representations and significations of cultural marginality (262-5).

Michel Foucault's argument in *The History of Sexuality* that, in the nineteenth century, identity was characterized by secrecy–the secret of sex–encourages those interested in studying representations of homosexuality to read all inscriptions of a secret, pathological identity as inscriptions of sexual identity, thus effecting another metaphorical imperialism (69-70). In researching a larger project that examines literary resistance to scientific constructions of sexuality and mixed-race identity in the nineteenth century, I am looking at many texts which were not written by self-identified gay and lesbian writers. A question occurred to me when reading nineteenth-century texts by African-American men and women, similarly not self-identified as gay or lesbian, who participated in this discourse of difference and secrecy: Is Foucault's idea about secrecy and identity applicable to nineteenth-century American culture, where African identity and racial equality were among the most controversial issues of the century?

I would argue that, particularly in the United States, the secret of identity, contrary to Foucault's suggestion, was not only the secret of sex, but also the secret of race. Foucault himself suggests that eugenics, as part of a technology made up of "perversion-heredity-degenerescence," was a major part of the technology of sex (118). But the specificity of race constituted as a secret, as well as what he means by race, is something he does not address directly. Given this complication of Foucault's thesis, I want to state something that, to some, may seem obvious; but I'll say it anyway because it has to be said as explicitly as possible: There is nothing absolutely unique to gay and lesbian literature about finding out your "true" identity, dealing with scientific representations of that identity as pathological, and fearing that others will detect your secret, pathologized identity.

During the Reconstruction, and continuing through the turn of the century, many African-Americans wrote novels or autobiographies about "passing." At the same time, informed by the interest in the "origin of man" and the discourses of scientific racism, genetics, evolution, and eugenics, there was an explosion in scientific writing about racial "inferiority" and the degeneration and imminent extinction of the Anglo-Saxon population. While homosexuals were seen as signs of the degeneration toward an original bisexuality or a kind of genetic mutation, an intermediate type between man and woman, African-Americans were seen as atavistic throwbacks to an earlier evolutionary stage, perhaps a separate species altogether. African-American "mulattoes" were thus an intermediate type, a type that confused the binary categories of the two-color system like the homosexual confused binary gender categories.

The political stakes involved in maintaining the hierarchy of these two-color and two-gender systems were, and continue to be, extremely high. With science becoming the culturally authorized discourse of knowledge in the nineteenth century, and biological concepts of purity, health, and pathology the dominant paradigms for this knowledge, the human sciences became the site of production for biological explanations of and justifications for social practices of oppression and exclusion.[1] Representing confusions of the binary paradigm of gender and race identification, homosexuals and mixed-race peoples were, by definition, pathological. For rather than prohibiting certain behaviors, the human sciences of the nineteenth century simply normalized certain identities and produced vast taxonomies for categorizing as pathological those who did not fit the norm (Martin 8). The construction of the individual, normal human subject, and the construction of all variations from this subject as pathological, are perfect examples of the operations of a science which has as its aim the production and naturalization of an order designed to ensure that, as Katherine Cummings puts it, "the outside(r) be kept out and the inside(r) in" (72).

By the early twentieth century, the eugenics movement was linked with sexology in an effort to regulate the population and maintain its racial and sexual purity by eliminating the proliferation of "racial hybrids" and the "third sex."[2] It should come as no surprise that the racially and sexually deviant, both "outcasts from evolution," would create literary representations of the self which have in common a thematic concern with resisting definitions of the self as pathological and fearing detection or exposure. This is not to say that representations of race and sexuality mean the same thing, or that African-American narratives about passing are really encoded representations of homosexuality, but rather that the discourses of racial and sexual identity, insofar as they are discourses about pathology or secrecy, are places where racial and sexual identity intersect, points at which they coincide, and also points at which they diverge. Pathology and secrecy are thematic sites where the discourses of racial science, racial identity, sexual science, and sexual identity cross over one another and interconnect, informing one another, developing similar representations of the self, meeting related ideological interests, and yet retaining a specificity which any simplistic conflation of the discourses and identities elides.

The subject of this chapter, then, is not so much the literature of gay or lesbian people of color, but the places where the discourse of race (in this case, a specific discourse about African-American "hybridity") and the discourse of homosexuality intersect. By choosing this as a focus I am not, of course, assuming that these identities cannot intersect in one subjectivity or one act of self-representation; nor am I suggesting that the racial sciences did not produce specific sexual constructions of race for, indeed, there are racialized sexes and sexualized races.[3] Rather, my aim is to suggest a way of including writers of color in the study of literature written when homosexuality was not institutionalized as an identity, or when self-identified gay or lesbian writers of color were rare. Rather than conflating racial and sexual difference, or making difficult biographical assumptions about writers of color on the basis of codified literary representations, we might look at the intersection of these discourses of identity. In what follows, I survey the discourse of nineteenth-century racial science, examine to what extent literature about mulatto racial identity resists the pathological model, and then conclude with a reading of a text about passing which could be read as codified homosexual panic, but which, I will argue, is clearly about the secrecy of race.

## II

The discourses of both racial and sexual identity grew from a common scientific conception of identity, difference, and pathology. At the heart of nineteenth-century human sciences was an attempt to constitute and differentiate the healthy and the sick, the normal and the abnormal. In the introduction to *Degeneration*, J. Edward Chamberlin and Sander Gilman note that "Nineteenth-century science combined a fiercely categorical instinct with a fierce interest in the nature of things" (x). This hunger took shape in the human sciences as a movement to categorize differences in the human species by multiplying the taxonomies of variation from an assumed, privileged norm (Stepan, "Race and Gender" 39-41). Informed conceptually by a belief in the normative western humanist subject—unitary, self-contained, and individualistic; white, male, and sexually attracted to the opposite sex—these scientific discourses operated to stabilize and maintain the health and purity of the human self, the human body, and the Anglo-Saxon human race.

Although the Caucasian male remained the point of reference for discussions of human variation, the sciences produced an enormous system of discrete categories for defining and describing the variations from this presumed normal human subject. Variants from this normative conception of the white male subject were not simply biological curiosities; their differences were, of course, invested with hierarchical meanings. Thus particular individuals, rather than retaining a universal signification, were invested with distinctions and identities which pathologized certain "types" of people, making them symptomatic of the threat to social progress, and evidence of the potential for the degeneration of the human race (Nye 50).

While women, the sexually "perverse," and the insane were the object of much of this discourse, at least as much scientific production was invested in situating African-Americans into an essentially inferior relation to the white, western enlightenment individual. Texts like *Types of Mankind*, the collection on biology and race edited in 1854 by Josiah Nott and George Gliddon, constitute the African-American as an essentially different subject, a "type of mankind" with a particular identity. If the enlightenment subject was a thinking, reasoning, unitary individual, the African-American must necessarily be instinctual, driven by the passions, and dependent upon others for survival (Nott and Gliddon 460-2).

Many nineteenth-century theories of race contended that the distinctions between all of the human races, and particularly the Caucasian and the African, were so great that they constituted unique types with differences in physical, moral, and intellectual capabilities (Stepan, "Biological" 100). Monogenist scientists contended that the races all originated from one type; all of the other races either evolved from this type or were the result of environmental conditions or regional variations. Other scientists founded their belief in the essential difference of the races on the polygenist hypothesis that there have always been separate races of man and we are all descended from various types which have been relatively stable over time (J. Haller 70-79). While there was little agreement between monogenists and polygenists on the specifics concerning the etiology of racial differences, their conclusions were similar: Caucasians and Africans were different in a fundamental way, either by design or by evolution, and these differences constituted them as separate species which must be kept socially, sexually, and genetically separate.

Since the eighteenth-century definition of species was that members of the same species were interfertile, the evidence of interfertility between blacks and whites implied that they belonged to the same species. Rather than accept this, the scientific community effectively re-defined what was meant by species in order to provide a biological rationale for the social and sexual segregation of the races. As Nancy Stepan notes, these manipulations of the terminology resulted in a "flexible biological theory of species and fertility, protean in its capacity to incorporate and interpret all the social and racial variations possible on the theme of mixing" ("Biological" 105-6). The terms "species" and "races," "hybrids" and "mongrels" were the subject of a great deal of discussion and definition, and became thoroughly confused by the various interpretations and schools of monogenist and polygenist thought. The result was a fusion of the terms such that, with the exception of a few specialists, to most people they signified the same thing: an essential biological, moral, intellectual difference between Caucasians and people of color, any genetic mixing of which would create monstrous biological aberrations (J. Haller 76; Stepan, "Biological" 105-8).

The mulatto was a primary focus of this discourse by the end of the nineteenth century. A denomination which was intended to associate etymologically the offspring of mixed-race unions with the mule, an infertile product of crossing between different species, the mulatto became the human example of racial instability in the zoological rhetoric of hybridization, an example which, it was hoped, would discourage interracial relations (Stepan, "Biological" 106-7). Characterized variously as weak and degenerate, or an intermediate between African and Caucasian saved from barbarism only to the extent of the infusion of Caucasian blood, the mulatto became the symbol of the consequence of transgressing the boundaries of species, either socially or sexually. Nott and Gliddon list the supposed weaknesses of "mulattoes," including their short life span, "intermediate intelligence," and physical delicacy; mulatto women are singled out as particularly weak, being "bad breeders, bad nurses," and "liable to abortions" (373). Paul Broca claims that mulattoes lack the fertility of "pure" Caucasians or "negresses," using this claim as evidence of their unnatural hybridity and as evidence that racial mixing itself is unnatural (32). As late as 1920, Lothrop Stoddard stated that the offspring of interracial union is "a mongrel–a walking chaos, so consumed by his jarring heredities that he is quite worthless" (166).

The mulatto shared this discourse of pathology with other human differences which confused the boundaries of the two-color or two-gender concept of the human species. The notion of inherited or ancestral pathology took on a life of its own. Eugene Talbot's *Degeneracy: Its Causes, Signs, and Results* (1898), as Nancy Stepan says, posited pathological degeneracy as any imaginable kind of difference which could be lurking unobserved in one's constitution. Stepan writes:

> Degeneracy in this sense was a pervasive, subtle decay of the individual or group, a deviation from a standard of normality, which was caused by some transgression of social, moral, or physical rules and which became established in the hereditary constitution of the individual. (112)

This specter of an undetectable, hidden taint was shared by racial and sexual minorities who, informed by the cultural paranoia about dormant but inherited, essential, and pathological identities, were encouraged to keep themselves under constant surveillance.

The construction of difference as biologically, and therefore essentially, pathological, and of difference and pathology as essentially degenerative, worked as a technology of control and regulation, constituting difference as a shameful secret and thus ensuring self-surveillance. Both racial and sexual identity were thus something you could discover about yourself and something you must keep secret from others. This is where the narratives of racial and sexual identities intersect and where the similarity between narratives about "passing" and narratives about "coming out" or being "outed" lies. African-Americans light enough in color to "pass" and homosexuals were both deemed pathological, intermediate types in the discourse of the nineteenth century. Racial hybrids were "perversions" of race and sexual perverts were, according to Eugene Talbot, "representative of a 'still blacker phase of biology'" (qtd. in Stepan, "Biological" 112-3). Thus, both homosexual and mixed-race African-Americans harbored a secret about the self, a secret which, if detected by others, could ruin one's life. For if, as Foucault asserts, homosexuality was constituted as the sexual secret of the century, mixed-race identity was constituted as the racial secret of the same period.

The two questions I want to pose, given these intersections in the construction of racial and sexual identity, are to what extent are scientific constructions of racial identity interpellated or resisted by African-Americans writing about the mixed-race African-American; and in narratives about passing, how is this narrative of surveillance and detection represented? My interest in the first question arises in connection with the thesis of a larger study on sexual and racial sciences and resistance in American Literature in which I argue that sexually and racially constructed subjects rarely interpellate unproblematically the scientific constructions of pathological identity, but rather engage in struggles for authority over representation. In my consideration of this question I will turn to Frances E. W. Harper's *Iola Leroy, or Shadows Uplifted* to suggest that Harper is simultaneously inscribing white middle-class values and resisting nineteenth-century racial discourses of pathological hybridity. In my examination of the narrative of secrecy and detection, I will focus on Alice Dunbar-Nelson's "The Stones of the Village."

## III

*Iola Leroy* maintains an explicit didactic impulse which makes it clear that race and gender are the central issues in the novel, suggesting that the novel is a site of struggle between self-definition, interpellation of the scientific construction of racial difference, and resistance to these scientific determinations. Harper's novel has been criticized for its representation of the "elite mulatto" as the new middle-class especially well-equipped to uplift the blacker members of the race (Christian 28-9, 33). I would argue something similar to Claudia Tate's suggestion that the representation of middle class concerns in post-bellum fiction by black women is a kind of protest (Tate 107). Given the scientific representations of mulattoes at the turn of the century, Harper's novel may have been more politically challenging then than its Christian assimilationist politics seem to us today. Historicizing its assimilationist representations of African-Americans reveals how mainstream the novel's

nineteenth-century middle-class values were, as well as how promoting these values in the black community conflicted with the
white supremist, separatist politics of scientific racism. For Harper
to suggest that African-Americans might identify with white,
middle-class, Christian values and participate as full citizens in
social and political culture was to suggest something unthinkable to
both the racial scientists and those who believed in the scientific
construction of the African-American.

The primary characters in Harper's novel–Iola, Harry, and their
uncle Robert–are of mixed-race ancestry. Although they are all light
enough to pass for white, and Iola and Harry spent most of their
youth under the impression that they were white, they all refuse to
pass, and none of them see "black blood" as a taint. Harper represents both mixed-race and black African-Americans as cultural
leaders. Miss Delany, one of the novel's few African-Americans
with no white blood, is described by Harry as "more than witty, she
is wise; more than brilliant, she is excellent"; he also says that she is
beautiful, or "well-formed . . . Neither hair nor complexion show
the least hint of blood admixture" (Harper 198-9). A graduate of a
major University, Miss Delany is described as a leader in the community who, as a symbol of black racial purity, is a "living argument for the capability which is in the race" (199). Iola herself says,
"The best blood in my veins is African blood, and I am not
ashamed of it" (205).

Harper's representation of both the mulatto and the pure-blood
African-American as leaders could be read as a daring resistance to
the racial scientists' construction of the mulatto as a pathological
figure. The "hybrid" mulatto whose health and competence are
fragile does not exist in *Iola Leroy*. In addition to her interest in
educating emancipated slaves and promoting Christian values, tem-
perance, and women's equality, Harper represented racially-mixed
African-Americans as healthy, industrious individuals connected to
the black community; they are proud and strong because of the
"black blood" in their veins rather than the "white blood." Although Iola adheres to the racialist idea of "black blood" and
"white blood" representing racial ancestry, she does not see that
ancestry as determining physical health or moral character. She
says, "When we have learned to treat men according to the com-

plexion of their souls, and not the color of their skins, we will have given our best contribution towards the solution of the negro problem" (212). The racial scientists of the nineteenth century believed that the color of one's skin determined the "complexion" of the soul; for Josiah Nott and George Gliddon, among others, the two were inseparable. But for Iola, the complexion of the skin did not determine the complexion of the soul.

Harper's awareness of the major debates in the racial sciences is further evident in the discussion she stages between Dr. Latrobe, Dr. Gresham, Dr. Latimer, and Rev. Carmicle in the "Open Questions" chapter, a title which suggests her resistance to the answers provided by scientific racism. Dr. Latrobe is a vehement white supremist who believes that Africans should be grateful to have been removed from heathenism in Africa and introduced to a higher civilization and the one true religion. He cannot conceive of differences without seeing them hierarchically, responding to the suggestion of equality between the races by saying "we Southerners will never submit to negro supremacy. We will never abandon our Caucasian civilization to an inferior race" (221). Equality is not a possibility in his view; where there is difference, there is "supremacy" and inferiority. His refusal to see the value of equality is summed up in his statement, "what kind of society would we have if we put down the bars and admitted everybody to social equality?" (228).

Dr. Gresham's amalgamationist response to the problem of equality is "the absorption of the negro into our race," a proposal to which Dr. Latrobe vehemently objects, seeing it as bringing on the potential degeneration of civilization (228). When Dr. Latimer, the only African-American doctor present, argues that this "absorption" was begun by the white slaveholders, Dr. Latrobe refuses to discuss the matter, asserting only that, although there are blacks as white as himself, "the taint of blood is there and we always exclude it . . . there are tricks of blood which always betray them. My eyes are more practiced than yours. I can always tell them" (229). Latrobe's confidence in this ability to detect the invisible taint is undermined when Dr. Latimer, who has been passing as white in this discussion with Dr. Latrobe, later discloses his own connection to the black race. Dr. Latimer, the only passing character in the novel, passes for educational effect only. He gets Latrobe's respect, then "comes out," proving wrong both Latrobe's belief in the inferiority of the race as well as his theory about detection.

Although the other debaters are not as vehemently racist as Dr. Latrobe, both Dr. Gresham, a white man who hopes to marry Iola, and Rev. Carmicle, a black Christian reformer, maintain a degree of white, Western supremacy. Dr. Gresham thinks he is progressive on the race issue; yet he sees Africa as a heathen land with a barbaric influence on Southern culture: "the young colonies could not take into their early civilization a stream of barbaric blood without being affected by its influence, and the negro, poor and despised as he is, has laid his hands on our Southern civilization and helped mould its character" (217). His suggestion that the atrocities committed by white Southerners are an effect of their association with the barbarism of Africa reveals how twisted his so-called "progressivism" is. Ultimately his amalgamationist, assimilationist politics call for the eradication of racial differences, resulting in the maintenance of white skin and western culture. But, in a significant commentary on her commitment to the black race, Iola refuses to marry him. Reverend Carmicle, who has "no white blood in his veins," also seems to stand for the rights of African-Americans; but his emphasis on Christian assimilation and his admiration for Western civilization suggest that he believes to some degree in the inferiority of African culture, though not in the biological inferiority of the race.

The focus on medical and religious professionals in this debate calls attention to the novel's intersection with professional discourses and the discursive struggles concerning the "open questions" about race which post-bellum culture had to confront. Dr. Latimer, Iola, and Miss Delany, all hoping to educate blacks, both men and women, for participation in American culture, are the most "progressive" thinkers in the novel. While there are obviously controversial issues involved in their focus on assimilation and integration, it nonetheless represents a distinct resistance to scientific racism's account of African peoples as an essentially different, separate species, biologically unfit for the full responsibilities of citizenship in a democracy. Harper's representation of mulattoes, as well as blacks with no white ancestry, as strong and capable leaders in the political struggles of the Reconstruction challenges the position of racial scientists like Nott and Gliddon. Harper suggests that not only are Africans capable, so are mulattoes; and they are not a separate species, but an integral part of the human race and the social and political culture in the United States.

Harper thus resists the racial scientists' claims about the incapable African and the degenerate mulatto, but she does not effect a subversion of their ideas of difference and separation which might turn separateness, difference, and specificity into sources of empowerment. African-American politics of difference, which perhaps has its most visible expression in the Harlem Renaissance, the black nationalism of the 1960s, and contemporary black feminist discourse, was not recognized as productive in late nineteenth-century culture. During the Reconstruction the political aim of most African-American reformers was to participate in the culture into which they were "emancipated." Perhaps the absence of passing characters in Harper's novel is a testament to her hope and optimism shortly after the Reconstruction. Twentieth-century writers who made passing characters central to their work may have recognized what Harper perhaps did not. The end of chattel slavery did not mean the beginning of social justice, nor did it ensure the cohesiveness of a variety of mixed- and "pure-blood" African-Americans.

## *IV*

Alice Dunbar-Nelson's "The Stones of the Village" is a perfect example of the narrative of passing, secrecy, and the fear of detection. In Harper's *Iola Leroy*, Iola and Harry decide not to pass, and talk of how living "under a veil of concealment, constantly haunted by a dread of detection" is not worth the added status, since it is preferable to "walk the ruggedest paths of life a true man than tread the softest carpets a moral cripple" (Harper 266). Dunbar-Nelson's Victor Grabért makes a different choice. As a young boy, he does not fit into any of the racial categories in his small southern town. When he plays with the "little black and yellow boys of his own age," Grandmère Grabért, his West Indian grandmother, strikes him, saying "What you mean playin' in de strit wid dose niggers?"

When he plays with some other boys "whose faces were white like his own," they call him "nigger" and run away from him (Dunbar-Nelson 5). Neither white nor black, speaking a mix of English and Creole patois, Victor finds himself a complete outsider, the white, yellow, and black kids alike calling him "white nigger," a name which exemplifies the complexity of his racial identity. Grandmère Grabért finally sends him to New Orleans where she says he may be able to "mek one man of himse'f" (6). It is not clear whether she intends for him to pass in order to become one unitary man, a man with a simple relationship to the two-color system. But her recognition that he is not "one man" in this village where children of all races throw stones at him suggests her awareness of the impossibility of his subject position.

In New Orleans, Victor works for a bookseller who, upon dying, leaves him enough money to live off the interest and, through his will, provides for Victor to attend Tulane and become a lawyer. Realizing for the first time that no one in New Orleans has suspected his racial ancestry, Victor Grabért resolves to pass. But once a highly reputable lawyer, married to Elise Vannier, a white woman from one of the best families in town, he often finds himself on the verge of losing control when witness to the injustices faced by people of color. He becomes "morbidly nervous lest something in his manner would betray him" (13). He repeats to himself "I must be careful, I must be careful . . . I must go to the other extreme if necessary," while looking in the mirror, musing "You poor wretch, what are you?" (19).

Grabért's paranoia about confessing or disclosing his secret becomes so obsessive that it actually leads him to risk betraying himself. In scenes very similar to those which Eve Kosofsky Sedgwick identifies as "homosexual panic," Grabért makes every effort to conceal his identity and fears the penetrating "flash" of eyes that may recognize what he so desperately hopes to conceal (Sedgwick, *Between Men* 89, *Epistemology*, 20-21). His eyes "had acquired a habit of veiling themselves under the lashes as if they were concealing something which they feared might be wrenched from them by a stare" (Dunbar-Nelson 21). But Pavageau, a black lawyer in New Orleans who often represents people of color in civil suits, has an insight into Victor Grabért's "true" identity. When Grabért makes a legal decision against allowing the light-skinned grandchild of a black woman to attend the public schools, Pavageau meets his gaze with a "penetrating flash" and asks him whether he would remove his own child from school (26). Although Pavageau only wants him to be fair in his judgments, to do what he knows is right, Grabért has been so fearful of detection that he has become a relentlessly racist, and prominent, judge.

When he must give a speech at a campaign banquet, he fantasizes what a "sensation" he could make if he were to stand up and tell the entire hall what fools he has made of them, that he is "one of the despised ones" (31). As Grabért begins to address the campaign chairman, he hallucinates Grandmère Grabért sitting on the porch of the old two-room house he lived in as a child, and begins to choke as he talks to her softly, until he cannot breathe. His "descent into psychosis and madness," as Gloria T. Hull describes this scene, is the madness of paranoia and panic, panic over the fear that he will betray himself, since nobody else has disclosed his secret (Hull 36). When the men at the banquet rush to his aid, he runs wildly from them believing they are the boys of his old village who threw stones at him and called him "nigger." He stumbles as far as the doorway, where he falls and dies, presumably of a heart attack.

Grabért's experience of passing, while fearing detection and the threat of extortion and blackmail which a flash of penetrating, knowing eyes signals, reminds us of the fear of blackmail or extortion in texts as various as E.M. Forster's *Maurice*, Earl Lind's *Autobiography of an Androgyne*, and Blair Niles' *Strange Brother*. It also reminds us of the contemporary practice of "outing," disclosing the sexual identity of gay or lesbian people who hold positions of power but do not use their power to further gay rights. But far from a codification of the secret of homosexual identity, Grabért's racial identity is central to his panic, showing that, contrary to Foucault's argument in *The History of Sexuality*, sexual secrets are not the only secrets of identity. Although Foucault suggests that the discourse of identity was essentially a discourse about sexuality, and that the dominant theme of this discourse was secrecy and disclosure, a close look at narratives about racial passing indicates that, in the United States especially, the skeletons in the closet were secrets about race as well as secrets about sex.[4]

Written between 1890 and 1920, a period during which the various discourses of evolution, scientific racism, and eugenics reached their height of legitimacy and popular currency prior to their frightening results in the nationalism of Nazi Germany, both *Iola Leroy* and "The Stones of the Village" are part of an important discourse of racial identity. To read these texts as encoding the secret of sexual identity, simply because they represent resistance to pathological identification or passing, secrecy, and the fear of being discovered as, in some way, "queer," neglects the specificity of the narratives. The co-incidence of the crystallization of sexual identity in the discourses of nineteenth-century human sciences and in the popular imagination with the development of ideas about racial identity and the emancipation of African-Americans from slavery provides us with a way of understanding the similarity between these texts and gay or lesbian narratives about coming out, passing, and fearing exposure. But these discourses of identity intersect rather than parallel or encapsulate each other. Pathology and secrecy, both as technologies of control and as thematic concerns in literary and scientific discourses of identity, are shared by racial and sexual minorities. As technologies of control which ensure the maintenance of the two-color, two-gender system, these scientific discourses, and the places where they intersect, are important areas of study for those interested in the intersection of race and sex.

While I have suggested that it would be simplistic to assume that secrecy and sexual difference are one and the same, I recognize that I too have presented a somewhat simplified survey of this intersection, having merely pointed to a certain critical danger and an alternative critical focus which require further inquiry. We might look more closely into the subtleties of these representations of pathologized and secret identities, investigating both the differences and similarities in the rhetoric of scientific racism and sexology. I am interested in historicizing the construction of sexualized races (races represented as having specific sexual characteristics) and racialized sexes (sexualities represented as a different race) as well as the specific ways that constructions of gender work in these representations. Finally, we might do more to find self-identified gay or lesbian people of color who were writing in the late nineteenth and early twentieth century. For in order to be serious about inclusiveness in gay and lesbian studies we will have to resist the formation of new gay and lesbian canons, always asking ourselves what such canons exclude; and when we discover the writers and texts that these canons risk excluding, our incorporation of them should not subsume their differences under newly constructed universals.

## NOTES

1. Louis Althusser argues that science is the only thing outside ideology in "Ideology and Ideological State Apparatuses," *Lenin and Philosophy* (New York: Monthly Review Press, 1971) 171. De Lauretis critiques this in "The Technology of Gender," *Technologies of Gender: Essays on Theory, Film, and Fiction* (Bloomington: Indiana UP, 1987) 9.

2. For histories of scientific racialism and eugenics see Mark Haller (1963), John S. Haller, Jr. (1971), and Daniel Kevles (1985).

3. I consider these issues more directly in a larger project of which this article is a small part. The work of Gloria Anzaldúa, Cherríe Moraga, and Audre Lorde, among others, addresses the problem of constituting race and sexuality as discrete categories of identity. The historical work of Sander Gilman and Nancy Stepan, and theoretical work of Norma Alarcón and Chela Sandoval, among others, provides helpful ways of talking about this. Yvonne Yarbro-Bejarano used the terms racialized sexes and sexualized races in "The Lesbian Body in Latina Cultural Production: Expanding Race and Gender Categories in Gay and Lesbian Studies," a talk she gave at the University of Oregon in April 1992.

4. Sedgwick lists the definitions of closet from the OED in *Epistemology*, 65. This particular usage means "a private or concealed trouble in one's house or circumstances, ever present, and ever liable to come into view."

## WORKS CITED

Abraham, Julie. "History as Explanation: Writing About Lesbian Writing, or 'Are Girls Necessary?'" *Left Politics and the Literary Profession.* Ed. Lennard J. Davis and M. Bella Mirabella. New York: Columbia UP, 1990. 254-83.

Alarcón, Norma. "The Theoretical Subject(s) of This Bridge Called My Back and Anglo-American Feminism." *Haciendo Caras–Making Face, Making Soul: Creative and Critical Perspectives by Women of Color.* Ed. Gloria Anzaldúa. San Francisco: Aunt Lute, 1990. 356-69.

Althusser, Louis. "Ideology and Ideological State Apparatuses." *Lenin and Philosophy.* New York: Monthly Review Press, 1971.

Anzaldúa, Gloria. *Borderlands/La Frontera: The New Mestiza.* San Francisco: Aunt Lute, 1987.

Broca, Paul. *On the Phenomena of Hybridity in the Genus Homo*. London: Longman, Green, Longman, and Roberts, 1864.

Chamberlin, J. Edward, and Sander Gilman, eds. *Degeneration: The Dark Side of Human Progress*. New York: Columbia UP, 1985.

Christian, Barbara. *Black Women Novelists: The Development of a Tradition 1892-1976*. Westport, CT: Greenwood, 1980.

Cummings, Katherine. "Of Purebreds and Hybrids: The Politics of Teaching AIDS in the United States." *Journal of the History of Sexuality* 2 (1991): 68-94.

De Lauretis, Teresa. *Technologies of Gender: Essays on Theory, Film, and Fiction*. Bloomington: Indiana UP, 1987.

Dunbar-Nelson, Alice. "The Stones of the Village." *The Work of Alice Dunbar-Nelson*. 3 vols. New York: Oxford UP, 1988. 3:3-33.

Foucault, Michel. *The History of Sexuality*. 1978. Trans. Robert Hurley. New York: Vintage, 1988.

Gilman, Sander. *Difference and Pathology: Stereotypes of Sexuality, Race, and Madness*. Ithaca: Cornell UP, 1985.

Haller, John S., Jr. *Outcasts from Evolution: Scientific Attitudes of Racial Inferiority, 1859-1900*. Urbana: U of Illinois P, 1971.

Haller, Mark H. *Eugenics: Hereditarian Attitudes in American Thought*. New Brunswick: Rutgers UP, 1963.

Harper, Frances E. W. *Iola Leroy, or Shadows Uplifted*. 1892. Boston: Beacon, 1987.

Hull, Gloria T. "Shaping Contradictions: Alice Dunbar-Nelson and the Black Creole Experience." *New Orleans Review* 15.1 (1988): 34-7.

Kevles, Daniel J. *In the Name of Eugenics: Genetics and the Uses of Human Heredity*. New York: Knopf, 1985.

Lorde, Audre. *Sister Outsider*. Trumansburg, NY: Crossing, 1984.

Martin, Biddy. "Feminism, Criticism, and Foucault." *New German Critique* 27 (1982): 3-30.

Moraga, Cherríe. *Loving in the War Years: lo que nunca pasó por sus labios*. Boston: South End, 1983.

Nott, Josiah, and George Gliddon, eds. *Types of Mankind*. Philadelphia: Lippincott, Grambo, 1854.

Nye, Robert. "Sociology and Degeneration: The Irony of Progress." *Degeneration: The Dark Side of Human Progress*. Ed. J. Edward Chamberlin and Sander Gilman. New York: Columbia UP, 1985. 49-71.

Sandoval, Chela. "U.S. Third World Feminism: The Theory and Method of Oppositional Consciousness in the Postmodern World." *Genders* 10 (1991): 1-24.

Sedgwick, Eve Kosofsky. *Between Men: English Literature and Male Homosocial Desire*. New York: Columbia UP, 1985.

_____ . *Epistemology of the Closet*. Berkeley: U of California P, 1990.

Stepan, Nancy. "Biological Degeneration: Races and Proper Places." *Degeneration: The Dark Side of Human Progress*. Ed. J. Edward Chamberlin and Sander Gilman. New York: Columbia UP, 1985. 97-120.

_____ . "Race and Gender: The Role of Analogy in Science." *Anatomy of Racism*. Ed. David Theo Goldberg. Minneapolis: U of Minneapolis P, 1990. 38-57.

Stoddard, Lothrop. *The Rising Tide of Color Against White World-Supremacy*. New York: Scribner's, 1920.

Tate, Claudia. "Allegories of Black Female Desire: Or, Rereading Nineteenth-Century Sentimental Narratives of Black Female Authority." *Changing Our Own Words: Essays on Criticism, Theory, and Writing by Black Women*. Ed. Cheryl A. Wall. New Brunswick: Rutgers UP, 1989. 98-126.

Yarbro-Bejarano, Yvonne. "The Lesbian Body in Latina Cultural Production: Expanding Race and Gender Categories in Gay and Lesbian Studies." Presentation delivered at the University of Oregon in April 1992.

# Premature Gestures:
# A Speculative Dialogue on Asian Pacific Islander Lesbian and Gay Writing

Alice Y. Hom, PhD (cand.)

*University of California, Los Angeles*

Ming-Yuen S. Ma, MFA (cand.)

*California Institute of the Arts*

**SUMMARY.** A collaborative exploration of the political realities and implications faced by self-identified Asian Pacific Islander lesbian and gay writers. Mixed-genre piece combining the essay and dialogue form, it contains sections co-written as well as individual pieces by the authors. The issues touched upon through this discussion are: available community-based and mainstream publishing venues, development of community-based writing, relation between grassroots political organizing and writing, API and lesbian/gay identity issues, internalized racism and homophobia, and other barriers for API lesbian and gay writers.

Correspondence may be addressed to Alice Y. Hom at: Claremont Graduate School, History Department, 1027 N. Dartmouth, Claremont, CA 91711-5908. Correspondence may be addressed to Ming-Yuen S. Ma at: 1530 North Myra Avenue, Los Angeles, CA 90027.

[Haworth co-indexing entry note]: "Premature Gestures: A Speculative Dialogue on Asian Pacific Islander Lesbian and Gay Writing." Hom, Alicy Y., and Ming-Yuen S. Ma. Co-published simultaneously in the *Journal of Homosexuality* (The Haworth Press, Inc.) Vol. 26, No. 2/3, 1993, pp. 21-51; and *Critical Essays: Gay and Lesbian Writers of Color* (ed: Emmanuel S. Nelson) The Haworth Press, Inc., 1993, pp. 21-51. Multiple copies of this article/chapter may be puchased from The Haworth Document Delivery Center [1-800-3-HAWORTH; 9:00 a.m. - 5:00 p.m. (EST)].

## I. INTRODUCTION: MULTIPLE OPENINGS WITH(IN) A DIALOGUE

*What, then, are the limitations of our practice? How is our practice complicit with certain established societal structures?*

–Ming-Yeung Lu[1]

**MING-YUEN S. MA:** This quote brings up many of the questions that keep coming up in my mind as I work on this project, and I think that they point out the uncertainties in my motives: who am I, a first generation Chinese gay man, who was born but did not grow up in the United States, whose higher education was enabled by my privileged, upper-middle-class background, to write about Asian lesbian and gay writers? What is my placement in the text? What does it mean for us to be writing about works by persons of Asian and Pacific Islander descent in a language that is not our own–though most of us communicate by it?[2]

**ALICE Y. HOM:** As a second-generation Chinese American, raised in a working-class immigrant family but educated in an Ivy League college, I think there are some complexities to the language issue. Many second-, third-, and fourth-generation Asian Americans do not feel their native language is an Asian language. When talking about Asian Pacific Islander lesbian and gay writing, we have to address the definition of "Asian Pacific Islander." In this case we are speaking of Asian and Pacific Islander immigrants and those born in the United States. The diaspora is limited to the United States although some of the Asian Pacific Islander lesbian writings are coming from Canada. For the most part, we will concentrate in this United States-centered context because most of our research and experiences are from here.

**MM:** We first have to define the parameters we are operating in: to be discussing an "Asian and Pacific Islander lesbian and gay literature" at this point is a premature gesture. Not only has there not been much attention paid to this specific area by both Asian American Studies and Lesbian and Gay Studies, and by extension, gay presses and publishers who publish Asian American writers, but even within our communities there had not been much support for our writers in the form of publishing venues. This, of course, extends to the larger question of our visibility in society at large, which brings up the questions around (our) identity politics, and how that politics has impacted the "mainstream," and how it has been processed and incorporated/assimilated by dominant culture.

**AH:** To give a background of my placement within this text, I am familiar with the poetry, short stories, and the few novels written by Asian Pacific Islander (API) lesbians. My personal search to find anything by, about, and for API lesbians stems from the scarcity of such written documents. Through the research for my thesis on the Asian Pacific Lesbian Network (APLN), I have come into contact with many API lesbian writers. I have come to their works through a personal network as well as chance sightings in feminist or gay/lesbian bookstores. These writers, whose ethnicities include Korean, Chinese, Japanese, Filipino, Vietnamese, and mixed heritage, are in their twenties to early forties. The more established American-born and immigrant writers, in terms of works published and popularity, are living in the United States, and there are a few writers who live and were born in Canada as well.

**MM:** My research was conducted more by personal contacts and referrals due to the lack of published API gay writers. I have come across a number of emerging writers who are in their twenties and early thirties, all currently living in the United States, but balanced in terms of American-born and immigrant. Their ethnicities are predominantly Filipino, Chinese, and Vietnamese. They all write in English, although some of them are of a bilingual background. Due to the scarcity of published works, I have chosen to focus on the circumstances faced by these emerging writers. I will analyze the venues available to them and the factors that have affected the (lack of) development of API gay men's writing(s).

**AH:** We need to recognize diversity as a factor in the development of writing. While we are aware of our class and ethnic background, how do we bring our awareness into writing this essay? We are still informed by our past experiences, our schooling, and it is hard to pull away from that.

**MM:** We are operating within a predetermined premise, and yes, we are privileged persons, but there are also political realities and experiences of oppression that we have gone through and are aware of because of our particular positions as persons of color, as lesbians and gay men, and you as a woman in academia; we do have something to offer to our readers. I think that just because we realize our privilege, it doesn't necessarily mean that we have to withdraw from these discussions because we are claiming a space for ourselves in academia and on our own terms. This space we can then offer to others who do not have the access that we have and keep expanding it. Therefore, we need to be constantly aware of the terms we are operating in. This project, for instance, should define its own terms. There have been black people writing about black people, and Asians writing about Asians, and who is to say that I cannot comment on black gay writers as an Asian gay man? Black gay writers are in many ways our predecessors because the development of their writing, and its acceptance within the lesbian and gay community at large, defines the terms under which API gay writers will or will not be accepted. These are valuable lessons to us, just as the Civil Rights Movement is a model for the Asian American and gay liberation movements. There is also the question of coalition building as well, and I believe that if we are to build effective coalitions between groups of so-called marginalized peoples, we must cease to operate within the boundaries defined for us, because it is this which is keeping us apart in the most profound sense. It is a question of paradigms–the best and the worst of multiculturalism as we know it today.

**AH:** Because we are seen as the "model minority," we are often perceived by other people of color as part of the problem; we are perceived as more white than colored, and are often cast in the role of the oppressor.[3] This has to do with stereotypes of us being successful and obedient, stereotypes that we also buy into. However, there are Asian Americans who believe we could make links with other people of color because we have similar experiences (of oppression), and through them we can come together as a multiracial coalition. It is necessary to make connections with other people of color in this essay, because we would then not be speaking specifically to an API and white audience, but the other people of color who read this journal can make links to us as well. I do not want this essay to address specifically white audiences; I want us to speak to other API lesbians and gays, so they can see a part of themselves represented.

## II. CONDITIONS

In view of the recent boom in the gay presses, and the increasing popularity and visibility of some API American writers such as Amy Tan (*Joy Luck Club* and *The Kitchen God's Wife*, published by Putnam Press), Maxine Hong Kingston (*The Woman Warrior, Tripmaster Monkey, China Men*, and others, published by Alfred A. Knopf), Jessica Hagedorn (*Dogeaters*, published by Penguin Books), David Wong Louie (*Pangs of Love*, published by Alfred A. Knopf), Gus Lee (*China Boy*, published by A. Dutton), and the playwright David Henry Hwang (*M. Butterfly* and *F.O.B.*), the question, "Why not Asian and Pacific Islander American lesbian and gay writers?" seems relevant. Given the advent of multiculturalism and its emphasis on inclusiveness and the re-incorporation of the "marginalized Other" into the "mainstream," the fact that API lesbians and gay men transverse the two categories of Asian Pacific Islander and lesbian/gay should mean that we, as triply and doubly marginalized groups, would enjoy an increasing visibility within both our communities and the "mainstream."[4] This has not been the case. API lesbian and gay writers occupy an intersection between these two categories that does not exist. We have, in effect, "slipped through the cracks." Which leads us to ask: Whose categories are these? Why organize one's identities and affiliations around them? And what are the stakes involved in identifying ourselves with these categories? What is gained and what is lost? These are questions that will surface under different contexts throughout this paper. However, before we can speculate on them, we must explicate the conditions faced by and venues available to API lesbian and gay writers working in a contemporary context.

> *For me personally, my writings have been in about 40 anthologies, but I have always fought to be in them and I feel that I have always been fighting. I fought to be visible. I fought to be heard. I fight to be included.*
>
> –Kitty Tsui[5]

Much of the contemporary writing produced by API lesbians has been facilitated and expressed in feminist presses and in feminist and women-of-color newsletters and newspapers. Anthologies are the best places to find a poem or short story here and there by API lesbians. Writers such as Chea Villanueva (*Girlfriends*, published by Outlaw Press, and *The Chinagirls*, Lezzies on the Move Publications–self-published), Kitty Tsui (*The Words of A Woman Who Breathes Fire*, Sinister Press–self-published), Merle Woo (*A Yellow Woman Speaks*, Radical Women–self-published), and Willyce Kim (*Eating Artichokes* and *Under The Rolling Sky*, The Women's Press Collective; *Dancer Dawkins and the California Kid* and *Dead Heat*, Alyson Publications) have published their fiction, short stories, and poetry collections either through publishing houses or by self-financed efforts. These writers, as well as Canyon Sam and Barbara Noda, have also been included in women-of-color, lesbians-of-color, and Asian women anthologies and compilations, such as: *This Bridge Called Our Back* (Kitchen Table Women of Color Press, 1983), *Making Waves: An Anthology of Writings By and About Asian American Women* (Beacon Press, 1989), *Without Ceremony* (IKON Journal #9, 1988), and *The Forbidden Stitch* (CALYX Books, 1989). These women are a part of the first wave of writers whose work appeared as early as 1972 to the late 1980s.

The anthology *Between the Lines: An Anthology by Pacific/Asian Lesbians of Santa Cruz, California* (1987) by Santa Cruz API lesbians is the first publication of Asian Pacific women's writings, but because of its limited release it has not been identified as such. The editors, sponsored by local San Francisco Bay Area community fund-raisers, went on a book tour in 1987 promoting it in various cities around the country. They were helped through the API contacts made at the March on Washington for Lesbian and Gay Rights in 1987. Through this network of making friends in API lesbian communities around the country, the editors were able to bring the anthology directly to API women. The personal ties and contacts further underscore the kind of networking that takes place in distributing and making visible API materials.

In the introduction to *Piece of My Heart: A Lesbian of Colour Anthology* (1992), Silvera Makeda wrote of the difficulty in producing this book that took nearly six years because, in part, many lesbians of color were not ready to break out of the fear of loss of family and community and she was not personally prepared to devote her time when other projects needed attention. A crop of API lesbian writers has emerged in this latest lesbian of color anthology, such as: Lanuola Asiasga, Michelle Chai, Chan Kit Yee, Chen Ling Hua, Ritz Chow, Nila Gupta, Tomai Kobayashi, C. Allyson Lee, Patrice Leung, Sharon Lim-Hing, Mona Oikawa, Noriko Oka, Midi Onodera, and Indigo Som. The issues addressed in their writings are similar to the ones written by the first wave of writers, which include themes such as self-representation, identity, sensuality, and feminist and women-of-color politics.

The difficulties Makeda experienced are similar to the problems Sharon Lim-Hing and Mi Ok Bruining are feeling with their Asian Pacific Islander anthology.[6] With both women extremely busy with their own school work, writing, and limited funds, they are in the beginning stages of their collecting process. According to Bruining, the anthology has been a word-of-mouth effort since there are no available funds for a widespread call for submissions as of yet. They hope to begin a nationwide call, including Canada, for submissions of prose, poetry, essays, photographs, and visual art by, about, and for Asian Pacific Islander lesbians and bisexuals. A question that they as editors have been grappling with is how to represent the diverse and varied ethnicities, histories, and experiences of API lesbians? They have asked interested API lesbians to join an advisory board in order for it to reflect the diversity of its communities. Members of the advisory board are responsible for recruiting contributors of their own ethnic group in their local area and promoting the book in their network of friends. This way the various communities of Asian Pacific lesbians can be closely integrated in the process and will feel included in a work that is for them. Sister Vision Press will publish this anthology.

Another personal project-in-process is Ingin Kim's solicitations for any doodles, writings, and drawings by API lesbians and bisexuals to be included in a visual magazine-inspired format. This smaller project has had difficulty in getting submissions which could be explained by the hesitancy that some API lesbian writers feel about their work. API lesbians have published elsewhere in newsletters, journals, and other such venues, but it is difficult to

keep track of newsletters, small-press newspapers, feminist journals, and dyke magazines. We are sure there are other API lesbian
writers out there that we are not aware of at this time.

Comparatively, contemporary venues that specifically feature
writings by API gay men are virtually non-existent. The venues
created by feminist presses, and the women-of-color, lesbians-of-
color, and Asian women's anthology projects that gave a number of
API lesbian writers exposure do not exist for API gay writers.[7]
There are, for sure, a number of journals, such as *In Your face* (San
Francisco) and *Queer City Anthology* (published by The Portable
Lower East Side, New York City), that have published contemporary works by API gay writers, but these are either one time "special issues" that do not provide a sustained support system, or they
are non-specific venues that nevertheless publish works by API gay
writers along with works by other writers of diverse ethnic backgrounds and sexual identities. Similar to some API lesbians, a number of API gay writers have also had their work published in newsletters and newspapers produced and circulated by API lesbian and
gay organizations. However, being self-financed publications that
are put out by social, support, and/or political groups relying on
their members volunteering, these publications are often erratically
produced–depending on the availability of time and money of the
group's members–and are distributed only through that particular
group's mailing list and local distributors. *Phoenix Rising* (published by Asian Pacifica Sisters in San Francisco), *Lavender Godzilla* (published by Gay Asian Pacific Alliance in San Francisco and
the Bay Area), *CelebrAsian* (published by Gay Asians Toronto),
and the AMALGM Newsletter (published by Alliance of Massachusetts Asian Lesbians and Gay Men in Boston) are examples of
newsletters published by API lesbian and gay groups. There are
also newsletters that are published by mixed API and non-API gay
groups, such as Asians and Friends/New York and Chicago, that
sometimes feature writings by API gay men, but since they are not
API-specific venues, they will not be discussed in this essay.

*Lavender Godzilla* is an interesting case among these newsletters
mentioned above. It is currently undergoing a change in its focus,
shifting from a newsletter format to that of a literary journal. In
terms of its production it has remained on a volunteer basis with

funding from both Gay Asian Pacific Alliance (GAPA) and outside sources such as the Out Fund. Its distribution still remains primarily in the Bay Area, where it is carried by some bookstores and distributed among GAPA members. Two recent issues (Fall 1991, Spring 1992) were produced as magazines, and featured prose, poetry, essays by API gay writers, and interviews with community organizers. The different issues are organized around theme issues such as Asian parents/gay sons, eroticism and sexuality, and immigration/homophobia/racism. Forthcoming issues will focus on erotica, family, and media representation. Although its contributors are still primarily from the Bay Area, it has begun to broaden its scope by soliciting material from API gay writers in other cities and states. Of the publications I have come across, *Lavender Godzilla* seems at the moment to be the most likely publication to develop into a sustainable venue for Asian Pacific Islander gay writers; it enjoys a relatively wider distribution than the other newsletters. It also has the most Asian Pacific Islander gay writers I have seen in one publication, many of whom–Pablo Tapay Bautista, Gilbert Chan, Rafael Chang, Justin Chin, Jesse Cortes, Vince Crisostomo, Voltaire Gungab, Dirk Jang, Steve Lew, Edward Lim, Franklin Lim Liao, Ming-Yeung Lu, Welmin Militante, Nilo Salazar, Vince Sales, Paul Shimazaki, Andy Spieldenner, Rafaelito V. Sy, Trac Vu, and others– have first been published here, and now have their work featured on a consistent basis. Joel Tan, Han Ong, and Henri Tran are writers based in Los Angeles who have been published in local venues. Joel Tan and Han Ong (interview) have also been published in *Lavender Godzilla*.

Another related project is an anthology of API gay men's writings that is currently being compiled by John Manzon (New York City; affiliated with Gay Asian Pacific Islander Men of New York) and Fernando Chang-Moy (Washington, D.C., Gay Asian Pacific Islander Network). This is a long-term project that will feature works by 20-30 API gay men of Chinese, Japanese, Korean, Filipino, and Vietnamese descents, as well as API gay men from other ethnic groups. The writers are both immigrant and American-born, their ages range from 20 to 50. Most of the submissions to date are from urban centers such as New York, San Francisco, Los Angeles, Boston, Washington, D.C., Chicago, and Toronto, where there are visible and organized groups of API gay men active in the communities.

The writings in this anthology will include poetry, prose, critical and theoretical essays, historical essays, interviews, and informational pieces that will deal with issues such as immigration and AIDS/HIV prevention. A bibliography of gay Asian Pacific Islander writing and related source material, and photographs and artwork that are relevant to the project will complete this compilation. Given the fact that this is the largest and most extensive compilation of writings by API gay men to date, and that it is likely that this anthology will be published by a major publishing house, which means that it will be distributed nationally in bookstores, it will be an important and historical step towards our visibility in both the Asian Pacific Islander American and Lesbian and Gay communities. In the context of our discussion, this project is significant in that it is a community-generated effort that has accessed a distribution network previously not available to projects of this nature. In this sense, this anthology is similar to other anthology projects that feature works by gay men of color.

## III. BETWEEN WRITING AND POLITICAL ORGANIZING

*If there is to be evidence of our experiences, we learned ... that our own self-sufficiency must ensure it*

–Essex Hemphill[8]

**MM:** There are a number of black gay writers' anthologies published by publishing houses with a national and international distribution.[9] A number of black gay writers, such as Essex Hemphill and Assoto Saint, have become increasingly visible figures in the cultural and critical sectors of both the African American and lesbian and gay communities due to their exposure through these publications. I think this is a precedent and a model for API gay writers. However, what I want to stress is that before the embracing of black gay writers by the "mainstream" gay press, there was already a strong community-based support network.[10]

The support system and venues created within a self-identified community of individuals is a key factor in the emergence of a generation of black gay writers. It is also important to note that these black gay writers had adopted this model from the pioneering cultural organizing done in the feminist and women-of-color communities, where community-based publishing and literary activities have been developed and created as alternatives to the hegemonic "mainstream."

The community-based support systems that enabled the emergence of black gay writers and lesbian-of-color writers are not present within API gay communities; we are not yet able to provide venues for our own writers.[11] The lessons we can learn from both black gay writers and our API lesbian sisters is that community-based support and development contribute to a vital basis from which the "mainstream" can be approached. Given the historical exclusion of self-identified API gay men from both the gay presses and the ranks of Asian Pacific Islander writers, it seems only logical, if not necessary, that we organize and empower ourselves through creating our own support systems and broaden that basis through coalition building with those who are our potential allies.[12]

**AH:** One writer whose work challenges the mainstream heterosexual and lesbian publishers is Chea Villanueva. Her writing, including *Girlfriends* (1987) and *The Chinagirls* (1991), is interesting in this light because there is never an identifiably white woman in it; her characters' dialect, dress, and mannerisms reflect working-class women-of-color and their everyday lives. Villanueva has given interviews where she speaks of her lack of interest in writing about white lesbians because her work reflects her experiences which is very women-of-color identified. In part, her work might not be published or reviewed because her work does not have a white lesbian character. Villanueva was asked by one of her publishers to add a white lesbian character, to make the characters more monogamous, and to cut out the dildo scenes, which she refused to do. At her readings, some white lesbians said that they did not understand what she was saying or they did not know when to laugh, while the women-of-color in the audience would burst out laughing and praise her work as wonderful and meaningful to them. There is something about audience reception that we need to talk about.

**MM:** The question of audience reception also brings up the issue of economics. It is very important for us to realize who buys from the gay press, who is targeted through the gay press, and who runs the gay press. The support from women-of-color communities and the presence of writing within women-of-color communities provide a lot of spiritual and intellectual, as well as financial support for API lesbian writers–exemplified by the inclusion of their work in women-of-color anthologies. This is not the same in the gay men's communities.

**AH:** If I did a survey of 50 API gay men and asked them to name some Asian Pacific Islander lesbian writers, I do not think they could come up with any. A number of API gay writers do not know of API women's writings because it is not very visible or they are not aware of it. They look to other lesbians-of-color or women-of-color for that precedent. There is a lack of awareness between the two groups.

**MM:** This is partially due to the different identification between the men and the women. We do not know what others are doing unless there are personal friendship or political ties, and this kind of exchange is beginning to happen. It is true in terms of your statement about the lack of awareness between the two groups. However, I do see many API gay writers of my generation who are very influenced by feminism, by women-of-color writers like Audre Lorde and Gloria Anzaldúa. This influence has shown itself through a prevalence of the testimonial format among these writers.

**AH:** With respect to organizing, it is really difficult to have a co-gender group that is evenly balanced, where all the issues come out. The men work in different ways from the women. Some API lesbians say that men know how to work together because of their socialization with teamwork in sports and leadership roles and because men often act in this capacity, while women share everything and play support roles. Consensus is the method of decision making for many lesbians and some women think that is not a practical method. I know some API lesbians who do not want to be with gay men, although they recognize the solidarity among all gay people because of a common oppression on a theoretical level. We also have to identify the sexism within our own cultures, where fathers and sons hold and are given more power and respect in API families.

**MM:** There is also a specific kind of misogyny that exists among gay men, who are raised as men in a sexist society, but are made to feel inadequate as homosexuals in a heterosexist society, which results in a kind of paranoia where you have to "dis" women to be gay. On the other hand, gay men are also more likely than heterosexually-identified men to question the dominant gender structure and are consequently more receptive to feminist ideas. In terms of class, most API gay men who are organizing and writing come from an upper/middle-class background like myself. We have the access to write: our English is "good" enough, we have the education, the connections . . . For me what it points to is this: now we are being solicited by the larger gay and lesbian community, we are invited to be on panels, to be in publications, but only a selected group is invited, and this has much to do with one's class background.

**AH:** Even the organizing (among the API lesbians) is usually done by students and educated professional women. It is difficult for a working-class woman to take time out to be a part of an organization or to come out and write for a journal, although there are some women who do. Issues of practical survival might be foremost in their minds. I think that in the writings that we see, and the retreats that happen, many class issues are not brought out at all. The whole notion of retreats, that you can take time out from work, pay $100 to register and then fly somewhere is a luxury or a huge sacrifice. Some organizers work to correct or alleviate the financial situation, but it is difficult, given the limited funding for lesbian organizations; women get paid less than men on the whole, and there are not many rich lesbian philanthropists.

**MM:** Since we are anxious to not fall into the trappings of our upper/middle-class background, we develop this class guilt which translates very easily into a fear of saying and doing the wrong thing, which can lead to a paralysis in our organizing work. We do have more resources, and that can be aggressively distributed among identifiable individuals and groups that need it. I am not talking about charity, but a kind of leveling of our resources, our knowledge, and an exchange of experiences among the different groups, a dialogue. Of course, there are going to be differences and arguments, but our differences are still going to be there even if we choose to ignore them. How else can we grow as a group except by coming to terms with our diversity? A community-produced publication, for instance, can be a more inclusive venue than outside ones, but this is not to say that we should turn down outside invitations, because there are also issues of visibility. We can also redirect and refer some of these invitations to other people. That is happening already, but people still shy away from it; we are reluctant to share information and resources. The building up of a sustainable system that can facilitate exchange and distribute resources, at least within an identifiable group, should be one of our major goals.

**AH:** There is a move towards that in the women's community, but the differences among the women and the enormity of the task can be paralyzing. Some women are now reviving Asian Pacifica Lesbian Network because they want to be part of that support system. When someone needs information and contacts, the Network can serve as a resource and offer support to alleviate her loneliness. People recognize that a strong visible support system needs to be established.

**MM:** Effort is being made to create a support system, and they remain predominantly upper-middle-class initiated efforts. I often see a denial of our class bias in predominantly middle-class organizations–a delusion that we somehow "transcended" our class background by our realizing it. This is not the case. Awareness without concrete actions does not create changes. Therefore, we have to be extremely self-aware of our methodology in organizing, and of how much we have come to accept as the norm. We do not want to make this into a self-perpetuating closed system that only benefits ourselves, and even worse, to believe that we are serving others.

**AH:** It is extremely hard to be self-critical. In the context of my writing and research on API lesbians, I find myself often caught up in certain ways of thinking. It is not until someone points out a different perspective that I realize my immersion into the topic has sometimes left some things undefined.

**MM:** In the women's communities, there is a pre-existing model of grassroots organizing developed by the preceding feminist movements, which is not present in the men's communities. When we are faced with these issues of difference, we have no background in dealing with them. So we deal with them in very stereotypically male ways–we break off from the group, we vie for control, we create this paralysis that is very destructive on the movement as a whole. Our differences do not get incorporated into the movement as a whole; instead, they become wedges between the factions. A more productive approach would be to build upon our commonalities while recognizing the differences that exist among groups: a politically and ideologically sophisticated Pan-Asianism.

**AH:** The idea of Pan-Asianism has been a topic that has come up in various contexts.[13] So even within a group where we ostensibly belong, there are contestations as to where we should identify ourselves. The whole notion of us coming together as a racial and sexual minority is one that is rife with contradictions, and many organizations have fallen apart in the face of these tensions. The coming together and breaking down of our identities happened at the Asian Pacifica Lesbian Network sponsored retreat in Santa Cruz in 1989, where some women felt at home, both in terms of race and sexuality. Yet, there were others of different ethnicities and backgrounds who felt left out and voiced their concerns. Some women felt stronger afterwards because it allowed them to voice their criticisms; it was very empowering to see "Asian women" talking about their feelings of invisibility, talking about their needs because Asian Pacific Islanders are never perceived to be vocal about our needs or about being critical. Many women felt that it was a great thing, while others felt that it was divisive–why can't our commonalities be stressed instead of differences?

**MM:** Many of these "coming together" type organizing efforts are "reactive" in the sense that our terms are being defined for us as we organize. In much of our organizing, we only pay lip service towards addressing the issue of difference, which does not lead to

actual changes. Our modes of organizing are still very much the same thing. We need to take a more in-depth look at our difference and develop ways to use that to our advantage.
*An Aversion to (Our) Longing* by Ming-Yuen S. Ma

> *This is the body that hears BROTHERHOOD like screeching nails.*

> –Justin Chin[14]

Compared to the African American identities, API identities are more elusive and harder to come to grips with. This is so because Asian Pacific Islanders, as a group, are rife with contradictions.[15] The circumstances under which most API immigrants arrived in the United States are different from the circumstances under which most Africans were brought here. Temporally, African Americans had been in this country longer and in larger numbers than Asian Pacific Islanders. There is also a more dynamic relationship between African American cultures and the dominant culture in the United States. Therefore, African American cultures are more pronouncedly different from African cultures in Africa when compared to API American cultures and API cultures in Asia and the Pacific Islands. Language, for instance, is a good indicator of this point; there are considerably more Asian Pacific Islander languages spoken in the United States than African languages. Furthermore, although there are certain similarities between slavery and immigration, given the continual economic as well as military exploitation of the "Third World" by the "First World," these two are different experiences that cannot be equated. The forcible erasure of the slaves' indigenous cultures that happened during the late 1700s and 1800s is a more brutal and abrupt process than the assimilation process experienced by most API immigrants in the United States. Slavery has produced a more clearly demarcated break between Africa and African Americans. This, along with the factor of time, has made the African American communities more ethnically homogeneous than Asian American communities.[16]

As the heterogeneity among different API ethnicities is more pronounced than that among African Americans, this makes the grouping of these ethnic categories under the homogenizing term of Asian Pacific Islander more problematic. Also, as the "model minority," we are under the most pressure to assimilate into "mainstream" society. This social pressure not only affects the treatment and attitude towards APIs by non-Asians, but it also affects how we see ourselves. The education system and mass media in this country generally conform to the value-system of the dominant culture, in fact, they are also the chief channels through which these values and standards are disseminated. Through these channels, a standard of normality is created and promoted among its audiences, who, in different degrees, adopt these values as their own. Images of APIs in these venues are scarce, and the ones that are shown are extremely problematic because they are one-dimensional and are created according to the stereotypical assumptions about APIs in the dominant culture.[17] The effects these stereotypes have on anti-Asian violence and the level of self-esteem among APIs, which has a direct correlation to suicide rates, substance abuse, and violence in our communities, has been discussed and elaborated upon by others.[18] What I want to point out here is how these dynamics manifest themselves among API gay men and how those manifestations affect our self-esteem, our social interaction, and our organizing work.

*Do you cruise me / cause I'm somewhere between black and white / new flavor / outside your color schemes?*

                                        –Andy Spieldenner[19]

If we look at commercial gay sexual representation, it appears that the antiracist movements have had little impact: the images of men and male beauty are still of white men and white male beauty. These are the standards against which we compare both ourselves and often our brothers–Asian, black, native, and Latino. Although other people's rejection (or fetishization) of us according to the established racial hierarchies may be experienced as oppressive, we are not necessarily moved to scrutinize our own desire and its relationship to the hegemonic image of the white man

                                        –Richard Fung[20]

Since many of us "came out" in the Euro/American gay context, our ideals of male beauty are necessarily influenced by the dominant cultural standards of beauty and desirability. On the other hand, our (presumed) racial characteristics are fetishized by the non-API gay communities as a frozen form of desirability–one that is derived from an Orientalist perspective.[21] In this economy of desire, the trade is almost always unidirectional; where APIs are encouraged to use our "exotic appeal," our "Oriental sensuousness," to maximize our attractiveness to other–non-Asian and usually white–men. Not only do we not see other API men as desirable; they are almost always perceived as competition because those who are like us undermine our exoticism and our "specialness" in the eyes of the (desirable) white man.

> *share those same looks i get as i walk down the Castro / from my own brothers proudly flaunting their white boys / white men with them / giving me the eye which says because he is white and he is beautiful and he is mine so keep away from me.*
>
> –Justin Chin[22]

This rivalry among ourselves is a result of our sexual colonialization. Not only does it affect our sexual object choice, these internalized racist beliefs and notions extend beyond our choice of sexual partners and manifest themselves in our interactions with each other. In social situations, they often manifest themselves as unnecessary hostility towards each other. In political organizing work, initiatives to organize are often met with mistrust and apathy. The negativism and reluctance that we so often come across among ourselves, and the vicious and disrespectful manner with which we put down and silence each other are truly disturbing to me as I, too, participate in it. Frantz Fanon, in his discussion of the psychological effects of colonialism on the black population of Antilles, cites a passage from Anna Freud's description of the phenomenon of ego withdrawal: "a method of avoiding 'pain,' ego restriction, like the various forms of denial, does not come under the heading of neurosis but is a normal stage in the development of the ego. . . . But, *when it has become rigid or has already acquired an intolerance of 'pain' and so is obsessionally fixated to a method of flight, such withdrawal is punished by impaired development. By abandoning one position after another it becomes one-sided, loses too many interests and can show but a meager achievement*" (my italics).[23]

Fanon then goes on to describe how "black man cannot take pleasure in his insularity," because he "requires white approval." From another viewpoint, E.S. Hetrick and A.D. Martin have reached similar conclusions in their study of the effects of internalized homophobia upon the behavior among gay teenagers: "the homosexual desires that prevent complete identification with the dominant group can lead to that self-hatred labeled by the American Psychiatric Association as ego dystonic homosexuality. Ego dystonic homosexuality, in turn, stimulates futile attempts to change sexual orientation, *provokes aggression against one's group,* and again can lead to reckless and dangerous behavior."[24] Furthermore, "homosexual self-hatred and identification with the dominant group may lead to acceptance of the belief that [suffering] is "God's punishment" or a natural consequence of 'unnatural behavior' . . . *It may also lead to a fatalism, an acceptance of one's doom with a concomitant belief that changes in [our lives] will make no difference"* (my italics).[25]

Drawing from the above sources, and concurring with the theories of internalized racism and homophobia, I would argue that in our social and sexual interactions, even though our white master is often not bodily-present, we are still fighting each other for his attention. He is, in fact, within us. So perhaps, the problems that we come up against in our attempts to organize is not due solely to the problem of our difference and our (lack of) assimilation into Euro/American cultures, but that there are mechanisms of colonialism working within us which prevent us from coming together as a group. In this light, it is more productive for API gay men to claim our identit(ies) not as fixed, essential notions of who we are and what we (should) do, but as a political act. Then, our claiming and defining of our identities will not be seen, both by ourselves and others, as prescriptions of how to act as API gay men, but rather, as moments of articulation through which we constantly negotiate our various positions both within and outside of dominant culture.

To speak of API gay writing in this context automatically and necessarily categorizes it as a genre. However, if we can claim that term for ourselves, and define it with our own (lack of) definitions, then it, too, becomes a political act: to see the development of our writing, both in the aesthetic and the practical sense, not as a process of qualifying what is or isn't API gay writing, but as an opportunity to claim our voices and create channels through which more of us can speak. Our identity politics are then constantly articulated, debated, and strengthened and expanded through our writings. It is certainly an arena in which questions of (our) identities and (our) placement within different communities can be considered, and that will be on our own terms.

> *Do we explore these questions or do we settle for that secret isolation which is the learned tolerance of deprivation of each other–that longing for each other's laughter, dark ease, sharing, and permission to be ourselves that we do not admit to feeling, usually, because then we would have to admit the lack; and the pain of that lacking, persistent as low-grade fever and as debilitating?*

–Audre Lorde[26]

*Between Worlds: Identity Issues* by Alice Y. Hom

> *My father has this fear that I am going to end up homeless. Little does he know that I already am.*

–Alice Y. Hom[27]

I begin with the above quote because the themes of "home" and "place" strike a deep chord within many API lesbians because the communities that we ostensibly belong to do not necessarily acknowledge or affirm our presence. Asian American communities rarely or never address lesbian issues and sometimes go to great lengths to deny our existence. Lesbian communities do not reflect our presence nor do they deal with concerns we have, such as anti-Asian violence or immigration issues. Where do we belong? is a difficult question to answer when on the whole this society does not validate gays and lesbians or people of color. Since APIs have historically been excluded and buried in history, and women fall in the same category, it is no wonder one is unable to find much documentation on API women, much less lesbians–a minority within a minority within a minority. To break down the invisibility, one must examine the obstacles that API lesbians face within the contexts of self-identity, their families, and larger lesbian communities.

Specifically, there is conflict between Western beliefs and values and Asian beliefs and values. The tension among these two can cause an API lesbian to experience much inner turmoil in expressing her sexuality. Pamela H., in "Asian American Lesbians: An Emerging Voice in the Asian American Community," states that to straight Asian Americans "homosexuality is seen as a Western concept, a product of losing touch with one's Asian heritage, of becoming too assimilated."[28] For some APIs homosexuality is seen as "a white disease." Although homosexuality is common in all societies and cultures, it is experienced and manifested in a variety of ways. Immigrant lesbians often bring the knowledge that there is a place for same-sex relationships in their native countries which validates their existence and dismantles the notion that homosexuality is a white, Western characteristic.

One reason for the difficulty in coming out to API families is the fear of rejection and loss of family support and network. Living in a society where racial/ethnic support is valuable and necessary, an API lesbian might not want to jeopardize those ties. Maintaining the family structure is still felt keenly by us since coming out might also break up or strain relations among the family members. The lesbian daughter is seen as rebelling against traditional Asian values and following supposedly "outside" values, if she does not follow the traditional path of marriage and starting her own family.

Another difficulty lies in the language barriers that might prevent disclosure, a parent might not understand the statement, "I am a lesbian." And she might not be able to say it in her native language. There are no directly translatable words that describe "lesbian" in most Asian languages, although there are some phrases that imply same-sex love or friendship. Despite the absence or unfamiliarity of a word that describes lesbian, it does not mean lesbianism does not exist. Since API lesbians are not going to learn or hear about homosexuality within their family (which is one source of language perpetuation), they also might believe that their lesbianism is not a part of their culture. Indeed, in most Asian immigrant families the topic of sexuality is rarely discussed, thus homosexuality will rarely surface. The context in which API lesbians (all APIs for that matter) will hear or see lesbianism is mostly in an English language and white framework.

There is also the opinion of outside API communities to contend with. They place a heavy burden on an API lesbian because they could negatively pass judgment on the family. To lose "face" or stature in the community would be a blow to the family and family name. Some parents do not want to reveal their daughter's lesbianism to other relatives or friends for fear of stigma. In some cases, a family denies and remains silent among themselves about their daughter's sexual orientation. Of course not all families express the actions described above since there is a spectrum of responses, ranging from denial to acceptance.

An API lesbian might not have access to outside lesbian support or social groups because of communication difficulty and lack of cultural sensitivity in white networks. Additionally, an Asian immigrant lesbian has a different set of issues to contend with if she is not of legal status in this country. She might hide her sexual orientation for fear of deportation. Also the lesbian community is seen usually as a predominantly white group. The invisibility and lack of lesbians of color in these movements prevents some API lesbians from getting involved because they do not want to be token members in the group, which some have experienced. Their issues regarding immigration, racism, language, and cultural sensitivity might not get addressed in most lesbian organizations.

In some respects an API lesbian feels torn between choosing her racial/ethnic community over her sexual community or vice versa. Although this does not and should not be the case, there are times when this false choice is put upon a lesbian. The goal should be the integration and affirmation of multiple identities that API lesbians have, rather than the splitting or choosing among them. African American and Latina writers, such as Audre Lorde, Barbara Smith, Gloria Anzaldúa, have written about race, gender, and sexuality as closely intertwined constructs. A similar view toward multiple identities also informs API lesbian writing in general.

Some of the major themes in API lesbian writing revolve around self-identity, self-representation, exploration of political and cultural issues, immigration, mixed heritage, and adoption issues which are expressed through poetry, prose, erotica, essays, plays, and short stories.

## IV. IDENTITY AND WRITING

**AH:** Internalized racism and homophobia are two of the main factors that inhibit many API lesbians and gay men from identifying with the term Asian Pacific Islander. Obviously, cultural factors play a part in that self-identification. I noticed that a number of women have different consciousness about how they see themselves in relationship to society at large, in relationship to the API communities, and in relationship to the lesbian communities. There are some API lesbians who see other API lesbians, but because of internalized homophobia and racism, won't identify with them. The issue of identity is very interesting because a lot of the writing reflects whether they can be "out" in their own communities or whether they can promote and affirm their cultural differences in the lesbian communities–issues that face API gay men as well. However, sexual stereotypes prevalent about API men and women play a role in our different identity formations. The stereotypes of API men as passive, weak, and effeminate are equivalent to the stereotypes of gay men, in general, thus making it easier to conceive of an API gay man. API women, whose stereotypes are sexual in nature and related to men, for instance exotic prostitutes and submissive, obedient servants to men, make it difficult to envision an Asian lesbian.

**MM:** Other factors, such as the prominence of the sex industry in Thailand and the Philippines, where a number of Euro/American gay men go for sex, contribute to both the stereotypes and relative visibility of API gay men. You could step into a "rice bar"[29] and no matter where you are, and even if you are an MIT graduate or a lawyer, you are automatically transformed into a "shower dancer," or an "off-boy." The transition between the boundaries is so acute that it is astonishing. Among my peers, it seems that we are all going through a process: at one point, we all had this realization that we have been objectified and stereotyped by the gay (white) community, and as a result, we have come to idealize Asian/Asian relationships. Some of us realize now that there are other factors, such as class and politics, that could and do influence a relationship; even if a person has the same skin color or ethnicity as we do, it does not mean that he will share our political beliefs or understand our class backgrounds. But then again, there is still the overwhelming pressure in the gay community for API men to go with white men. Whenever I go out, I still see API gay men with white men or other men of color, very seldom do I see a group of API men hanging out together except in rice bars, but even there, you seldom see API men cruise each other.

**AH:** The situation is quite different among lesbians. For the most part, API lesbians are with other API lesbians, or with other women-of-color–one might not see them with white women. I think this has a lot to do with the feminist movement of the 1970s, that it was a white middle-class women's movement, which was very apparent to a lot of women-of-color. So there is a political stance among some lesbians of color that one should go with another woman of color. Because an individual white lesbian does not always identify her racism, or her racist behavior, the whole movement is seen as racist. We have to be very specific about how we define feminism. I think this sentiment played a major role in the formulation of relationships among lesbians-of-color. We always have to go through so much to make ourselves visible in the lesbian community, that most of us don't want to deal with a white lover, that would be too hard. There is also peer pressure: your friends might say, "Why are you going out with a white dyke?" For the majority of the women you see, it is always a "sticky rice" situation.[30] That is a big difference that I see between API gay men and lesbians. How do interracial relationships affect what we are talking about here? I think it is a side issue.

**MM:** Because what we are really discussing here are identity issues, and a large part of our identity is defined by our sexuality, so who you sleep with (and who you don't) does influence our self-perception.

**AH:** API lesbian writers are often prone to self-censorship, we are often too self-critical; we think that what we have to say is not worth anybody's time, not literary enough. Many of us are not trained to be writers, so there is tremendous self-doubt and self-censorship. This, in part, might be the reason why submissions to anthologies are few.

**MM:** In my attempts to solicit writings for this essay, the response has been disappointingly low. Of all the writers I came into contact with, many are just emerging, many also have other commitments, such as doing AIDS work, that take up all their time. I have also heard the argument of "ghettoization" used as a reason to not identify oneself as an API gay writer. While there are very real issues concerning the limited interpretation of one's work because of one's race and/or sexual identit(ies), the alternative is to measure oneself against the norm, which is Eurocentric and heterosexist. Since we are the model minority, this aversion to identifying oneself with a "marginalized" identity, the pressure to assimilate, is also the strongest among us.

**AH:** There seems to be a nebulousness to an Asian American identity. It is often a reactive situation, an unjust incident or a negative occurrence, which makes us formulate, think about, and claim our identities. A discriminatory action committed against you makes you realize your disempowered position. These are indications that we are somehow considered "different" by other people's standards. It is important to realize the differences that we have within an ostensibly identifiable group, such as the gay and lesbian communities. There are different styles of activism that reflect a range between an assimilationist perspective and a confrontational stance.

**MM:** For us, militancy is not possible without the ground work done before us by our predecessors. I don't think that the connections between the generations are being recognized enough. I see other young activists making grandstanding statements about their work; about how "revolutionary" they are compared to their "moderate" predecessors. For me, this is an ahistorical and self-defeating approach.

**AH:** There is a lot of collective non-memory; people just don't remember their roots and from where they have come. I don't know if the younger people know that maybe just 25 years ago, you could not dance in public with a member of the same sex, that you could be arrested. There were regular raids in gay bars. There are gay people today who do not know that. I think this is partially due to the lack of education on gay and lesbian history. Some people do not know where to go for resources and information, especially if they live in areas where there are no accessible lesbian and gay communities.

**MM:** Our writing, acting as documentation of our existence and as articulations of our experiences, can play an important role in the passing on and building of our histories. In this sense, it is an important component to be developed by "marginalized communities" such as ours. However, we have also pointed out and examined some of the contradictions and difficulties involved in the development of an identity-based writing. In drawing attention to them, we hope that current and forthcoming API lesbian and gay writers can become more conscious of these issues and will actively engage with them in their work. We realize that while it is important to continue to empower ourselves through the articulation of our experiences, it is equally crucial to realize the paradigms in which these forms of (self) representations are operating. Perhaps different forms of writing can then be developed so that they can be both self-empowering testimonies and forms of representation that resist the cultural commodification of "marginal" experiences?

**AH:** The development of writing comes in stages; the early stage involves testimonial/experiential writing which is an integral phase in its development. API lesbian and gay writing is still evolving. Although much of the articulation has touched upon the testimonial/experiential form, other forms of writing are also being explored. In this essay we draw attention to this area, and by doing so, we hope to both support our writers and stimulate more activity. We realize that this is only a beginning.

## NOTES

1. In "Passion Tales: Allegories of Identity" by Ming-Yeung Lu.
2. "Asian" includes East Asians, South Asians, and Southeast Asians.
3. The "model minority" myth has been attached to Asian Americans since the late 1960s. Japanese Americans and Chinese Americans, specifically, were touted in many mainstream magazines and newspapers as being "whiz kids" or success stories. What the press and the perpetuators of these stories fail to address

is the diversity of ethnic, generation, and class differences that do exist for those who fall under the category of Asian American. The success stories might be about the Chinese or Japanese who came to the United States post-1965 Immigration Act which brought over a class of people distinct from the Chinese and Japanese who arrived in the late 1800s. Newer Asian ethnic immigrants and refugees make for a more complex situation that negates the assumption that all Asian Americans are successful.

4. Although I realize that Multiculturalism represents a much more complicated set of ideologies and strategies than "putting the marginalized in the mainstream," it is undeniable that its interpretation and application by institutions such as schools and universities have, for the most part, remained on the level of a sophisticated form of tokenism, where the discourses of the "Other" are studied and categorized by a methodology that still operates on the underlying paradigms of dominant cultural practices and beliefs.

5. From a roundtable discussion: ". . . But Some of Us Are Brave–Lesbians, Culture, and Politics."

6. At the time this essay was written, the API lesbian/bisexual anthology had two editors. However, Mi OK Bruining had to drop out and Sharon Lim-Hing is now the sole editor.

7. Interestingly, a number of "out" API gay men have been publishing within the academic and theoretical context, mostly in the context of lesbian and gay studies and cultural studies. These writers and theorists are Richard Fung, Jeff Nunokawa, and Martin Manalansan. Ming-Yuen S. Ma, Quentin Lee, and Ming-Yeung Lu also address theoretical issues in their work. Trinity Ordona, Connie S. Chan, Vivian Ng, and Alice Y. Hom are the API lesbians we have come across who do work in this context.

8. Essex Hemphill, from the introduction to *Brother To Brother: New Writings by Black Gay Men*, p. 25.

9. *In The Life: A Black Gay Anthology*, ed. Joseph Beam (Boston: Alyson Publications); *Brother To Brother: New Writings by Black Gay Men*, ed. Essex Hemphill (Boston: Alyson Publications, 1990); *The Road Before Us: 100 Gay Black poets*, ed. Assoto Saint (New York: Galiens Press, 1991).

10. Writers' collectives such as the Other Countries Collective organized and developed significant literary voices through a process of workshops in which black gay writers can read, discuss, and critique each other's works. This also provided a context in which these writers can find support and common interests from others like them. The collective also presented public readings to various audiences in both the African American and lesbian and gay communities. Community-based literary journals such as the *Pyramid Poetry Periodical* and the *Other Countries Journal* provided sustained support for emerging black gay writers. Furthermore, periodicals such as *BLK* and *Black/Out* featured literary materials alongside journalistic articles. These also served as channels through which events such as readings and book publications can be publicized. Furthermore, two film and video works produced and directed by black gay directors: *Looking For Langston* by Isaac Julien and *Tongues United* by Marlon Riggs, also utilized

the poetry and writings of black gay men and gave these writings a central place within their filmic narratives, thus bringing these voices into another medium, and to different audiences.

11. There are probably a variety of reasons why these venues are not present in our communities, some of which can be attributed to specific difficulties involved in organizing among API gay men, which will be discussed in the "An Aversion to (Our) Longing" section of this paper. The comparatively shorter period of organizing in our communities (GAPA has been in existence for five years, and Gay Asian Pacific Islander Men of New York for about four) can also be another factor. Also, at the moment many Asian Pacific Islander gay activists are focusing on the problem of AIDS and HIV within our communities. In fact, more than one of the writers I talked to are currently doing AIDS/HIV work full time, which prevents them from pursuing their writing.

12. I think that both black gay writers and other gay writers of color, as well as API lesbian writers and other lesbian writers of color are our obvious allies, but in this statement I do not exclude the possibility of building coalitions with heterosexually-identified API writers and Euro/American lesbian or gay writers. In some cases, such as with feminist writers, and especially API feminist writers, there is already much dialoguing going on.

13. Pan-Asianism is the concept of having a unified group of APIs working on common issues. However, given the heterogeneity of this grouping, "Pan-Asianism" has been successful mainly in single-issue oriented projects, such as anti-Asian violence.

14. From *The Song of Unending Desire* by Justin Chin. This portion of the work is unpublished.

15. This is to continue the comparison initiated in the dialogue. Among people-of-color groups, APIs are probably most similar to Latinos in terms of our demographics, recent immigration patterns, language, and cultural diversity. However, since African Americans are the most visible people of color in the United States, they do define many of the conditions in which all people of color operate; other people of color often find ourselves having to "measure up" to the terms defined by African American histories and cultures, which are political histories, experiences, and cultural traditions that we do not always share. There is the familiar black/white dichotomy in discussions of racial issues that often fails to account for other people of color–our dealings with white people, with each other, and the dynamics that exist within the presumably homogenous group of "white." This comparison, then, is made in order to articulate some of the differences that exist among people of color, thereby breaking this dichotomy into the more complex interactions that exist between the groups.

16. Although there have been recorded histories of APIs in the United States since the 1700s, our presence here has been a result of waves of immigration, unlike the massive importation of African slaves within a comparatively shorter period of time. Furthermore, legislation such as the Chinese Exclusions Act (1882) and the Gentlemen Agreement Act (1911), and other such laws that prohibited

APIs from entering the United States, as well as related legislation such as the alien land laws of 1920s, have prohibited APIs from settling in the United States.

17. Here, the word "stereotype" is not used in the sense that these representations are entirely false images, but that they are "arrested representations" in the sense that Homi Bhabha proposes because I feel that although these representations are one-dimensional and often "degrading," they nevertheless contain a small degree of "truth" that is distorted through misunderstanding. Therefore, this is not really a question of "good" versus "bad" images but a question of variety and breadth that exists within imaging.

18. Since there are many pre-existing texts that deal with this phenomenon from various viewpoints, I chose to focus on the specific circumstances within gay communities. For other discussions around the correlation between stereotypes of APIs in the media and how they affect the perception and treatment of APIs, look at Renee Tajima's "Lotus Blossoms Don't Bleed: Images of Asian Women," in *Anthologies of Asian American Film and Video* (New York: A Distribution project of Third World Newsreel, 1984), p. 28, and the videos *Slaying the Dragon* by Debra Gee and *Who Killed Vincent Chin?* by Christine Choy and Renee Tajima.

19. From *Race Relations Made Flesh* by Andy Spieldenner.

20. From Richard Fung's essay "Looking for My Penis: The Eroticized Asian in Gay Video Porn," p. 149.

21. The association of "orientals" with feminized exoticism and sensuality has been pointed out and analyzed by Edward Said in his book *Orientalism*. Although his text focuses more on Middle and Near Eastern cultures, and Richard Fung has made important distinctions between the construction of the Middle/Near Eastern "Oriental" and the Far Eastern "Oriental" in "Looking For My Penis," I feel that the discourse of Oriental/Occidental delineated by Said also applies to what I am discussing here. For an example of how such mechanisms of representation operate upon a Far Eastern subject, see the first chapter of Rey Chow's *Woman and Chinese Modernity*, in which she analyses the orientalizing mechanisms in Bertolucci's *The Last Emperor*.

22. From *The Song of Unending Desire* by Justin Chin. This part of the longer work was published in the Fall issues of *Lavender Godzilla* under the title "Doing It On The Oriental," Vol. 4, No. 2 (Fall 1991), p. 24. The entire work is unpublished.

23. The quote of Freud is from Anna Freud, *The Ego and the Mechanism of Defense* (New York, International Universities Press, 1946), p. 111, cited in Frantz Fanon, *Black Skin, White Masks*, trans. Charles Lam Markmann (New York: Grove Weidendeld, 1967), p. 51. Fanon's application of Freud's passage is also located on the same page.

24. In E.S. Hetrick and A.D. Martin, "Designing an AIDS Reduction Program for Gay Teenagers," in *Problems and Proposed Solutions in Biobehavioral Control of AIDS*, David G. Ostrow, ed. (New York: Irvington Publishers, Inc., 1987), p. 43. Although Hetrick and Martin's article focuses primarily on AIDS among gay teenagers, and Fanon's discussion on blacks in Antilles, I think that their in-

sightful discussion of self-hatred, denial, and self-destructive behaviors applies very succinctly to my discussion here. In the second quote from Hetrick and Martin, I have substituted AIDS-specific phrases with ones that are more lesbian and gay-specific. I am also aware of the problematic roles that the institutions of psychology and psychoanalysis have played in the construction of same-sex sexual relationships as a form of pathology. However, since we do live and operate within a society in which certain sets of ideologies, namely Patriarchy, Capitalism, and Eurocentricism, are privileged over others, and that we are all acculturated to these ideologies in different degrees, I do personally favor an approach of critical engagement over outright rejection. I chose these statements from Hetrick and Martin for their clarity in illustrating the murky emotional responses caused by self-hatred in a specifically "lesbian and gay" context. Their statements should be read in relation to the earlier statements by Fanon and Fung.

25. Ibid.

26. In Audre Lorde's "Eye to Eye: Black Women, Racism, and Anger," p. 164.

27. Alice Y. Hom, "Homophobia: The Fear of Going Home," unpublished essay.

28. Pamela H., "Asian American Lesbians: An Emerging Voice in the Asian American Community," p. 284.

29. A gay bar frequented by API gay men. It is often a venue for non-API men who fetishize API men to look for sex partners, but at the same time, it also offers a "safe space" for API gay men from predominantly Euro/American bars.

30. "Sticky rice" refers to an API gay man or lesbian dating another API gay man or lesbian. It is a play off of "rice queen," which denotes a non-Asian gay man who only dates Asian men.


# WORKS CITED

"But Some of Us Are Brave–Lesbians, Culture, and Politics," *San Francisco Sphere*, Nov. 1991.

Chin, Justin. *The Song of Unending Desire*, 1991, part of which was published as "Doing It On the Oriental" in *Lavender Godzilla* (fall 1991): 22-24.

Chow, Rey. *Woman and Chinese Modernity: The Politics of Reading Between West and East*. Minnesota: U of Minnesota P, 1991.

Chung, C., A. Kim, and A.K. Lemeshewsky, eds. *Between the Lines: An Anthology by Pacific/Asian Lesbians of Santa Cruz, California*. Santa Cruz: Dancing Bird, 1987.

Fanon, Frantz. *Black Skin, White Masks*. Trans. Charles Lam Markmann. New York: Grove Weidendeld, 1967.

Fung, Richard. "Looking for My Penis: The Eroticized Asian in Gay Video Porn." *How Do I Look? Queer Film and Video*. Ed. Bad Object Choices. Seattle: Bay, 1991. 145-168.

Kim, Willyce. *Dancer Dawkins and the California Kid*. Boston: Alyson, 1985.

_____ . *Dead Heat*. Boston: Alyson, 1988.

H., Pamela. "Asian American Lesbians: An Emerging Voice in the Asian American Community." *Making Waves: An Anthology of Writings by and about Asian American Women.* Boston: Beacon, 1989. 284-290.

Hemphill, Essex. Introduction to *Brother To Brother: New Writings by Black Gay Men.* Ed. Essex Hemphill. Boston: Alyson, 1990. xv-xxxi.

Hetrick, E.S., and Martin, A.D. "Designing an AIDS Reduction Program for Gay Teenagers." *Problems and Proposed Solutions in Biobehavioral Control of AIDS.* Ed. David G. Ostrow. New York: Irvington, 1987. 43.

*Lavender Godzilla,* c/o Gay Asian Pacific Alliance, P.O. Box 421884, San Francisco, CA 94142-1884.

Lorde, Audre. "Eye to Eye: Black Women, Racism, and Anger." *Sister Outside.* Freedom, CA: Crossing Press Feminist Series, 1984. 145-175.

Lu, Ming-Yeung. "Passion Tales: Allegories of Identity." *Lavender Godzilla* (Spring 1992): 6-15.

Makeda, Silvera, ed. *Piece of My Heart: A Lesbian of Colour Anthology.* Toronto: Sister Vision, 1992.

Noda, Barbara. *Eating Strawberries.* Berkeley: Shameless Hussy, 1979.

*Phoenix Rising,* c/o Asian Pacifica Sisters, P.O. Box 170596, San Francisco, CA 94117.

Robinson, Harold et al., eds. *Queer City.* New York: Portable Lower Eastside, 1991.

Said, Edward W. *Orientalism.* New York: Vintage Books, 1979.

Spieldenner, Andy. *Race Relations Made Flesh.* Unpublished, 1991.

Tsui, Kitty. *The words of a woman who breathes fire.* San Francisco: Sinister, 1983.

Villanueva, Chea. *Girlfriends* (#1 in the Girlfriends Trilogy). New York: Outlaw, 1987.

_____. *The Chinagirls* (#2 in Girlfriends Trilogy). Lezzies on the Move, 1991.

Woo, Merle. *Yellow Woman Speaks.* Seattle: Radical Women Publications, 1986.

# (Re)Locating the Gay Filipino: Resistance, Postcolonialism, and Identity

Martin F. Manalansan IV, Phd (cand.)

*University of Rochester*

**SUMMARY.** This paper attempts to critically analyze issues of postcolonial displacement, immigration, and homosexuality by examining the works of two Filipino gay immigrant writers, John Silva and Ralph Peña. Using postcolonial and critical theories, anthropological studies, and ethnographic fieldwork in New York City, this paper focuses on the role of language, memory, the body, race/ethnicity, and social class in the narrative strategies of the two writers. This paper argues that gay postcolonial writers such as these two relocate and reconfigure homosexual/gay identity in the face of new and oppressive hierarchies, identities, and practices.

## The Diasporic Deviant/Diva

When I came to America, ten years ago, *parang panaginip* [like a dream] . . . all the scenes I saw on American TV shows and movies were happening all at once.

*Renato, 32 years old*

Correspondence may be addressed to the author at: 129 West 20th St., New York, NY 10011.

[Haworth co-indexing entry note]: "(Re)Locating the Gay Filipino: Resistance, Postcolonialism, and Identity." Manalansan, Martin F., IV. Co-published simultaneously in the *Journal of Homosexuality* (The Haworth Press, Inc.) Vol. 26, No. 2/3, 1993, pp. 53-72; and *Critical Essays: Gay and Lesbian Writers of Color* (ed: Emmanuel S. Nelson) The Haworth Press, Inc., 1993, pp. 53-72. Multiple copies of this article/chapter may be purchased from The Haworth Document Delivery Center [1-800-3-HAWORTH; 9:00 a.m. - 5:00 p.m. (EST)].

The seven years before coming to America, before my father's [immigration] petitions for all of us [in the family] were approved by the embassy, were a preparation. Everything began here in America.

*Jake (a.k.a. Jasmine), 21 years old*

The first thing I realized here is that the gays are very different from the *bakla* in Manila. I met this gorgeous *afam* [American], macho '*day*, and we cruised each other, went home together and in bed, he lifted his legs up in the air like any bona fide hair stylist . . . *nakakaloka* [maddening]. But I went through it . . . *alam mo na* [you know] . . . when in Rome . . .

*Efren (a.k.a. Imelda), 43 years old*

The iconic quotations above are from "real" lives elicited in ethnographic interviews of Filipino gay immigrants living in New York City. These voices, like the works of John Silva and Ralph Peña, two Filipino immigrant gay writers whose works will be discussed in this paper, demonstrate the intricacies of postcolonial displacement, both physical and cultural.

This paper attempts to analyze two works which draw on the intersection of race/ethnicity/nationalism, economic status, and homosexual/gay identities and the processes of postcolonialism, immigration, AIDS, and mass media. This paper will map out the sociocultural milieu while setting forth the narrative strategies deployed by the authors. It utilizes multiple sources, such as interviews with Filipino gay men, ethnography, and critical theory in order to provide a symptomatic reading, that is, to identify and articulate the distinctive features of their postcoloniality (Ashcroft 115; see also McClintock; Shohat). In the first section, I will use the two texts to map out the role of language and memory in the imagination of spaces. I will provide a short historical cultural background of U.S.-Philippine colonial and postcolonial configurations. In the second section, Gay Desire and the Ineluctability of Class, I will attempt to fill the gaps about class that have always plagued gay critical writing. These two writers are seen in terms of how marginalization is a relative term and how access to and competence in American culture is facilitated by their upper- or middle-class upbringing and Western education. This section argues how class is oftentimes subsumed under the idioms of race and ethnicity. In the third section, the Deterritorialized Body, I will extend the notion of space into a notion of bodies. In this section, I will analyze the rhetorical strategies involved in presenting race, class, and sexuality through the medium of the body using Deleuze and Guattari's concept of deterritorialization. Of particular importance is the interaction of physical or corporeal conditions, such as complexion or HIV infection, with cultural displacement and differences. In the final section, I will attempt to sum up the interpretations and propose a way of reading particular kinds of gay immigrant writings.

People, ideas, and objects are in constant flux in a postmodern world. Perpetual diasporas, mass communication, and mass transportation establish what is called a "global ethnoscape." "Tourists, refugees, exiles, guestworkers, and other moving groups and persons" occupy this terrain in an increasingly unprecedented degree (Appadurai 192). In such a world, space and identity become increasingly problematic (Gupta & Ferguson 6-23). Cultural production therefore takes on a cosmopolitan character. The desire that many Third World people feel for the Western world, and the yearning that exiles and expatriates feel for their homeland are reflected in many themes of postcolonial writings. The influx of people and ideas continues to grow exponentially between different regions of the world. These "travels" have allowed people to expand their imagination about "other places." Fax machines, video cassette recorders, and other technological marvels allow people specifically of the Third World to see and hear the other side without having to leave their homelands.

Within such a background, gay postcolonial writers who have immigrated to the metropolitan center confront a multiplicity of identities, hierarchies, and dislocations. While U.S.-born gay writers of color face an oppressive white hegemony, the bifocality inherent in the postcolonial condition forces gay immigrant writers of color to face several sets of interconnected oppressive structures. The construction of their "otherness" takes on several levels of meaning and a profusion of practices and fractures. The works of gay immigrant writers of color attempt to bridge the disjunctures brought about by immigration, exile, or other transnational processes and more importantly the effects of western/westernized education and the adoption of such colonial languages as English.

The imaginings of the postcolonial immigrant gay writers involve the constantly shifting notions of "here" and "there." Mercurial concepts such as "homeland" and "new home" are among the central symbolic anchors for the works of gay immigrant writers. As such, they offer possibilities and strategies that shape the unique form of their writings. Edward Said writes about the qualities of the exile (the preeminent role of the postcolonial):

> 'Seeing' the entire world as a foreign land makes possible originality of vision. Most people are aware of one culture, one setting, one home; exiles are aware of at least two, and this plurality of vision gives rise to an awareness of simultaneous dimensions, an awareness that–to borrow a phrase from music–is contrapuntal. "Exile," 366

For gay writers from the Third World, immigration provides a multidimensional vision. For these men, the collision of ideologies and the ambivalence of attitudes and feelings (particularly towards the former colonial master) re-locate the place of sexual identity within their texts. In other words, the contestation of being gay is viewed concurrently with and through other kinds of oppressions and yearnings, both local and transnational.

In the case of Silva and Peña, the historical relationship between the Philippines and the United States becomes the grist for fabulating postcolonial gay selves. "Iyay," a story by John Silva which is basically an autobiographical memoir, is a reminiscence about his nanny who is affectionately called Iyay. The work interweaves snatches of Silva's childhood growing up in the Philippines, his homosexual desires, and his immigration to the United States. These experiences are set against the figure of Iyay who is an intrinsic part of his family and emotional life, but whose class and cultural difference set her apart from the author within the social hierarchy. In "Iyay," Silva constructs a narrative that meditates on the inequalities of class and race in the Philippines and in the United States.

The second work, *Cinema Verite*, is by Ralph Peña, a playwright living in New York City. *Cinema Verite* is a performance piece, a one-man monologue. It chronicles the travails of a Filipino gay immigrant named Gerry de la Cruz who dispenses his experiences and opinions in a campy, self-mocking, and poignant manner. It spans the times of sexual awakening in a Catholic seminary, his attempts at getting a visa to enter the United States, his escapades in bars and sex cinemas in the Big Apple, falling in love, and eventually becoming HIV infected. Peña approaches his narrative by showing the dynamics of homophobia, racism, immigration, and AIDS in the Philippines and in the United States and how these processes create multiple displacements.

## THE CARTOGRAPHIES OF DESIRE

To understand the two works one must understand the colonial and postcolonial configurations of power, culture, and desire between the Philippines and the United States. The relationship between the two countries is exemplified by what ABC correspondent Sam Donaldson said in a discussion during the 1986 Philippine revolution that ousted Ferdinand Marcos. When the other members of the panel started comparing the Philippines with Haiti and other countries undergoing massive political upheaval, Donaldson countered, "But the Filipinos are different, they are family."

Essentially, the web of relationships started more formally with the American annexation of the Philippines after the Spanish-American war. After suppressing military resistance by nationalist Filipinos, America started a rather incestuous kinship tie with the Philippines. The "years of Hollywood," with American colonization of the Philippines, have never abated, especially with the organization of military bases (Clark Air Force Base and Subic Naval Base among others) and the transplanting of American corporations. The relationship has been so close that anybody white was *Amerikano* or *Kano* and everything imported was PX (post exchange or the United States military commissary, which was at one time the only constant source of American and other western products).

The close articulation between Philippine and American cultures has created what could be considered a border culture (Gupta & Ferguson 18; Rosaldo 196-217). Unlike Mexico, the Philippines does not have territorial contiguity with the United States. However, the widespread use of the English language and American popular culture has produced a rarefied hybrid culture. Gupta and Ferguson said that borderlands are places of incommensurable contradictions and do not indicate a fixed topographical site (Gupta & Ferguson 19).

In this situation, imaginings and dreams about the center preoccupy the conscious and unconscious texts of the inhabitants of the periphery. This is illustrated by the way Silva and Peña utilize icons of American popular culture to frame their narratives whether the settings involve the Philippines or America. Tab Hunter and Rick Nelson inhabit Silva's homosexual fantasies and Doris Day sings "Que Sera Sera" to emphasize the inevitability of his immigration to the States. Peña picks camp figures such as Judy Garland and Bette Davis to boost the satirical and gay mood of the narrative, which is punctuated by Manhattan Transfer's "A Nightingale Sang in Berkeley Square."

To go abroad for most Filipinos means to go to America. Dreams of going to America are as ordinary as the shanties that line Manila's roads. The American embassy is always full of people lined up with the hopes of getting a visa. The steady flow of immigrants and temporary visitors has made Filipinos one of the fastest growing immigrant populations in the United States. Immigration therefore naturally extends the kinship ties with the mother country in more spatial terms.

In this context, the two works by Silva and Peña reflect the dreams of America as well as imaginings of the Philippines. Territoriality is eroded and contradictions are brought to light when "the imagined places become lived spaces" (Gupta & Ferguson 11). Indeed, what is perhaps striking in both texts is their attempt to meditate on the realities of living in one country while dreaming of another. These realities include homophobia, class inequality, and racism. Asymmetries occur not just in one but in both spaces.

Silva and Peña utilize language to delineate postcolonial displacement. It is language, whether English, Ilonggo (a language in south central Philippines), or Tagalog, which lays out the rough terrain of immigration, homosexual desire, class, and racial difference in the two works. Postcolonial linguistic issues revolve around the language hierarchy that mirrors the sociopolitical, economic, and cultural configurations of colonial history and multinational business (Said, "Figures" 10-11). In the Philippines, bilingualism or multilingualism is a reality as in any "Third World" country. English, which is one of the official languages of the country, is actually used more often than any other Philippine language. Many Filipinos switch between English and one of the native languages. All these realities are reflected in the strategic and critical use of language(s) in the postcolonial text.

Language plays paradoxical and multiple roles in the two texts. English is a stark temporal marker in both texts. Increasing fluency in English is seen as a period of radical change in the life trajectories presented in the two works. Silva recounts the time before immigrating to America as a time when there is a radical linguistic shift. His father forbade him and his sisters to speak Ilonggo and punished them by deducting a few centavos from their allowance if they did so. It was also at this time that he was weaned away from Iyay's care. This temporary separation was further aggravated by his speaking to her in English. He writes:

> To Iyay, cut off from the routine of caring for me, this new regime was distressing. And when I spoke to her in English, she kept silent, understanding little and unable to respond. She would often give me an angry smirk for making her feel stupid. (23)

This illustrates how language creates a gulf, distance, and asymmetry in a loving, seemingly equal relationship. This spatializing dimension of language is equally as important as its temporalizing one because they occur concurrently. In this instance, distance foretells the impending separation between the author and his nanny when he immigrates to the United States. Furthermore language also creates social distance as linguistic competence in English also marks the class differences between the nanny and her ward.

After years in America, Silva's homecoming is marked by another linguistic change when Iyay notices his American accent when speaking Ilonggo. This change in linguistic ability parallels the alterations in Silva's views about class hierarchy and oppression that occurs in the Philippines. He has come to re-view his relationship with Iyay within the framework of the class structure. The language in the text also shifts from a mnemonic rumination to an almost polemic one about the class realities in the Philippines.

Immigration reshapes the linguistic landscape in both texts and within the individual. Peña writes about the point when Gerry de la Cruz (the play's lone character) starts losing his links with the Philippines and losing his "Filipino-ness." It was at this time he started to gain confidence in speaking English:

> I had a heck of a time with English. I'd want to say something, think of it in Filipino, make the translation in my head, and then say it in English. By then, I've lost the momentum. Oh God, I've ruined jokes this way. After a while, with the help of *Sesame Street* and *Knotts Landing*, I got the hang of it. And the first indication that I may have lost some of my "Filipino-ness" was when I began to dream in English. (6-7)

Peña interconnects the expansion of the imagination and identity with linguistic ability and cultural competence. Throughout the play, Gerry performs verbal acrobatics, puns, and alliterations with gay white American camp idioms.

Language displays and revivifies the bifocal perspective and the experience of displacement. Silva utilizes English and Ilonggo when he writes about his beloved nanny. Like a primeval archeologist or antiquarian, Silva picks and lays out native words either untranslated or with parenthetical English translations to construct the place of his childhood, to "exhibit" to other readers his native culture and to evoke memory.

Memory is a tool for revivifying experience as well as for the re-construction of otherness. The Ilonggo word for remember is *dumdum*. This word is repeated throughout Silva's text. He writes, "To forget, you see was tantamount to ending one's love" (24). For Silva, memory is an act of love as well as a re-creation. In his text, memory or remembering acquires a new dimension, its fetishization. The sensory experiences Silva lays out for the reader in a diglossic fashion perform mnemonic and objectifying roles. For example, when he writes about the sweets that his Iyay would bring for him after her mahjong sessions and comes up with a list that resembles a catalogue of artifacts, *"Serg's chocolate bars, sugar coated peanuts, drops of molasses in little wooden globules dispar-*

*agingly called pungit sang Igorot (the snot of the Igorot) or Chinese dried plums called champuy"* (22).

This text, much like a museum guide, takes the non-native reader on a selective tour of another culture. Memory is heightened in order to convert sense experiences into quasi-lessons on Philippine culture. The objectification of memory results in the transfiguration of otherness. In this process of bringing sense experiences from the past, Silva at the same time creates a space between past and present. This distance between what happened "there" and his vantage point "here" imbues the past with an alterity. The familiar childhood objects and scenes are presented in a detached descriptive form very much like traditional ethnography.

Both Silva and Peña seem to find the need to formulate passages to locate themselves within the culture they left behind and to signify their differences within the culture in which they have been relocated. In Silva's text, alterity is presented through the invocation of words such as terms for his grandfather's mistress (*querida*), straw mats (*banig*), or names that are left untranslated or in the raw, as well as the juxtaposition of native terms with parenthetical translations. The blatant authorial intrusion brought about by word translations provides the impersonal air of traditional ethnography. Silva performs the role of cultural translator or pseudo-anthropologist by explaining some native customs such as *tanday* to provide both a sense of otherness and displacement. He also provides an opportunity for Filipino readers to trigger their own memories.

The persistent litany of native objects juxtaposed with the English translations performs metonymic functions, as it centers the realities of two cultures, nations, experiences, and languages (Ashcroft 51-77). Silva is like the primordial archeologist–the antiquarian–who fishes out of memory the keepsakes, and the marks and indexicals of life events in the Philippines.

Unlike Silva, Peña does cultural translations in an indirect way by refusing until in the middle of the play to locate his character's ethnographic pontifications. In this part of the play, Gerry narrates how he is led by a gorgeous white hunk from a New York gay bar out into the streets where the white man's friends are waiting. They surround him and he attempts to get out of the situation by saying he is not gay. They beat him anyway; all the while he is screaming.

But in the last moment, when his defenses are completely down, he screams, "*Hindi ako bakla*" (I am not homosexual). At his most naked and vulnerable moment, the main character reverts to his native language. While throughout the play, the verbal acrobatics are provided in trendy and campy English, the type that one hears from American stand-up comics, it is in this one scene when the lone Tagalog phrase is uttered. Violence and homophobia then reterritorialize the character and unmask both the mimicry and ambivalence inherent in the fluent and rapid English one-liners.

The experiences Peña recalls are humorous encounters of an openly gay man which when taken without the spatial references could possibly occur anywhere. The ironic mode employed by the author "signals real or feigned disbelief . . . towards [his] own statements; it often centers on the recognition of the problematic nature of language and so it revels or wallows in satirical techniques" (Fischer 224). The bashing scene brings the main character and the whole play back into its postcolonial core. Ambivalence is exposed with the single Tagalog utterance and reveals the colonial mimicry of the main character. Gerry de la Cruz is the quintessential postcolonial because he is like, as Gayatri Spivak has said, "the wild anthropologist" displaying the cultural savvy of a First World native while still being part of the Third World (165).

The persistent use of colloquial English throughout *Cinema Verite* encloses an attempt to deny one's racial/national/ethnic origins. This phenomenon is seen in many Filipino gay immigrants who deny their national or ethnic origins and say they are from Hawaii or Samoa or someplace "more exotic." In the case of Gerry de la Cruz, the switch from English to Tagalog involves a dual denial of being gay and of being Filipino. This duality represents how language, much like ideology, simultaneously obfuscates and reveals underlying conditions. It also shows how the inclusion of native languages within a predominantly English text is a strategic action aimed at resisting and subverting the hegemonic genres and narratives prevailing in cultural production.

## GAY DESIRE AND THE INELUCTABILITY OF CLASS

The cosmopolitan practices displayed in the texts are necessarily backed up by economic realities. The gay expatriates in the texts, both fictional and "real," do not have the financial stories of woe incessantly referred to by numerous other immigrants. They are upper-class gay men who came either to study, as in *Cinema Verite*, or because of links to America (Silva's father being an officer in the U.S. army).

What is striking in both texts are the strategies deployed in fashioning gay desire in relation to class and other inequalities. While Silva attempts to discuss the oppressive class structure in the Philippines, he is silent about its counterpart in the United States; Peña on the other hand refers tangentially to class. This is not to say, however, that they are impervious to the importance of the class nexus in understanding social realities. Rather, they are influenced by the processes of immigration, exile, and expatriation. These processes obscure class distinctions. The rhetoric of American immigration seems to imply that assimilation and citizenship involve shucking one's native values as well as status at the border. There is a popular conception that one comes to America naked from the trappings of class. Furthermore, there is a resistance in American popular discourse to any discussion of the topic (Ortner *passim*).

The texts show how class does not cross borders in the same form. While the two writers may not talk directly about class differences in the United States, they unwittingly include it in their discussion of gay desire and ethnic/racial alterity. The strategies involved in both texts dissolve the various inequalities of class, race, and/or ethnicity with each other across spaces. More specifically, class is processed through the lens of gay desire and ethnicity/race. Class position in the Philippines is juxtaposed with alien status in the United States.

In a pivotal scene, Silva visits Iyay with his lover Jonathan. During dinner, he sits Iyay at the head of the table or the *kabisera*, which is usually reserved for the most esteemed member of the family/head of the household. He marvels at the transformation Iyay undergoes when she sits down to dinner:

> I couldn't understand Iyay's coldness. Was it because she was thirty years older now from all that ribaldry? Was she uncomfortable with my egalitarian gesture of having her sit to dinner with us? Was it because she was shy not being able to speak to

> Jonathan in English? Was she ill? Then it dawned on me as I
> smelled the perfume she was wearing, Chanel was my lola's
> favorite . . . Now she was seated for the first time in my lola's
> chair, eating at the very table she had waited on. She was repli-
> cating my lola's actions, my lola, indifference to eating and to
> everyone else at the table, her habit of looking ahead, disdainful
> of the dinner conversation. (33)

Iyay's mimicry of Silva's grandmother (*lola*) an upper-class
woman is seen in corporeal terms. This class mimicry parallels the
cultural mimicry Silva develops during his stay in the United States.
The transformation in Iyay's appearance goes hand in hand with
Silva's light complexion after his U.S. sojourn. In a sense, this
transformation speaks of Silva own changes in the United States.

In America, class difference and gay desire attain the dimension
of "ethnic" otherness (Brennan 1-19). Immigrant gay desire is seen
as an intrinsic part of Silva's alterity. He writes:

> I soon developed my first childhood crush on a classmate named
> Edward Kowinski, a bright-eyed, blond, freckle-faced boy. I
> called him every night from the hall closet and ended my good-
> byes by boldly declaring my love for him. (He wouldn't re-
> spond, perhaps attributing my queer affection to my being a
> foreigner.) (24)

Silva reconciles the fact that because he is an alien or racial other,
the "queerness" of his desires may be seen through other forms of
alterities. His upper-class standing is virtually invisible. This is
illustrated by another situation when he runs into Tab Hunter, the
star of his (wet) dreams. Hunter knocks him over and Silva remains
unable to declare his love for him and to offer him rides on his
grandfather's Arabian horses. The man of his dreams merely picked
him up, "smiled apologetically and rushed off." Iyay, he contends,
would have corralled, scolded, and forced Hunter back to him, even
if she had to bribe him.

On one level of meaning, he uses Iyay as a contrasting figure to
Tab Hunter. Iyay is loving and more concerned about Silva's person. There is another level, however, in which Iyay is more cogni-
zant of Silva's importance within the Philippine social hierarchy.

For Tab Hunter, Silva is only a dark-complexioned "ethnic" fan. Hunter is unaware of Silva's prominent family, the hacienda, hundreds of farm workers, and the Arabian horses. Iyay, because of her position in the class structure, re-inscribes Silva's importance and self-esteem. It is evident in this section that there is a failure to transfer or translate the attractiveness, power, and allure of high-class standing across spaces.

While *Cinema Verite* is more silent about class issues in general, there are glimpses in which the rather tenuous interconnection of economy and gay desire are attempted. Gerry, the protagonist, describes himself as a middle-class person who inherits his grandfather's estate. This allows him to pursue his dream of studying in the United States. However, at the guidepost of the U.S. embassy, his visa application is rejected despite this economic windfall. Gerry confides that the consul was not amused at the corsage he wore in a graduation picture. He later gets his visa when he chains himself to the window bars and demands a transsexual operation screaming, "Long Live George Washington and Christine Jorgensen"(6).

While eligibility to enter the United States is usually seen in economic terms, this is displaced by sexual alterity. The extreme irony is that he is allowed to enter the borders of the United States because he wants to cross gender borders. The irony of the situation is that the American consul (the vanguard of the borders) only sees through Gerry's sexual alterity and desperation and approves his visa application. The erasure of class distinctions for expatriates from the Third World coincides with the substitution of other idioms of identity.

## THE DETERRITORIALIZED BODY

Deleuze and Guattari use the image of the rhizome to talk about the necessary rootless and mutable conditions in this postmodern world (Chapter 1). This botanical allusion goes further with the gay postcolonial body. This body is an anomaly in the taxonomy of global culture not only because it does not conform to the hyper-masculine white images such as the Terminator Man, but is decentered in both the native lands of the Third World as well as in the hegemonic white gay community of the First World. The postcolonial gay man faces a more intricate grid of hierarchies and oppressions. His body is both physically and culturally reconfigured by dominant cultural producers in porn films (Fung 145-168), in travel and tourism, or in ordinary interactions within what is called the gay community.

The gay postcolonial body is caught in the intersection of class, desire, and race. It is actively refashioned both by individuals and institutions. Class, for instance, as the texts will show, involves the imaginings of complexion, of scent, of demeanor. The somatic aspects of desire and cultural displacement can be seen in terms of what the expatriates feel the standards of desirability are within their adopted culture or to what they themselves aspire or imagine themselves to be. Deployment of various strategies of acquiescence and resistance are both employed in the two texts. Material forces such as the AIDS epidemic and economy also participate in the construction of this listless, rootless body.

In "Iyay," language and body reflect the changes wrought by immigration. In Silva's text, the changes focus on his imaginings about class. He reminisces about his first homecoming in this way:

> When we returned to the Philippines, there was Iyay, amidst hundreds of people at the Manila pier, as our ship, the President Wilson, slowly came to dock. It was not her uniform but her height, and her jumping up and down, that made me notice her immediately. She was so happy she was crying. She embraced me, kissed me and she looked me over, amazed how big I had grown and how my complexion had lightened like an Americano. She had a harder time understanding my Ilonggo, since it acquired an American accent. (30)

In coming back home, Silva comes face to face with the changes within himself through Iyay's observations. The lightness of his complexion is synchronous with the growing notion of differences between himself, his family, the "mestizos," and his class and those of the hacienda workers, the darker ones, and Iyay. The valorization of light skin is interpreted as freedom from manual work, a sign of upper-class breeding as well as an iconic marker of being western or nearly western (mestizo). The lightening of the skin on the other hand paradoxically unfolds with Silva's growing consciousness of the inequities of the class system in the Philippines. He agonizes over the treatment of the household help by his family and his friends, the dismal conditions of the field workers in his family's hacienda, and, most of all, the plight of his Iyay. The epidermal signs are indexical of more internal changes within Silva. Marxist classes in college as well as American society's seeming obsession with hiding class distinctions have molded Silva's own progressive ideas.

Richard Rodriguez, in an analogous situation with Chicano culture and class system, realizes that while his own hands may be as calloused and his skin as dark as *los braceros* and *los pobres*, *"what really made me different from them was an attitude of mind, my imagination of myself"* (278). The corporeal changes in Silva are subsumed in the changes in his own self-construction. He sees himself as a redeemer of people like Iyay, someone who would lift them out of the chaos and misery of poverty. He writes:

> The second time I left the Philippines for the United States, I had grown into an angry twenty-one year old radical. It was another tearful goodbye with Iyay but this time I was ideologically hardened. I promised her that the oppression she and her peasant class had faced for centuries would soon be over. Iyay was quizzical of my zeal. Her only response was that I should send for her once I got settled in the States so she could continue serving me! (30-31)

The effacing qualities of immigration are most striking in *Cinema Verite*. Peña uses language as a tool for the cultural obfuscation of identity within the text. He shows how Gerry attempts to re-work his individual identity by altering his physical appearance. The agony of the transplanted and its bodily manifestations are seen in these lines from *Cinema Verite*, when Gerry de la Cruz laments:

> Now, do I look Filipino to you? Do I? I mean, most times, I'm taken for any nationality but "Filipine," as some of them say. I myself am not sure if I am. I used to be . . . Oh I admit, I tried to hide my roots–literally. I dyed my hair red. I was going for

pale blond, but with blue contact lenses I looked like a Siamese cat. (16-17)

The problematics of identity are interwoven with the reconfiguring of the body. The quote above reveals the necessary ambivalence and instability of identity by Gerry's attempts to "pass" for a Caucasian man. The Caucasian man is seen as the desired image or standard by which to model oneself. The yearning for the West is translated into an "imagined and desired whiteness" (Fanon *passim*). The use of irony in the text and the sarcastic self-mocking attitude of the character index the heart of the postcolonial dilemma, the erasure (albeit unsuccessful) of the native self.

The reconfiguring of the body is reflected in particular standards of beauty and attractiveness. Asian men are not seen as viable objects of desire except in very specific "Orientalized" ways. Gerry is aware of this and he notes:

> It became embarrassingly clear that those [white men] who have a taste for Asians to begin with, were after just that. Smooth hairless body, almond eyes, and long straight black hair. So it's back to the Nancy Kwan look. (17)

The inscription of desirable bodily attributes is framed within what the West has prescribed. Gerry notes that the Asian man or woman must be an Oriental in order to be desirable. The Nancy Kwans of the world, whether men or women, have to subscribe to this tenet. The play *M. Butterfly* (Hwang) emphasizes Gerry's point but in a less campy way. The strategic use of camp in *Cinema Verite* extends the absurd and racist dimensions of this reality.

Gerry charts this issue in New York gay life. In the American gay community, there are bars which cater mostly to Asians and Caucasian men who desire them. These bars are called rice bars and these Caucasian men are called rice queens. These idioms are used by Gerry in the following lines to illustrate how race and desire construct the body within such a space:

> I go to this Asian bar in the Village, appropriately called: THE PADDY. Not to drink really. I'm not much for alcohol, you know, the svelte, starving, Third World look. Sometimes I meet

some very interesting men here. I remember this guy coming up
to me and asking me where I was from. "The Philippines," I
said. . . . He went on to ask why is it that Asians all look alike?
(10)

To designate a bar as a rice bar, as with dinge bars for Black gay
men or cha-cha bars for Latinos, obliterate the corporeality of Asian
men. The question, "Why is it that Asians look alike?" logically
follows the structures of racist sentiments and attitudes that have
given rise to such an institution. This is made more dramatic by the
fact that Gerry is a gay man who immigrated to America to find
these effacing institutions, persons, and practices (Fung 159-160).
Indeed, Gerry's question, "Do I look Filipino?" is a product of
erosions that have plagued him since he started imagining and
desiring America.

In the play, the question of physical appearance and the body is
complicated and in some way answered by the specter of AIDS.
Towards the end of the play, Gerry reveals that he has tested positive for the HIV antibody. His lover dies of AIDS and he himself
attempts suicide but botches it. Then he calls his estranged parents
in the Philippines who tell him to come home. He agrees with them.
The disease brings him back to his family and potentially re-patri-
ates and re-territorializes him.

However, he is unable to "come home" to either the Philippines
or the United States. He declares that because of U.S. and Philippine immigration and quarantine laws he is without a country.
AIDS reterritorializes the corpus, but the legalities and policies
regarding AIDS deterritorializes him again.

At the end of the play, the character distributes a flyer that starts
with "I am Gerry de la Cruz, I am a Filipino and I am HIV positive." The juxtaposition of identity and disease is telling. In some
way, it answers many of Gerry's rhetorical questions about being
(or looking) Filipino. The exigencies of the disease have forced him
to look into the possibility of repatriation, but it has also confronted
him with a blatant and literal kind of "homelessness" that mirrors
his own cultural homelessness as a gay postcolonial.

AIDS becomes the body and the individual becomes the disease.
Gerry embodies AIDS in several ways. AIDS perhaps is the best

allegory of gay postcolonial experience. It is a transnational occurrence, a pandemic that traverses borders and at the same time demarcates borders (between gay and straight, between foreigner and native). It performs within multiple levels of marginality that make up the complex grid of race, nationality, sexuality, and class that gay postcolonials face. The dilemma of AIDS contains the necessary conditions of the gay postcolonial body as it exists within the interstices of various discourses in the First and Third Worlds, and in gay and heterosexual communities. Gerry, as a gay postcolonial, physically and symbolically carries the trappings of the so-called scourge of the twentieth century as he stands on the edges of medical quarantine and cultural and political exclusion.

## READING "GAY" POST-COLONIALITY:
## LOOKING AT THE DIASPORIC DEVIANT

I do not propose a definitive theory of gay postcoloniality on the basis of my interpretation of the two works. I do suggest, however, that the two works provide distinct voices to the writings of gay men of color. Amidst the debate on multiculturalism, there has never been any effort to understand how transnational processes shape (racial/national/ethnic and sexual) identity and world view. It has always been taken for granted that a non-white male writer who has sex with other men and who lives in America will write about the duality of the experience, that is, being non-white (Black, Latino, Asian, or other ethnic/racial groups) and being gay. While these two identities are crucial in the texts of most gay postcolonials, these identities do not address the complexity of the problems and issues they face as individuals and as a group.

To properly understand the nature and dynamics of the two texts by Silva and Peña, it is enlightening to regard them as border texts or as border writings. Hicks defined border writings as deconstructing binarisms or dichotomies and "undermine the distinction between original or alien culture" (xxiii). She further characterized them as multidimensional in that the writings are able "to see not just from one side of the border, but also from the other side as well" (ibid.).

Gay postcolonial writings and authors are multidimensional in the sense that they provide oscillating views from several perspectives, such as disgruntled immigrants in the metropolis, resisting the coopting powers of the dominant culture, a wistful native dreaming of other lands, or a reconstituted native who has lived in both spaces and whose experiences continually connect and divide the contradictory, sometimes opposing, sometimes complementary transnational forces (see Anzaldúa). Silva's autobiographical self and Peña's protagonist Gerry are constructed out of such multifaceted vision(s) that emanate from postcolonial experiences. These textualized selves are embodiments of the complexity of living as a gay man in/from the Third World.

Unlike Western exilic writings (see Seidel), these gay postcolonial writings decenter utopic imaginings. Instead, gay postcolonial writings weld the experiences of oppression in native and adopted lands into discursive reflections on the self and the social world. Silva's and Peña's reflections are not easy polemical condemnations of the First World, nor the idealization of bucolic Third World homelands. Rather, they are raw glimpses into the diversity of oppressions and contestations that cut across boundaries. There is no promised land and no salvation in any one place. For these gay postcolonials, the only imminent vision is universal struggle.

## AUTHOR'S NOTES

A version of this paper was presented at the 3rd Annual National American Studies Graduate Student Conference, Boston University, October 1992. This paper was awarded the Kenneth W. Payne Student Prize for 1992 by the Society of Lesbian and Gay Anthropologists.

John Silva and Ralph Peña generously provided the manuscripts and time to discuss their works. Extended and lively discussions with numerous people allowed me to develop my ideas. Among these were Mary Jane Po, Robin Miller, Gregg Bordowitz, Joey Almoradie, Vince Sales, Bonnie Johnson, and several gay Filipinos living in New York City. David Mcdonagh and Ana Morais edited parts of the paper and gave valuable suggestions. Mike Tan wrote to me about what was happening to friends and the Manila gay scene I left behind (only physically). Rick Bonus, despite being on the other coast, has pushed me into thinking more critically about the similar experiences that have brought the two of us to America and provided the warmth of a friendship that spans the two countries and more than a decade. My family and friends in America and in the Philippines have provided both the memories and the continuity of home wherever "it" is.

# WORKS CITED

Anzaldúa, Gloria. *Borderlands/La Frontera: The New Mestiza.* San Francisco: Aunt Lute, 1987.

Appadurai, Arjun. "Global Ethnoscapes: Notes and Queries for a Transnational Anthropology. *"Recapturing Anthropology: Working in the Present.* Ed. Richard Fox. Santa Fe, NM: School of American Research Press, 1991. 191-210.

Ashcroft, Bill, Gareth Griffiths, and Helen Tiffin. *The Empire Writes Back: The Theory and Practice of Postcolonial Literature.* London: Routledge, 1989.

Brennan, Tim. "Cosmopolitans and Celebrities." *Race and Class* 31.1(1989): 1-19.

Deleuze, Gilles, and Felix Guattari. *A Thousand Plateaus: Capitalism and Schizophrenia.* Minneapolis: University of Minnesota Press, 1987.

Fanon, Frantz. *The Wretched of the Earth.* Harmondsworth: Penguin, 1961.

Fischer, Michael. "Ethnicity and the Postmodern Arts of Memory." *Writing Culture: The Poetics and Politics of Ethnography.* Ed. James Clifford and George E. Marcus. Berkeley: University of California Press, 1986. 194-233.

Fung, Richard. "Looking for My Penis: The Eroticized Asian in Gay Video Porn." *How do I Look.* Ed. Bad Object Choices. Seattle: Bay Press, 1991. 145-168.

Gupta, Akhil, and James Ferguson. "Beyond Culture: Space, Identity and the Politics of Difference." *Cultural Anthropology* 7.1 (1992): 6-23.

Hicks, D. Emily. *Border Writings: The Multidimensional Text.* Minneapolis: University of Minnesota Press, 1991.

Hwang, David Henry. *M. Butterfly.* New York: Plume, 1986.

Ortner, Sherry. "Reading America: Preliminary Notes on Class and Culture." *Recapturing Anthropology: Working in the Present.* Ed. Richard Fox. Santa Fe, NM: School of American Research Press, 1991. 163-189.

McClintock, Anne. "The Angel of Progress: Pitfalls of the Term 'Postcolonialism.'" *Social Text* 31-32 (1992): 84-98.

Peña, Ralph. *Cinema Verite.* Ms.

Rosaldo, Renato. *Culture and Truth: The Remaking of Social Analysis.* Boston: Beacon Press, 1989.

Rodriguez, Richard. "Complexion." *Out There: Marginalizations and Contemporary Cultures.* Ed. Russell Ferguson, Martha Gever, Trinh T. Min-ha, and Cornel West. Cambridge: MIT Press, 1991. 265-366.

Said, Edward. "Reflections on Exile." *Out There: Marginalizations and Contemporary Cultures.* Ed. Russell Ferguson, Martha Gever, Trinh T. Min-ha, and Cornel West. Cambridge: MIT Press, 1991.

————. "Figures, Configurations, Transfigurations." *Polygraph* 4 (1990): 10-26.

Seidel, Michael. *Exile and the Narrative Imagination.* New Haven: Yale University Press, 1986.

Shohat, Ella. "Notes on the 'Post-Colonial.'" *Social Text* 31/32 (1992): 99-113.

Silva, John. "Iyay." *Lavender Godzilla.* (Spring 1992): 20-25, 30-35.

Spivak, Gayatri. "The New Historicism." *The Postcolonial Critic: Interviews, Strategies, Dialogues.* Ed. Sarah Harasym. New York: Routledge, 1990.152-168.

# Myth Smashers, Myth Makers: (Re)Visionary Techniques in the Works of Paula Gunn Allen, Gloria Anzaldúa, and Audre Lorde

AnnLouise Keating

*Eastern New Mexico University*

**SUMMARY.** This paper examines the revisionist mythmaking strategies employed by three lesbian-feminist writers of color: Paula Gunn Allen (Laguna/Sioux/Lebanese/Scottish), Gloria Anzaldúa (Chicana *tejana*), and Audre Lorde (Caribbean/African/American). By incorporating creatrix figures such as the West African Mawulisa, the pre-Aztec *Coatlicue*, and the Laguna Pueblo Spider Old Woman/Thought Woman into their works, they challenge the cultural stereotypes that silence women of color by denying their access to language. Their use of nonwestern mythic material destabilizes monolithic definitions of (white heterosexual) female identity, yet their mythmaking goes beyond this challenge to hegemonic concepts of (white) womanhood. As they replace the Judeo-Christian worldview with modes of perception drawn from Native American, Chicana, and African mythic traditions, they offer a far-reaching critique of western culture's binary structures. By displacing the boundaries

---

Correspondence may be addressed to the author at: Department of Languages and Literature, Eastern New Mexico University, Portales, NM 88130.

The author wishes to thank Gloria Anzaldúa and Karen Hollinger for their comments and suggestions on earlier versions of this paper.

[Haworth co-indexing entry note]: "Myth Smashers, Myth Makers: (Re)Visionary Techniques in the Works of Paula Gunn Allen, Gloria Anzaldúa, and Audre Lorde." Keating, AnnLouise. Co-published simultaneously in the *Journal of Homosexuality* (The Haworth Press, Inc.) Vol. 26, No. 2/3, 1993, pp. 73-95; and *Critical Essays: Gay and Lesbian Writers of Color* (ed: Emmanuel S. Nelson) The Haworth Press, Inc., 1993, pp. 73-95. Multiple copies of this article/chapter may be purchased from The Haworth Document Delivery Center [1-800-3-HAWORTH; 9:00 a.m. - 5:00 p.m. (EST)].

73

between inner/outer, subject/object, spirit/matter, and other dichotomous terms, the new myths they create provide radical alternatives to the existing social structures.

I say *mujer magica*, empty yourself. Shock yourself into new ways of perceiving the world. Shock your readers into the same. Stop the chatter inside their heads.[1]

The rejection of traditional phallocentric values and the subsequent search for alternate descriptions of reality which affirm female experience has become a major theme in twentieth-century women's poetry and fiction.[2] Whether they explore the ways in which the dominant discourse silences women or appropriate and transform conventional stories and myths, a number of contemporary feminist writers have demonstrated the vital connection between narrative control and self-realization. In such works, only those female protagonists who can tell their own stories have the authority to define themselves. As several recent critics suggest, one of the most effective strategies employed in this effort to reclaim the power of speech involves the revision of patriarchal myths.[3] Because myths embody a culture's deepseated, often unacknowledged (and therefore unquestioned) assumptions about human nature, this narrative technique enables women poets and novelists to subvert hegemonic descriptions of female identity in two interrelated ways: To borrow Rachel Blau DuPlessis's terms, they "displace" the narrative voice by permitting the woman silenced in traditional accounts to tell her side of the story, or they "delegitimate"–alter and rearrange–the narrative events.

According to both DuPlessis and Alicia Ostriker, the motivating force behind women writers' revisionist myths is the subversion of the dominant ideology's hidden male bias. By rewriting the well-known tales of Eve, Lilith, Medusa, and other mythic figures, feminists challenge the traditional accounts' false representations of women. These alterations transform the original myths' structure and content so extensively that, as Ostriker asserts, "the old stories are changed, changed utterly, by female knowledge of female experience" (215).

But what happens when women mythmakers reject both the "old stories" and the Graeco-Roman tradition they reflect? If changing the content transforms the conventional myths into critiques of western civilization's masculinist bias, what implications arise when, instead of an "old vessel filled with new wine" (Ostriker 212), both the container and the wine are replaced? Do the resulting myths still function primarily as "the challenge to and correction of gender stereotypes" (216)? Or do they oppose other systems of oppression as well? According to Bonnie Zimmerman's analysis of recent lesbian fiction, revisionist mythmaking plays an additional role in the work of lesbians of color. By introducing issues of ethnicity into their texts, "third world" lesbians simultaneously reclaim the cultural specificity of their own female identities and expose the hidden racism often found in feminism itself: they "offer a political correction to the ethnocentric vision of white women as well as an affirmation of their own cultural traditions" (203).

An examination of the revisionary strategies employed by Allen, Anzaldúa, and Lorde both illustrates and extends Zimmerman's assertion. As lesbians of color, these writers negotiate diverse sets of socially constructed spaces: Allen, a professor of Native American studies at UCLA and the Laguna/Sioux/Lebanese/Scottish daughter of shopkeepers was born on the Cubero land grant in New Mexico; Anzaldúa, a cultural theorist and Ph.D. candidate at Santa Cruz, is the Chicana *tejana* daughter of farm workers from south Texas; and Lorde, the daughter of working-class Caribbean immigrants and a self-described "Black woman warrior poet," was born and raised in New York City. To borrow Victor Turner's phrase, they are "threshold people" who "elude or slip through the network of classifications that normally locate states and positions in cultural spaces" (95). Although the socially constructed spaces each writer "slips through" and the revisionary myths she invents reflect the specificity of her regional, ethnic, and economic background–as well as other differences like native languages, religion, education, and skin color–Allen, Anzaldúa, and Lorde employ similar revisionist strategies. As Zimmerman suggests, their use of non-western mythic material destabilizes monolithic definitions of (white heterosexual) female identity, yet their mythmaking goes beyond this challenge to hegemonic concepts of (white) womanhood. As they replace the Judeo-Christian worldview with modes of perception drawn from Native American, Chicana, and African mythic traditions, they offer a far-reaching critique of western culture's binary structures. By displacing the boundaries between inner/outer, subject/object, spirit/matter, and other dichotomous terms, the new myths they create provide radical alternatives to the existing social structures.

Like other revisionist mythmakers, Anzaldúa, Lorde, and Allen reject the false images of women embodied in phallocentric narratives, but they take this revisionary process even further. Rather than "displace" or "delegitimate" specific stories and myths, they replace the Graeco-Roman tradition itself. By incorporating nonwestern creatrix figures such as the West African Mawulisa, the pre-Aztec *Coatlicue*, and the Laguna Pueblo Spider Old Woman/ Thought Woman into their works, they challenge the cultural stereotypes that silence women of color by denying their access to language.[4] As they "remythologize" their work, their writing becomes a powerful tool for self-discovery, political resistance, and social change. Because they maintain that alterations in the social structure begin within each individual, they describe their writing as a transformational process which empowers them to (re)create themselves, their readers, and the external world. As they write, they undertake what Anzaldúa describes as a "spiritual excavation, . . . (ad)venturing into the inner void, extrapolating meaning from it and sending it out into the world" ("Haciendo caras" xxiv). Their revisionist mythmaking becomes a call to self-reflection and action; by exploring their own inner shadows they challenge their readers to do so as well.

Yet this combination of politics, spirituality, and mythology seems untenable to many contemporary critics. Indeed, even the term "mythology" can be problematic, for it implies a metaphysics—a synthesis of psychic, supernatural, and material forces—often seen as irrelevant to twentieth-century concerns. As both Anzaldúa and Allen point out, because scholars frequently equate tribal myths with superstitious beliefs, they regard nonwestern mythico-religious systems as unsophisticated, inaccurate, and naive.[5] Even those who acknowledge the importance of mythic tales often identify them with a timeless realm and universal truths disconnected from everyday life.[6] However, by separating people's actions in the material world from the symbolic freedom contained in the mythical, such definitions do not account for the role mythic images play in the (de)construction of gender and other systems of difference. As Houston A. Baker, Jr., notes, the dichotomy between "mythic/literary and sociohistoric domains" restricts mythic power to an "ahistorical symbolic universe of discourse." Baker suggests that although these domains *"are distinguishable, they are not mutually exclusive"* (his emphasis) and locates Afro-American literary criticism at the "mediational juncture" of the literary/mythic and sociohistoric worlds of discourse (116-17).

Although Baker restricts his discussions of myth, history, and liminality to the "creative symbolic potency of Afro-American art," I believe that his description of the critic's liminal status illuminates the work of Allen, Anzaldúa, and Lorde. Like his "historically grounded critic" who functions as "a mediator–as an agent who summons and interprets for a human audience the symbolic force of literary or mythic narrative," they too mediate between historic, mythic, and contemporary worldviews. Each writer locates herself at cultural and interpretive crossroads "where new meanings are stunningly generated" (117). More specifically, their positions "betwixt and between"[7] established social structures, customs, and conventional belief systems enable them to reject the traditional dualisms between internal and external forms of reality. They synthesize spiritual, political, and mythic worldviews to create new myths and new theories of writing. As William G. Doty points out, "[i]t is especially in the freedom of liminality that new metaphors are born, revisions of the social structure are first attempted, and creative insights are developed" (91). By replicating their own liminal states in their revisionary myths, Allen, Anzaldúa, and Lorde challenge their readers to rethink the dominant culture's sociopolitical inscriptions. They destabilize the "networks of classification" which hold each individual in her or his own culturally constructed space. In so doing, they create what Trinh Minh-ha describes as "a ground that belongs to no one, not even to the 'creator'" (71). It is this space which cannot be possessed by any single person or group, I would argue, which allows them to simultaneously spiritualize and politicize their works.

Whereas Turner describes the liminal period as a temporary stage which results in the individual's "reaggregation," or return to the social structure, for Paula Gunn Allen liminality represents a permanent (yet constantly changing) way of life. In a 1990 interview she associates her lesbianism with the Native American worldview and explains that "perversity (transformationality) . . . constitutes the sacred moment, the process of changing from one condition to another–*life-long* [her emphasis] liminality" (Caputi 56). Indeed, Allen's entire cosmology reflects this perpetual liminality, a condition of constant transformation which she elsewhere describes as "the fluidity and malleability, or creative flux, of things" (*Sacred Hoop* 68). This belief in a dynamic, living universe shapes Allen's work as a poet, fiction writer, and Native American literary scholar. She locates herself on the interface between internal and external realities and likens her writing process to a vision quest in which she attempts to "pull the vision out of" herself; and the "trick," she maintains, "is to get back to our origins, to know what it knows or what she knows" (qtd. in Eysturoy 99).

This search for the origin–which for Allen represents "our mother," the Laguna Pueblo Thought Woman–does not imply a retreat into a mythical prehistorical past; it is, rather, a political act. Indeed, in "Who Is Your Mother? The Red Roots of White Feminism," Allen emphasizes that her interest in recovering the "red roots" of Anglo feminism is not motivated by "nostalgia." She maintains that until mainstream and radical U.S. feminists recognize that their efforts to establish egalitarian social structures represent the "continuance" of native gynecentric traditions, they overlook important models for political change (*Sacred Hoop* 214). But what, exactly, is the difference between "continuance" and "nostalgia"? After all, both terms seem to indicate the desire to recapture an earlier era. Yet Allen's theory of "life-long liminality" or change, coupled with her insistence that history is nonlinear and each individual is "a moving event in a moving universe" (*Sacred Hoop* 149), makes such interpretations untenable. In a dynamic, constantly changing, organic world, we cannot repeat the past; nor can we escape it. Instead, she explains, we use the past both to understand present conditions more fully and to direct future actions.

Allen's revisionist mythmaking reflects this view of the past. Because she believes that "the loss of memory"–the erasure of tribal and gynecentric traditions–represents "the root of oppression" (*Sacred Hoop* 213), she sees her work as an act of resistance. In essays such as "Grandmother of the Sun: Ritual Gynocracy in Native America" and "Kochinnenako in the Academe," for example, she associates heterosexual, white, male ethnographers' distortions of woman-identified Native American myths with contemporary forms of oppression experienced by indigenous peoples and women of all colors. She reinterprets central female deities such as the Hopi's Spider Woman, the Navajo's Changing Woman, and the Keres Pueblos' Thought Woman in order to demonstrate their significance for twentieth-century feminists. Furthermore, by emphasizing the central role Native American women have played in social, political, and religious structures, she challenges contemporary constructions of female identity.[8]

Unlike many feminist revisionist mythmakers who primarily identify goddess imagery and female power with childbirth,[9] Allen associates women's creativity with the intellect. Thus she opens *The Sacred Hoop*, her collection of scholarly essays, by declaring: "In the beginning was thought, and her name was Woman" (11). Similarly, she begins her novel, *The Woman Who Owned the Shadows*, by retelling the American Indians' creation story of Old Spider Woman, whose "singing made all the worlds. The worlds of the spirits. The worlds of the people. The worlds of the creatures. The worlds of the gods" (1). According to Allen's own tribal tradition–that of the Laguna Keres Indians–the creatrix, Spider Old Woman/Thought Woman, does not give birth to the universe but rather thinks and sings it into existence. By repeatedly emphasizing this point, Allen rejects western culture's hierarchical dichotomy which equates the masculine with the intellect and the feminine with the physical. Yet she does not simply replace one dualism with another. As "the necessary *precondition* [my emphasis] for material creation," Allen's Thought Woman represents a dynamic holistic power, the source of both "material and nonmaterial reality" (*Sacred Hoop* 14-15).

This primary identification of a female creatrix with intellectual power enables Allen to redefine women's roles in society. By emphasizing that female-gendered mythic figures served as the foundation for many tribes' legal, societal, and religious structures, she challenges U.S. stereotypes of women as the "sexually charged" yet passive bearers of (male) culture (*Sacred Hoop* 43-44). She rejects sentimental notions of motherhood and maintains that women's power is not exclusively biological but rather "the power to make, to create, to transform." Allen further destabilizes western culture's equation of motherhood with biological birth by asserting that in many tribal cultures the terms "Mother" and "Matron" represent "the highest office to which a *man* [my emphasis] or woman could aspire" (*Sacred Hoop* 28-29).

Allen's goal is transformation. As she recovers Native American female creatrix figures, she attempts to alter her readers' worldviews. Thus in "Something Sacred Going on Out There: Myth and Vision in American Indian Literature" she equates myth with metamorphosis and change by defining it as a unique mode of communication, "a language construct that contains the power to transform something (or someone) from one state or condition to another." She challenges western conceptions of mythic stories as falsehoods or lies and argues that they embody a mode of perception–"the psychospiritual ordering of nonordinary knowledge"–shared by all human beings, "past, present, and to come." For Allen, myths are "teleological statements" which have a direct bearing on the ways people conduct themselves in the physical world. By affirming each person's "most human and ennobling dimensions," she explains, mythic tales provide human beings with new possibilities for action (*Sacred Hoop* 103-6). Allen's confidence in myths' transformative power has its source in their liminal status–their position "betwixt and between" societal conventions and rules of behavior. As Doty points out, by offering participants a way to distance themselves from everyday experience, myths give them entry "into realms other than the workaday." When readers or listeners imaginatively enter these mythic worlds, they can "play out alternate possibilities that would be impossible" in everyday life (130).

Allen illustrates myths' transformational power in *The Woman Who Owned The Shadows* where her halfbreed protagonist, Ephanie Atencio, remains alienated and unable to control her own life until she rediscovers her role in the sacred stories of her people, the Guadalupe Indians. Throughout most of the novel Ephanie experiences extreme self-division and despair as she attempts to understand the ways her identity has been shaped by childhood events, patriarchal western culture, and Native American traditions. She moves several times, joins a therapy group, attends powwows, studies, and reads, yet psychic wholeness eludes her. Only when she perceives the parallels between her own childhood and the mythic story of the Iroquois Sky Woman can she make sense of her life; as Allen elsewhere explains, she acquires "a point of entry into the ritual patterns of her people" (*Sacred Hoop* 100). It is important to recognize that this "point of entry" does not signal escape into the past; it is, I believe, the reverse. Ephanie's insight transforms her; as she finally understands her own personal and mythic past(s), she learns how to live her life in the present:

> Knowing that only without interference can the people learn and grow and become what they had within themselves to be. For the measure of her life, of all their lives, was discovering what she, they, were made of. What she, they, could do. And what consequences their doing created, and what they would create of these. (212)

Like Paula Gunn Allen, Gloria Anzaldúa utilizes revisionist mythmaking to simultaneously politicize and spiritualize her work. She identifies her task as a writer with that of the Aztec *nahual*, or shaman; she too is a "shape-changer" who uses language to reinvent herself and her world. In *Borderlands* and again in her preface to *Making Face, Making Soul/Haciendo Caras,* she insists that each reader is "the shaper of [her] flesh as well as of [her] soul."[10] This ancient Nahuatl proverb supports her conviction that the inner and outer dimensions of life are intimately related. For Anzaldúa, this interrelationship implies that "making soul," writing, and building new forms of culture are synonymous. Just as the Aztecs believed that "the religious, social and aesthetic purposes of art were all intertwined," so she sees third world women artists as political activists who synthesize the spiritual and material dimensions of life (*Borderlands* 66). Because she maintains that alterations in the social structure have their source in the individual, she encourages women of color to reject external authority and look within. To successfully challenge the existing forms of oppression, they must "break the false mirrors in order to discover the unfamiliar shadows, the inner faces, las caras por dentro" ("Haciendo caras" xvii).

Anzaldúa depicts her own spiritual exploration–her journey into the "unfamiliar shadows" and her discovery of an alternate source of creative power–in *Borderlands/La Frontera*. In fact, this work can be read as her *Künstlerroman*, for in chapters such as "How to Tame a Wild Tongue," "*la herencia de Coatlicue*/The Coatlicue State," and "Tlilli, Tlapalli: The Path of the Red and Black Ink" she explores the obstacles she and other *mestizas* encounter in their efforts to reclaim the written word. Unlike conventional accounts of an artist's struggles to achieve self-autonomy, however, Anzaldúa's narrative blends autobiography with history and social protest with poetry and myth. Even her style–most notably her abrupt shifts between first and third person narration and her code-switching, her transitions from standard to working-class English to Chicano Spanish to Tex-Mex or to Nahuatl–indicates the simultaneous growth of an individual and collective identity.[11]

By interweaving her own story with historical accounts, Anzaldúa rejects western culture's dichotomy between the private and public spheres. As Chandra Mohanty notes, many autobiographies and testimonials produced by third world women challenge traditional theories of selfhood and sociality. These narratives do not emphasize the development of the individual self; instead, they suggest "the possibility, indeed the *necessity* [her emphasis], of conceptualizing notions of collective selves and consciousness as the political practice of historical memory and writing by women of color and third world women" (36). However, because Anzaldúa's conception of a collective self includes a spiritual component as well as the sociopolitical and historical elements Mohanty describes, revisionist mythmaking plays an important role in *Borderlands*. By reclaiming and reinterpreting the figure of *Coatlicue*, she invents an image of female identity which simultaneously reaffirms her ethnic roots and politicizes her work.

Historical and contemporary issues of gender, race, sex, and class converge in Anzaldúa's use of this ancient meso-American goddess. As she traces *Coatlicue*'s descent from her pre-Columbian role as the central creatrix to her current status as the demonic Serpent Woman, she charts the transition from matrifocal to phallocentric social structures which occurred when the indigenous Indian tribes were conquered by the Aztecs and Spaniards. Stripped of her all-inclusive, cosmic powers, this goddess–who originally "contained and balanced the dualities of male and female, light and dark, life and death"–was divided in half: as *Tlazolteotl/Coatlicue*, she was banished to the underworld where she became the embodiment of darkness, materiality, and female evil; and as Tontantsi/Guadalupe, she was purified, Christianized, "desexed," and transformed into the virgin mother (*Borderlands* 32). By associating this primary split with western culture's dual consciousness, Anzaldúa utilizes mythic narrative to critique twentieth-century sociopolitical conditions. As she re-members and reinterprets *Coatlicue*, she challenges the hierarchical oppositional mode of thought which divided this pre-Christian mythic figure into parts.

Anzaldúa's most extensive revisionist mythmaking occurs in "*la herencia de Coatlicue*," *Borderland*'s central chapter. As Cherríe Moraga notes in her review of the book, this chapter is extremely perplexing: "the prose disorients, jumping around from anecdote to philosophy to history to *sueño*, seldom developing a single topic" (152). And indeed, "*la herencia de Coatlicue*" consists of abrupt shifts and puzzling metaphors, but I believe that an analysis of Anzaldúa's revisionary tactics reveals an underlying design. By adapting the figure of *Coatlicue* to represent a central "archetype" in her psyche (*Borderlands* 46), she creates a metaphor which simultaneously depicts her own development as a *mestiza* artist and offers her readers an alternative to western culture's exclusive emphasis on rational thought.

Even the disorienting prose furthers Anzaldúa's revisionist myth, for it replicates the fragmentation which characterizes the *Coatlicue* state. Just as her *Coatlicue* myths symbolize both the descent into double consciousness which occurred under colonial rule and the "fusion of opposites" (*Borderlands* 44-47), the *Coatlicue* state represents periods of intense inner struggle which can entail the juxtaposition, the synthesis, and the transcendence of contrary forces. In its earliest stages, Anzaldúa's *Coatlicue* state is the writing blocks which inhibit her creative energy, and the resistance to growth which prevents her from achieving new states of awareness. She attributes these conflicts to her identity as a *mestiza* and explains that the opposing Mexican, Indian, and Anglo worldviews she has internalized lead to self-division, cultural confusion, and shame. On the one hand, she is drawn to nonrational native traditions which posit the validity of psychic events and the supernatural; on the other, she has been trained to rely solely on reason and dismiss such beliefs as "pagan superstitions." These two modes of perception–"the two eyes in her head, the tongueless magical eye and the loquacious rational eye"–seem to be mutually exclusive; they are separated by "an abyss that no bridge can span" (*Borderlands* 45).

As Anzaldúa's autobiographical description of her first encounter with *Coatlicue* suggests, this extreme dualism–coupled with the subsequent feelings of inadequacy and shame–lead to the *Coatlicue* state. Near the chapter's opening she explains that she began menstruating at a very early age and felt that "[h]er body had betrayed her. She could not trust her instincts, her 'horses,' because they stood for her core self, her dark Indian self" (*Borderlands* 43). Anzaldúa's use of third person narration to describe her own experience replicates the double consciousness which triggers the *Coatlicue* state, as well as the self-alienation which results. To gain distance from the physical, emotional, and psychic pain, she began identifying "the conscious I" exclusively with her intellect. This self-division gave her a (false) sense of autonomy: although she could not control her emotions, she could try to ignore them by focusing entirely on her conscious thoughts.

It is this self-denial which signals entry into the *Coatlicue* state, and Anzaldúa explains that each time she attempts to ignore her psychic or physical fears she experiences an extreme inner conflict which leads to depression, paralysis, and despair. Resolution cannot occur until she acknowledges and begins to explore these previously suppressed emotions. Significantly, she does not *abandon* the "rational eye" in order to rely exclusively on the "magical eye," the emotional/intuitive mode of perception. Instead, she begins using her intellect differently: rather than struggle to maintain self-autonomy, she consciously struggles to let it go. Thus she opens "Letting Go" by asserting that

> It's not enough
> deciding to open.
>
> You must plunge your fingers
> into your navel, with your two hands
> split open (*Borderlands* 164)

As this graphic imagery indicates, Anzaldúa believes that the transition from double consciousness to new states of awareness entails intense, often painful, self-excavation: the *mestiza* must "shake," "rip," and "split open" the protective false masks she normally wears. Only then can she truly "let go. / Meet the dragon's open face / and let the terror" engulf her. Although she "dissolve[s]" into her fear, this self-loss is only a temporary stage which initiates transformation; she has "crossed over" and entered an alien new place: "All around [her] space. / Alone. With nothingness" and no one to save her, she must rely exclusively on herself. But she has entered a liminal space which makes transformation possible, and the self she relies on is different: she is evolving new powers ("gills / grow on [her] breasts") which enable her to survive in this "vast terrain." This poem illustrates transitional states analogous to Allen's "life-long liminality," for Anzaldúa emphasizes that "letting go" and "crossing over" are not isolated discrete events: "It's not enough / letting go twice, three times" or even "a hundred" (*Borderlands* 164-66).

Similarly, in "Poets have strange eating habits" Anzaldúa adopts a series of metaphors such as horseback riding and human sacrifice to illustrate the poet's use of conscious thought. In this poem writing becomes a wild "nightride" over the edge of a cliff. Rather than surrender the reins and let her instincts or emotions entirely control her, she must "coax and whip" the "balking mare / to the edge." Once again, the decision to "let go" is presented as a deliberate choice, and she asks: "Should I jump face tumbling / down the steps of the temple / heart offered up to the midnightsun." Her decision to leap over the edge makes self-change possible:

Suspended in fluid sky
I, eagle fetus, live serpent
    feathers growing out of my skin[.]

As in "Letting Go," Anzaldúa describes this transition in terms which imply perpetual liminality: "Taking the plunge" becomes habitual, as "routine as cleaning [her] teeth," and "jumping off cliffs" is "an addiction" (*Borderlands* 140-41).

The conscious decision to "jump"–which, paradoxically, entails relinquishing conscious control–initiates what I will describe as the second major phase of Anzaldúa's *Coatlicue* state. Her exploration of previously suppressed emotions leads to the evolution of an alternate mode of perception, one which synthesizes rational and nonrational thought. In *"La conciencia de la mestiza/*Towards a New Consciousness," she attributes this synthesis to the *mestiza*'s ability "to break down the subject-object duality that keeps her a prisoner and to show in the flesh and through the images in her work how duality is transcended" (*Borderlands* 80). As in "Letting Go" and "Poets have strange eating habits," Anzaldúa maintains that this new mode of perception often entails intense emotional, psychic pain as the *mestiza* attempts to reconcile apparent opposites. Yet it is this willingness to confront, rather than reject, the cultural ambiguities and immerse herself in the *Coatlicue* state which enables her to perceive reality differently. Thus in *"la herencia de Coatlicue"* she emphasizes the painful nature of this transition to *mestiza* consciousness by describing it as "a dry birth, a breech birth, . . . one that fights her every inch of the way." As in the poems, however, she implies that this "screaming birth" is transformative; "the repressed energy rises, . . . connects with conscious energy and a new life begins" (*Borderlands* 49).

Although not always identified as such, the *Coatlicue* state–with its "decision to take a flying leap into the dark" (*Borderlands* 49) and the subsequent transformations which occur–plays an important role in Anzaldúa's theory of artistic expression. In "Speaking in Tongues: A Letter to Third World Women Writers," for example, she emphasizes the risks involved in writing and likens her own experience as a writer to "leap[ing] into a timeless, spaceless noplace." Once again, this entry entails both self-loss and self-transformation: she "forget[s] [her]self and "feel[s] [she is] the universe" (172). As this non-temporal, non-spatial, non-place suggests, for Anzaldúa writing, like the *Coatlicue* State itself, is a (perpetually) liminal activity: "It is always a path/state to something else" (*Borderlands* 73). Thus she describes the writing process as "learning to live with la Coatlicue" and explains that the *mestiza* writer must repeatedly "jump blindfolded into the abyss of her own being and there in the depths confront her face, the face underneath the mask" (*Borderlands* 74-75).

By identifying this hidden "face" both as the "alien other" and as her own "inner self, . . . the godwoman . . . *Antigua, mi Diosa*, the divine force within, *Coatlicue-Cihuacoatl-Tlazolteotl-Tonant-zin-Coatlalopeuh-Guadalupe*" (*Borderlands* 51), Anzaldúa utilizes revisionist myth to displace the conventional boundaries between inner/outer, subject/object, and self/other. She locates the "alien other"–the objectified outsider–within herself and dissolves the borders between writer, reader, and text. Writing becomes, both literally and figuratively, self-inscription: it is "making soul" and "carving bone, . . . creating [her] own face" (*Borderlands* 73). As these metaphoric descriptions imply, Anzaldúa takes Cixous's injunction to "Write yourself: your body must make itself heard" (97) to new levels by writing her soul as well as her body. Indeed, she insists that it is this fusion of body and soul which makes the *mestiza* "*nahual*, an agent of transformation . . . able to change herself and others." By repeatedly associating body with soul, Anzaldúa deconstructs and reconstructs her readers' identities as well as her own. When she writes, she explains, her "soul . . . is constantly remaking and giving birth to itself through [her] body" (*Borderlands* 73-75).

This equation of writing with perpetual physical/spiritual self-birth is disruptive. As Trinh observes, "a subject who points to him/her/itself as a subject-in-process . . . is bound to upset one's sense of identity–the familiar distinction between the Same and the Other since the latter is no longer kept in a recognizable relation of dependence, deviation, or appropriation" (48). By deconstructing the image of a monolithic self and destabilizing the boundaries between body/soul, inner/outer, and other dichotomous terms, Anzaldúa challenges readers to examine their self-conceptions and redefine their own borders.

For Anzaldúa, there is no permanent division between inner and outer realities. Because she believes that "[n]othing happens in the 'real' world unless it happens in the image in our heads" (*Borderlands* 87), she develops new configurations of psychic and political power, such as the Borderlands, the *Coatlicue* state, and the notion of a *mestiza* consciousness itself. These graphic metaphors invite readers to imaginatively reconstruct their worldviews and envision alternate ways of living. As Doty explains, because mythical symbols contain units of information that are not bound up by the immediate contours of what presently is being experienced, . . . [they] provide concrete conveyances for (abstract) thought. Alive in a world of metaphoric and symbolic meanings, they allow experimentation and play with images, ideas, and concepts that otherwise would remain too incorporeal to be engaged. (20)

Using mythic metaphors which "concretize the spirit and etherealize the body" (*Borderlands* 75), Anzaldúa builds a new culture, *una cultura mestiza*. Her words incite us to actively create a complex mixed-breed coalition of "queers"–the outsiders who, because of race, gender, sexual orientation, or class position, refuse to conform to the dominant cultural inscriptions.

For Audre Lorde as well, writing, "making soul," and building culture are intimately related. By fully integrating her personal experience as a black lesbian feminist with her public role as a writer, she demonstrates her conviction that self-discovery, art, and social protest are inseparable. As she explains in an interview with Claudia Tate, she believes that societal change begins within the individual: "our *real power* [her emphasis] comes from the personal, [and] our real insights about living come from that deep knowledge within us that arises from our feelings" (106). Lorde's work is shaped by her belief that poetic expression and political action have their genesis in each individual's emotional life. In *The Cancer Journals*, for example, she examines the anger, sorrow, and loss she felt after her mastectomy in order to learn "who [she] was and was becoming throughout [that] time" (53). For Lorde, self-expression and self-discovery are never ends in themselves. Because she sees her desire to comprehend her battle with cancer as "part of a continuum of women's work, of reclaiming this earth and our power," she is confident that her self-explorations will empower her readers (17).

Like Anzaldúa and Allen, Lorde associates her theory of writing with nonwestern traditions. In the interview with Tate, she defines art as "the use of living" and explains that, whereas the European worldview depicts life as a series of conflicts,

African tradition deals with life as an experience to be lived. In many respects, it is much like the Eastern philosophies in that we see ourselves as a part of a life force. . . . We live in accordance with, in a kind of correspondence with the rest of the world as a whole. And therefore living becomes an experience, rather than a problem, no matter how bad or painful it may be. Change will rise *endemically* from the experience fully lived and responded to. (112, my emphasis)

By defining her own life as integrally related to an over-arching "life force," Lorde can experience each event as a lesson to be learned from rather than an obstacle to be overcome. Furthermore, by positing each person's interconnection with this holistic life force, she acquires both the courage to explore her emotions as she writes and the confidence that this exploration leads inevitably to personal and communal transformation.

As Lorde herself points out, this approach to life is not uniquely African. Yet by attributing her organic worldview to her nonwestern roots, she subtly emphasizes the political implications of her work. According to Patricia Hill Collins, black U.S. women activists' preservation of African cultural traditions has enabled them to successfully resist the dominant society's attempts to destroy their sense of community: "By conserving and recreating an Afrocentric worldview women . . . undermine oppressive institutions by rejecting the anti-Black and anti-female ideologies they promulgate" (144). I see Lorde's revisionist mythmaking as an important dimension of this political activism. As she incorporates Yoruban and Dahomean *orisha*, or spiritual forces, into her poetry, fiction, and prose, she reclaims a tradition which has been almost entirely erased by western culture.[12]

This mythological erasure parallels the experience of African American women who, as Collins demonstrates, are objectified–both by the dominant U.S. culture and by the black community itself–through a series of overwhelmingly negative stereotypes such as the matriarch, the welfare mother, and the sexually promiscuous woman (67-90). Although these doubly oppressive images make each woman "invisible as a fully human individual," Collins asserts that many African American women have transformed their status as "invisible Other" into a source of tremendous inner strength (94). By developing a "private, hidden space of . . . consciousness," they successfully have defied the externally imposed labels and maintained their authority to define themselves (92-93). Indeed, one of Collins's main arguments throughout *Black Feminist Thought* is that African American women's ability to create a unique self-defined standpoint has been essential to their survival. However, because they often mask their resistance with outward conformity, this inner dimension of their lives has received little recognition (91). As Collins suggestively notes, "far too many black women remain motionless on the outside . . . but inside?" (93, her ellipses).

Revisionary mythmaking enables Lorde to *externalize* the "inside ideas" Collins sees as a hallmark of black U.S. women's resistance to dominant groups (92-93). In her work, West African mythic images serve as vehicles for establishing self-affirmative definitions of black womanhood. By expressing her own self-defined standpoint through the figures of Aido Hwedo, Seboulisa, and other African *orisha*, Lorde offers her black female readers new ways to perceive themselves and new ways to act. It is this trajectory from "inside ideas" to outer forms she refers to in the interview with Tate when she describes her attempt to develop a voice for African American women. When she writes, she explains, she "speak[s] from the center of consciousness, from the *I am* out to the *we are* and then out to the *we can*" (105, her emphasis).

Revisionist mythmaking plays a vital role in Lorde's ability to speak both for herself and for other black women. Karla Holloway makes a similar point in her recent study of West African and African American women writers' use of nonwestern mythic material. As Holloway demonstrates, by incorporating metaphoric ancestral and goddess figures into their work, contemporary black women writers have created both a gendered, culture-specific voice and a "collective consciousness" (30). In their texts, mythology serves as a cultural and linguistic bridge: it is "the meta-matrix for all uses of language and the primary source of a literature that would recover a historical voice that is at once sensual, visceral, and real" (107). Black women writers of the diaspora cannot physically reclaim the African culture–the "language, religion, political independence, [and] economic policy"–lost during the Middle Passage and slavery; however, their revisionist mythmaking enables them to "spiritually" re-member and reconstruct their cultural past (20).

Although Holloway restricts her analysis to the aesthetic dimensions of black women writers' fictional narratives, her emphasis on the interconnection between mythic metaphors, voice, and "spiritual memory" (20) has important implications for Lorde's poetry.[13] In *The Black Unicorn*, Lorde's 1978 collection of poems thematically unified by references to Yoruban and Dahomean *orisha*, mythology serves as the "meta-matrix" for her development of a culture and gender-specific voice. In the first section, she reshapes West African myth to define herself as a black woman warrior poet. Throughout the remaining sections, she enlarges this original definition to encompass a network of mythic, historic, and imaginary women extending from the Yoruban goddesses–through the ancient Dahomean Amazons, her family, friends, and female lovers–to the "mothers sisters daughters / girls" she has "never been" (48). Because myth provides the basis for "the community's shared meanings [and] interactions with both the spiritual and the physical worlds" (Holloway 31), Lorde's retrieval of West African mythic figures enables her to create a liminal space where new possibilities–new definitions of black womanhood–can emerge. Thus Pamela Annas locates the poems in *The Black Unicorn* "at the *boundary* between unnaming and renaming" (23-24, my emphasis).

As Annas's emphasis on unnaming and renaming implies, in *The Black Unicorn* Lorde's revisionary myths are both deconstructive and reconstructive. By replacing white Euro-American goddess figures with metaphors of the black goddess, she rejects ethnocentric concepts of womanhood for a culture-based model of female identity formation. The title poem, for example, concludes with her "redefinition of woman, a necessary naming through unnaming, since in Western literature 'woman' has historically meant 'white'" (Annas 24). Lorde's revisionist mythmaking challenges other hegemonic concepts as well. In "A Woman Speaks," she spurns the image of feminine power as a gentle nurturing force and warns readers to "beware [of her] smile": she is "treacherous" and angry, filled with "old magic" and "the noon's new fury" (5-6). Similarly, in "The Women of Dan Dance with Swords in Their Hands" Lorde's revisionist myth subverts the dualistic notion of a transcendent deity. She declares that her power, although divine, is not other-worldly: she "did not fall from the sky," nor does she descend gently "like rain." Instead, she "come[s] like a woman"–like an Amazon warrior woman–with a sword in her hand (14-15).

Whether she refers to black women warriors dancing with swords in their hands or to goddesses "bent on destruction by threat" (88), Lorde's mythic figures have little in common with those reclaimed by Anglo cultural feminists. This difference reflects the specific conditions faced by contemporary black women. As Holloway notes, "[t]he African deity imaged in black women's literature is very different from the highly romanticized versions of goddesses rediscovered by Western feminists. The African deity is a figure of both strength and tragedy–like the women whose lives echo hers" (154-55). In both "Dahomey" and "125th Street and Abomey," for instance, Lorde depicts Seboulisa, the Dahomean creatrix figure, with "one breast / eaten away by worms of sorrow and loss" (10, 12). Yet these poems are not elegies; they are, rather, assertions of power in the face of tremendous cultural deprivations. By identifying herself as Seboulisa's "severed daughter," Lorde underscores both the cultural loss she has experienced as a black woman of the diaspora and her discovery of a personal, communal, and mythic voice. In a stanza which illustrates Collin's description of black women's "inside ideas," Lorde writes that, although separated by "[h]alf earth and time" from this single-breasted black goddess, her own "dream" reunites them. She has inscribed Seboulisa's image "inside the back of [her] head." Through imaginative reconstruction, Lorde adopts the ravaged goddess's name as her own; by so doing, she acquires "the woman strength / of tongue" which empowers her work. She projects her speech outward and boldly declares that she will laugh "*our* name into echo / all the world shall remember" (12-13, my emphasis).

Like Anzaldúa and Allen, Lorde rejects the cultural inscriptions which attempt to silence third world women by negating their subjecthood. As they reclaim nonwestern creatrix figures like Seboulisa, *Coatlicue*, and Old Spider Woman/Thought Woman, these lesbians of color challenge hegemonic definitions of white, heterosexual, middle-class womanhood. Although the revisionary myths each writer invents reflect the specificity of her historical, material, and ideological conditions, all three women develop writing strategies which expose the arbitrary nature of western classifications. By deconstructing and reconstructing mythic images of female identity, they translate their liminal status into their revisionary myths. In so doing, they break down the binary divisions between inner and outer modes of reality. As they simultaneously spiritualize and politicize their work, they create what Trinh describes as "a new in-between-the-naming space" (112), a place where new definitions–and new coalitions–can emerge.

## NOTES

1. Anzaldúa, "Speaking in Tongues" 172.
2. See DuPlessis; Frye; Rubenstein; Walker; and Greene.
3. See DuPlessis 105-41; Ostriker 210-40; and Walker 49.
4. See, for example, Alarcón and the essays collected in Moraga and Anzaldúa.
5. Anzaldúa, *Borderlands* 36-37; Allen, *Sacred Hoop* 103-17.
6. See Doty's overview of scholars' separation between myth and science (2-40).
7. The phrase is Turner's. See 95-96.
8. Allen, *Sacred Hoop* 13-29 and 222-24.
9. See, for example, Gadon and Rabuzzi.
10. Anzaldúa, *Borderlands* 66 and "Haciendo caras, una entrada" xvi.
11. For examples of Anzaldúa's shifts between first and third person narration see *Borderlands* 42-43 and 140-41. For a discussion of her code-switching see the preface to *Borderlands* (n.p.).
12. See Lorde's "Open Letter to Mary Daly" in Moraga and Anzaldúa 94-97. See also Sojourner and Bádéjó.
13. Revisionist mythmaking also plays a significant role in Lorde's "biomythography," *Zami: A New Spelling of My Name*. See Keating.

## WORKS CITED

Alarcón, Norma. "The Theoretical Subject(s) of *This Bridge Called My Back* and Anglo-American Feminism." Anzaldúa, *Making Face* 356-69.

Allen, Paula Gunn. *The Sacred Hoop: Recovering the Feminine in American Indian Traditions*. Boston: Beacon, 1986.

————. *The Woman Who Owned the Shadows*. San Francisco: Spinsters/Aunt Lute, 1983.

Annas, Pamela. "A Poetry of Survival: Naming and Renaming in the Poetry of Audre Lorde, Pat Parker, Sylvia Plath, and Adrienne Rich." *Colby Library Quarterly* 18 (1982): 9-25.

Anzaldúa, Gloria. *Borderlands/La Frontera: The New Mestiza.* San Francisco: Spinsters/Aunt Lute, 1987.

————. "Haciendo caras, una entrada." Anzaldúa, *Making Face* xv-xxviii.

————, ed. *Making Face, Making Soul/Haciendo Caras: Creative and Critical Perspectives by Women of Color.* San Francisco: Aunt Lute Foundation, 1990.

————. "Speaking In Tongues: A Letter To Third World Women Writers." Moraga and Anzaldúa 165-73.

Bádéjó, Diedre L. "The Goddess Osun as a Paradigm for African Feminist Criticism." *Sage: A Scholarly Journal on Black Women* 6 (Summer 1989): 27-32.

Baker, Jr., Houston A. *Blues, Ideology, and Afro-American Literature.* Chicago: U of Chicago P, 1984.

Caputi, Jane. "Interview With Paula Gunn Allen." *Trivia* 16 (1990): 50-67.

Cixous, Hélène. "Sorties: Out and Out: Attacks/Ways Out/Forays." *The Newly Born Woman.* Hélène Cixous and Catherine Clement. Trans. Betsy Wing. Minneapolis: U of Minnesota P, 1988.

Collins, Patricia Hill. *Black Feminist Thought: Knowledge, Consciousness, and the Politics of Empowerment.* Boston: Unwin Hymen, 1990.

Doty, William G. *Mythography: The Study of Myths and Rituals.* Tuscaloosa: U of Alabama P, 1986.

DuPlessis, Rachel Blau. *Writing Beyond the Ending: Narrative Strategies of Twentieth-Century Women Writers.* Bloomington: Indiana UP, 1985.

Eysturoy, Annie O. "Paula Gunn Allen." *This Is About Vision: Interviews with Southwestern Writers.* Ed. John F. Crawford, William Balassi, and Annie O. Eysturoy. Albuquerque: U of New Mexico, 1990. 95-107.

Frye, Joanne S. *Living Stories, Telling Lives: Women & the Novel in Contemporary Experience.* Ann Arbor: U of Michigan P, 1986.

Gadon, Elinor W. *The Once and Future Goddess: A Symbol For Our Time.* San Francisco: Harper & Row, 1989.

Greene, Gail. *Changing the Story: Feminist Tradition and the Tradition.* Bloomington: Indiana UP, 1991.

Holloway, Karla F.C. *Moorings & Metaphors: Figures of Culture and Gender in Black Women's Literature.* New Brunswick: Rutgers UP, 1992.

Keating, AnnLouise. "Making 'our shattered faces whole': The Black Goddess and Audre Lorde's Revision of Patriarchal Myth." *Frontiers: A Journal of Women Studies* 13 (1992): 20-33.

Lorde, Audre. *The Black Unicorn.* New York: Norton, 1978.

————. *The Cancer Journals.* San Francisco: Spinsters/Aunt Lute, 1980.

————. *Zami: A New Spelling of My Name.* Freedom, CA: Crossing P, 1982.

Mohanty, Chandra. "Introduction: Cartographies of Struggle: Third World Women and the Politics of Feminism." *Third World Women and the Politics of*

*Feminism*. Ed. Chandra Mohanty, Ann Russo, and Lourdes Torres. Bloomington: Indiana UP, 1991.

Moraga, Cherríe. "Algo secretamente amado." *Third Woman: The Sexuality of Latinas* 4 (1989): 151-56.

Moraga, Cherríe, and Gloria Anzaldúa, eds. *This Bridge Called My Back: Writings by Radical Women of Color*. 2nd ed. New York: Kitchen Table: Women of Color, 1983.

Ostriker, Alicia. *Stealing the Language: The Emergence of Women's Poetry in America*. Boston: Beacon, 1986.

Rabuzzi, Kathryn Allen. *Motherself: A Mythic Analysis of Motherhood*. Bloomington: Indiana UP, 1988.

Rubenstein, Roberta. *Boundaries of the Self: Gender, Culture, Fiction*. Urbana: U of Illinois P, 1987.

Sojourner, Sabrina. "From the House of Yemanja: The Goddess Heritage of Black Women." *The Politics of Women's Spirituality: Essays on the Rise of Spiritual Power Within the Feminist Movement*. Ed. Charlene Spretnak. New York: Doubleday, 1982. 57-63.

Tate, Claudia. *Black Women Writers at Work*. New York: Continuum, 1983.

Trinh T. Minh-ha. *When the Moon Waxes Red: Representation, Gender and Cultural Politics*. New York: Routledge, 1991.

Turner, Victor. *The Ritual Process: Structure and Anti-Structure*. Chicago: Aldine, 1969.

Walker, Nancy A. *Feminist Alternatives, Irony and Fantasy in the Contemporary Novel by Women*. Jackson: U of Mississippi P, 1990.

Zimmerman, Bonnie. *The Safe Sea of Women: Lesbian Fiction 1969-1989*. Boston: Beacon, 1990.

# The House of Difference:
# Gender, Culture,
# and the Subject-in-Process
# on the American Stage

Lou Rosenberg, PhD (cand.)

*Claremont Graduate School*

**SUMMARY.** A lesbian woman of color is often defined by her multiple differences as "other" and/or "object." Yet these very differences can also allow her to challenge culturally held notions of gender, subjectivity, and representation. This article examines one such example, Cherríe Moraga's teatro *Giving Up the Ghost* where, for the first time, the issue of Chicana lesbian sexuality is addressed on the stage.

As the position of speaking subject is taken by ones who are defined as object by gender and as other by culture, not only are the cultural practices that inscribe those definitions confronted, but the subject itself as cultural construct is challenged, destabilized, and questioned. The position of unified speaking subject is not always one to aspire to; instead, it can be regarded with suspicion and replaced with a Kristevan "subject-in-process."

---

Correspondence may be addressed to the author at: Department of English, Claremont Graduate School, Claremont, CA 91711.

[Haworth co-indexing entry note]: "The House of Difference: Gender, Culture, and the Subject-in-Process on the American Stage." Rosenberg, Lou. Co-published simultaneously in the *Journal of Homosexuality* (The Haworth Press, Inc.) Vol. 26, No. 2/3, 1993, pp. 97-110; and *Critical Essays: Gay and Lesbian Writers of Color* (ed: Emmanuel S. Nelson) The Haworth Press, Inc., 1993, pp. 97-110. Multiple copies of this article/chapter may be purchased from the The Haworth Document Delivery Center [1-800-3-HAWORTH; 9:00 a.m. - 5:00 p.m. (EST)].

Theatre provides an especially rich medium for encounters between such subjects and the definitions of difference imposed on
them; it is a setting where questions of representation, boundaries,
and the body intersect. When this space is entered by "subjects-in-
process" struggling against the web of differences that has previously defined them, all the terms that have inscribed these differences come into question. A woman in such a position not only
challenges being an object of representation but can critique the very
notion of representation. A lesbian woman of color, defined by multiple differences, can challenge the very deep culturally held notions
of bipolar definition. Such questions and challenges are of course not
restricted to the inhabitants of what Audre Lorde has termed the
"house of difference," but the "house" itself seems a likely place for
such questions to occur. One such example is Cherríe Moraga's
teatro *Giving Up the Ghost* where, for the first time, the issue of
Chicana lesbian sexuality is addressed on the stage. In *Giving Up the
Ghost* four characters struggle with issues of gender, sexuality, and
identity. The construction of these characters, her treatment of the
audience, and her explorations of language and desire are Moraga's
challenges to a representational system that has contributed so
heavily to the pain and confusion that the play explores.

Before we examine how Moraga specifically uses theatrical performance to expose the inherent problems in the notion of unified
subjectivity, we must first clarify what the term subject means.
Although there is much to argue with in Althusser's definition, it is
still a useful place to start. Althusser's subject is linguistically
constructed by ideology, a process called interpellation. In his well-
known example, an "individual" is hailed by the police. Whether
one responds by complying, fleeing, or even ignoring this call, one
cannot escape the identification of "you" or suspect. Interpellation
thus positions the individual inescapably within the ideological system, simultaneously the subject *of* ideological address and subjected *to* the ideology inherent in such address.

Although there is much that is valuable in Althusser's theory of
interpellation, there are significant problems. For example, Althusser's subject is raceless, genderless, with no stated sexual orientation, hence "always already" a straight white male. Since subjectivity is one's position in language, this places many people

significantly at odds with the "I" that is somehow supposed to represent them, the position they speak from and from which they are addressed. Moreover, since even the act of refusal further embeds one within the interpellative address, this deterministic view of interpellation allows little room for agency or the possibility of change. There are, however, less restrictive ways of looking at the subject. A more satisfactory description may be offered by Julia Kristeva's term, the "subject-in-process." The Kristevan subject position is open to change, seen as "the place not only of structure and its repeated transformations but especially of its loss, its outlay" (Kristeva 52).

Paul Smith takes Kristeva's definition of the subject-in-process a step further when he demonstrates that a constructed subject can possess several not necessarily complementary "structures"; it is a condition he calls "colligation," the overlapping of subject positions. Smith does not confuse the subject with the individual as Althusser does, but attempts to show how one individual may simultaneously experience several different and often conflicting subject positions. Smith's position can also be extended by Trinh T. Minh-ha's concept of identity *as* difference in which she challenges whatever hints of a core or "essential" self that might remain in the term "Individual." As she states, "the 'I' is not a unified subject, a fixed identity or that solid mass covered with layers of superficialities one has gradually to peel off before one can see its true face. 'I' is, itself, infinite layers" (27).

An unsettling question often arises from this attempt to redefine a subjectivity based entirely on unquestioned assumptions of a white male Eurocentric heterosexist norm: Is destablizing the privileged position of the "I," what Lacan calls the speaking subject, yet another way of denying less privileged "others" such as lesbian, gay, people of color a voice? Indeed, at first, this radical view of the "I" may seem to defeat the goal of political agency. How does such a "layered" decentered being take action? How can one work for the benefit of a particular "identity," such as feminism or gay rights, if "identity" itself is in question? This would seem to be Kristeva's position when she argues, "What can 'identity,' even 'sexual identity' mean in a new theoretical and scientific space where the very notion of identity is challenged?" (209).

This notion seems to lead Kristeva into a political paralysis; she is unable to assume a feminist position because to do so would be to reinscribe a notion of identity that she no longer believes in. Is this because Kristeva can only conceive of political action as something undertaken by one who believes herself or himself to be a unified subject? If so, she is clearly in error, for this is simply not the case. One can act on behalf of a position while not claiming it as an exclusive identity. Indeed this view of non-unity seems to answer the helplessness implied by Althusser without raising the idea that political action depends on an ideologically free space from which to operate. A further caution must be added, however. Certainly, the idea that one can somehow choose or negotiate between subject positions is appealing; but, as Moraga shows us, these choices or negotiations can often be difficult and painful, depending on the conditions of the choice. Therefore, we need to look more carefully at some of the inherent tensions generated by multiple subject positions as illustrated in Moraga's teatro.

A woman in minority culture appears to be caught in a web of conflicting positions, all of which seem to deny her subjectivity; denied a voice in the dominant culture by virtue of her race (and, possibly, class), she is often further silenced within her own culture by the patriarchal values inherent within it. If she is to claim subjectivity in the world of the dominant culture as a member of her own culture, must she also uncritically espouse all the values of the culture she seeks to valorize and preserve? Will not a critique of a culture already endangered be seen as an attack, as complicity with those who would destroy it? Such questions seem urgently engraved in Moraga's struggles to reconcile the plural subjectivity she experiences as a lesbian, a feminist, and a Chicana.

In her first depiction of this plural subjectivity, Moraga has two characters, Corky and Marisa, represent one person at different stages of her life. These conjoint characters often occupy the stage at the same time, and at one point playfully acknowledge each other's presence–thus portraying "Corky/Marisa" as a subject-in-process. Corky, Marisa's younger self, is a would-be tough "chaparitta" in her early and then late teens who struggles against being defined by the passivity, helplessness, and vulnerability culturally embedded in the sign "woman." She attempts uncomfortably and unsuccessfully to inhabit a "tough" male role. Marisa, a woman in her late twenties, is concerned with the "ghosts," her past, and questions of gender, desire, and identity, that have divided and destroyed her relationship with the more heterosexually oriented Amalia.

The fourth character is "the People," those viewing the performance who are also included as characters in the play. Moraga employs this tactic as a further challenge to the representational conventions that deny her experience and allow no place for their expression. By redrawing the border between audience and performers, Moraga thus problematizes the image of representation which posits a single, detached, isolated viewer. She also directly speaks to the issue of community. As Yvonne Yarbro-Bejarano states, "The Chicana writer finds that the self she seeks to define and love is not merely an individual self, but a collective one. In other words the power, the permission, the authority to tell stories about herself and other Chicanas comes from her cultural, racial/ethnic, and linguistic community" (42). Moraga's inclusion of "the People" uses this device to simultaneously challenge the standards of her community that isolate and silence her, and at the same time affirm and reincorporate herself into that community. Since this device is to be repeated whenever the play is staged, it can also be a way of building, albeit in a limited sense, community. Thus, the structure of the play creates a context that engages in what Marisa calls, "making familia from scratch."

Moraga uses the theatre to make familia because it is a potential locus for cultural self-reflexivity; it is a place to examine and call into question the "truths" that imprison her by revealing the inherent paradoxes within them. The theatre is an especially good place to examine these paradoxes because of its innately "double" nature–what critic/director Richard Schechner has termed the "not-not." As Schechner points out, an actor, such as Olivier portraying Hamlet, is in a paradoxical state: he is "not-not Hamlet and not-not Olivier." This complex and seemingly contradictory condition, though often elided, is the ontological basis of theatre. As a spectator accepts the provisionally double nature of the theatrical experience, she is also temporarily more open to other alternative possibilities. Expecting the unusual, she is thus more ready to entertain new ideas for, as Victor Turner reminds us, performances are "occasions in which as a culture or a society we reflect upon and define ourselves, dramatize our collective myths and history, present ourselves with alternatives and eventually change in some ways while remaining the same in others" ("Social Dramas" 1).

What then are the "alternatives" that Moraga presents through performance? As a woman who wishes to explore and develop subjectivity or a "voice" that has never been heard in either the dominant culture or her own, who attempts to simultaneously critique and preserve her culture, Moraga opens up a difficult, complex, rich, and potentially dangerous field of cultural reflexivity. What is the effect on both her own and the dominant culture when such a person reveals private, previously inarticulated experience? What is the relationship of that experience to articulation, to culture? If a culture depends on silence, to break that silence is to alter that culture. However such questions, eruptions, or "attacks," can also be seen as agents of reform, the basis for cultural transformation and change. As Turner informs us: "New ways of modeling or framing social reality may actually be proposed and sometimes legitimated in the heat of performance, emerging as a sort of artifact or popular creativeness" ("Frame, Flow" 39). While Turner's claim of "legitimation" may seem somewhat idealistic, it is certainly not unrealistic to see performance as enabling new issues to be considered.

One of the central issues Marisa is therefore able to discuss with her "familia" is an attempt to understand her sexuality. At a crucial point in the play she simultaneously proclaims her suspicion of her bisexual lover Amalia's desire for her, her belief that Amalia's desire for a man would be greater, and her knowledge that while her life with Amalia would be easier if she were a man, Amalia actually does want her more as a woman. Marisa's problem lies not in her inadequate reasoning powers; rather, her conundrums are insolvable because the terms that she uses deny her experience and her desire. Specifically she encounters two significant obstacles to articulation: gender and representation. First, as a woman, and even more specifically a Chicana feminist, she can't speak at all since the position of "speaking" subject has been almost entirely denied to her and second, as a lesbian, she can't speak about her attraction to women because representation, as we shall see, denies any expression of female desire.

Corky/Marisa's initial difficulties stem from the conflation of gender, sex, and desire. Although the two are often conflated, gender, the cultural representation of sexual difference, comes after and is not the same as biological difference. As Teresa De Lauretis explains, "Gender is not sex, a state of nature, but the representation in each individual of a particular social relation which pre-exists the individual and is predicated on the conceptual and rigid (structural) opposition of two biological sexes" (5). As we will see, the confusion engendered by seeing the social construction of gender as a biological given is a central paradox explored in Moraga's work.

As a social construction, gender is also used to dictate and "naturalize" social behaviour. In this instance, Corky's female gender is used to ensure that she cannot speak her desire; for in her world, as Norma Alarcón informs us, there is a "fantastic cultural silence, religious or Freudian with regard to what the girl's position is in the Holy Family or the Oedipal triad." It is only permissible, Alarcón concludes, for a girl child to speak as a "would-be mother" (153). Corky rejects this role, but cannot find a way to express her desire for women as a woman, a problem that continues to trouble her when, as Marisa, she attempts to understand her relationship with Amalia.

Corky's prohibitions may shed some light on Marisa's riddle: that she suspects Amalia's desire for her is weak, believes that Amalia's desire for a man would be greater, but knows that while her life with Amalia would be easier if she were a man, Amalia actually does want her more as a woman. The problem, as we can see by Corky's silencing, lies in the way that representation undercuts any expression of female desire. And here, despite claims of Eurocentrism and latent homophobia that may unfortunately not be entirely without justification, it is still useful in this situation to invoke Irigaray's explanation of representation.

Irigaray claims that representation in Eurocentric culture is based on hom(m)o sexuality. This term, a pun on the words "homme" for man and "homo" the same, represents the male desire for the same. In *This Sex Which Is Not One,* she states, "The feminine occurs only within models and laws devised by male subjects which implies that there are not really two sexes, but only one. A single practice and representation of the sexual" (86). Irigaray sees Freud's theory of penis envy, in which a woman sees herself as castrated, as a projection of the male fear of castration. As long as the woman is thought to envy the man's penis he can rest secure in the knowledge that he must have it after all. If woman is defined only by being other than man, different from man, then what that "other" and "different" being lacks, man must certainly possess. Irigaray states, "To castrate the woman is to inscribe in her the law of the same desire, of desire for the same" (86).

Therefore, in the patriarchal logic of representation, woman can only be seen as man's other, his negative or mirror image. Woman is situated outside of representation as absence, as negativity, or at best, as a lesser man. In such a system woman's desire for another woman is unthinkable, unrepresentable. Female homosexuality is therefore misinterpreted in terms of male homosexuality, that is, a woman's desire for another woman is still seen in terms of male desire. Therefore, lesbian desire is both beyond and outside of representation and we can see that Marisa's attempts to understand her desire in terms that were never made to accommodate it expose the inadequacy of those terms.

As Irigaray has shown, in the system of representation that Corky inhabits self-representation is denied to women. Under the "logic of the same" there is no such thing as female desire; since Corky experiences desire she concludes that she must not be a woman and thus represents herself as male, dressing in the "cholo" fashion of the sixties: khakis with razor-sharp creases and a pressed white undershirt, hair short and slicked back. This self-authorship is also expressed through her streetwise speech and her attempts to imitate both the cowboys in the movies and the rebellious young men of her culture. As a woman in patriarchal culture she occupies a marginal position; in her attempts to gain subjectivity she represents herself not only as a man, but one in partial rebellion against the patriarchal order, an outlaw straining at the limit of cultural constraints.

The concept of representation as unproblematic depends on a continuing female silence. Once this silence is broken, representation itself is undermined and disturbed. Corky's speech must therefore be heard not only against the silence demanded by the claims of her culture which offer her a very limited range of expression but also by the larger Eurocentric demands of representation which allow no voice at all for her desire. Rejecting these limitations, but finding no "voice" of her own, Corky speaks instead with the exaggerated toughness of a cholo:

> sometimes I even pack a blade  no one knows
> I never use it or nu'ting but can feel it there
> there in my pants pocket run the pad of my thumb over it
> to remind me I carry some'ting am sharp  secretly. (Act I. p. 4)

It is tempting here to "read" Corky as a covert phallus-packing Lacanian, secretly running her thumb over the incisive, potentially castrating signifier that allows her to speak her desire by giving her both identity and alienation. The blade, her own castration fetishized, allows her, temporarily, to "speak" but not as a woman. She realizes that her toughness, her subjectivity, depends on the existence of suppressed other: the category of woman. The desire for freedom and the desire for women are both culturally defined as male; Corky therefore bases her attempts to express her desires for both as a male: the bato and the cowboy. She recalls:

> In my mind I was big 'n tough 'n' a dude
> in my mind I had all their freedom
> the freedom to really see a girl
> kinda  the way  you see
> an animal  you know? (Act I. p. 5)

Corky has internalized culturally stereotyped polarities of essentialized masculine and feminine behavior at odds with her feelings. At this point she does not so much question these definitions as she does her own identity. If women are silent and passive, then she is not a woman. This self-denying role is difficult to maintain, for she knows that she herself is a woman and that women do have feelings.

> always knew I was a girl
> deep down inside
> no matter how i tried to pull the other
> off
> I knew
> always knew
> I was an animal that kicked back
> cuz it hurt. (Act I. p. 6)

These contradictions inherent in Corky's attempts to establish an identity that reconciles her gender and her desire are magnified shortly thereafter when she is unable to victimize a younger, defenseless child to reinforce her own sense of power. Corky fails to properly enact the predatory "Cowboy" role she has learned so well from the movies and learns that whatever her desire does consist of, it does not include victimizing another person. This point is ironically underscored when, recounting the story of her own terrified passivity during her childhood rape, she recalls her attacker and poignantly cries, "He made me a hole" (43).

As Marisa, still struggling to understand and articulate her feelings, she decides that she does not want or need a male persona; still she cannot express or comprehend her feelings within the "logic of the same." She declares: "I never wanted to be a man, I only wanted a woman to want me that bad" (13-4). Marisa knows what she wants–female desire directed towards her, but the only terms she has to describe this compromise her chances of ever attaining it.

Although she now believes she can desire women without playing a male role–one which she rejects since, for her, it involves power, dominance, cruelty–Marisa continues to read desire as male. If she no longer believes that she must be a male in order to desire women, she now believes that she must be a male in order to be strongly desired by a woman–even though she knows it is actually her own "femaleness" that makes Amalia desire her (28). Further complicating this with the logic of the same where all desire is male she ponders:

> Its odd being queer
> its not that you don't want a man'
> you just don't want a man in a man
> You want a man in a woman. (Act I. p. 29)

But what "man" does Marisa want? It is not a biological one, she does not want the body of a man. She wants some one capable of desiring her. She wants a woman who desires her, and as woman's desire exists outside of representation, Marisa calls this desire "man." It is this, desire for her, that she calls a man in a woman. Strangely enough, Amalia provides this when she expresses her desire for Marisa as male. Amalia, speaking directly to the People, recalls her dead lover Alejandro and remarks, "I feel him in me every time I touch la Marisa." She feels, after his death, that she incorporates him, that it is as Alejandro that she makes love to Marisa (27-8).

There is no room in these linguistic equations for Corky/Marisa's or Amalia's feelings, and yet these feelings exist. Marisa and Amalia's relationship is a given, although its articulation is, for the characters at least, an impossibility. By staging this unresolved contradiction Moraga has given us, the audience, "the people," a chance to witness or perhaps participate in this struggle that exposes the insufficiencies of representation.

Later the lovers experience a momentary breakthrough when their identities temporarily coalesce. For one moment desire is wholly female as Marisa inquires:

> Who was the beautiful woman in the mirror of the water,
> you or me?
> Who do I make love to
> Who do I see in the ocean of our bed? (27)

The language in this passage with its mirrors, water, and oceans, is fluid and unrestricted, evoking easily transgressable dissolving boundaries. Finally the lovers conclude that when they made love to each other, "Everything was changing in both of us" (32).

Except for a few brief, epiphanic moments such as these there is always something intangible between Marisa and Amalia that distorts, impedes, and finally destroys their relationship. One such illustration occurs in a poignant moment when Amalia, who we the audience know will leave Marisa, dreams that she and Marisa are lovers in a semi-Edenic tribe that reflects their ethnicity but ultimately cannot withstand their relationship. Realizing that the expression of their desire violates a taboo in a society that she both loves and is in conflict with, Amalia wonders:

> If this law nearly transcribed in
> blood could go . . .
> then, what else?
> What was there to hold on to?
> What immense truths were left? (Act II. p. 52)

Further complicating this cultural impediment, the "logic of the same," desire as male, slips in and out of their language like the "ghost" that Moraga struggles so hard to renounce. Like a ghost, it is elusive, insubstantial, haunting, persistent, and enduring; it transcends time and space and can "slip in" anywhere. As we have seen, neither Marisa nor Amalia can speak directly of their desire for each other without using the word "man." Marisa, for example, wants a "man in a woman," and when Amalia makes love to Marisa, it is somehow "really" her dead lover Alejandro who is doing so. Moreover, after the relationship is over, Marisa carries within her another, internalized impediment. She often refers to the "rocks" in her legs, her memories and anger that weigh her down and keep her "bolted to this planet." Both of these obstacles, one so immaterial and inescapable and the other so obdurate and dense, are used to illustrate how the logic of the same obscures Marisa and Amalia's ability to articulate their desire. This imagery is clearly established when the teatro begins and Marisa, sitting back to back with Corky, informs us:

> I always see that man–thick-skinned, dark, muscular.
> He is a boulder between us.
> I cannot lift him and her, too, carrying him.
> He is a ghost, always haunting her . . .
> lingering. (3)

Here male desire, personified as Alejandro, Amalia's dead lover, is imaged as both obstacles, the boulder and the ghost. Both are powerful symbols of natural and spiritual opposition–the boulder, like the rocks in Marisa's legs, can be seen as the weight of internalized oppression, while the ghost is, like ideology, intangibly, inextricably, interwoven between subjects. A boulder, like a strongly held belief system, is intractable, dense, solid, and hence hard to move, change, or attack. Only an extreme, violently destructive change like an explosion can shatter it, or it may be eroded over a long period of time. Perhaps most importantly, a boulder has the power to crush and oppress.

Boulders and ghosts are hard to fight because they are inanimate and hence invulnerable. They are either impenetrable or amorphous and hence are difficult to break apart or change. But perhaps these "strengths" are also their weaknesses; although they are powerful, both are also arid, for they can deny life but cannot create or sustain it. Boulders and ghosts are not alive, have no warmth, and, finally, are not human. And while "humanity" is a much debated term, it is precisely that–her standing as a member of the human community, as a part of a familia–that Marisa will not renounce.

Jane Gallop has asked if our desire for closure, for a resolution effected by the union of opposites, is a heterosexist assumption? If so, it is a desire that *Giving up the Ghost* leaves unfulfilled. As Marisa declares at the beginning, "It is not clean, nothing neat. It's about a battle I will never win and never stop fighting." Still unresolved, conflicted, raw, and alive, Marisa, left with her ghosts at the end of the teatro, decides:

> It's like making familia from scratch
> each time all over again . . . with strangers
> If I must, I will.

## AUTHOR NOTE

The author wishes to acknowledge Dorrine Kondo, David Román, and Gregory Bredbeck for their insightful comments. She is further indebted to Rosann Simmeroth for her perceptive comments, feedback, and support.

## WORKS CITED

Alarcón, Norma. "Making Familia from Scratch: Split Subjectivities in the Work of Helena Maria Viramontes and Cherríe Moraga." *The Americas Review: A Review of Hispanic Art and Literature of the USA* 15.3-4 (1987): 147-159.

De Lauretis, Teresa. *Technologies of Gender: Essays on Theory, Film and Fiction.* Bloomington: Indiana University Press, 1987.

Irigaray, Luce. *This Sex Which is Not One.* Ithaca: Cornell University Press, 1985.

Kristeva, Julia. Quoted in Moi, Toril. *Sexual/Textual Politics: Feminist Literary Theory.* New York: Metheun, 1985.

Moraga, Cherríe. *Giving Up the Ghost: A Teatro in Two Acts.* Los Angeles: West End Press, 1984.

Smith, Paul. *Discerning the Subject.* University of Minnesota Press, 1988.

Trinh T. Minh-ha. "She, the Inappropriate/d Other." *Discourse: Journal for Theoretical Studies in Media and Culture* 8 (Fall-Winter 1986-7): 21-35.

Turner, Victor. "Frame, Flow and Reflection: Ritual and Drama as Public Liminality." *Performance in Postmodern Culture.* Ed. Michel Benamou. Madison: Center for Twentieth Century Studies, 1977,

_____ . "Social Dramas and Ritual Metaphors." *Ritual, Play, Performance: Readings in the Social Sciences/Theatre.* Ed. Richard Schechner. New York: Seabury Press, 1976.

Yarbro-Bejarano, Yvonne. "Chicana Literature from a Chicana Feminist Perspective." *The Americas Review: A Review of Hispanic Art and Literature of the USA* 15.3-4 (1987): 139-45.

# Sexuality Degree Zero: Pleasure and Power in the Novels of John Rechy, Arturo Islas, and Michael Nava

Ricardo L. Ortiz, PhD

*San José State University*

**SUMMARY.** "Sexuality Degree Zero" explores common themes and formal strategies in the fiction of three prominent gay Chicano writers: John Rechy, Arturo Islas, and Michael Nava. Employing the concept of a politicized textual "pleasure" as theorized by French critic Roland Barthes, the study argues for the political efficacy of aesthetic choices characteristic to the three authors. Analyses of Rechy's use of pornography, of Islas' transgressive use of cultural iconography, and of Nava's use of sexual "perversions" in the context of classic crime fiction, all go to demonstrate the various uses of pleasure in the construction of a doubly marginalized but defiant self and voice in fiction by gay Chicano men.

The writer is always on the blind spot of systems, adrift; he is the joker in the pack, a *mana*, a zero degree . . . his place, his (exchange) value, varies according to the movements of history

---

Correspondence may be addressed to the author at: Department of English, SJSU, One Washington Square, San José, CA 95192-0090.

[Haworth co-indexing entry note]: "Sexuality Degree Zero: Pleasure and Power in the Novels of John Rechy, Arturo Islas, and Michael Nava." Ortiz, Ricardo L. Co-published simultaneously in the *Journal of Homosexuality* (The Haworth Press, Inc.) Vol. 26, No. 2/3, 1993, pp. 111-126; and *Critical Essays: Gay and Lesbian Writers of Color* (ed: Emmanuel S. Nelson) The Haworth Press, Inc., 1993, pp. 111-126. Multiple copies of this article/chapter may be purchased from The Haworth Document Delivery Center [1-800-3-HAWORTH; 9:00 a.m. - 5:00 p.m. (EST)].

> . . . he is asked all and/or nothing. He himself is outside ex-
> change, plunged into non-profit . . . desiring nothing but the
> perverse bliss of words . . . the writer suppresses this gratuitous-
> ness of writing . . . he stiffens, hardens his muscles, denies the
> drift, represses bliss: there are very few writers who combat both
> ideological repression and libidinal repression.
>
> *Roland Barthes[1]*

John Rechy's early fiction, especially *City of Night* and its redux
variation, *Numbers*, marks him as a rare specimen of the doubly
resistant writer Barthes lauds at the end of this passage.[2] Indeed, if
few writers combat both ideological and libidinal repression, even
fewer are as ostentatious as Rechy in doing so. I will devote most of
this chapter to a general analysis of Rechy's powerful if conflicted
negotiation of this common space, especially in his early fiction.
Rechy's work, as the one outstanding career-long oeuvre by an
arguably "gay" Chicano writer, will in turn stand as the test case
for an emerging body of work by other gay Chicano men, notably
Arturo Islas and Michael Nava, who will receive more attention at
the conclusion of this discussion.[3]

Rather than merely describing each writer's attempt to reaccess
the past through the kind of semiotic, iconographic play I will
describe below, I intend to ask why, as novelists, these three writers
have chosen such radically different formal paradigms, why they
take such different positions vis-à-vis the mainstream literary tradition. Implicit in this last question is the assumption that aesthetic
strategies, by telling us something of the writer's orientation toward
pleasure, inscribe into his or her text a structure of desire which in
turn tells us as much about the construction of political and cultural
subjectivity as about sexual subjectivity.

Aesthetically, *Numbers* (1967) raises the question of the function
of pornography as a limit-case of the intersection of content and
form, of sexual (and even cultural) politics and the question of
artistic value. Anyone who has read the more popular *City of Night*
(1964) will recognize in Rechy's later *Numbers* an attempt to disen-
cumber *City of Night*'s "male hustler as existential drifter" model
of the rhetorical excesses couching it in the earlier text (without,
that is, sacrificing its psychological complexity). What remains in

*Numbers* has, for worse rather than better, been taken for a slightly more sophisticated instance of gay male pornographic fiction. Rechy tells us in the 1984 Foreword to *Numbers* that at least two early readers "warned [me] that the book's concentrated sexuality might harm me as a serious writer," warnings which anticipated the book's "largely hysterical critical reception," a reaction aimed primarily at its "highly graphic" sexual content.[4] It is a text which, ostensibly at least, makes no bones about its sexual content, even as it does no better job than its predecessor of elaborating on the significance of its protagonist's (Chicano) ethnic identity, or on the intersection of the ethnic and sexual dimensions of that identity in a common symbolic space we might call political or ideological.

While some may argue that in later works, especially *Sexual Outlaw* and his most recent *The Miraculous Day of Amalia Gómez*, Rechy manages to break free of the ideological closets restricting the earlier fiction, I would respond that even these ostensibly "out," activist texts bear an anxiety about their political projects, an anxiety which evidently stems from the manner in which *desire* in Rechy's texts plays more often against than with itself in the construction of a subject at once libidinally and ideologically "free." Rechy's apparent foregrounding of sexual over ethnic difference in his early protagonists, for example, does not simplify his being categorized as an unambiguously "gay" writer, especially given the conflicted nature of those protagonists' desire. His hustlers, never mincing words over the homosexual nature of their exploits, check whatever may be celebratory about their homoeroticism with an insistent, self-hating, apologetic stance which disavows at every turn the play of their own desire in their sexual performances.

We might locate here one of those interesting sites of pleasurable disjunction between Rechy and his putatively autobiographical protagonists. One of the striking features of Rechy's authorial posturing is indeed his willingness to expose himself, more so than his characters, to the admiring gaze of his readers. Rechy has Johnny Rio, his alter-ego in *Numbers*, enact a number of curiously narcissistic scenes. For example, while driving through the desert to Los Angeles in Chapter One, Johnny "tries to shut . . . thoughts [of death and self-destruction] off [by looking] down at his shirtless chest, which–deeply, deeply tanned–gleams with sweat. Pleased by the sight, he runs his hand over it, brings that hand to his mouth, and licks his own perspiration, feeling the excitement burgeoning between his legs. . . . Triumphantly, the thought of sex has driven away the thought of death, at least for now."[5]

Clearly, Rechy's text wants to derive its ontological value from its analogous relation to body, albeit one "without organs," that is, as a disorganized amalgamation of sites of pleasure. Indeed, Barthes reminds us that "the pleasure of the text is not necessarily a triumphant, heroic, muscular type" which requires that the writer "throw out [his] chest." The reader's "pleasure," Barthes insists, "can very well take the form of a drift," which in turn poses a challenge for the writer, who must allow the reader the autonomous enjoyment of an ineradicably "local" effect. Writing "in pleasure," Barthes warns, does not "guarantee . . . me, the writer . . . my reader's pleasure." The writer "must seek out this reader (must 'cruise' him)," must elicit from him that intense but momentary double-take in order to create in the text "a site of bliss."[6] This pleasure is, then, profoundly informed by the simultaneous operations of siting and sighting, that is, by an act of self-exposure which, in eliciting the desiring gaze of its audience, creates a space defined by this exchange of desires, of looks.

Rechy loves to offer himself up as an erotic image, even to the manner in which he is photographed for jacket covers.[7] While there is nothing absolutely revelatory about this posturing, it is nevertheless helpful to discuss Rechy's retreat into his text as a function of his relationship to his body. In *Numbers*, for example, Johnny Rio undertakes a self-fashioned therapeutic regimen in his years of isolation in Laredo, a regimen which involves intense physical training. This program clearly functions as an image of literal self-composition easily translatable into textual terms.

Rechy's obsession with his heroes as erotic objects does, for this reason, go a long way toward explaining how he limits their development as ethnically specific characters. Johnny's retreat to Laredo receives the following treatment from Rechy: "'Away' means Laredo, in Texas, his hometown in the beautiful purple, blue and golden Southwest: Laredo–which, on the one side–toward the border–is still very Mexican, as colorful as a sarape. . . . [Johnny] has lived there alone in his apartment . . . working hard . . . saving all his money; in his leisure time exercising compulsively with weights . . . avoiding people . . . [until] one day . . . as he stood looking at himself in the mirror, he felt curiously that he had ceased to exist, that he existed only in the mirror. He reached out to touch himself, and the cold glass frustrated him."[8] To some extent the true alienation here is Rechy's unwillingness to explore the "Mexican side" of his own psyche; he makes passing mention of Johnny's "dreary fatherless Mexican Catholic childhood: poor, poor years and after school jobs," but only as the source of "unpleasant memories" he tolerates during his three-year hiatus in Laredo. Little is made of the connection between this alienated sense of cultural identity and the more vague existential trauma Johnny will try to overcome sexually by challenging himself to turn thirty tricks during his brief stay in Los Angeles.

Rechy thus hides a good deal more than he shows, particularly when we look at the manner in which specifically ethnic questions are almost simultaneously invoked and covered up in his early fiction. Elsewhere I have looked more closely at this issue.[9] For here it suffices to say that Rechy's flagrant sexuality more often than not serves to distract him, and his reader, from looking too closely at the disturbingly sexual dimension of his cultural, familial background.

What pleasure, on the other hand, a reader may be said to derive from the inscription of a (reformed) drifter like Johnny Rio into the Rechean text has more to do with more elusive forms of semiotic play than with the semantic description of any of his sexual encounters, the episodic units of his picaresque erotic journey. One example of this kind of pleasurable textual play can be found in Rechy's use of names. As Johnny speeds toward Los Angeles in the first chapter of *Numbers*, "not so much . . . driving as . . . being driven," Rechy informs us that "'Rio' is not actually his last name–it's not even his mother's maiden name," and that, instead, he "assumed [it] in Los Angeles because, especially in a world where no last names are given, it sounded romantic, like a gypsy's."[10] "Johnny Rio," though technically as anonymous a name as the generic "John" given to the protagonist of *City of Night*, is nevertheless no simply "empty" signifier.

Like a variable in an algebraic formula, its value is wholly determined by its context. In this case, the name of a "stock" Latin lover or exotic lead from some grade-B Hollywood film remains a fully motivated choice; in a specifically south Texan, Chicano context, it situates Johnny precisely on "*el río*," the border, the fluid no-place between places whose symbolic and practical value as origin, as source of derivation, has been so productively articulated recently by Gloria Anzaldúa.[11] While Johnny's name has no derivation (specifically, he did not derive it from his *mother*), Rechy's simultaneous naming and unnaming of Johnny does give a value to his protagonist's anonymity, a value that does not extend to the nameless (but not numberless) tricks Johnny will encounter in his sexual odyssey through the parks and theatres of Los Angeles.

Generically, *Numbers* exhibits some of the markedly parodic tendencies of pornographic fiction and film, but it bears them in a more playful, though no less critically self-conscious way. Rechy's text offers us a post-modern inversion of both picaresque and pastoral forms. Like Rechy's other protagonists, Johnny Rio is clearly anti-heroic in the "classic" mode of existential, Beat-generation writing. This creates some tension between his often narcissistic exhibitionism, left over from a more traditionally heroic paradigm, and his rôle as a drifter over a post-modern, apocalyptic landscape, which is, if anything, pastoral in its emphasis on secret places in public parks, leafy grottoes and caves where the "phallic" hero both exposes and hides himself. This subtly androgynous indeterminacy of genre is literally reflected in Johnny's body-type; his "is an easy masculinity–not stiff, not rigid, not blundering nor posed . . . [and] as with all truly sexually attractive men, there is something very, very subtly feminine about him, . . . [which] has to do with the fact that he moves sensually, that his eyes invite, that he is constantly flirting . . . and that he is extremely vain."[12] For this reason, despite its ostensible phallo-worship, *Numbers* remains a complexly gendered text. The phallic trajectory of Johnny's erotic quest is often delayed and suspended by enclosures (the "grottoes" or "caves" of trees and shrubs in Griffith Park, the balconies of "open all night" theatres), frozen stages of unreproductive sexual play.

The movie theatres in turn offer another paradoxical reversal of representational space. These all-night B-movie houses are not porn palaces *per se*; what "obscene" activity Rechy does stage in them occurs in the literally ob-scene space, that is, in the seats, where the audience enjoys itself, invisibly, unseen. And, like the novel, these theatres become for Rechy the site of a decadent (not to say decayed or "fallen") aesthetic; "Quite probably," the narrator speculates, "these theatres once housed elaborate ['live'] productions . . . vaudeville, perhaps even opera."[13]

Walking the streets near Pershing Square, Johnny also notices "stores displaying hundreds of magazines showing naked bodies in garish color" alongside "rancid fried-chicken counters" and "leathery army-and-navy outlet stores," all suggesting varying manifestations of the rank commercialization of decadent culture, in a manner that establishes some critical distance between *Numbers* and the "mere" pornography Johnny observes on the magazine racks. Curiously, it is in this decrepit commercial/cultural scene that Rechy chooses to inscribe himself, to inject a little intertextual blood into a vein of his text: a downtown character accosts Johnny and recounts to him the "stir" occasioned by the "young number" who "used to hang around the bars and Pershing Square" and "wrote a book about Main Street and hustling and Pershing Square and queens," inspiring "tourists" to come "down looking for Miss So-and-So that he'd written about!"[14]

It is not, therefore, in the hyper-frequent presentation of sexual encounters that Rechy engages his readers, catching us in our voyeuristic fascination with his most seductive, pleasurable moments of self-exposure as *textual* effect. Pornography as such does not guarantee its audience anything like the readerly pleasure defined by Barthes; and certainly one can argue that it does not even guarantee any more banal sorts of pleasure either. It does, however, seem to me that in Rechy's case the pornographic dimension of *Numbers*, especially as it anticipates the overt activism of *Sexual Outlaw*, provides us with a way of exploring one simultaneously aestheticized and politicized gesture on Rechy's part, one which takes the reader in, educating him politically by appealing directly to his erotic investments.

In *The Sadeian Woman*, Angela Carter offers the following extremely useful analysis of the political potential in pornographic writing. Despite its characteristic insistence on the Utopian, Carter argues, porn can never be purely "art for art's sake" because it is always "art with work to do."[15] Porn's "sensationalism . . . suggests the methodology," and the effectiveness, presumably, "of propaganda." The moment porn abandons its conventional idealism and begins to aspire to any kind of realism, "the more likely it is to affect the reader's perception of the world . . . [through] the total demystification of the flesh and the subsequent revelation . . . of the real relations of man and his kind." The pornographer, Carter concludes, therefore "has it in his power to become a terrorist of the imagination."

As "applied art" with a built-in taste for efficient, pragmatic effect (titillation, orgasm), porn more than any of the "fine arts" bears a significant subversive potential whenever it decides to work against the interests of the status quo.[16] Pornography thus allows us to construct pleasure as a transgressively productive (and not conservatively reproductive) labor, encumbered but also charged, like any socially and historically conditioned behavior, with a complex arrangement of values and investments. *Numbers*, in the way that it anticipates in its pornographic discourse the more politicized *Sexual Outlaw*,[17] suggests that Rechy understood, long before the generation of politicized writers, performance artists, and filmmakers coming under fire of censorship in our own day, that he could put the shock-value of porn in the service of salutary political ends.

While literal pornography does not enter into the formal aspirations of writers like Islas and Nava, both of them exhibit a marked fascination with the obscene. This fascination, I would argue, has as much to do with the way they negotiate the ambivalence they feel toward the past, toward their origins in both their cultural and sexual dimensions, as Rechy's marked pathologies have to do with his.

In Islas this fascination too often relegates the sexual histories of his characters to the level of innuendo, to the "obscene" space off the stage of explicitly narrated events. In *The Rain God*, the narrative of Felix Angel's murder at the hands of a young serviceman he tried to seduce reads almost like a cautionary tale of the grave cost of taking any kind of sexual risk. Islas devotes the chapter entitled "The Rain Dancer" to Felix's life, framed by the events leading directly to his death.[18]

Typical of Islas' prose, the chapter is beautifully modulated between present and past experiences, elegantly understated, if perhaps then a little coy about the manner in which it represents characters' sexual behavior through symbolic displacements and verbal sleights of hand. Felix, we are told, "spent most of his life" in a "border town" where "traffic flows from one side of the river to the other," and where, "from the air, national boundaries and differences are indistinguishable." While Islas inhabits the same symbolic territory that Rechy does in his fiction, the displacing language of borders in Islas favors making cultural rather than sexual distinctions explicit.[19]

Felix is inscribed in an emphatically Chicano cultural text from which his sexuality marks him, very discreetly, as different. "Felix was not a respectable man," Islas tells us; he frequented a "serviceman's bar" with "enough of an ambiguous reputation to be considered an interesting or suspicious place by the townspeople on the 'American' side of the river." While Felix's sexual taste is touchingly idealistic ("Constantly on the lookout for the shy and fair god who would land safely on the shore at last, Felix searched for his youth in obscure places on both sides of the river"), his practices are a bit more jaded; he takes advantage of his ability to offer work to young Mexican men to require that they undergo physical examinations with him. "The physical," Islas tells us, "consisted of tests for hernias and prostate trouble and did not go beyond that unless the worker . . . expressed an interest in more." Felix's predilections in turn take on the socially "safe" status of gossip, of mere rumor; the workers largely "forgot the experience, and [only] occasionally referred to him behind his back but affectionately as *Jefe Joto.*"

The generation following Felix's has the better fortune of being able to lead more openly gay lives. As treated by Islas in *Migrant Souls*, however, Miguel Chico and Serena's experiences as gay people still remain largely in that marginalizing closet-space of silence that marks Islas' suggestive, understated style. Serena, for example, "small, robust and perfectly suited to her job as a P.E. teacher," accomplishes the astonishing feat of making a "Boston marriage" for herself in El Paso ("Del Sapo" is its anagrammatic foil in Islas' fiction). She "lives in an apartment" with "Mary

Margaret Ryan, an algebra teacher from Boston" and performs good works which hold "at bay the judgment of those Angels who were suspicious about the erotic lives of others because their own were so dull."[20]

Serena, though important to any reading of sexuality in Islas' texts, is generally less important a character than her outspoken sister Josie and their cousin Miguel Chico. Unlike Serena, who finds her life "Wonderful," Miguel Chico is Islas' most tormented character, the one closest in life-story to Islas' own personal history. Miguel Chico spends most of *Migrant Souls* in the thrall of his alcoholism and in despair at his estrangement from his former lover. We should not be surprised, then, that Miguel Chico's life receives so muted a treatment from Islas; part of it has to do with the larger problem of Islas' negotiation of his profoundly homophobic culture, a culture he wants to record both lovingly and critically. When his aunt Eduviges, responding to the news of Felix's death, declares, "I don't believe a word of it. There are no homosexuals," Miguel Chico sits in "grief-stricken" silence, leaving it up to his more vocal cousin Josie to taunt her mother in anger. Serena, surprisingly, even defends Eduviges, reminding Josie, "You know what it's like in Del Sapo," and suggesting that she more than Josie knows what it means to confront a cultural attitude insistent on her nonexistence, and what it takes to survive nevertheless within that culture.

Despite the melancholic, almost tragic cast of Islas' work, there remains a significant yield of pleasure to be procured from the kinds of semiotic play in which Islas allows himself to indulge. For Islas, as for Rechy, nomination becomes a chief tool in accessing the most potent semiotic resources of his cultural environment; indeed, this is one of the rare instances in which Islas' symbolism achieves a kind of Rechean excess.[21] The matriarch of Islas' Angel clan, Encarnación Olmeca Angel, incarnates "nominally" much of the cultural complexity of Islas' fictional world; but even her nickname, Mama Chona, has a good deal to tell us about the larger psychological complexity that informs Islas' treatment of his culture. Mama Chona stands for the "big mother," or better put, the mother-in-excess; she is at once authoritarian and nurturing, a figure whose power, both positive and negative, permeates both texts in the manner that the image and iconographic power of the Virgin/Madonna permeate the culture they describe.[22]

Mama Chona's spiritual foil in Islas' fiction is the rebellious, cynical, wisecracking Josie, whose full name, "Josefa" after St. Joseph, signals the larger contrast she poses for Mama Chona. Josie's character, however, suffers from a kind of masculinization also signalled by her name. Islas, like Rechy and Nava, seems, in his attempts to explore the construction of femininity in his culture, to revert occasionally to an almost drag-style performance; this limitation suggests even more clearly that often their explorations of feminine experience are actually displaced attempts to address issues too intimately threatening to the construction of masculinity to be treated openly as masculine problems.

While the potency of the Marian symbol permeates Rechy and Islas' fiction, it is less pronounced but certainly there in Michael Nava's. Nava's women are less dimensional than the more elaborately developed women characters in Islas and Rechy, but this can only be partially explained as a necessary function of the generic demands of detective fiction, which is Nava's specialty. *How Town* is the third and latest in Nava's series of texts involving investigative attorney Henry Rios, who is gay and Chicano. The latina women in *How Town* run the gamut from Rios' religiously fanatical mother to his sister Elena, a former nun who is lesbian. "Our mother," Rios tells his reader, "retaliated" against their father's alcoholism "with religious fanaticism. As she knelt before plaster images of saints, in the flicker of votive candles, her furious mutter was more like invective than prayer."[23] And Elena's brief, important appearances in the novel, though they suggest something of the emotional complexity that alienates her from her brother, present her to the reader as little more than a caricature of the dour Berkeley lesbian.[24]

In Elena's house, however, Rios observes telling vestiges of his sister's cultural and familial past. "An oil painting of a nude above the fireplace," he tells us, "showed a desiccated woman with a flat Indian face, standing with her hands at her breasts, as if to protect herself. There was nothing soft about her nudity; its graphic, painful clarity denied any sensuality–she was a Madonna for whom giving birth had been an act of self-obliteration. I wondered," Rios concludes, "if this represented our mother to Elena."[25] Regardless of its significance to Elena, the image of a too-delineated, "painful" nudity speaks directly to the sin from which *How Town*'s intricate morality play originates. Again, as an image of great semiotic power, it organizes questions of origins, both political and sexual, around the problematic of desire, around the complex construction of pleasure.

Like any good postmodern detective, Nava's Rios is intimately implicated in the sin he is enlisted to uncover and expiate, and in *How Town* that sin is pedophilia. The case takes Rios back to his home town of Los Robles in Northern California, and, as more clues emerge about the pedophile brother of Rios' best childhood friend, the clearer it becomes to the reader that Nava has made pedophilia the informing metaphor for one's relation to one's own past, to one's own childhood, to oneself as a child. It also serves as a test case for Rios' own moral limits; Rios' first interview with Paul Windsor, whom he has been hired to defend, brings all these questions together, and it is to Nava's credit that he does not opt for easy answers to the moral problems his dramatic situations raise.[26] The most complex maternal figure in *How Town* is Ruth Soto, the thirteen-year-old daughter of the Windsors' maid, and the mother of Paul Windsor's child. The child-mother Ruth, who lives in Rios' old neighborhood, suffers multiple layers of abuse (sexual as well as economic) at the hands of white, wealthy Paul Windsor; his crime, his violation of her body, realizes all the horror represented in the earlier image of childbirth, and yet she survives, ironically in the maternal care of Henry's own sister, Elena, and Elena's black lover Joanne.

It is tempting to argue, in conclusion, that Henry Rios has a good deal to teach the more alienated or anguished gay characters in Rechy and Islas' fiction.[27] Rios' openness about his sexual and cultural identity allows Nava to demonstrate the ease with which these differences can acquire the status of significant but not incapacitating circumstance in the larger cultural and political environment in which Rios lives, and this without indulging in a too-stylized detective-fiction treatment, which would strain our ability as readers to suspend our disbelief. Nava's fictive world is very recognizably contemporary California in all its complexity–sexual, cultural, and political. This does not, however, suggest that Nava intends to make Henry Rios a Utopian model of perfect self-acceptance. Rios never entirely resolves his problems with either his sister or his past, and his disturbing fascination with Paul Windsor's sexuality ironically gets the last word.[28]

Like Rechy and Islas, Nava recognizes that, despite the importance for gay people, and for people of color, of achieving a stable, resistant political identity, identity as such is fundamentally an effect of the self's troubled relation to memory and desire, that is, to language.[29] What Rechy does most effectively with the subversive elements of porn, and Islas with the elegance of lyrical reminiscence, Nava achieves through that paradoxical turn most postmodern detective fiction takes in its profound exploration of the detective's psyche, as he searches for the author, the culprit, the inscriber of clues who inevitably turns out to be some version of the detective himself. And it is here, in this troubled intersection of power and pleasure, of history and desire, that writers as disparate as Rechy, Islas, and Nava inscribe themselves and perform, each in his own different manner, that doubled resistance of ideological and libidinal repression with which this chapter began.

## NOTES

1. See Barthes, p. 35. No one other theorist will inform the following reading as much as Barthes; *The Pleasure of the Text* in particular seems to me to offer a strategy for the implementation of a politically informed semiotic reading of Chicano/a texts complementary to the Jamesonian model proposed by Ramón Saldívar in *Chicano Narrative: the Dialectics of Difference*.

2. While I intend to focus this discussion around Rechy's novel *Numbers* (reprinted with new foreword, 1984), I will make occasional comparative references to three of his other novels: *City of Night* (also reprinted with a new introduction, 1984), *Sexual Outlaw: A Documentary*, and *The Miraculous Day of Amalia Gómez*.

3. See Islas' novels *The Rain God* and *Migrant Souls*, and especially *How Town*, Nava's third installment in his series of Henry Rios mysteries.

4. Foreword to *Numbers*, pp. 3-4.

5. *Numbers*, pp. 13-4.

6. See Barthes, pp. 18, 4.

7. See Rechy's Foreword to *Numbers* (1984), where he cites "anger conveyed in reviews" aroused by "the use of my photograph on the front of the book's jacket" (p. 3).

8. *Numbers*, pp. 22-3.

9. See Ricardo L. Ortiz, "Rechy, Isherwood and the *Numbers* Game," forthcoming in the published proceedings for the Fifth International Congress on Hispanic Cultures in the United States, Fall 1992.

10. *Numbers*, pp. 15, 18. We must not underestimate the importance of naming, especially in ethnic American literature. See William Boelhower, p. 81. Boelhower's reading of ethnic American literature hinges on the presupposition that, "According to ethnic semiosis, in the beginning was the name."

11. Rechy especially, but even Islas and Nava, seem to acknowledge both the power of, and the problems resulting from, Hollywood-generated images of latino/as in general and of chicano/as in particular. For a cursory but comprehensive inventory of mainstream Hollywood's mishandling of latino figures and culture, see George Hadley-García.

12. *Numbers*, pp. 16-7.

13. *Numbers*, p. 40.

14. *Numbers*, p. 25.

15. See Carter, pp. 19-21. In a telling aside, Carter argues that the best pornographers usually demonstrate a surprisingly sophisticated understanding of their project. Sade's libertines, for example, after endless dissertations on the philosophical underpinnings of their predilections, would command the turning of theory into practice with the reflexive imperative, "Let's to work!" Pleasure was work for the libertine inasmuch as it constituted the ultimate duty or obligation one owed by necessity to the nature which had made one sentient.

16. Witness the recent controversy surrounding Marlon Riggs and Essex Hemphill's film, *Tongues Untied*, which should leave us asking what precisely shocked Jesse Helms and his fellows more: explicitly presented sex between black men, or the politically revolutionary message conveyed by the film in both words and images.

17. In some ways *Sexual Outlaw* would be a better test case for Carter's arguments; as a self-styled "fictional documentary" its language is even closer to a bare-bones realism than that of *Numbers*, whose hyper-reductive prose seems to me as close to one kind of zero-degree writing, to "mere" writing, as writing ever gets. See especially Rechy's own discussion of the relation of his aesthetic strategies to his political ends in the Foreword to the 1984 edition of *Sexual Outlaw*.

18. *The Rain God*, pp. 113-138.

19. See *Migrant Souls*, pp. 164-5, for a fascinating discussion of the cultural and political status of Chicanos, which Islas stages between Rudy, Miguel Grande, and other members of the "first" and "second" generations of Angels. Chicanos, Rudy argues, "don't know what we are because we don't know where we are . . . between two countries completely different from each other," his sardonically offered solution to this crisis of identity being to "keep the border and give both lands back to the Indians!"

20. See *Migrant Souls*, pp. 103-7, for Islas' brief treatment of Serena's history.

21. While Rechy's early fiction relies mostly on the symbolic fecundity of anonymity, in *Amalia Gómez* he makes heavy if often ironic use, especially, of

religious names in weaving his larger symbolic tapestry. While Nava exercises a bit more restraint on this score, we could make a similar argument for his naming his hero Henry Rios as I do for Rechy's Johnny Rio in *Numbers*.

22. The Marian symbol could, indeed, serve as an illustrative point for a study contrasting their literary treatments of the feminine as such in the cultural and familial life of the Chicano community. Rechy's Amalia Gómez, for example, understands her attractiveness, one of the chief ways she understands her*self*, period, not only as a function of her resemblance to both María Félix and Elizabeth Taylor, but also through her chief iconographic model, Jennifer Jones' Bernadette of Lourdes.

23. See *How Town*, p. 2.

24. See Chapters 1 and 21 of *How Town* for scenes involving the siblings.

25. *How Town*, pp. 5-6.

26. See Chapter 5 of *How Town*. Nava is noted for the powerful efficiency of his dialogue, and this interview is one of the best examples in his work of the psychological complexity he can create with astonishingly few words.

27. One friend of Rios praises him thus for his unwillingness to compromise himself professionally: "A gay public figure, a criminal defense lawyer and a Chicano—you didn't choose an easy road. . . . You could have stayed closeted and gone for the big money on Montgomery Street as some huge firm's token minority partner" (pp. 21-2).

28. After an argument with his much younger lover, Josh, Rios describes their conciliatory embrace thus: "He got up and held his hands to me and pulled me up to my feet from the bed, like a child" (p. 243).

29. For Nava this even takes the form of the relationship he wishes to develop vis-à-vis the mainstream Anglo-American literary tradition. *How Town*'s title refers to a poem by cummings, and in the text there are scattered references to Stevens, Eliot, Bishop, and even a comical one to Jane Austen.

## WORKS CITED

Anzaldúa, Gloria. *Borderlands/La Frontera*. San Francisco: Spinsters/Aunt Lute, 1987.

Barthes, Roland. *The Pleasure of the Text*. Trans. Richard Miller. New York: Noonday Press, 1975.

Boelhower, William. *Through a Glass Darkly: Ethnic Semiosis in American Literature*. Oxford: Oxford University Press, 1987.

Carter, Angela. *The Sadeian Woman and the Ideology of Pornography*. New York: Pantheon Books, 1978.

Hadley-García, George. *Hispanic Hollywood: The Latins in Motion Pictures*. New York: The Citadel Press, 1990.

Islas, Arturo. *Migrant Souls*. New York: Avon Books, 1990.

Islas, Arturo. *The Rain God*. Palo Alto: Alexandrian Press, 1984.

Nava, Michael. *How Town*. New York: Ballantine Books, 1990.

Rechy, John. *City of Night*. New York: Grove Press, 1963.

Rechy, John. *The Miraculous Day of Amalia Gómez*. New York: Arcade Publishing, 1991.

Rechy, John. *Numbers*. New York: Grove Press, 1967.

Rechy, John. *The Sexual Outlaw: A Documentary*. New York: Grove Press, 1977.

Saldívar, Ramón. *Chicano Narrative: the Dialectics of Difference*. Madison: University of Wisconsin Press, 1991.

# Gay Re-Readings of the Harlem Renaissance Poets

Gregory Woods, PhD

*The Nottingham Trent University, England*

**SUMMARY.** In the light of the long-established fact of their homosexuality or bisexuality, it is high time for the cluster of "Negro Renaissance" poets, Countee Cullen, Langston Hughes, Claude McKay, and Richard Bruce Nugent, to be reappraised by and for gay readers. This paper seeks to develop gay reading strategies in relation to the poems of these writers, in order to reveal for contemporary readers likely subtexts which, at the time of their writing, were publicly read as bearing on race alone. It is often possible to read a particular poem as referring (in images such as that of the social outcast) to either racial or sexual oppression, interchangeably; and possibly, therefore, to both at once, by way of an implicit comparison. Likewise, poems on miscegenation can just as well be read, via the theme of forbidden love, as referring to homosexuality. The fact that most published critical readings deal only with the racial issue does not invalidate the likelihood that the poem can be, and indeed requires to be, read as referring, also, to sexuality. Gay readings emerge, then, not merely from these writers' representations of attractive men and boys, but also in the midst of their most famously anti-racist themes.

Eric Garber has spoken of "a homosexual subculture, uniquely Afro-American in substance," which took shape in Harlem after the

Correspondence may be addressed to the author at: Department of English and Media Studies, The Nottingham Trent University, Clifton Lane, Nottingham, NG11 8NS, England.

[Haworth co-indexing entry note]: "Gay Re-Readings of the Harlem Renaissance Poets." Woods, Gregory. Co-published simultaneously in the *Journal of Homosexuality* (The Haworth Press, Inc.) Vol. 26, No. 2/3, 1993, pp. 127-142; and *Critical Essays: Gay and Lesbian Writers of Color* (ed: Emmanuel S. Nelson) The Haworth Press, Inc., 1993, pp. 127-142.

First World War (318). To speak of the Harlem Renaissance and its participants in a gay cultural context is to speak, uniquely, of a cohesive gay community whose texts have been inherited not only by its most legitimate heirs–lesbian and gay African-Americans today–but, indirectly, by gay communities throughout the Western world. I mean "texts" in the broadest sense, including languages and styles, songs and fashions, as well as novels and poems.

However, this unique subcultural heritage has gone largely un-recognized, even by African-American commentators, whose criti-cal practice tends to be no less heterocentric than that of their white equivalents. As Emmanuel Nelson has written, "Almost all the major figures of the Harlem Renaissance were gay: Alain Locke, Countee Cullen, Langston Hughes, Claude McKay. Yet among black scholars of the Harlem Renaissance there is a remarkable reticence about the sexualities of these pioneering artists and a determined unwillingness to explore the impact of their gayness on their literary constructions and on the forms and directions of the Renaissance" (92).[1]

It is high time for the Harlem Renaissance poets to be reappraised by and for gay readers. I am persuaded of the urgent need for such action when a gay black writer like Daniel Garrett says, of the Harlem writers, that "many . . . were homosexual, though none but for Bruce Nugent expressed this in his work" (17). In the following essay I intend to explore various gay reading strategies in relation to these writers, to suggest to contemporary readers likely subtexts which had to be kept concealed at the time of their writing–con-cealed, that is, from hostile readers, but always accessible to percep-tive, sympathetic readings. Such readings must be carried out, even today, in the face of obstruction on the part of some of the writers' estates, which would seem to prefer questions of non-standard sexuality to remain buried in obscurity. The case of the Langston Hughes Estate's interference in Isaac Julien's film *Looking for Langston* is only the most visible example of this tendency.[2]

The simplest way to begin a search for "gay poems" by the Harlem writers is to consult them on the topic of attractive men and boys. There are many such figures in Langston Hughes's poems, but it should be remembered that they appear among at least as many, if not more, beautiful women. In a sense, to turn some of these poems into "gay poems" one must take the simple, and entirely excusable, step of isolating them from the rest. Disapproving heterosexual readers may complain that this is cheating, and that it has the effect of falsifying Hughes's output. My considered reply is that gay readers have had to make themselves, with practice, adept at such strategies, in order to step around the barriers which gay poets have often been forced to erect around themselves. If anyone is involved in the falsification of gay poets' work, it is the censorious and homophobic critical voices within the dominant, heterosexual community.

Hughes is particularly good on sailors. Like Billie Holiday, he covers the waterfront–that site of promiscuous social interaction and continental drift, where heavy labor and frantic leisure are equally at home, and where violence is no more than an expression of passionate release, no less than a way of life. As glimpsed in "Water-Front Streets" (*Selected* 51), this is potentially an ugly place, yet its ugliness is tempered by its conduciveness to dreaming. The waterfront is, by definition, on the margin of the city. It is also, by temperament, on the margin of urban social structures. Although the city's wealth must pass through this place, it does not itself accumulate wealth. Most who work here are poor. But they are rich in experience. Some have travelled on ships; others, who have had to stay behind, have travelled in the mind. It is its association with travel, its links with the rest of the world (in the present context, with Africa in particular), that make this a place in which the imagination holds sway, and even in which reality itself can meet the standards of the imagination. The dreams Hughes has in mind seem to be distinctly un-American. They are dreams of another place, where "life is gay."

One can read this poem as a slight lyric of rather sentimental Garveyism. But the language in which it is expressed is clearly intended to take us further. The poem's adjectives are "beautiful," "dream," "rare," gay," and "beautiful" again. The adverb "wondrous" qualifies and intensifies "rare." This is no picture of squalor or poverty. As the imagery solidifies in the second stanza–with two of the adjectives becoming nouns, "beauties" and "dreams"–one receives an impression of nothing less than glamour; not so much the glamour of the water-front streets themselves, which are "not so beautiful," as that of the "lads" who embark from here and who, in due course, will disembark again, laden with fresh experience.

The ships on which these sailors sail are "dream ships" to those who stay behind, not only because of the exotic places they sail to, but also because of their exotic cargo, the sailor "lads." Like ships themselves, these boys' hearts are freighted with "beauties" and "dreams." In such dreams, they reimagine the amorous encounters they enjoyed in port and conjure up hypothetical future encounters. In the last two words, "like me," the speaker both compares his experience with theirs–he, too, is laden with dreams since encountering beauty–and identifies himself as the possible subject of an absent sailor's dream.

The international trade in dreams is also, of course, a trade in flesh.[3] Whether the sailors are buying or being bought, they participate physically in a commodification of dreams, of which Hughes seems heartily to have approved (but which was deplored by his critics in the black bourgeoisie, which was so earnestly trying to underpin its limited economic successes with racial "respectability"). In other poems, then, sailors are associated with cash: when they hit the waterfront they have both energy and money to burn. So "Port Town" is spoken, jauntily, by a whore of unspecified sex, to a sailor, enticing him with promises of a night of alcohol and "love"(*Selected* 71). This jovial little poem, luxuriating in its own unapologetic shallowness, is a typical product of pre-Stonewall homosexuality: safe in the complacent assumption that it is spoken by a woman, but daring in the possibility that it is not. The distance between its two possible versions produces an ironic, stereoscopic effect which is authentic camp.

"Young Sailor," too, concerns the moment when a man on shore leave tries to decide what to spend his accumulated wages on (*Selected* 73). Alcohol and women are the two alternatives mentioned. But remember that the gay mythology of available sailors, while acknowledging that such men generally consider themselves heterosexual, depends on frustration and drunkenness to deliver the prize. Hughes's sailor goes to sea for "strength" and returns to port for "laughter." At the point where sea and land so productively meet, on the waterfront, he "carries" both strength and laughter, in a balanced combination which makes him irresistible. While the strength of his physique may be menacingly attractive, his relaxed laughter is positively inviting. It may be that he will continue to laugh while one engages with his strength. So be it. Both sailor and poem ignore the future, focused as they are on momentary delight, having "nothing hereafter."

Interestingly, these poems do not specify the skin color of the sailors. On the other hand, for obvious reasons, the politicized Harlem street-poems often depend for their persuasiveness on Langston Hughes's clear attraction to young black men and his concern at their plight. I do not necessarily mean that these are all "gay poems" in the narrow sense of statements of homosexual attraction; but there is, surely, a gay element to the poet's attitude to his male subjects. In the long sequence of poems "Montage of a Dream Deferred," for instance, the recurrent evocation of "Little cullud boys" is deeply affectionate. Hughes likes them. The tone of his voice wears a smile, even as he acknowledges their anxiety at reaching their "draftee years." As much as they may be a part of his own dreams, his poem concerns their dreams of genuine access to opportunity in the United States, and the deferral thereof (*Selected* 221-272).

The readings one performs on such texts depend on the degree of investigative creativity one is willing to exact upon them. In the case of Hughes's "Trumpet Player," it could be judged both impertinent and counter-productive, not to mention heavy-handed, to read the whole poem as a conscious or unconscious paean to orality, and to oral sex in particular. The man in the poem is, after all, blowing a trumpet, not a penis. The fact remains, however, no matter how tactful the reader wishes to be, that the poem expresses its celebration of jazz in terms of ecstasy, desire, and pursed lips. (We should also remember that the word "jazz" itself has sexual origins.) In other words, the trumpeter may not be having sex—or not at the moment of the poem—but he is sexy: both desirous and desirable (*Selected* 114-115).

Another textual homage to black manhood, Claude McKay's poem "Alfonso, Dressing to Wait at Table" (76), might be read as having an exclusively "racial" agenda, to the extent that it protests the confining of an active, black life to the service of rich white people. But the degree of its admiration for Alfonso, long prior to its mildly politicized, racial ending, leaves an impression more of an erotic frisson than of protest. The two aspects are, in the end, inseparable: for it is the sheer beauty of Alfonso's life and liveliness that makes his confinement especially shocking. Although his eyes are "made" to attract women, it is clear that they have a similar effect on such men as the poet. While preparing to wait at table, Alfonso sings in a revealingly versatile voice which rises from mellow and seductive low notes to a trilled falsetto. And while singing, he blows "Gay kisses" in the direction of "imaginary lasses"–either he imagines women he might be kissing; or his audience wrongly imagines he intends his kisses for women; or the members of his audience, men like the poet, imagine themselves in the place of the women he likes to kiss. Whichever way one reads the scene, it constitutes a moment of shared joy which is interrupted by the greed of white people and the consuming culture they dominate.

Countee Cullen's long poem "The Black Christ" (104-137) also routes its anti-racist message through a paean to the beauty of the black man Jim. Although its speaker is Jim's brother, the whole text is essentially a love poem. When Jim is lynched, Cullen gives the subsequent lament a homo-erotic cultural focus by referring to the dead man as Lycidas (Edward King, the beloved college friend of John Milton), Jonathan (lover of David), and Patrocles (Patroclus, lover of Achilles), all prematurely dead and volubly mourned by the men who loved them. The death itself is also eroticized: Jim is "raped" by sleep; even when hanged, his corpse is "lusty." Jim's brother adorns him with such adjectives as "young," "beautiful," "comely," and "lovely" (132-133). His moral force is conveyed, almost entirely, in terms of wasted physical beauty.

A characteristic which all these writers share with white gay writers, but which is given a doubled intensity by the context of racism, is their interest in the related themes of oppressed beauty and of love under threat. White lesbian and gay readers are likely to be able to follow, and quite readily comprehend, the logic of the thought that leads, by however circuitous a route, from beauty to tragedy. There is an early, fictionalized version of a white gay man's response to Countee Cullen in the novel *Strange Brother*, by the pseudonymous Blair Niles (1932). The book's central character,

June Westbrook, visits her homosexual friend Mark Thornton in his apartment. He has a copy of Alain Locke's anthology *The New Negro* (1925), from which he reads out Cullen's poem "Heritage." He is moved to tears when he comes to the lines in which Cullen speaks of finding no relief, day or night, from the heavy tread of footsteps "through my body's street." June understands that Mark has "identified himself with the outcasts of the earth. The negro had suffered and that bound Mark to him" (234). This sympathetic identification with oppressed African-Americans intensifies Mark's anti-racism, but also suggests that he will find in Harlem–as he has already found, in the book's scenes in the Harlem clubs–a return of sympathy from black people for his own anomalous relation to the dominant order.

Clearly, this episode posits a reading stratagem based on solidarity. It suggests, furthermore, that a black gay reader should be encouraged to make cross-references between his own racial and sexual status, identifying not only directly with the poet's disadvantaged race, but also making Mark's transverse association of America's racism with its homophobia. Had Blair Niles known (as she may have done), or been able to state, that Cullen was homosexual, she might have pointed out that he, doubly oppressed, was able to express himself openly only in reference to race, but that he may be assumed to have invested in this expression the frustration and anger generated at the other source, his sexuality. If he could construct a text in this manner, it follows that, working in reverse, the black gay reader should be able to extrapolate from the "racial" text the sexuality-based anger which he and the author share.

If such associative readings work, for both white and black gay readers, I see no reason why one should not apply them, also, to other famous statements of racial oppression by gay black authors. It should be possible, for instance, to read Claude McKay's defiantly angry "If We Must Die" as referable to homosexual oppression. Given the author's own sexuality, such a reading would do far less damage to the text, which is usually and sensibly read in reference to racial prejudice (or, more specifically, to race riots of 1919), than Winston Churchill did it when he used it to represent the situation of Britain forced into a corner by Nazi Germany.[4]

In a similar way, there is no reason why one should not apply

Countee Cullen's "From the Dark Tower" (47) to both racism and homophobia. While the imagery of light and dark is clearly intended to refer to white and black, it also works well as a representation of openness and enforced closetry. Taking the latter view of the poem, one can effortlessly read it as celebrating the hidden "twilight world" of homosexuality. Moreover, not only does Cullen deplore oppression and celebrate the concealed lives which resist and survive it, but he also, in the closing couplet, offers some hope for the future, however distant. We "hide," he says, and "wait." But our waiting is not without purpose: we bide our time and pass the time by tending our "agonizing seeds." Of course, this last image, for all its assertion of pain, promises future growth and an emergence into light and life.[5]

When writers' enumerations of the absurdities of race prejudice focused–as they often did–on the miscegenation taboo, their texts inevitably arrived at a theme which was of particular interest to those of them who were homo- or bisexual: forbidden love. McKay's poem "The Barrier" (80), for instance, could seem to be addressing any barrier to love in the first ten of its twelve lines. By repetition of the phrase "I must not," the poet reminds someone he loves that neither sight nor speech–still less touch, which is not mentioned–may be exchanged by them on any but the most formal basis. Only in the final two lines does he make it explicit that this embargo on love is caused by racial difference: the poet is "dark," the loved one "fair." Until this point, the reader has been free to perform a gay reading. Indeed, even after the poem has imposed its closure, conclusively focusing on the one social issue rather than the other, one is left with an impression of the ambiguity which has thus been disengaged. As a gay reader, one may at least derive from the poem an associative reading which results in a comparison of the effects, on love, of racism and homophobia.

McKay's poem "Courage" (110) has a similar theme, and both gains and loses by treating it with consistent ambiguity. Neither the racial nor the sexual reading is closed off, but the sexual prevails. Much of the imagery corresponds with that of other poetry by homosexual men in this period: a "lonely heart," warm but sad glances, a "guarded life," the forlorn search for a shared refuge, and so forth. Yet, for all its conventional distress, the poem does reach quite a positive and assertive conclusion in the image of a joined pair of "understanding hands." This determined clasp is what is referred to in the poem's title. Despite all forces to the contrary, the speaker and his beloved courageously link hands, thereby affirming their "ardent love and life." Whether this courage is enforced by racist or homophobic objections to the affair is not stated, and is therefore, although not immaterial, generously left to the focus of the individual reader.

Nathan Huggins has said, of Countee Cullen's "Harsh World That Lashest Me," "There is, here, no real evidence that the poet is black, yet one has to know that fact to have the romantic sentiment make any sense" (212). In relation to the generalised complaints about oppression, one could say the same about his homosexuality.[6] One should add the caution, however, that this kind of transference between race and sexuality depends on ambiguity in the text–or on vagueness, to put it more negatively. White gay readers, in particular, should not be tempted to believe that their homosexuality necessarily gives them much of an insight into the oppression experienced by black people. Race and sexuality are transferrable terms only in the most general sense. As soon as one approaches the specifics of either, one begins to see the dangers in the tendency to confuse the two. We need to be continuously aware of and awake to the dangers of appropriation. To read the work of writers like Hughes as "gay poetry" alone would be offensively reductive, yet little more so than to read it as "black poetry" alone. A new wave of readers is now prepared to perform creative re-readings on a literature which must be seen *fully*, as poetry *by gay men of color*, if it is to receive the value and respect it deserves. After all, a readerly practice which involves denial as one of its principal strategies can hardly be called "reading" at all.

Among the most accomplished of the ambiguous poems is Countee Cullen's elegant and unfussy "Tableau" (7), which celebrates the sight of a black boy and a white boy crossing the street, arm in arm, followed by disapproving glances. The poem offers a perfectly harmonized counterpoint of the two themes, sexuality and race, in a manner which, while saying nothing explicitly gay to the inattentive reader, nevertheless broaches the scandalous topic of homosexual miscegenation without subterfuge or disguise. To be so discreetly indiscreet is an excellent feat of anti-homophobic irony only rarely achieved in the pre-Stonewall conditions which provoked it. No amount of paraphrase can do it justice. The poem manages to negotiate its passage between safety and risk in a manner which seems almost as light as it is actually solid and secure.

Another text which manages this balancing trick is Hughes's "Joy" (*Selected* 57), a poem which presents itself as a rudimentary narrative, in the first person and past tense. The speaker goes looking for a certain vibrant, young woman, and finds her in scandalous circumstances and bad company–in the arms of the butcher's apprentice. Thus far–and here the story has already ended–the poem is a lilting, merrily hetero tale. But read it again; read its *title* again. The poem is called "Joy" because the young woman's name is Joy. It is also called "Joy" because it is not merely about a young woman, but about *joy.* On this second reading one sees the point: a male speaker celebrates the fact that he has found *joy* in the arms of the butcher's boy.

The heterosexual poem becomes a no less explicit homosexual poem by means of a sophisticated but uncomplicated reversal. The heterosexual poem depends upon its personification of joy as a young woman; the homosexual poem depends on the young woman's *un*personification as the abstract noun, joy. The woman is, as it were, the poem's cover. While she acts as decoy to inattentive homophobes, who are led up the garden path of their own complacency, the speaker is free to assert the joy of homosexual desire to those readers whose trained ears are receptive to the modulations of his camp tone.[7]

More clearly autobiographical lyrics, no matter how discreet, should supply fruitful material to the active gay reader, particularly when they concern the growth from childhood, through adolescence, into maturity. In the wistful poem "Home Thoughts" (21), McKay remembers the joys of his native Jamaica in terms of named schoolfriends: Davie, Cyril, and Georgie, one agilely shinning up mango trees, the second hauling bananas on his back, and the third stripping off his clothes for a swim. This celebration of the physical activities of boys is, of course, a straightforward instance of nostalgia: that of the adult for boyhood, and that of the exile for his boyhood home. However, in the poem's final couplet, McKay

briefly switches from reminiscence to a moment of associative eroticism, in which, between a gasped "Oh" and the terminal exclama-
tion mark, he indulges in the realist daydream of a new generation
of boys, all climbing trees, hauling weights, and taking off their
clothes, now, at the very moment of the poem. This closing line
conveys a great intensity of desire and despair. Home is a place the
poet has left (Jamaica and boyhood), which he might possibly re-
visit (Jamaica), but to which he can never return (boyhood).

McKay creates a similar mood in "Adolescence" (27), a recol-
lection of a remarkably untroubled period, through which he claims
to have drifted as if in a state of suspension, an idyllic interim
between childhood and adulthood, rather than the difficult metamorphosis which so many other writers describe adolescence as
being. The poem situates the youth, prone and semi-naked, under a
sky which deepens continually into warm, moonlit, and starry
nights. These are not nights of writhing, frustrated sleeplessness,
endured on sheets reeking of semen and sweat; on the contrary, they
bring peace and peace brings sleep, undisturbed by dreams.

The sense of balance and order which McKay thus imparts to the
experience of puberty, is strongly contrasted, in the third and last
stanza, with his mood at the time of writing. Here, where he speaks
of having to endure nights of feverish restlessness which neither
drink nor drugs can calm, he appears to have exchanged an adolescence of sagacious equilibrium for a distinctly lonely and embit-
tered adulthood. The principal effect of the difference is located on
his palate: whereas his youth was "sweet," his present condition
fills his mouth with "acrid brine." Whereas sleep used to be as
delicious as "early love," the lack of it is now–and "forever"–a
source of agitation and enforced nostalgia. The solipsistic joy of
youth has turned into a kind of lonely resentment–even, once
McKay has emigrated to the great northern city, in the midst of
crowds.

The theme of loneliness recurs in the poem "On Broadway"
(67), where McKay describes feeling excluded from the vibrantly
"gay" (in both senses?) street life of Broadway by the youth and
carelessness of the crowd. Indeed, the adjective "careless" seems
to be the crux of the matter: for McKay is in an inhibited mood.
What he sees on the sidewalk is a couple, represented by the whole

of the youthful crowd: personifications of Desire and Passion, the former "naked," both "brazen." There is at least a hint, here, of the discomfort of closetry. The poet is lonely because he cannot make an open declaration of himself. Carefulness has been imposed on his emotions to an extent that serves to stifle them. All that he can do, the only response available to him, is to "gaze" at the sheer glamour of Broadway, as if it were the creation of his own deprived but fertile imagination, a "dream." No doubt, the social geography of Manhattan should also be taken into account when one reads this poem. The theme of race is inevitably suggested by the fact that Broadway is not Harlem. It may be that the young people in this crowd are not only "brazen" in their heterosexuality, but also brazenly, carelessly white. The poem conveys a sense of multiple exclusions, of exile.

This century's literature by homosexual men often raises the theme of exile, even if only of the internal sort. At its most intense, this association of outlawed sexuality with exile leads to a self-pitying view of homosexuality as *meaning* the enforced exclusion from love itself. Love, at best, is seen as being beset by difficulty. Langston Hughes's post-coital poem "Desire" (*Selected* 90) speaks of the "double death" of consummation, involving a dying away of breath and the evaporation of the partner's disconcertingly unfamiliar scent. It is not clear whether this refers to the estrangement of an established couple or a one-night-stand between literal strangers. In "Café: 3 A.M." (*Selected* 243) he mentions the "sadistic eyes" of vice squad members whose job it is to entrap and harass "fairies." The former of these poems utilises a poetic cliché, common since before the time of Shakespeare. The latter is much more to the point: for all its brevity, it exposes with a sudden crystal clarity the reality of how lesbians and gay men have to love in the face of adversity. Countee Cullen, in one poem's title and substance, calls on the reader to "Pity the Deep in Love" (54). Possible reasons for this may be found in other poems which depict lovers who must bury their love in order to allow it to grow–see "The Love Tree" (59)–or deny it altogether–see "Magnets" (143). Similarly, in the "Song in Spite of Myself" (note the reference to Whitman), Cullen personifies love as a male, but claims that it inevitably falters, to end in "aching" (98). You can love Love, but, as like as not, he will repay you with shame and heartbreak.

David Levering Lewis has said "Cullen's homosexuality was to be a source of shame he never fully succeeded in turning into a creative strength" (77).[8] It may be that, in the last analysis, we shall have to say much the same of McKay. Both poets chose the line of least resistance: discretion; and while their sexuality did, as we have seen, find expression in their work, it does not seem to have functioned therein as a major shaping or modulating force. Both wrote poetry whose formal constraint does, to be sure, give an impression of voices stifled and held back—even at the same time as it expresses itself with perceptible passion and daring on racial matters. Only Langston Hughes managed a sassy and incisive voice, with many tonal levels, which he appears to have developed, not by reading Shakespeare and Keats, but by allowing himself to relax into the very different (and thoroughly American) influences of Walt Whitman and the Blues. The result is often recognizable to the trained ear as intentionally camp.[9]

However, it feels appropriate to conclude this essay with a brief reference to the prose poems of the gay maverick Richard Bruce Nugent. Nugent provided an exotic and evocative story, "Sahdji," for Alain Locke's anthology *The New Negro* (113-114), in which one man who loves another, unbidden, kills for him, but thereby effectively kills him. Yet it was the story "Smoke, Lillies, and Jade" which won notoriety for Nugent when it was published by Wallace Thurman in the first and only issue of the journal *Fire!!* Langston Hughes later called it, rather coyly, "a green and purple story . . . in the Oscar Wilde tradition" (*Big Sea* 237). What such texts and the reactions to them demonstrated then, and remind us now, is that the voices of out gay men can often be heard over even the most strident demands that they be silenced.[10]

Nugent was the exception. When reading the writers of the Negro Renaissance we should not expect, nor be disappointed by the lack of, the kind of openness we now reasonably demand of gay writers. Our re-readings should never be impatient. If, on the other hand, one gives the likes of Cullen, McKay, and Hughes the attention and respect which are their due, one sees that contemporary gay African-American voices—as have been gathered in anthologies like Assoto Saint's *The Road Before Us*–are not, simply, bursting fully formed out of silence. They are following a tradition secured in Harlem in the third decade of this century. The Harlem writers may have had to remain closeted, but they were no less gay for that.

## NOTES

1. This should not distract us from the fact that the main impetus behind the current recovery of the Harlem Renaissance as a gay cultural phenomenon is coming from gay African-American critics. The record of white gay critics has not always been impressive. To give myself as an example, my book *Articulate Flesh* names only one black poet, Langston Hughes, in a primary bibliography of over a hundred poets. The text itself does not refer to Hughes once. For a trenchant report on many issues raised by white critical responses to black cultural products, see Michael Awkward's essay "Negotiations of Power."

2. See Essex Hemphill's interview with Isaac Julien (Hemphill 174-180) and Hemphill's short essay "Undressing Icons" (181-183). In the latter, Hemphill refers to the Langston Hughes Estate as Hughes's "sacred closet" (181) and reaches the following angry conclusion about the Estate's involvement in the affair: "Perhaps black assimilation into Western culture is more complete than we realize. It was common at one time to openly silence and intimidate outspoken black people. Now black people practice these tactics against each other–just like white men" (183). See also Bad Object-Choices (17-19).

3. Langston Hughes shows no sign of linking this trade, ironically or otherwise, with the commodification of flesh which first brought African slaves on ships to the Americas.

4. When McKay introduced his own reading of the poem on Arna Bontemps' disc "Anthology of Negro Poets" (Folkways Record, FP91) he spoke of it as a universal poem, intended for all people who are "abused, outraged and murdered, whether they are minorities or nations, black or brown or yellow or white, Catholic or Protestant or Pagan, fighting against terror" (Huggins 72).

5. Cullen uses the seed image again in "Ultimatum" (69), where he states his determination to plant his chosen seed–an activity which inevitable has a sexual resonance–regardless of whether it will subsequently grow upwards ("to heaven") or downwards ("to hell"). I am inclined to read this as a moment in which the poet decisively washes his hands of the "moral" issues which other people have imposed on his life. In any case, as one sees in the perversely paradoxical "More Than a Fool's Song" (67), Cullen was happy to hypothesize that the people who are commonly thought virtuous may actually be vicious, and vice versa.

6. This argument can also be applied to non-specific love lyrics. Wayne Cooper mentions poems by McKay which "celebrated brief affairs with partners whose sex is never explicitly stated. They could well have been either men or women" (75). Cooper lists the following poems, all in *Home to Harlem*, as exam-

ples: "Romance," "The Snow Fairy," "Tormented," and "One Year After" (388, n. 39).

7. Eric Garber's assertion that "Even Langston Hughes touched upon the topic" of black lesbian and gay experience in the poem "Café: 3 A.M." takes an unnecessarily narrow view of what constitutes a reference to the topic (33). While it may be true that, as Allen D. Prowle has said, "Hughes rarely allowed himself to indulge in personal poetry" (84), I would argue that the sensuality and enthusiasm which Hughes conveys in his work are easily read as representations of the atmosphere of subcultural life in Harlem as he experienced it.

8. There are even more negative ways of putting this. For instance: "Nor can there be any doubt that his feeling of inferiority is also derived . . . from his partial or total inability to lead a normal sex life" (Wagner 295).

9. I do not mean to endorse what Amitai Avi-Ram has rightly referred to as "the relatively simplistic association of 'conventional' poetic forms (such as the sonnet) with political conservatism and of 'free verse' with liberation"(33). But there is, arguably, a real problem of inappropriate archaisms in Cullen and McKay's formal verse, especially when they force themselves into awkward inversions, which makes Hughes, by contrast, seem far more in touch with the *Zeitgeist* of modernist Harlem.

10. Nugent himself has said, of the *Fire!!* story, "I didn't know *it was gay* when I wrote it" (Smith 214). But his readers could then, and can now, immediately perceive a clearly gay voice which, in its unguarded flamboyance and flair, even in its breathily queeny ellipses, briefly defied the dominant culture's threats to voice the desires of the emergent gay sub-subculture.


## WORKS CITED

Avi-Ram, Amitai F. "The Unreadable Black Body: 'Conventional' Poetic Form in the Harlem Renaissance." *Genders* 7 (Spring 1990): 32-46.

Awkward, Michael. "Negotiations of Power: White Critics, Black Texts, and the Self-Referential Impulse." *American Literary History* 2.4 (Winter 1990): 581-606.

Bad Object-Choices, eds. *How Do I Look? Queer Film and Video.* Seattle: Bay Press, 1991.

Cooper, Wayne F. *Claude McKay: Rebel Sojourner in the Harlem Renaissance, A Biography.* Baton Rouge and London: Louisiana State University Press, 1987.

Cullen, Countee. *On These I Stand: An Anthology of the Best Poems.* New York: Harper and Row, 1947.

Garber, Eric. "A Spectacle in Color: The Lesbian and Gay Subculture of Jazz Age Harlem." *Hidden From History: Reclaiming the Gay and Lesbian Past.* Ed. Martin Bauml Duberman, Martha Vicinus, and George Chauncey, Jr. Harmondsworth, Middlesex: Penguin, 1991. 318-333.

Garrett, Daniel. "Other Countries: The Importance of Difference." *Other Countries: Black Gay Voices* 1 (Spring 1988): 17-28.

Hemphill, Essex, ed. *Brother to Brother: New Writings by Black Gay Men.* Boston: Alyson, 1991.

Huggins, Nathan Irvin. *Harlem Renaissance.* New York: Oxford University Press, 1971.

Hughes, Langston. *The Big Sea.* London: Pluto, 1986.

————. *Selected Poems.* London: Pluto, 1986.

Lewis, David Levering. *When Harlem Was in Vogue.* New York and Oxford: Oxford University Press, 1989.

Locke, Alain, ed. *The New Negro.* New York: Boni, 1925.

McKay, Claude. *Selected Poems of Claude McKay.* New York: Harcourt, Brace and World, 1953.

Nelson, Emmanuel. "Critical Deviance: Homophobia and the Reception of James Baldwin's Fiction." *Journal of American Culture* 14.3 (Fall 1991): 91-96.

Niles, Blair. *Strange Brother.* London: T. Werner Laurie, 1932.

Prowle, Allen D. "Langston Hughes." *The Black American Writer, Volume II: Poetry and Drama.* Ed. Chris Bigsby. DeLand, FL: Everett/Edwards, 1969. 77-87.

Saint, Assoto, ed. *The Road Before Us: 100 Gay Black Poets.* New York: Galiens Press, 1991.

Smith, Charles Michael. "Bruce Nugent: Bohemian of the Harlem Renaissance." *In the Life: A Black Gay Anthology.* Ed. Joseph Beam. Boston: Alyson, 1986. 209-220.

Thurman, Wallace, ed. *Fire!!* 1.1. New York: The Fire!! Press, 1926.

Wagner, Jean. *Black Poets of the United States From Paul Laurence Dunbar to Langston Hughes.* Urbana: University of Illinois Press, 1973.

Woods, Gregory. *Articulate Flesh: Male Homo-eroticism and Modern Poetry.* New Haven and London: Yale University Press, 1987.

# Countee Cullen's Uranian "Soul Windows"

Alden Reimonenq, PhD

*St. Mary's College of California*

**SUMMARY.** Although Countee Cullen was once hailed "poet laureate" of the Harlem renaissance, today his reputation has waned due, in part, to the absence of biographical study which would elucidate the relationship of his life and literary output. One consequential component of Cullen's life–his homosexuality–played an integral part in the creation and development of his poetry. To miss this significant aspect of Cullen's artistic life is to invite misinterpretation. Unfortunately, most African American scholars of the Harlem Renaissance have dismissed, ignored, or denied Cullen's homosexuality. Yet, this weighty element of his life was at the core of his literary imagination. This bio-critical study examines the import of Cullen's homosexuality on his poetry in an attempt to position the poet as the inaugurator of Black gay poetry in the United States.

At a time when there is a welcomed explosion of interest in gay literary studies, David Bergman issues a sobering caution: "So spotty is the critical work even today, so incomplete the published record, so unexplored are the archives, that we are very far from ready to write a history of gay American literature" (11). Investiga-

Correspondence may be addressed to the author at: English Department, Dante 312, St. Mary's College of California, Moraga, CA 94575.

[Haworth co-indexing entry note]: "Countee Cullen's Uranian 'Soul Windows'." Reimonenq, Alden. Co-published simultaneously in the *Journal of Homosexuality* (The Haworth Press, Inc.) Vol. 26, No. 2/3, 1993, pp. 143-165; and *Critical Essays: Gay and Lesbian Writers of Color* (ed: Emmanuel S. Nelson) The Haworth Press, Inc., 1993, pp. 143-165. Multiple copies of this article/chapter may be purchased from The Haworth Document Delivery Center [1-800-3-HA-WORTH; 9:00 a.m. - 5:00 p.m. (EST)].

tions of the lives, cultures, and subcultures of American writers serve as ballast in the development of such a sound history. Yet, archival research is lacking generally and is woefully scant in African American studies where a minimum of scholarship is the result of plumbing repositories of personal papers. Thus, it is not surprising that recently, in the span of less than a year, two publications on Countee Cullen present opposing claims on the poet's sexuality.

Amitai Avi-Ram's analysis, which depends absolutely on "[t]he fact of Cullen's homosexuality" (45), is pitted against Gerald Early's discussion which marginalizes the poet's sexuality in a footnote asserting that "no evidence" exists to prove that Cullen had "homosexual relations with any other figures of the Renaissance" (19). Basing his argument on imagined evidentiary problems, Early revokes Cullen's homosexuality by proclamation. Ironically, both critics cite the same scholars to support their arguments: Avi-Ram cites Jean Wagner, David Lewis, and Arnold Rampersad as contributors to the growing "acceptance" of Cullen's homosexuality; Early lists these scholars as those who "have read letters and poems that seem suggestive in this regard but have offered nothing conclusive" (19).

Even a cursory excursion through the bank of correspondence which survives Cullen eliminates doubt about his sexuality. For instance, in an early letter to Alain Locke, Cullen wrote:

> I secured Carpenter's "Ioläus" from the library. I read it through at one sitting, and steeped myself in its charming and comprehending atmosphere. It opened up for me *soul windows* which had been closed; it threw a noble and evident light on what I had begun to believe, because of what the world believes, ignoble and unnatural. I loved myself in it. (my emphasis)[1]

If Edward Carpenter's *Ioläus: An Anthology of Friendship* (1902) opened "soul windows" for Cullen when he was only nineteen and before he had published his first book of poetry, one wonders why scholars still choose to treat Cullen's homosexuality as an insignificant or tenebrous facet of his life. Cullen's jubilation over finding *his* homosexual self represented in *Ioläus* is testimony to his acceptance of his gay identity.

Antihomosexual bias has precipitated the critical neglect and concomitant relegation to the literary minor leagues of many African American gay writers. Emmanuel S. Nelson, in a denunciatory review of the critical reception of James Baldwin's novels, proves that the literary establishment is discriminatory. Nelson targets the "African-American critical tradition" which "offers many classic examples of heterosexist bias." Providing a modest list of Renaissance gays, Nelson assaults the lethargy of Black scholars, pointing to their "remarkable reticence about the sexualities of these pioneering artists and a determined unwillingness to explore the impact of their gayness on their literary constructions and on the forms and directions of the Renaissance" (92). Homosexuality, in the creative lives of Renaissance artists, must be underscored if we are to understand fully this stage in the development of African American literature.

Dismissing Cullen's homosexuality has thwarted comprehensive evaluations of his poetry. Tracing where and how his gay life intersected and shaped his creativity is an integral part of historicizing Cullen's art. Such biographical mapping is a foundational step upon which any demonstration of Cullen's intrinsic distinction as a poet must rest. This biographical essay aims to represent, through a selective review of extant correspondence, the unseen, homosexual side of Countee Cullen in order to invite dialogue on the poet as the inaugurator of African American gay poetry.

## *I*

Efforts at historicizing Harlem Renaissance literature provide valuable biographical, political, and sociological studies; however, scholars have generated few inquiries on the influence of same-sex relationships and artistic creativity. Jean Wagner published the first criticism on Cullen's homosexuality; his discussion, however, reneges on its promise to link the poet's gayness and his works. Although they include Wagner's book (in French) in their bibliographies, neither Blanche Ferguson (206) nor Margaret Perry (109) even mentions Cullen's homosexuality. David Lewis's celebrated study treats Cullen and Locke's homosexuality rather insensitively. In a groundless assertion, Lewis labels Cullen's homosexuality as "a source of shame he never fully succeeded in turning into a creative strength" (77). Similarly, Alan Shucard glosses over Cullen's homosexuality in one paragraph riddled with quotations from Lewis's mistreatment of the subject (70-71). Conversely, Arnold Rampersad and Gloria T. Hull, through meticulous archival research, offer objective portraits of Renaissance gays. Especially noteworthy is Rampersad's handling of Cullen as Locke's pander in a pursuit of Langston Hughes (66-69). Given Rampersad's subject, however, he only considers Cullen's gayness as it intersects with Hughes's questionable sexuality. Not until Avi-Ram has any scholar advanced Wagner's argument to yoke biography and creativity. Scholarship on Cullen's homosexuality and its impact on his art remains checkered and skimpy.

There is a paralysis on the part of scholars who cannot discuss a text except in terms of how it either conforms to or departs from established literary norms. Houston Baker, Jr., comes to a similar conclusion in his revisionist essay that suggests the necessity of perceiving Cullen as a *race* poet despite his claims against such pillorying. Baker revises his critical approach and maintains that his "interpretation is a contextualization" (99)–that is, understanding the "demands of the 1920s" and what he terms "cultural spirit work" has allowed him to hear the "inaudible" "sounds of the lowground that comprises a black cultural geography" (97). Baker's argument forcefully silences those critics who, using inadequate critical yardsticks, have devalued Cullen as a racial poet. Understandably, Baker criticizes Shucard's thin study citing the limitations of the New Criticism. Baker's approach widens the critical vision, and

> Cullen, thus, becomes a veritable sign of struggle, a poet *malgré lui*, encoding inaudible reaches of the low and common valley of *blackness*. His ironic confessionals, rewritings of the old legacies of color, and invocations of Afro-American religious testimonial forms bespeak his downward journey toward a place that *hurts*, but also heals. (Baker's emphasis, 100)

Baker is, of course, making the case for rereading Cullen in view of the fullest context of the poet's racial struggle. But Cullen used poetry also to record and encode the deeper and therefore more inaudible–troubled and celebrated–sounds of his homosexuality. Cullen's poetry is to a great degree constituted with cultural affirmations and denunciations, especially as regards class, race, *and* sex. Scholars are only beginning to develop a critical taxonomy for homosexual texts; thus, they have been unable to hear Cullen's barely audible gay voice.

Eric Garber reconstructs Harlem gay life as Cullen knew it by focusing on how African American intellectuals tolerated, indulged in, and even celebrated homosexuality. Garber's cinematic look at gay life and culture pauses here and there to capture the details of the night club scene, the art work, and the personalities of the 1920s and 1930s (318-319). While it cannot be gainsaid that Cullen closeted his homosexuality, it is also undeniable that he was a known member of the underground social network of gays and lesbians.

Cullen's fear of discrimination surely triggered his secretiveness; fortunately, through the prescience of some notable individuals, we have an intriguing personal record–often marked with a codification difficult to crack–of Cullen's homosexual associates, male lovers, and their influence. Cullen dedicated or wrote poems for all of the men who were his lovers, with the exception of his gay French associates or lovers–presumably those men listed by Michel Fabre as "lesser-known friends and lovers" (89-90). Cullen also dedicated poems to his closest homosexual friends: Alain Locke, Harold Jackman, Carl Van Vechten, and Leland Pettit. Thus, Cullen's personal history is not an anomaly; he blended into a secret society in which gay life was commonly reified.

## II

When the center of this gay coterie is established, it will, no doubt, prove to be Alain Locke. Although Locke held a professorship at Howard, he had many contacts in Harlem and exercised immeasurable influence on young *male* artists, actively encouraging and supporting them spiritually and, in some cases, financially. This fulgent portrait of Locke's generosity contrasts boldly with his misogyny, as Hull describes accurately (7-11). Locke's relationship with Cullen, although not sexual, was extremely close as their numerous letters affirm. From Cullen's first letter of introduction to the last which solicited Locke's advice on the failing *St. Louis Woman*, we have the chronology of a friendship between two gay men, cemented in love, loyalty, trust, and secrecy.

In 1922, Cullen's first letter to Locke was an inquiry about a Rhodes scholarship.[2] By the next letter, Locke and Cullen had met and discussed their homosexuality; Hughes was already an object of their mutual curiosity; and, Cullen coaxed Locke, "Write to him, and arrange to meet him. You will like him; I love him; his is such a charming childishness. . . ."[3] Early on, homosexuality had brought Cullen and Locke together.

Cullen appreciated Locke's counsel and expressed gratitude for "proffers of advice." He also wrote candidly about "questions of moral and social conduct."[4] Locke responded: "I think I may assure you of but one standard of judgment,–and that is the law of a man's own temperament and personality. But one cannot often discover this, especially if there are convention-complexes except through confessional self-analysis."[5] If Cullen heeded any advice, it was surely derived from this statement; for, his is an androcentric poetry replete with overt confessional self-analysis–a feature most evident in *Copper Sun* (1927) and *The Medea and Some Poems* (1935).

Locke's association with Cullen clearly went beyond professional advising. They had many mutual acquaintances, and their relationship was strong enough to address candidly the success and failure of finding lovers. More importantly, they introduced each other to potential lovers. In the letter in which Cullen thanked Locke for Carpenter's *Ioläus*, he also mentioned a prospective lover, Ralph Loeb. Cullen was disappointed and rationalized repeated rebuffs:

> I believe the cause may be defined as parental, for I feel certain that the attraction was as keenly felt by Loeb as by me. . . . I suppose some of us erotic lads, vide myself, were placed here just to eat our hearts out with longing for unattainable things, especially for that friendship beyond understanding.

After imploring Locke to intercede, Cullen closed with the postscript, "Sentiments expressed here would be misconstrued by others, so this letter, once read, is best destroyed."[6] Cullen's quest "for unattainable things" and "that friendship beyond understanding" found its way into his poetry as a common theme and integral aspect of his homosexual aesthetic. "For a Poet" demonstrates this personal philosophy of hiding unachievable homosexual dreams (*Color* 45).

The Loeb alliance was dalliance; in less than a month, Cullen wrote: "Ralph came to see me yesterday, and sang for me. We are getting along famously."[7] Shortly thereafter, Cullen felt "compelled to relinquish all hope in that direction. . ." and reasoned: "I am afraid to attempt to bend the twig the way I would have it go, lest my way be the wrong way for it. . . . So I am going to allow it to grow at will. But there is *D*."[8] Loeb was easily replaced, or as Cullen wrote: "Unless Fate reopens it, the chapter of my life in which R. figured is irrevocably closed."[9] Cullen recovered quickly and moved on to a white lover, Donald Duff.

Cullen's relationship with Duff was more serious as revealed in the steady mention of him to Locke. Even when his attention was sidetracked by Friedrich, a German student, Cullen did not abandon Duff. Of Friedrich, he wrote, "Nothing definite has been spoken of yet, but how I would love to make such a trip!"[10] And later when the affair was foiled, Cullen resigned himself that "everything from now on is going to be fatalistic" and ". . . I am afraid to form any new friendships."[11] Two months later, Cullen expressed "disappointment in not being chosen for the German trip." In the same letter, he mentioned Yolande DuBois who had drawn him "near the solution of [his] problem." Yet Cullen claimed: "But I shall proceed warily." Together with entertaining thoughts of Friedrich, Yolande DuBois, and his "problem," Cullen wrote in a postscript, "I have lost track of Donald, although I have written several letters to him."[12]

At age twenty, Cullen was developing a reputation as a fine poet, but these letters show that he was quite troubled with his sexuality. The failures at finding suitable male partners distressed Cullen, and his turning to Yolande DuBois can be seen as a chance at mainstream acceptance. His fear, depression, and loneliness can be seen in:

You will recall that in my last letter I spoke of a presentiment of happiness with a certain young lady. All that has come to nought [sic]–as yet. And then there are complications–her age and experience above my own, and then *that fear which is always at my heels.* Add to this that Langston has written me but once, that Donald has apparently cut me, and you will see what a happy time I am having. (my emphasis)[13]

Early refers to Duff as "a pacifist and a literary-fringe type who, apparently, was friendly with a number of artists" (86). Clearly, for Cullen, Duff meant more. That Cullen dedicated the homosexual poem "Tableau" to Duff is a measure of how much he invested emotionally. The poem announces Cullen's awareness of the impending discrimination for those who dared to secede from the ranks of "normalcy." Under the poetic veil of speaking out against racism, Cullen achieves a larger purpose by also criticizing antihomosexual bigotry. In the last amazing stanza, the speaker imagines the Black and white lovers–who have been described walking "Locked arm in arm"–as,

> Oblivious to look and word
>> They pass, and see no wonder
> That lightning brilliant as a sword
>> Should blaze the path of thunder.

*(Color* 14)

"Lightning" here suggests passion; more importantly, the lovers, as lightning, symbolize the illumination or knowledge that will "blaze" a "path" to understanding. As unconventional lovers, they are "oblivious" to the stares of the "dark folk" and the jibes of the "fair folk"; in both cases, they must, as the storm imagery suggests, use knowledge ("lightning") as power against such ignorance. In this way, Cullen implies that that which is seen and understood will "blaze the path of thunder"; that is, illumination will ultimately give way to voicing that understanding–which the poem does self-referentially. The path-blazing is a road to freedom from the ridicule perpetrated by racists and heterosexists. Further, the poem is reminiscent of Walt Whitman's "In Paths Untrodden" in which the speaker is alone contemplating "manly attachment" and "athletic love" in order to "celebrate the need of comrades" (146). Cullen dramatizes Whitman's imaginings in "Tableau," and even the title–translated as "scene"–suggests that the lovers are putting on a public show for the unenlightened. Here we have an early example of the connectedness of Cullen's homosexuality and his literary imagination. It matters little whether Duff or the poetic idea came to Cullen first. What is important is the evidence of the inextricable interweaving of the two.

Young Cullen, troubled by his gayness, had to struggle with mostly Locke's nurturing. Given the fundamentalists' exhortations against sex, in general, and homosexuality, in particular, Cullen could not turn to his father (an African Methodist Episcopal minister). Locke's wisdom on this score, his advising Cullen toward "confessional self-analysis," and his generosity in securing lovers, all contributed to Cullen's perseverance. "The Wise," dedicated to Locke, demonstrates Cullen's penchant for equating wisdom with the accumulation of knowledge not from experience in this world, but from understanding derived from the supernatural. Thus, dead men, who experience other worlds, know things we cannot. Just as dead men, under the cover of earth, know how deep roots grow, so also gays, behind closet doors and in the world as well, have a unique perspicacity. The poem is a fitting tribute to Locke, the philosopher, who was Cullen's only confidant until he met Harold Jackman, his lifelong soulmate.

Jackman and Cullen became friends in November 1923 while Cullen attended New York University. Imparting to Locke that "differences were patched up" with Duff, Cullen also announced, "My greatest fraternal solace just now is a friend Harold Jackman by name. Although I do not believe that he and I have any *spiritual affinity*, yet he has endeared himself mightily to me, and I am anxious for you to meet him" (my emphasis).[14] Cullen's enthusiasm aside, it is apparent that he and Jackman had not yet confessed their gayness as evidenced in his voicing uncertainty over "any spiritual affinity" between them. Cullen often used the word "spirit" and its derivatives as a codification for homosexuality. Cullen wrote to Locke, "I feel toward him as David toward Jonathan."[15] These sentiments are echoed years later, when Arna Bontemps, in a memoir, calls Cullen and Jackman "the David and Jonathan of the Harlem twenties" (12). Cullen and Jackman surely discussed their gayness after their friendship was galvanized; however, there is still no written evidence that the relationship was ever sexual.

In Jackman, Cullen found a Harlemite near his age and the start of a community in which he could find some freedom without fear of repudiation or public exposure. After meeting Jackman, Cullen's letters are more honest even in their being more discreet; that is, letters to Locke and Jackman–while still codified–are more direct and self-assured. The camaraderie among the members of this emerging gay coterie is best described, through oxymoron, as marked by a closeted openness.

Not all of Cullen's lovers inspired poetry; some had an adverse sway, as he wrote Locke about "Knapp" who was a member of the "order" whose eyes were blue. Because Knapp had "exalted ideas of constancy," Cullen decided to content himself with only "spiritual sympathy."[16] Cullen's resolution suggests that, at this time, although both men were gay, Knapp's wish for constancy was problematic. Moreover, the association was another letdown for Cullen; the sheer work of sustaining the affair interfered with his writing. In completing the poem "Spirit-Birth" and sending it to Locke for suggestions, Cullen explained that he would not have completed the poem "had not *K* and I severed all relations." Cullen complained of "depression" and rationalized it as "good for my verse." He vowed: "I shall never again love any one with all my heart and soul. If I must be a libertine in order to preserve my health, my sanity, and my peace of mind, I shall do so; I shall make no further sacrifices."[17]

Predictably this was a promise Cullen could not keep; for, just a few months later, he wrote to Locke: "Roy, will you tell me, in strict confidence just how sincere Llewellyn Ransom is? I am not aughing [sic] for deep sea secrets–merely enough to teach me how to act. . . . Just how much have I to gain or lose through his observation?"[18] Locke took some time to intervene; in exasperation, Cullen wrote, "my need deepens" in a letter describing a car trip to Boston with Jackman and Eric Walrond. Cullen called the trip "a revelation" regarding Walrond whom he found "most surprisingly sympathetic and aggressive" but offered "no lasting solution. . . ."[19] Cullen abhorred flagrant displays of sexual prowess. He was very private; a point which is substantiated in a letter to Locke about their progress with Ransom. Cullen rejoiced over "[t]he prospect of a mutually sincere adjustment" and urged Locke to press on:

> How long will it be before you see L.R. again? If it will be over a week, you might enclose a sealed note to him in your next letter to me, with instructions for him to read and destroy in my presence. Please pardon my urgency, but I *must* have an adjustment as soon as possible, or I shall be driven to recourse with *E. W.* and *that* I fear. (Cullen's emphasis)[20]

Clearly, an "adjustment" (a code word for gay sex) could be had for too exacting a price from Walrond or others, but Cullen was in search of a more "mutually sincere" relationship. After meeting him on several occasions, Cullen questioned whether Ransom was expressing "mere kindness or what [he] most desired it to be." Cullen related how dependent he was on Locke to push the relationship toward "permanent understanding"; for, nothing would suit him better, "not even H.J."[21] The comparison to Jackman underscores just how much Cullen desired in his match with Ransom. Locke was eventually successful, and Cullen's excitement and happiness resounded: "L.R. was here last night, and we quite conclusively understand one another. . . . I shall write now, I am sure. . . . There is so invigorating a relief in being happy!"[22] Cullen's homosexual emotional state clearly affected his creative temperament and output.

It is critical to note that Cullen changed the title of "Spirit-Birth" to "The Shroud of Color" when it was published without a dedication in the *American Mercury* (November, 1924). He then made revisions to the poem and published it again in *Color* (1925) with the dedication "For Llewellyn Ransom." Again, Early gets it wrong by guessing that Ransom was "simply a neighbor" or that his name was "possibly a pseudonym" (97). Knowing that Ransom was Cullen's lover allows us to hear the heretofore inaudible sounds (to borrow Baker's term) of the anguish and torment over self-acceptance in "The Shroud of Color." This idea is corroborated in view of the title change and Cullen's addition of the following seven lines in the third stanza:

> There is no other way to keep secure
> My wild chimeras; grave-locked against the lure

Of Truth, the small hard teeth of worms, yet less
Envenomed than the mouth of Truth, will bless
Them into dust and happy nothingness.
Lord, Thou art God; and I, Lord, what am I
But dust? With dust my place, "Lord, let me die."

Just before these lines, the speaker begs God for one thing only: "To dream still pure all that I loved, and die" (*Color* 28). The seven additional lines declare a dream as the only province where the speaker can exist without pain. There "wild chimeras" can be kept secure against the ravages of Truth. Truth is a culprit here because it (racial and sexual self-acceptance) imposes cruel realities and value judgments on "wild chimeras." Cullen's word choice here is apt: the mythological chimera (a grotesque monster comprised of various animal bodies or a beast with male and female parts) symbolizes the wild or unconventional imaginings of a marginalized other and, as such, can exist only in the fabric of a dream. This notion is echoed in "For A Poet" in which homosexual feelings must also be hidden. The inaudible sounds have to do with the homosexual connotation Cullen attached to "spirit"; thus, the battle with Truth takes on sexual as well as racial significance. By the end of the poem, we witness the birth and acceptance of not only race but also the soul as an expression of the homosexual self. As in "Tableau," the argument against racism and heterosexism coexist neatly.

Cullen found love with Ransom, and even Loeb's reappearance in 1925 posed no threat; he assured Locke that he would steel himself against further hurt:

I am beginning even now to school myself to a casual interest—but do you recall the closing lines of my poem "The Spark?"—

I knew a man
Thought a spark was dead,
That flamed and ran
A brighter red,
And burned the roof
Above his head.

Being so wise, whom shall I blame if I am burned?[23]

Although this poem (*Copper Sun* 31-32) can be given a hetero-sexual reading, this letter is Cullen's admission that his poems are given to homosexual interpretations and show his penchant for submerging gay themes. Later, writing to Locke about his content-ment with Ransom, Cullen said, "L. is a godsend. And I don't forget your part in directing the gift my way."[24]

Although Cullen and Locke remained close friends, there is a noticeable independence in Cullen after he received a master's de-gree from Harvard in 1926. This independence was surely a mark of maturation, and as Cullen grew less dependent on Locke, he strengthened and deepened his enduring friendship with Jackman.

### III

During the period of gay relationships with Loeb, Duff, Knapp, and Ransom, Cullen corresponded simultaneously with Yolande DuBois. In fact, Cullen gave his prospective bride a ring, took it back, was engaged, broke it off, and finally, with Jackman as best man, married Yolande DuBois on 9 April 1928. Lewis details the events of the marriage, hints at Cullen's inability to perform a husband's sexual duties, and points to W. E. B. DuBois's domi-nance over and insensitivity toward his daughter (201-203). Jack-man certainly knew that Cullen was staging a drama with a predict-ably bad ending. By Thanksgiving, the union had definitely soured, and Jackman advised Cullen "to get a divorce over there" so as "to come back to America a free man." Jackman voiced displeasure over Yolande DuBois's pettiness, "You're too nice for her, but I think one of these days you'll give way to your feelings–you'll break loose; it will eventually reach that stage."[25] Jackman's sex-ism notwithstanding, the marriage had not lasted a year, and he supported Cullen unconditionally through this troubling time.

From Yolande DuBois's perspective, Cullen's homosexuality was *the* reason for their divorce. In a startlingly frank letter to her father, she mentioned that she and Cullen tried in vain to reconcile because he told her "something about himself that just finished things." After this discussion, Yolande DuBois realized she would have to leave Cullen and claimed that, although she respected him enormously, she had never loved him. Having lost respect and "having an added feeling of horror at the abnormality of it" led her to the determination:

> I knew something was wrong–physically, but being very igno-rant & inexperienced I couldn't be sure what. When he con-fessed that he'd always known that he was abnormal sexual-ly–as far as *other men were concerned* then many things became clear. (DuBois's emphasis)

Yolande DuBois understandably felt deceived; yet, her "horror and disgust" did not stand in the way of her humanity. She prom-ised Cullen she would not use his homosexuality as grounds for their divorce and urged her father to "tear this [letter] up." Clearly, she meant to protect Cullen, and the promise was kept.[26] With the dissolution of the marriage Cullen developed stronger gay relation-ships, particularly with Jackman.

Cullen depended on Jackman not only for advice but also for all the Harlem "dirt." In particular, Jackman's letters provide eyewit-ness chronicles of the very spirit of the age and inner workings of Harlem society. Jackman recounts the gay lives of Wallace Thur-man, Richard Bruce Nugent, Edward Perry, Caska Bonds, Claude McKay, Eric Walrond, Richmond Barthé, Alain Locke, Carl Van Vechten, and most of Cullen's male lovers. Research into the period would be incomplete without Jackman's informal, "newsy" histo-ry–albeit often rife with camp.

In one letter, Jackman reported: "And there is a rumor in Harlem that Pettit committed suicide–I spoke to your father about this and he said it wasn't true. But the niggers have it that Pettit committed suicide over some boy. Ask Caska about it–I got it from him."[27] This bit of Harlem gay history was later fictionalized in Blair Niles's novel, *Strange Brother* (1931), in which Leland Pettit looms transparently behind the character of Mark Thornton. Pettit who was white and from Milwaukee, fell in love with a Black youth in Harlem. Cullen dedicated "Colors" to his friend Pettit (*Copper Sun* 11–12)–a poem that argues for the insignificance of color through an ironic display of the dangers of prizing "Red" and "Black." The last stanza, "The Unknown Color," describes a peculiar fear caused by the unseen which can be seen as racism and homophobia. This stanza is, perhaps, an allusion to Pettit's interracial and homosexual relationship.

Through Jackman's letters, we learn that Cullen traveled to London before returning home from France. He went there to see *Porgy*–the 1927 play based on Du Bose Heyward's 1925 novel of the same name–in which Edward G. Perry was appearing as a dancer. It is my contention that Perry and Cullen were lovers in the late twenties and early thirties before Cullen took his French lovers. Jackman often referred to Perry; for example, ". . . . did Edward tell you he sold a story to 'True Story?' Now, he *didn't* tell me to write and tell you this. . . . I don't know how confidential you two are anyway. I mean outside of —."[28] This is a codified reference to being gay and, more importantly, to Jackman's acknowledgment of them as a couple. Their relationship was strong enough for Cullen to dedicate the very successful poem, "More Than a Fool's Song," to Perry. The poem owes a literary debt to John Donne's "Song" ("Go and catch a falling star"), patterned after medieval lyrics of impossibility, and is a diatribe against those who interpret the world erroneously. Further, it criticizes the orthodoxy of Christian beliefs and argues that we may all be fooled that the world we believe to be one way is really quite different. On another level, the poem suggests that homosexuality might not be the heinous sin it is proclaimed to be, and that homosexuals may be the "souls" who "are climbing up" rather than those who "are hurtling down" (*Copper Sun* 67).

In addition to the dedication of "More Than a Fool's Song," Cullen gave Perry his original, handwritten copies of several poems. Van Vechten (collecting for Yale's future James Weldon Johnson archive) asked Cullen to send him any original writings; Cullen responded, "The originals were usually sent to friends or destroyed. So these I am sending you are about as original as they can be according to my way of working."[29] Cullen's "way of working" was to write his drafts by hand and then to type them when he was sure of making only minor revisions. On five of the typed copies he sent to Van Vechten, Cullen wrote "Sent to E. G. P." That Cullen sent these handwritten originals to Perry is telling indeed.

All five poems are published in *The Medea and Some Poems* and, most importantly, they are, as a group, gay in theme, imagery, and argument. The poems are "Sonnet Dialogue" (initially entitled "Discourse in a Sonnet"), "These are no wind-blown rumors," "Interlude," "Any Human to Another," "Bilitis," and "I would I could." In earlier gay poems, Cullen used race to blur the focus; in these poems, there is no such poetic dodge. Reading Cullen's translation of Pierre Louÿs's French poem "Bilitis," one is struck by the honesty of the description of lesbian love. In Cullen's own poems, this frankness abounds, and we are tempted to hear Cullen as speaker pouring forth directly to Perry on the impermanence of love, the poet's frustration in amorous expression, and the necessity of cooling passion's heat. A fuller examination of these poems and others in the collection will reveal that by the mid-thirties, Cullen had found and fine-tuned his gay poetic voice. Here are the most manifest indicators of androcentricity as a component of Cullen's gay literary imagination. Judging from the lack of references to Cullen's love interests in letters to Jackman, one can conclude, with some surety, that Cullen did not have long-term male partners for some time after Perry. This period coincides with Cullen's summer trips to France and the correspondence with his French lovers.

No one wrote more letters to Cullen than did Jackman, and to him Cullen dedicated most of his work. Signing his name "Countée P. Cullen," he dedicated an early handwritten copy of "Advice to Youth" to Jackman (*Color* 80).[30] To Jackman, Cullen dedicated: "Heritage"–one of his most famous and successful poems; *The Black Christ and Other Poems* (1929) (with Edward Perry and Roberta Bosley); and his only novel, *One Way to Heaven* (1932). Cullen's death was a shock to Jackman, as he wrote to Locke: "I am still dazed by Countee's death: it will be some time before I realize it. . . ."[31] Jackman went to his grave with knowledge of Cullen's birth and natural parents;[32] Cullen died with the secret of Jackman's daughter "Diana"–celebrated in "Three Nonsense Rhymes for My Three Goddaughters" (*The Medea and Some Poems* 78-9)–born to a Viennese woman named "Anne."[33] Toward the end of his life, Cullen found love and trust again in Edward Atkinson, a young man fourteen years his junior.

## *IV*

Cullen and Atkinson enjoyed a mature and sustained homosexual partnership. Because Cullen married Ida Roberson in 1940, his relationship with Atkinson was as closeted as previous ones; again, the lovers' history is found in secret correspondence. Cullen was aware that these letters could be damaging; he signed many simply "C" or using the alias "Charles Crawford." Cullen presumably destroyed most of Atkinson's letters; for, only a few survive. Nevertheless, these letters are the lovers' history from March 1937 through December 1945, merely a month before Cullen died.

Cullen and Atkinson met early in 1937, and their relationship grew quickly; by summer, Cullen, writing from France, missed Atkinson: "These are really what one may call halcyon days. And yet so ungrateful is the heart of man, that I am not completely satisfied. *There is a great void that cannot be filled on this side. . .*" (my emphasis). The "great void" Cullen alluded to is complicated. Surely he missed Atkinson and their gay community, but he also pined for their shared experiences in art, music, and literature. Of particular note, is Cullen's response that he could not find a copy of *Revelation* which Atkinson requested. The novel by André Birabeau (translated from French into English in 1930 by Una, Lady Troubridge) is the story of a mother who, after her son is killed in an auto accident, finds out that he was homosexual. Eventually the angry mother is redeemed by her son's lover who helps her to transform her rage into love. As regarded his own writing, Cullen bemoaned his "poetic output" being "very little" as he had only translated two stanzas from the French of the gay poet Paul Verlaine and "two acrostics." He ended the letter, "Yo te . . . tan mucho."[34] The ellipsis marks the most significant part of the "great void"– Cullen's love for Atkinson.

By 1941, Cullen's constant migraine headaches often foiled the lovers' customary Friday meetings. Cullen's illness slowed his writing, but his relationship with Atkinson remained stable. Cullen did not publish any poems dedicated to Atkinson, but he alluded to having written verse for him in a letter referring to pictures Van Vechten had taken of Atkinson in a monk's garb–resembling Brother Martin de Pores, a Peruvian saint. Cullen and Van Vechten used "Brother Martin" as a pseudonym for Atkinson: Van Vechten hoped Cullen would "some day indite a sonnet to Holy Brother Martin." Cullen wrote: "I have recently spent several hours in an attempt to invest his name [Brother Martin] with whatever slim aura of immortality my own may achieve."[35] Cullen also mentioned how he enjoyed Atkinson's birthday celebration; previously, he had sent a poem penned just for the occasion. Never published, the entire poem appears here for the first time.

Song For July 15

Blest be the day!
Let the bells ring!
Let them convey
What I would sing:
Blest be, alway,
Both night and morn
Blest be the day
That You were born![36]

Cullen shakes no great poetic ground here, but the poem's very existence provides yet another example of the close knitting of the poet's homosexual and artistic life. The poem also indicates how the love relationship had grown since 1937.

Dating Cullen's other poem to Atkinson is difficult. He wrote of working on verses in July 1942; it is probable that it was completed that year. The untitled poem was donated to Yale by Atkinson and is being published here for the first time in its entirety.

Because I voice this mild complaint,
Don't think I'm mad, because I ain't;
I'm just a wee bit roiled and riled
At your indifference, my child.
If you were sick and I were well,
I'd swell the stores of A. G. Bell;
I'd do no disappearing trick,
If I were well, and *you* were sick.
I have no malady outrageous,
Nothing infectious or contagious.

If you should give my hand a shake,
There's nought with which you would outbreak.
If you should come and wish me well,
That would not sound your final knell.
If you should stand beside my bed,
And lay a cool hand on my head,
I think my ills would disappear
As quick as that, yes instanter;
And you would find no rash infection
Resulting from such close connection!
Then there's the phone; I will admit
The fees are rising bit by bit,
But surely, child, you can afford
One little jingle, 'pon my word!
Because I voice this mild complaint,
Don't think I'm mad, because I ain't.
But, damn it, I am hurt![37]

Reminiscent of lover's complaints from the English Renaissance, this poem echoes sentiments found in many of Cullen's letters in which he upbraids Atkinson for not expressing affection or not communicating frequently enough. The poem records part of the history of their gay relationship in a playful and serious way, wavering between reprimand and love song. The poem also echoes a letter which evinces the older Cullen's caution set against the younger Atkinson's free spirit: "Will you do something for me? Try not to live your *entire* life during this decade. I admit that my reasons are to a large extent selfish; I want to feel that you will be here for a long time to come."[38] By the end of 1942, Cullen's health worsened, and Friday meetings were missed more frequently. The relationship was still secure, however, as seen in the change of salutation in Cullen's letters; he greeted Atkinson as "D. B." or "Dearest and Best."[39]

By August 1943, Atkinson was in the army. He wrote Cullen from Camp Upton, New York, sore from injections and depressed: "I feel that my moments of severe dejection here would be more severe if I didn't have the memories of all the pleasant & thoughtful acts you did for me. They had a kind of fatalistic quality about them and I am not too sure that they were not prophetic." As usual, he signed, "EIII."[40] Cullen responded immediately with reassurance: "The same day you left I translated a poem from the French of Baudelaire. I send it to you. Read in it whatever you care to." The Baudelaire poem is "Tout Entière" ("All in One" or "Altogether"), a dramatic lyric in which the Devil asks the speaker to single out the most captivating and inspiring of his lover's attributes. The speaker's soul replies that it is impossible to separate such qualities in her, and thus there is no one preferred part. Cullen translated the French pronouns as Baudelaire used them, thus the poem is, on the surface, heterosexual. But Cullen chose this poem for Atkinson at a time when the young soldier was in need of a pledge of their love. The poem was Cullen's warrant that he loved Atkinson *entirely* and that that love had not been shaken by absence or distance. The invitation to Atkinson to interpret the poem however he pleased allowed the lover to reaffirm their union through the permanence of art. Here, again, we find the tight weave of Cullen's homosexuality and his literary imagination. By extension, contemporary readers have Cullen's endorsement to find valid homosexual readings in his poems.[41]

Atkinson was transferred to Camp Wheeler, Georgia, by September 1943. His letters depict how doubly trying it was for a Black gay male during World War II. He wrote: "I am so choked with ill-feeling, deep-seated resentment, unpremeditated sadness that it's hard to be coherent." Atkinson longed for music and literature and imagined that when Cullen played *Dein Blaues Augen* they both heard and enjoyed it; he thanked Cullen for the Baudelaire poem and called it "balm from Gilead."[42]

In 1944 and 1945, Cullen's health declined, and the very few letters show Cullen's mounting problems with producing *St. Louis Woman*, managing finances, and finding a suitable place to meet his lover. The letters are short and lack the vitality of earlier ones. The last of these is a typical apology for missing Atkinson due to illness and a wish for a date at Jackman's.[43] Cullen died 9 January 1946, and Atkinson attended the funeral.

In reclaiming Cullen's gay life, it is difficult not to focus on the angst commonly associated with the oppressed. Cullen surely, as the undertones of many poems verify, suffered because of his sexual preference. The combination of machismo and fundamentalism in the Black community militated against any open homosexual activity. However, among Harlem intellectuals, gay freedom existed because secrets were kept. Fortunately, Cullen was a reputable poet; for, his very status mitigated the insularity and inner torment experienced by other gays. Poetry also provided an expressive outlet for the pain *and* pleasure of gay love in lyrics like "Tableau," "Interlude," "Every Lover," the beautiful "These are no wind-blown rumors," and the bold "Song in Spite of Myself" in which Love is a male. Even during his heterosexual marriages, it is not an exaggeration to suggest that Cullen *enjoyed* his gay life despite all the pressures against perceived opprobriousness. With the support of male lovers and gay friends all of his adult life, Cullen engendered happiness in the face of pain; in this way, he was also able to represent poetically a homosexual self, in its complexity, in some of his best work. Having opened his Uranian soul windows at an early age, Cullen succeeded indeed in integrating his homosexuality as a forceful–though sometimes inaudible–dimension of his literary imagination.[44]

## NOTES

1. Cullen's personal papers are housed mostly in the Amistad Research Center (ARC) at Tulane as The Countee Cullen Papers (CCP). Additional pertinent correspondence was acquired from the Alain Leroy Locke Papers (ALLP) in the Moorland-Spingarn Research Center (MSRC) at Howard and the James Weldon Johnson Collection (JWJC) in the Beinecke Rare Book and Manuscript Library (BRBL) at Yale. Citations will appear as notes, abbreviated as indicated above. Cullen to Locke, 3 March 1923, ALLP, MSRC, Howard.

2. Cullen to Locke, 24 Sept. 1922, ALLP, MSRC, Howard.

3. Cullen to Locke, 12 Jan. 1923, ALLP, MSRC, Howard.

4. Cullen to Locke, 29 Jan. 1923, ALLP, MSRC, Howard.

5. Locke to Cullen, 3 Feb. 192[3], CCP, ARC, Tulane.

6. Cullen to Locke, 3 Mar. 1923, ALLP, MSRC, Howard.

7. Cullen to Locke, 5 Apr. 1923, ALLP, MSRC, Howard.

8. Cullen to Locke, 30 Apr. 1923, ALLP, MSRC, Howard.

9. Cullen to Locke, 31 May 1923, ALLP, MSRC, Howard.

10. Cullen to Locke, 8 June 1923, ALLP, MSRC, Howard.

11. Cullen to Locke, 21 June 1923, ALLP, MSRC, Howard.

12. Cullen to Locke, 26 Aug. 1923, ALLP, MSRC, Howard.

13. Cullen to Locke, 30 Sept. 1923, ALLP, MSRC, Howard.

14. Cullen to Locke, 24 Nov. 1923, ALLP, MSRC, Howard.

15. Cullen to Locke, 7 Jan. 1924, ALLP, MSRC, Howard.

16. Cullen to Locke, 1 Apr. 1924, ALLP, MSRC, Howard.

17. Cullen to Locke, 4 May 1924, ALLP, MSRC, Howard.

18. Cullen to Locke, 29 July 1924, ALLP, MSRC, Howard.

19. Cullen to Locke, 20 Sept. 1924, ALLP, MSRC, Howard.

20. Cullen to Locke, 27 Oct. 1924, ALLP, MSRC, Howard.

21. Cullen to Locke, 31 Oct. 1924, ALLP, MSRC, Howard.

22. Cullen to Locke, 1 Nov. 1924, ALLP, MSRC, Howard.

23. Cullen to Locke, 30 Mar. 1925, ALLP, MSRC, Howard.

24. Cullen to Locke, 27 May 1925, ALLP, MSRC, Howard.

25. Jackman to Cullen, 29 Nov. 1928, CCP, ARC, Tulane.

26. Yolande DuBois to W. E. B. DuBois, 23 May 1929, Archives and Manuscripts, Univ. of Mass., Amherst.

27. Jackman to Cullen, 20 Sept. 1929, CCP, ARC, Tulane.

28. Jackman to Cullen, 17 Mar. 1930, CCP, ARC, Tulane.

29. Cullen to Van Vechten, 21 July 1942, JWJC, BRBL, Yale.

30. "Advice to Youth" and "Query," n.d., CCP, ARC, Tulane.

31. Jackman to Locke, 25 Feb. 1946, ALLP, MSRC, Howard.

32. Jackman to Cullen, 20 Dec. 1928, CCP, ARC, Tulane.

33. Jackman to Cullen, 20 Sept. 1929, CCP, ARC, Tulane.

34. Cullen to Atkinson, 1 Aug. 1937, JWJC, BRBL, Yale.

35. Cullen to Atkinson, 24 July 1942, JWJC, BRBL, Yale.

36. Cullen to Atkinson, 14 July 1942, JWJC, BRBL, Yale.

37. Untitled poem, JWJC, BRBL, Yale.

38. Cullen to Atkinson, p.m. 15 Mar. 1943, JWJC, BRBL, Yale.

39. Cullen to Atkinson, n.d., Thursday, JWJC, BRBL, Yale.

40. Atkinson to Cullen, 10 Aug. 1943, CCP, ARC, Tulane.

41. "Tout Entière" (enclosure), Cullen to Atkinson, 12 Aug. 1943, JWJC, BRBL, Yale.

42. Atkinson to Cullen, 5 Sept. 1943, CCP, ARC, Tulane.

43. Cullen to Atkinson, p.m. 10 Dec. 1945, JWJC, BRBL, Yale.

44. Financial support for the research presented here issued from the generosity of the Faculty Development Fund and Alumni Association of St. Mary's College of California.

## WORKS CITED

Avi-Ram, Amitai F. "The Unreadable Black Body: 'Conventional' Poetic Form in the Harlem Renaissance." *Genders* 7 (1990): 32-45.

Baker, Houston A. *Afro-American Poetics: Revisions of Harlem and the Black Aesthetic.* Madison: University of Wisconsin Press, 1988.

Bergman, David. *Gaiety Transfigured: Gay Self-Representation in American Literature.* Madison: University of Wisconsin Press, 1991.

Bontemps, Arna, ed. *The Harlem Renaissance Remembered.* New York: Dodd, Mead and Company, 1972.

Cullen, Countee. *Color.* New York: Harpers, 1925.

_____ . *Copper Sun.* New York: Harpers, 1927.

_____ . *The Black Christ and Other Poems.* New York: Harpers, 1929.

_____ . *The Medea and Some Poems.* New York: Harpers, 1935.

Early, Gerald. "Introduction." *My Soul's High Song: The Collected Writings of Countee Cullen.* New York: Anchor Books, 1991.

Fabre, Michel. *From Harlem to Paris: Black American Writers in France, 1840-1980.* Urbana: University of Illinois Press, 1991.

Ferguson, Blanche. *Countee Cullen and the Negro Renaissance.* New York: Dodd, Mead, and Co., 1966.

Garber, Eric. "A Spectacle in Color: The Lesbian and Gay Subculture of Jazz Age Harlem." *Hidden from History: Reclaiming the Gay and Lesbian Past.* Ed. Martin Duberman, Martha Vicinus, and George Chauncey, Jr. New York: New American Library, 1989. 318-31.

Hull, Gloria T. *Color, Sex, and Poetry: Three Women Writers of the Harlem Renaissance.* Bloomington: Indiana University Press, 1987.

Lewis, David Levering. *When Harlem Was in Vogue.* New York: Knopf, 1981.

Nelson, Emmanuel S. "Critical Deviance: Homophobia and the Reception of James Baldwin's Fiction." *Journal of American Culture* 14.3 (Fall, 1991): 91-96.

Perry, Margaret. *A Bio-Bibliography of Countee P. Cullen, 1903-1946.* Westport: Greenwood, 1971.

Rampersad, Arnold. *The Life of Langston Hughes.* Volume 1: 1902-1941. New York: Oxford University Press, 1986.

Shucard, Alan. *Countee Cullen.* Boston: Twayne Publishers, 1984.

Wagner, Jean. *Les Poètes Nègres des États-Unis.* Paris: Librairie Istra, 1963.

_____ . *Black Poets of the United States.* Trans. Kenneth Douglas. Urbana: University of Illinois Press, 1973.

Whitman, Walt. *The Complete Poems.* Ed. Francis Murphy. New York: Penguin, 1975.

# "Being Bridges": Cleaver/Baldwin/Lorde and African-American Sexism and Sexuality

Shelton Waldrep, PhD (cand.)

*Duke University*

**SUMMARY.** In an attempt to place James Baldwin and his ideas within the context of a debate on black sexuality and sexism, this paper begins with a section on Eldridge Cleaver and his critique of Baldwin's position on sexuality and race. Cleaver's own homophobia and misreading of Baldwin's essays and published comments on Richard Wright contribute to his inability to grasp Baldwin's sophisticated analysis of race/sexuality/sexism within Western culture. The second section takes up Baldwin explicitly and attempts both to outline his position more fully and to suggest the breadth and depth of his analysis of sexuality and the work yet to be done to chart it. In the final section of the paper I turn to Audre Lorde in order to update the critique of Baldwin's position within the debate. Lorde, like many other contemporary writer-theorists, sees the terms of the discussion differently from Baldwin. She agrees with his hatred of racism, homophobia, and sexism, but she disagrees with his solution that acceptance and "brotherly" love are a solution to the real prob-

---

Correspondence may be addressed to the author at: Department of English, Box 90017, Duke University, Durham, NC 27708-0017.

[Haworth co-indexing entry note]: "'Being Bridges': Cleaver/Baldwin/Lorde and African-American Sexism and Sexuality." Waldrep, Shelton. Co-published simultaneously in the *Journal of Homosexuality* (The Haworth Press, Inc.) Vol. 26, No. 2/3, 1993, pp. 167-180; and *Critical Essays: Gay and Lesbian Writers of Color* (ed: Emmanuel S. Nelson) The Haworth Press, Inc., 1993, pp. 167-180. Multiple copies of this article/chapter may be purchased from The Haworth Document Delivery Center [1-800-3-HAWORTH; 9:00 a.m. - 5:00 p.m. (EST)].

lems facing black (and gay) people today. She posits a belief in the necessity for delineating the particular subject position she holds: black, lesbian, female, Western, etc., and she is wary of any allegiances that might elide the clues to her oppression. The paper attempts to demonstrate that these differing positions are, nevertheless, linked in ways historical and otherwise.

## I. CLEAVER

Afro-American letters has always existed as a dialogue with itself. Du Bois carefully answered Washington, Ellison was always aware of the figure of Wright, Malcolm X knew King, and so on in a dynamic relationship that only increases in complexity as time moves on and African-American writers become more numerous and prominent. In the late 1960s this family discussion had become a cacophony of voices reasoning and arguing the important themes and sub-themes of intellectual and practical survival. One of the newly prominent discussions was that having to do with African-American gender construction and its concomitant parts: sexuality and sexism within the race and without. In 1968, with the publication of *Soul on Ice*, Eldridge Cleaver ignited a fierce argument about where the politically savvy African-American man stood on the topics of race and gender. By simultaneously crystallizing through elegant articulation the correct position for the Panther-leaning new black revolutionary and setting up a sexist/homophobic paradigm aching to be broken, he established a milestone in African-American gender debates. Aspects of his more negative ideas may cling to discourse even today (his updating of the image of the emasculated African-American man, for instance), but his immediate concern involved creating new ways for defining oneself using gender, sexuality, and race as self-conscious ideologies.

Cleaver's critique of gender and sexuality within *Soul on Ice* attempts to establish various dialectics and dichotomies. By developing a semiotic system whose codes include gender, race, sexuality, and, especially, masculinity, Cleaver tries to come to terms with his own position. However, his methodology is such that he is often the most contradictory when he deals with the most complex and crucial issues. For instance, he discusses his simultaneous love for and hatred of white women. He pens poems to the abstract "White Woman" and loves her just because she is white, but he also admits to raping white women in order to, as he explains, make society pay for various injustices–including not allowing him to love white women and to have access to them without stigma. Similarly, during the course of the book, he develops the idea of the "New Black Woman," the Queen of Sheba who will stand beside the "New Black Man" after the revolution is complete. Yet this mythic figure is in contradistinction to the real (white) Beverly Axelrod with whom he is deeply in love.

At one point Cleaver quotes from a letter to Axelrod: "I have had a bad habit, when speaking of women while only men are present, of referring to women as bitches. This bitch this and this bitch that. . . . And I felt very ashamed of myself. . . . I passed judgement upon myself and suffered spiritually for days afterward. This may seem insignificant, but I attach great importance to it because of the chain of thought kicked off by it" (140). This passage may be the only one in *Soul on Ice* where Cleaver actually questions his attitude toward women. Otherwise, he seems to believe that he must help to rethink the role they will play in the future, but that this process does not require that he consider any unconscious prejudices he might have himself. On the subject of gay men there is not a hint of even this much doubt. Cleaver attacks James Baldwin in particular with a vicious combination of misogyny and homophobia. His attitude toward Baldwin's masculinity and sexuality can be summed up in the comment that "he [Baldwin] cannot confront the stud in others–except that he must either submit to it or destroy it" (106). Cleaver seems never to conceive of the idea that being female or gay does not necessarily mean being jealous of others' machismo.

In fact, his misreading of Baldwin reveals Cleaver's codes and standards in such a way as to show their shortcomings for critiquing Baldwin's sexuality. More than once Cleaver calls homosexuality a sickness, and he implicitly contrasts it with the image of a black male boxer in top form on which he cathects his own desire for a perfect example of African-American masculinity.[1] Cleaver seems to buy into the intellectual macho cult of Norman Mailer, LeRoi Jones, and William Burroughs that was ripe at the time he was writing. Though Cleaver's ideas on sexuality are more complicated and somewhat less prejudiced than those of these other writers, his writing does contain many parallels with theirs.[2]

The central concept that can be said to be held in common by this group is that men suppress their feminine side because they must be strong in order to protect themselves from the weakness and decay that comes from age, women, and, except for Burroughs, gay men. This theory has lost most serious favor that it once had and has been lampooned by various women writers and even men of their generation such as Gore Vidal. As early as 1970, Kate Millet, in *Sexual Politics*, identifies Mailer's absurd propositions and analyzes their relationship to his fiction. Millet's book is perhaps the most famous critique of this hyper-male strain, but a counterforce was already present earlier in the thinking of Baldwin. Indeed, Cleaver's attack on Baldwin brings to the fore his courage and opposition to Cleaver's ideal of male sexuality.

Millet demonstrates the incredibly illogical and contradictory aspects of Mailer's musings on sexuality and gender and shows that, although there is a type of self-consciousness in his writing, the sexual themes tend to be, finally, frighteningly misogynist and homophobic. She contrasts Mailer to Jean Genet, whose writing in many ways parallels Baldwin's in the working out of theories of maleness–especially homosexuality–in fiction. According to Millet, Genet's novels overturn accepted ideas concerning men and women by showing that gender is more an invention of society than a predestined biological fact. This redefinition of sexuality as social construct shifts the theoretical emphasis from biology towards an exploration of society's means of oppression and conditioning. In other words, one does not have to remain a prisoner of a scientific definition of one's sex, but can instead come to terms with one's identity while trying at the same time to understand how society functions.

Cleaver, however, repeatedly privileges the pseudo-scientific approach.[3] His belief that some men are effeminate by nature, and therefore predestined to be gay, is a specious assumption that actually supports the racist idea that African-American men must be primarily physical. Cleaver knows that theories of sexuality are complicated by race, but his thinking shows a paranoia that evolution damns African-American men to a constant battle for mascu-

linity as they can be emasculated by not only women and homosexual men, but also by envious white heterosexual men who
attempt to usurp their sexual power.

If women and heterosexual white men are complicated entities
for Cleaver, they are really nothing compared to the phenomenon of
the homosexual African-American man whose very existence represents hopelessly conflicting energies for Cleaver. His primary
argument, once unpacked, can be summarized in this quasi-syllo-
gistic way:

> African-American people hate themselves.
> African-American people want white-skinned babies.
> White men dilute the blood of African-American men by di-
> luting the African-American gene pool with white blood by
> impregnating African-American women.
> African-American gay men also want brown babies from
> white men.
> The African-American intellectual is an enemy because he
> assumes the white man's traits.
> Therefore: an African-American/male/gay/intellectual is the
> antithesis of a true African-American man, the nemesis con-
> taining all of the wrong traits and desires.

Although Cleaver's comments on Baldwin are scattered throughout the episodically organized *Soul on Ice*, many are concentrated in
the chapter "Notes on a Native Son." Here he criticizes Baldwin
for what he thinks is criticism by Baldwin of Mailer in the former's
"The Black Boy Looks at the White Boy."[4] In fact, Baldwin does
not dissect Mailer's work or the attitudes reflected in them like
Millet, but instead writes a memoir of his friendship with Mailer
and only critiques his ideas enough to say that their relationship was
often strained by disagreement. Cleaver, nevertheless, seems determined to see Baldwin as a threat and to be sensitive to any attacks
on Wright, Mailer, or anything that is important to the shaping of
the ideas that make up his identity at the time of *Soul on Ice*.

Cleaver's misunderstanding of Baldwin's general attitude toward
African-American writers also appears when he characterizes Bald-

win's comments on the famous Conference of Black Artists and Writers held in Paris in 1956:

> Baldwin, the reluctant black, dragging his feet at every step, could only ridicule the vision and efforts of these great men and heap scorn upon them, reserving his compliments . . . for the speakers who . . . were themselves rejected and booed by the conferees because of their reactionary sycophantic views. (98)

Actually, Baldwin wrote that he was excited and supportive of the conference. He simply–as always–raised points about the African-American situation that were not usually noticed. Most participants probably came to the conference expecting the prevailing ideas of the revolution to be praised and support for them strengthened. Baldwin did not attack the idea of a black revolution, but advanced original ideas that critiqued contemporary African Americans in addition to whites. This approach turned out to be prophetic, not unconstructively critical.

Cleaver launches his most vociferous attack against Baldwin on the subject of Richard Wright. Cleaver seems to think that Baldwin, in his essay "Alas, Poor Richard," acted as Brutus to Wright's Caesar by conjuring the image of Baldwin turning on his master with a vengeance. Baldwin acknowledges that he looked up to Wright; however, nowhere in either of his essays on him does he attack him in the way that Cleaver thinks. In *Notes of a Native Son*, Baldwin comments on Wright's work, but it is hardly an attack. "Alas, Poor Richard" is a biographical piece about the man Baldwin knew, but it is also in many ways a selfless homage. When Cleaver quotes from Baldwin's essay, "I was exasperated by his [Wright's] notions of society, politics, and history, for they seemed to me utterly fanciful. I never believed that he had any sense of how a society is put together," he fails to realize that Baldwin is giving the opinion of a younger self and that he is advancing his own notion that society is based upon relationships, not societal forces (an important contrast between the two writers that can be seen in their novels, among other places). This is a necessary outlining of difference that the young Baldwin had to make in order to function within Wright's shadow. Although Cleaver sees Wright as a mentor, he cannot accept Baldwin's comments as complex, tempered opinion in part because he does not understand Baldwin or his essential project.

It is debatable, anyway, whether Baldwin needed a real father figure like Wright. After all, the relationship between father and son is purposefully ironic in *Go Tell It on the Mountain*. Nevertheless, the main attack on Wright of which Cleaver accuses Baldwin is his comment on Wright's tendency to replace sex with violence in order to avoid what Baldwin saw as the true terms of racial/intra-racial debate: sexuality/gender/sexism. Cleaver is correct in saying that Baldwin criticizes Wright for doing this, but Baldwin did not attempt to discredit him. Baldwin does not write about sex simply because, as Cleaver implies, his sexual practices were not "normal." Instead he believed that examining sex and sexuality is more constructive than accepting masculinity as the embodiment of violence.[5] Baldwin's interest in sexuality as opposed to violence was a part of his overall belief that examining relationships among people–as he does in his novels–is the best way to advance theories about society. Baldwin does, however, understand and agree with Cleaver that racism and sexuality are inextricably linked and that the African-American man has often been the double subject of violence because of his color and how it intersects with representations of his sexuality. Cleaver's own example of this double bind is police brutality–one of the few subjects discussed in both *Soul on Ice* and his religious autobiography *Soul on Fire*. Baldwin, likewise, observes in *Nobody Knows My Name*:

> I think that I know something about the American masculinity which men of my generation do not know because they have not been menaced by it in the way I have been. It is still true, alas, that to be an American Negro male is also to be a kind of walking phallic symbol: which means that one pays, in one's personality, for the sexual insecurity of others. (17)

In a later interview, Baldwin echoes himself:

> The society makes its will toward you [gay person] very, very, clear. Especially the police ... or truck drivers. I know from my own experience that the macho men ... are far more complex than they want to realize. That's why I call them infantile. They

> [Americans] have needs which, for them, are literally inexpress-
> ible. They don't dare look into the mirror. And that is why they
> need faggots. They've created faggots in order to act out a
> sexual fantasy on the body of another man and not take any
> responsibility for it. . . . (Goldstein 13)

Baldwin sees violence against African-American males (and unlike
Cleaver, gay men and women) in psychoanalytical terms. For him
violence against male homosexuals is society's acting out of a collective mirror stage of infantilism. It is a fear of confrontation with
oneself and a fear of touch from others. Because he thinks that the
taboo against homosexuality may not be as great in African-American culture, he sees this as primarily an aspect of white American
culture. For him, members of white Western culture will remain
stuck in this condition and, therefore, violent as long as they believe
that their concept of civilization equals innate sophistication and
superiority.

Baldwin's gloss on white, logocentric European civilization be-
lies another of Cleaver's criticisms—namely, his attacking Baldwin
because he chose to live much of his life in France. According to
Cleaver, Baldwin was running away from America and from being
black because he wanted to appropriate Western European whiteness in the guise of intellectualism. On the contrary, anyone who
examines Baldwin's *oeuvre* can easily conclude that he always
remained self-consciously African and American. He always
looked back toward America from Europe. If this looking toward
was also a looking at, this is only part of his attempt to expand and
liberate African-American studies by providing the perspective of
an African-American man living in Europe. This is certainly not
original. Paris has been a liberating place for African-American
writers as diverse as Chesnutt, Holmes, Toomer, and, of course,
Wright. The ritual expatriation to France has become a common
part of African-American intellectual culture. Even though, in *No
Name in the Street*, Baldwin acknowledges that France has its own
racism, and he recognizes it as severe in its own way, his biography
indicates that when he sailed for Paris as a young writer he needed
psychological distance from his roots in Harlem and the ministerial
life he was leaving behind for the pursuit of writing. In Paris he

discovered that an African-American (or gay) person could fit more easily into urban society than in New York. Of course, it is to Paris that Cleaver flees when faced with jail again after writing a best-selling book in prison: *Soul on Ice.*

## II. BALDWIN

In *The Devil Finds Work*, Baldwin analyzes the American cinema's portrayal of African-American sexuality, the privacy of African-American lives, and American masculinity and homophobia. In *No Name in the Street*, he discusses the killing and castration of African-American men because they love white women. In his explicitly gay novels, such as *Giovanni's Room* and *Another Country*, he creates his most complex dissection of race, sexuality, and gender through fiction. And Baldwin even writes about Cleaver's writing on him and about Cleaver himself: "I was very much impressed by Eldridge . . . it's impossible not to be. . . ." In his essays, novels, and interviews, therefore, Baldwin discusses many of the same topics that Cleaver approaches in *Soul on Ice.* In developing his ideas about maleness and sexuality, however, he obviously took a position radically different from Cleaver's.

Baldwin's analysis of these topics is personal and penetrating. One typical example is the essay "The Male Prison" where he discusses Gide's double life of having sex with male prostitutes while professing love for his wife.[6] Baldwin comments on what he sees as the factors that formed Gide's predicament:

> Gide's relations with Madeleine place his relations with men in rather a bleak light. Since he clearly could not forgive himself for his anomaly, he must certainly have despised them [the prostitutes]–which almost certainly explains the fascination felt by Gide and so many of his heroes for countries like North Africa. It is not necessary to despise people who are one's inferiors–whose inferiority, by the way, is amply demonstrated by the fact that they appear to relish, without guilt, their sensuality. (*Nobody* 160)

Baldwin blends biography with cultural analysis in order to elucidate Gide and in the process makes a point about the gay subculture's pre-AIDS fascination for Tangiers. He continues by expanding the scope of his critique to suggest that Gide's struggle was not so different from "the heroes of Mickey Spillane" who are unable to communicate with women. This condition affects their relations with other men and thus "makes their isolation complete" (162).

This argument demonstrates two principles that are necessary for an understanding of Baldwin's approach to sexuality. First, Baldwin was an individualist. He did not follow a strict methodology, but rather wrote criticism that was an eclectic blend of textual analysis, biography, history, and pure speculation. He was a maverick not only because he dared to be considered an outsider, but because he relished his individualism, his marginal view. Second, Baldwin was a strong supporter of communication between women and men. For him, being a male homosexual did not mean losing contact with the other side–how women actually think and feel (a lesson that he sincerely believed could be learned even by macho men). These distinctions are important because they illustrate his differences with many of the critics who have approached the subject of African-American sexism and sexuality in the 1970s and 1980s. Few contemporary critics have been as progressive as he, but many have been more self-consciously theoretical. Baldwin concludes in the essay on Gide: "How to be natural does not seem to me to be a problem–quite the contrary. The great problem is how to be–in the best sense of that kaleidoscopic word–a man" (157). Baldwin's stance does not toe a theoretical line. He is unafraid to seem, by the 1970s, slightly old-fashioned in order that he might seem humanistic. He does not proclaim a gay identity, but accepts homosexuality as a part of his overall personality. In an interview conducted late in his life, Baldwin was asked, "What do you think gay people will be like then [in the future]?" He answered, "No one will have to call themselves gay. [The term] answers a false argument, a false accusation" (Goldstein 14). Baldwin does not attempt to prove anything by being out about his sexuality. He has said that he would never write a book about homosexuality per se. In his mind, *Giovanni's Room* and *Another Country* use homosexuality as a vehicle (as *Go Tell It on the Mountain* uses religion) to discuss his notion of universals. Not gay love, but love.

## III. LORDE

Perhaps. Many African-American writers, however, feel the necessity of dealing with the reality of sexuality and sexism differently. Audre Lorde is an African-American poet who has helped to develop a self-conscious, highly theoretical approach to politics within her life and art. She consciously identifies herself with labels–African American, woman, lesbian, etc.–and uses theoretical strategies similar to those used by feminists in France (such as writing from the body) to examine her situation within society. Lorde and theorists like her map the uncharted aspects of their lives to begin an articulation of their situation because African-American women are, in a sense, blank spaces within society.

For Lorde what is important is a thorough examination of power and an excavation of what is truly hers. She must consciously separate herself from white women, from men of both races, and, because her project is aimed at white women of the "First World," from mainstream feminism as well. Race and sex are thus elements in the system of binary oppositions that keep her marked as the ultimate outsider. She must construct paradigms of her situation in the hopes of better understanding her oppression.

Although Lorde consented to accept the symbolic distinction of sharing the National Book Award for Poetry with Adrienne Rich, a white lesbian poet, in the name of all women, her concepts of group and individual are quite different from Baldwin's. Any claim to universality or common humanity, such as he has made, would appear to her naive. She feels that she must write poetry that attempts via self-reflexiveness to come to terms with basic questions about sexuality by isolating the experience of African-American women in order that it might be analyzed. She must, therefore, keep her work free from heterosexist and masculinist domination. She must, in other words, always rewrite her history.

Baldwin has said that homosexuality is ultimately private. Lorde would say that identity is always already political and public. Society molds one's rights and identity if not explicitly one's sex life. As Lorde explains in her essay "Scratching the Surface: Some Notes on Barriers to Women and Loving," male-female communication must be subordinated to "female bonding" which "is self-protec-

tive and necessary to black women's self-definition." Lorde sees
this bonding as reflecting a material reality and it is "only to those
black men who are unclear as to the paths of their own self-definition that the self-protective bonding of black women [can] be seen
as a threatening development" (433). In fact, "the red herring of
homophobia and lesbian-baiting is being used in the black community to obscure the true double face of racism/sexism. Black women
sharing close ties with each other, politically or emotionally, are not
the enemies of black men" (433). She continues by noting that
African-American women are made to feel that African-American
men are a "prize" for which they must "compete" and that this
system keeps African-American women from communicating with
each other and recognizing their common strengths and interests
(434).

Essential to Lorde, therefore, is the belief that self-conscious
separation is necessary if she is to understand her place and identity.
That this process can also be a way for understanding how society
works is an idea that is antithetical to those held by Baldwin. This
difference came out markedly in a published conversation between
them in which he notes that African-American people have always
had to know how white people think, and she responds that African-
American women have always had to know what African-American men think–for survival. But now, says Lorde:

> We're finished being bridges. We're saying, "Listen, what's go-
> ing on between us is related to what's going on between us and
> *other* people," but we have to solve our own shit at the same time
> we're protecting our Black asses, because if we don't we are
> wasting energy we need for joint survival. ("Conversation" 74)

Later Baldwin voices his belief in the necessity for a link between
women and men and adds, "what I really think is that neither of us
has anything to prove" (129). Lorde counters: "We have to redefine
ourselves for each other because no matter what the underpinnings
of the distortion are, the fact remains that we have absorbed it"
(129-130).

Lorde's position does not promote separatism so much as separate understanding as a first step toward the decoding of gender,
sexuality, and race. Her approach is in sharp contrast with Bald-

win's method, if not his ultimate intentions, and is diametrically opposed to Cleaver's. Cleaver, however, helped to forge the way for Lorde's type of theoretical exhumation by dealing seriously with race and gender and by establishing a new model for discussing them. Baldwin's own brilliance is not only as a superb essayist but as a theoretical link between Cleaver's male-oriented sexist world and Lorde's theoretical lesbian enterprise. Baldwin's work demonstrates how Cleaver's masculinity is a blindness–a tough stance attempting to cover over homophobia. He was unafraid to look at what Cleaver would only consider the other, the enemy. Yet Lorde's comments show that Baldwin ignores much complexity within gender debate by his positing of brotherly love as a panacea for society's ills. She would say that Baldwin is too brotherly and leaves the unique experiences of women out of the picture.

As the current reexamination of classic African-American works continues, Lorde's approach will become increasingly useful. For instance, the early work of Jones, such as *The Toilet* and *The Baptism*, seems to require the developing of new paradigms for the untangling of homophobia/philia and race. All three of these writers, however, have helped to establish a dialogue on sexuality and sexism in an attempt to help African-American men and women come to terms with the brutal society into which they have been forced. By modeling their critiques as a dialogue to and about each other, these writers seem to share Cleaver's dream that "through the implacable march of history to an ever broader base of democracy and equality, the society will renew and transform itself" (175).[7]

## NOTES

1. Cleaver's own homoerotic impulse surrounding this construction is not addressed in his book. It remains an interesting point for further study, however.

2. Cleaver quotes a passage from Jones' *The Dead Lecturer* and this infamous statement by Mailer: "For being a man is the continuing battle of one's life, and one loses a bit of manhood with every stale compromise to the authority of any power in which one does not believe" (106). The theme of castration–impotence–brought about by women or the "effeminate" man remains little changed when it appears in Burroughs' writing in his collection *The Job* or in Mailer's again in 1976: "I think that before there were any kinds of contraception, women had the ability not to conceive. There was some signal they could send into their body. . . . And they would conceive only where there were great fucks. . . . Which is one of my little

thoughts" (Scavullo 128). Mailer went on to write and film a book entitled *Tough Guys Don't Dance.*

3. See especially the chapter "Primeval Mitosis."

4. A response to Mailer's essay "The White Negro."

5. Certainly the Black Panthers, of which Cleaver was once a part, were, as Baldwin says, no flower children (*No Name* 185), and Cleaver supported the violence-for-self-defense of Malcolm X over the peaceful resistance of King.

6. It might be significant to note that in *Corydon* Gide had already established himself as a sexual theorist of the biological kind (like Cleaver and Mailer). He was also paranoid about his sexuality and came to it late, and carefully, like Forster.

7. For further study of Baldwin and his relationship to race and sexuality, see "The Evolution of James Baldwin as Essayist" by Nick Aaron Ford in *James Baldwin: A Critical Evaluation* (1977) and two essays from *James Baldwin: A Collection of Critical Essays* (1974): "James Baldwin" by Robert A. Bone and "The Lesson of the Master: Henry James and James Baldwin" by Charles Newman. Useful more for its commentary on Cleaver rather than Baldwin is Georges-Michel Sarotte's *Like a Brother, Like a Lover: Male Homosexuality in the American Novel and Theater from Herman Melville to James Baldwin* (1976, French; 1978, English). For further discussion of Mailer, Millet, and male fears of castration/impotence and homosexuality refer to Paul Hoch's *White Hero, Black Beast: Racism, Sexism, and the Mask of Masculinity* (1978). A helpful current approach is provided in Emmanuel Nelson's "Critical Deviance: Homophobia and the Reception of James Baldwin's Fiction," *Journal of American Culture*, Fall 1991, Vol. 14, No. 3. For further reading on Lorde's theories of identity there is her essential *Sister Outsider: Essays and Speeches* (1984).

## WORKS CITED

Baldwin, James. *No Name in the Street*. New York: The Dial Press, 1972.

Baldwin, James. *Nobody Knows My Name: More Notes of a Native Son*. New York: The Dial Press, 1961.

Cleaver, Eldridge. *Soul on Ice*. New York: Dell Publishing Co., 1968.

"Conversation Between James Baldwin and Audre Lorde," *Essence* December 1984: 72+.

Goldstein, Richard. "'Go the Way Your Blood Beats.'" *The Village Voice* 26 June 1985: 13-14.

Lorde, Audre. "Scratching the Surface: Some Notes on Barriers to Women and Loving." *Feminist Frameworks: Alternative Theoretical Accounts of the Relations Between Women and Men*. 2nd ed. Ed. Allison M. Jagger and Paula S. Rothenberg. New York: McGraw-Hill Book Co., 1985. 432-436.

Scavullo, Franscesco, et al. *Scavullo on Men*. New York: Random House, 1977.

# "The Very House of Difference": Zami, Audre Lorde's Lesbian-Centered Text

Cheryl Kader, PhD (cand.)

*Beloit College*

**SUMMARY.** Locating the feminist subject at the intersection of shifting social groups, or "homes," allows me to explore the connections between concepts of home and identity in Audre Lorde's "biomythography," *Zami: A New Spelling of My Name.* While Lorde's writing attends to the complex intersections of race, gender, and sexuality, as the prologue to the text makes apparent, it also testifies to the "naturalness" of lesbianism as the ground of writing, thinking, and acting. In Lorde's text, the lesbian body figures neither as an essential or fixed identity nor as the site for a unified conception of community or home, but rather, as a paradigm for a new kind of writing–one which inhabits the very house of difference.

In the 1980s, Anglo-American feminism experienced a crisis of meaning. A movement–never coherent, feminism was from its inception always plural–grounded in the particularity of "women's experience" or "sexual difference" was forced to recognize the

---

Correspondence may be addressed to the author at: Women's Studies, Beloit College, 700 College Street, Beloit, WI 53511.

[Haworth co-indexing entry note]: "'The Very House of Difference': *Zami*, Audre Lorde's Lesbian-Centered Text." Kader, Cheryl. Co-published simultaneously in the *Journal of Homosexuality* (The Haworth Press, Inc.) Vol. 26, No. 2/3, 1993, pp. 181-194; and *Critical Essays: Gay and Lesbian Writers of Color* (ed: Emmanuel S. Nelson) The Haworth Press, Inc., 1993, pp. 181-194. Multiple copies of this article/chapter may be purchased from The Haworth Document Delivery Center [1-800-3-HAWORTH; 9:00 a.m. - 5:00 p.m. (EST)].

variability of gendered experience. The belief in universal, or even common areas of experience among women would become increasingly unraveled throughout the decade, with the result that gender as an analytical category now appears multiply encoded and mediated (not always unselfconsciously) by other dimensions of difference. Initial demands for more complex approaches to women's experience were motivated less by the desire to defer "gender" than by a concern with the inter-connections among various systems of power that shape women's lives.[1] That is, questions of feminism and feminist "identity" would henceforth be taken up in order to more adequately reveal their inherence in the world rather than to renounce gender-based interrogations altogether. Recognizing the ethnocentrism of gender theory means being attentive to the locatedness and the limitations of embodied existence. In place of a monothematic model of feminist identity, it means we begin, in the words of Minnie Bruce Pratt, "to stretch the borders of the self," to make space for a multifaceted and multicultural perspective conscious of the meanings attached to gender in specific social and historical locations.[2] This model turns on questions of accountability, or on what Adrienne Rich calls "a politics of location."

As articulated in "A Black Feminist Statement" by the Combahee River Collective in 1977, the concept of identity politics implies that neither "politics" nor "identities" is singular or fixed. The embodied, "interested" discourse which evolves out of Black women's experience is, in the words of the Collective, the product of a shared legacy which, while irreducible to sameness, is exemplified by a rupture with white "norms" *and* Black male experience. "Identity" and the practices engendered in its name are constituted along multiple axes–social and discursive–which often appear contested and in contradiction.[3]

The concept of identity politics can be evoked, therefore, as the site of multiple voicings for it demands recognition of the ways in which identity is fashioned by our various social locations across the terrain of difference and heterogeneity. Similarly, it speaks to the breakdown of *feminism* as a self-identical, unified entity and the instability of *gender* as its primary or privileged term. Any notion of a secure, romanticized HOME within feminism is attenuated by a politics of location which implies dislocation and partiality.

It should be noted that the concept of identity politics is itself currently under interrogation since, in the view of some theorists, it accords specific identities an excess of unity–of referentiality–that forecloses discussion and re-establishes "gender," "race," and "sexuality" as monolithic categories superimposed upon indeterminate "selves." Calling for a politics of performance which would sever the field of identification from any trace of an "essentialist" bias, critics of identity politics advocate a less determining role for identity.[4] As seductive as these arguments are, I am not yet willing to relinquish the concept of identity politics or my faith in its destabilizing effect on gender as an analytical category. As a vehicle for negotiating meaning and cultivating new discourses, the spatialization of identity into its multiple and shifting determinants serves neither to deny "the multilayered texture of [our] lives" (Combahee 214) nor to erase the still substantial effects of "identities"– both disenfranchised and agentic–upon the real.

Since my project addresses the social production of space–the ways in which space is invested with constantly evolving social actions and relationships–specifically, the production of feminist or gendered social space, the collapse of a unified and unifying feminism, a feminism in which gender is no longer the sole defining term, provides a fitting point of demarcation. For the purposes of this essay, the term "feminist space" will be employed to signify just one of numerous locations for the production and reproduction of culture: an apparatus for the reinvention and reorganization of subjectivity and for the generation of new meaning and/or popular knowledge(s). Feminist spaces are politically charged environments, oriented toward the dislocation of established frontiers and boundaries.

What concerns me here are the gendered, "elsewhere" or borderland spaces–social, discursive, and bodily–that serve as media for negotiating and fashioning new social (female) subjectivities. In this essay, I propose a reading of Audre Lorde's "biomythography" *Zami: A New Spelling of My Name* to illustrate the ways in which the "problem" of gender and the concept of identity politics not only inform the unfolding of Lorde's narrative but are inscribed in writing itself, invoking the possibility of a new discursive and historical subject.

Lorde's attention to "multiple registers of existence" (Alarcón 365) is evident in the prologue to *Zami* when she states: "I have always wanted to be both man and woman, to incorporate the strongest and richest parts of my mother and father within/into me" (7). In her essay "'A Nutmeg Nestled Inside Its Covering of Mace': Audre Lorde's *Zami*," Claudine Raynaud develops the idea–and the ideal–of androgyny, the mythic resolution of male and female, to explicate Lorde's text. In spite of Raynaud's lucid analysis, I suspect that Lorde is less interested in "reconciliation" than in the radical potential of "difference"–in keeping separate (unmaking) rather than rendering coherent the complexities of identity and history. Nevertheless, at the same time as Lorde insists upon the irreducibility of difference, she advances her body–the lesbian body in/of writing–as the very ground of meaning. It is this "contradiction" between lesbianism as an apparently stable identification and those multiple and intersecting differences which interrupt the possibility of any one secure "home" that I shall explore in this essay.

The lesbian body as signifier of a sexual difference sustained in the disjuncture with heterosexual "norms" is at the core of *Zami*. Lorde's text articulates the primacy of sexual desire which is from the beginning coded as "lesbian." The prologue's erasure of the paradigmatic Freudian triangle of mother, father, child–the Oedipal constellation which "authorizes" heterosexuality–in favor of "the elegantly strong triad of grandmother mother daughter" installs "woman forever" as arbiter of text/sex-uality. A far cry from the "woman-bonding" or "woman-loving" described by Faderman and others, *Zami*'s powerful, women-oriented women, women who can "enter a woman the way any man can" (7), are irreducibly *sexual*.[5] As Nicole Brossard writes (in another context), "[i]f it were not lesbian, this text would make no sense."

The lesbian body of Lorde's text is marked not only as the "site" of sexual pleasure, but is equated with the emergence of the *liminal* or *migratory* figure: ". . . when I was growing up, *powerful woman* equalled something else quite different from ordinary woman, from simply 'woman.' It certainly did not, on the other hand, equal 'man.' What then? What was the third designation?" (15, emphasis in the original). This, then, is the "I"/subject of the prologue–"the 'I' [that moves] back and forth, flowing in either direction or both directions as needed" (7). The liminal figure is lesbian–is liminal as a result of being lesbian. This is "sexual difference" as Teresa de Lauretis recognizes it: homosexual as distinct from hommo-sexual, the latter representing "sexual INdifference . . . a single practice and representation of the sexual" (156).[6]

*Zami* is shaped by the articulation of gender and sexuality. An attempt to redesign gender through the lens of sexuality, Lorde's narrative undoes the fixity of "gender identity," invoking a border-land space of performance, costume, theater, and roles as a land-scape for shifting permutations of the feminine.

For the space of one summer, Audre and Gennie, her first friend, transform New York into a threshold space, a world of their own making, fashioning a world of possibilities out of their experience as outsiders/outlaws:

> That summer all of New York, including its museums and parks and avenues, was our backyard. What we wanted and couldn't afford, we stole money from our mothers for.
> Bandits, Gypsies, Foreigners of all degree, Witches, Whores, and Mexican Princesses–there were appropriate costumes for every role, and appropriate places in the city to go to play them all out. There were always things to do to match whomever we decided to be. (88)

New York is converted into a play space, its streets–a theater, the girls–tricksters, deliberately assuming the masquerade for their "assaults" on the city. Tricksters are liminal figures who "emerge from or imply anti-structural states."[7] Their strategies reverse the order of things, subverting the meanings that govern the systems within which we live and work.

Inserting the body into history (her story) means historicizing the body–making the lesbian body an historical force. Consequently, the lesbian body participates in the transformation of meanings; it becomes a point of articulation for new meanings. In *Zami*, the lesbian body dislodges the "reliability" of gender as fixed and knowable, exposing the plural, contested meanings that converge on the term and the ways in which gender is determined in different cultural discourses. For Monique Wittig, lesbian desire transforms "gender"–the mark of heterosexuality and the agent of women's oppression: "Gender is the linguistic index of the political opposition between the sexes" (64). For both Wittig and Lorde, foregrounding the discontinuity between sex and gender augments lesbian desire as an intervention into knowledge which illuminates the play of meanings negotiated across bodies. For Lorde, however, it is the *specificity* of lesbian difference, not sexuality alone, which establishes gender as a site of indeterminacy: ". . . Muriel seemed to believe that as lesbians, we were all outsiders and all equal in our outsiderhood. . . . It was wishful thinking based on little fact, the ways in which it was true languished in the shadow of those ways in which it would always be false" (203).

In Lorde's text, it is a lesbian frame of reference that operates, not as a consistent and coherent identity but rather, as a discursive and conceptual "ground" for mediating social meanings and cultural practices. And this frame of reference is always intersected by race, class, ethnicity, and personal history. Since it is there at the beginning and origin of writing, at first glance, Lorde's lesbianism might appear to undercut the otherwise partial, constructed, and historically located "self" articulated in *Zami*. Lorde presents her sexuality as *defining*, as central to experience and identity. How, then, to explain these tensions between the fixity of lesbianism and the mutability and multiplicity of subject positions as they are taken up in Lorde's text?

In *Zami*, language is linked inextricably to memories of the mother, to the bodies of women–most specifically to memories of the mother's body–and to the primacy of sexual desire and pleasure:

> The click of her wedding ring against the wooden headboard. She is awake. I get up and go over and crawl into my mother's bed. Her smile. Her glycerine-flannel smell. The warmth. She reclines upon her back and side, one arm extended, the other flung across her forehead. . . . Her large soft breasts beneath the buttoned flannel of her nightgown. Below, the rounded swell of her stomach, silent and inviting touch. (33)

Her mother, too, is "different"–not like other mothers–and while Audre's relations with her mother are volatile and full of misunderstandings, it is from her that Lorde acquires the skills to survive in an alien environment (104). These connections with women signal moments of safety and security, of "home-comings": "Loving Ginger that night was like coming home to a joy I was meant for" (139). But these gestures, like writing itself, are always contextualized; they arise out of history–or "histories"–and they call attention to the ways in which the subject is constituted through/in language: being "Black, female and gay" meant that "we could not afford to settle for one easy definition, one narrow individuation of self" (226).

Audre Lorde's *Zami* speaks to the complex permutations of the self–to plurality *and* specificity. For while it is the specificity of lesbianism that is at the forefront of, that governs, writing/the rhetorical "body" of *Zami*, nevertheless, lesbianism is never an essential or totalizing identity. It is always intersected and traversed by shifting and often contradictory matrices of "difference." Lorde locates and relocates herself and her narrator within the different but overlapping histories of the people and communities among whom she lives, showing that we are the products of multiple and various "homes":

> Being women together was not enough. We were different.
> Being gay-girls together was not enough. We were different.
> Being Black together was not enough. We were different.
> Being Black women together was not enough. We were different.
> Being Black dykes together was not enough. We were different.
> (226)

*Zami* follows Audre Lorde, its author/narrator, on a journey from Harlem to Stamford, Connecticut, on to Mexico, and back to New York City. Informed and nourished by her mother's stories of Carriacou, Audre's "geography" traces the contours of a longed-for world–a home deferred, elsewhere. This proliferation of homes constitutes the text itself as a space of multiplicity and heterogeneity, and its narrator as an *exile*, moving between various configurations of power and meaning: "This now, here, was a space, some temporary abode, never to be considered forever nor totally binding nor defining" (13).

It is the impossibility, perhaps inadvisability, of any one "home" that undermines the essentialist project of reducing lesbianism or the lesbian body to a single signifier. As Joan Nestle brilliantly demonstrates in her essays on butch-femme relationships, continued attempts to reduce the plurality of meanings attached to lesbianism will have to contend with the inadequacy of former categories of sex and gender which all too often efface subtleties of history and lived experience.[8] While Lorde celebrates the "images of women, kind and cruel, that led me home" (3), "home" for the narrator of *Zami* remains elsewhere: a liminal, in-between space, unattainable except provisionally during moments of connection to other women. The instability of "home" in this text illustrates how the production of a "safe home," sanctuary, or immune space displaces discussion of the exclusions required in its name.[9]

Lorde's "journey to this house of myself" maps identity as migratory and fugitive–a refusal to submit to any position or location as final or static. Traveling to Washington, D.C., with her family on her graduation from eighth grade, Audre experiences segregation first-hand when her family is refused service in an ice-cream parlor, an event which sharpens her own growing awareness of racial "difference." Later, when she travels to Washington again, this time with the Committee to Free the Rosenbergs, her "difference"–racial, sexual–is converted into political activism. Nevertheless, even their common political struggle proves insufficient to the formation of close bonds between Lorde and her "progressive" colleagues:

> But my feelings of connection with most of the people I met in progressive circles were . . . tenuous. . . . I could imagine comrades, Black and white, among whom color and racial differences could be openly examined and talked about, nonetheless, one day asking me accusingly, 'Are you or have you ever been a member of a homosexual relationship?' For them, being gay was 'bourgeois and reactionary,' a reason for suspicion and shunning.[10] (149)

The intersections of race, sex, "politics," and location–historical and geographical (re)connections–traverse *Zami*. For example, in Mexico among the American colony in Cuernavaca, victims, many of them, of McCarthyist purges, Audre discovers political courage in excess of sexual openness. While in New York, "[d]owntown in the gay bars I was a closet student and an invisible Black, uptown at

Hunter I was a closet dyke and a general intruder" (179). Nowhere, however, is "the field of difference as a net of power," in Katie King's words, more marked and troubling than in Lorde's anatomy of lesbian life as it unfolded in the lesbian bars of the 1950s.

Lesbianism was uncharted territory. The bars–places of temporary refuge–were often raided by the police, who subjected their occupants to intermittent surveillance and censure, checking to make certain that women were dressed "appropriately."[11] In the bars, Audre was known as Ky-Ky, neither butch nor femme, and thus too unconventional even for the gay community. Her rejection of roles and her presence as one of few Black lesbians in predominantly white bars meant that, once again, Lorde's "identity" could not be unproblematically accommodated. Her "difference" interrupted the network of codes that sustained the social organization of the lesbian bar, establishing the gendered social space of the bar as a contested domain rather than a condensed symbol of sexual identity: "This was the first separation, the piece outside love. But I turned away short of the meanings of it, afraid to examine the truths difference might lead me to" (204).[12]

In spite of a shared sexuality, lesbian identity, even in the bars, derived from difference and displacement. While Lorde's project seems to be how to signify "lesbian" in white America, Black lesbians, as Katie King has persuasively demonstrated, were also kept from one another by complex structures of race and power. King shows how, in the contested space of the lesbian bar, "the structures keeping black women from each other is represented by the color-coding of butch/femme, the codes of race and power" (327). The "attraction and terror" of roles lay in their potential to echo and thus expose the social dynamics of white/black relations and in their internalization as "effective strategies of survival" (328).

*Zami* narrates the journey of a woman unwilling "to relinquish any of the complicated parts of herself." Neither her mother's home nor the home she makes with her lover, Muriel ("No more playing house"), do more than hold alienation temporarily at bay, for Lorde is painfully aware of her "differences," of an identity constituted in response to the various spaces she inhabits but always exceeding and thus dislocating their boundaries. Lorde's pursuit of "safe space" is attenuated by conflict, loss, and silence–the inevitable repressions demanded by nostalgia and the desire for sameness/ community. The only possibility is a community of exiles and outcasts: "However imperfectly, we tried to build a community of sorts where we could, at the very least, survive within a world we correctly perceived to be hostile to us" (179). At times, "home" may provide its residents with support and security, even intimacy; at other times, however, it operates as an obstacle to self-expression and desire.

In place of any permanent "home"–home as a fixed referent– Lorde exploits the partiality of home. Her text enacts Rich's "politics of location," continuously staging and restaging the construction of identity within different and fluctuating social and discursive domains. She writes: "In a paradoxical sense, once I accepted my position as different from the larger society as well as from any single sub-society–Black or gay–I felt I didn't have to try so hard. To be accepted. To look femme. To be straight. To look straight. To be proper. To look 'nice.' To be liked. To be loved. To be approved" (181).

*Zami* is no conventional lesbian autobiography. As Biddy Martin effectively demonstrates in a recent essay, "Lesbian Identity and Autobiographical Difference(s)," recent autobiographical writings by lesbians "take up, even as they work against, already conventional lesbian-feminist narratives of lesbian experience" (82). Arguing against totalizing concepts of lesbianism which posit lesbianism as a "profoundly life-saving, self-loving, political resistance to patriarchal definitions and limitations" (88), Martin points to collections like *This Bridge Called My Back* and essays like Minnie Bruce Pratt's "Identity: Skin Blood Heart" as examples of the ways in which lesbianism figures as the basis for "communities" forged not in essential identities or natural unities but in liberation, however temporary, from uniformity to general norms. The possibility of enacting lesbian desire sets the stage for the dissolution of boundaries around "identity" and for the relocation of meaning "elsewhere"–in resistant or counter-discourses which challenge the hegemony of heterosexuality.

The critical and epistemological juncture instantiated by *Zami*'s migratory lesbian body (the "absolute" subject of the text) undercuts gender identity from a discursive position outside of/eccentric to heterosexuality. While this is reminiscent of Wittig's "perspective given in homosexuality" which deterritorializes the economy of the same (the phallic economy), Lorde's text diffuses lesbian identity into difference and diversity. She celebrates (without romanticizing or reifying) the lesbian body, not the "essential" or authentic body of much lesbian autobiography but the lesbian body constructed "[in] desire and across multiple locations of class, race, language, [and] social relations" (Zita 342). Within the erotic economy of Lorde's autobiography, lesbian meaning begins with the body but is annexed to an interrogation of the multiple determinants that figure in any one woman's social position and which inscribe gender as a relational category dependent upon a politics of difference and location. In *Zami*, the lesbian body dislodges the "reliability" of gender as a fixed, knowable category, exposing the plural, contested meanings that converge on the term and the ways in which "gender" is determined in different cultural discourses.

Inventing history–bioMYTHography–as the context within which the self is forged yields a popular or collective memory, a new kind of knowledge generated in specific, localized spaces. Within this context, "home" is recast as a frame of reference–a location with respect to knowledge and meaning. In *Zami*, "real homes" are temporary, impoverished, and uncertain. There is no privileged space, no privileged discourse–only "the very house of difference." When, as an adult, Lorde discovers her mother's home (her "geography") on a map, she writes, "Once *home* was a long way off, a place I had never been to but knew out of my mother's mouth. I only discovered its latitudes when Carriacou was no longer my home" (256). As a resident of various "homes," *Zami*'s narrator actualizes Rich's claim that "a place on the map is also a place in history" (212). To the extent that "[her] life had become increasingly a bridge and field of women" (255), Lorde's thinking and writing are informed by her lesbian identity. Acknowledging the simultaneity of identities, however, complicates the ideology of lesbian subjectivity as authentic, unified, and waiting to be discovered. In its place is a lesbian body constructed across a plural and complex social, historical, and cultural "ground"; it is the vantage point from which the Black lesbian poet tells her story.

# NOTES

1. Challenges to the unity of feminist approaches to "identity" grew out of concrete experiences of exclusion. The focus was–and continues to be–on difference as an effect of social relations, that is, on a *politics* of difference. Consequently, the critics of gender theory insist upon the ways we are constrained and *liberated* by identity. As Susan Bordo puts it: "To deny the unity and stability of identity is one thing. . . . [T]he dream of limitless multiple embodiments . . . is another" ("Feminism, Postmodernism, and Gender-Scepticism" 145).

2. Pratt's groundbreaking essay, "Identity: Skin Blood Heart," which explores the construction of "identity" across multiple locations and cultural contexts, occupies a central place in my work. In her autobiographical intervention into the dynamics of inclusion-exclusion, Pratt writes about the lack of protection provided by "home": "I had expected to have that place with my children. I expected it as my *right*. I did not understand I had been exchanging the use of my body for that place" (27).

3. The Combahee River Collective was concerned with the question of "difference" in both a practical and theoretical context. The multiple determinants that figure in any woman's social position are organized around the body; while the body cannot be reduced to a fixed location, "multiple embodiments" is not a synonym for no body at all.

4. See, for example, Judith Butler, *Gender Trouble: Feminism and the Subversion of Identity*, for a restaging of the "order" of sex, gender, and desire. Butler calls for a new politics of subjectivity which would not foreclose its multivalent "cultural articulations." Butler's highly sophisticated readings of feminist theory caution against normative or exclusionary practices and/or categories–an approach her work shares with mine. Nevertheless, while the performative aspects of gender–gender as artifice–undo gender as a fixed, stable category and demonstrate the discontinuity between sex and gender, the female body has profound consequences for all those who live in it.

5. Among the best-known proponents of a lesbian "essence" are Lillian Faderman, *Surpassing the Love of Men: Romantic Friendship and Love between Women from the Renaissance to the Present*; Sarah Hoagland, *Lesbian Ethics: Toward New Value*; Adrienne Rich, "Compulsory Heterosexuality and Lesbian Existence"; and Sheila Jeffreys, *The Spinster and her Enemies: Feminism and Sexuality, 1880-1930*.

6. Cited in de Lauretis, "Sexual Indifference and Lesbian Representation," the phrase is attributed to Luce Irigaray. De Lauretis looks at the ways in which lesbian writers have attempted to separate gender (sexual difference organized around the phallus) from sexuality. She provides a thoughtful analysis of the current impasse of lesbian representation caught up in the discourses and practices of "hommo-sexuality."

7. For a modern-day report on "tricksters," see Sharon Thompson, "'Drastic Entertainments': Teenage Mothers' Signifying Narratives." The concept of the trickster is evoked when Lorde writes, "Muriel and I were reinventing the world together" (209).

8. For Joan Nestle's rewriting of the sex-gender "connection," see *A Restricted Country*. Nestle's essays, especially those which explore butch-femme relationships in the 1950s, are attentive to history without claiming any direct or "natural" juncture between sex, gender, and desire. While seeking to expand the horizons of representation, Nestle foregrounds the discontinuities between sex and gender and the ways in which lesbians negotiate the meanings of "bodies."

9. For more on "home" and the exclusionary practices carried out in its name, see Pratt, "Identity: Skin Blood Heart" and her breakdown of the imaginary unity and homogeneity of space.

10. In "This Huge Light of Yours" in *A Restricted Country*, Joan Nestle reveals the contradictions and intersections "between kept silences and new honesties." Her negotiation of the closet of (self)-representation during her participation in the Civil Rights Movement illuminates the shifting effects of space on identity.

11. Nestle's "Lesbians and Prostitutes: An Historical Sisterhood" (*A Restricted Country*) demonstrates the part played by dress codes in the lesbian bar: ". . . I was reminded of the warning older Lesbians gave me in the fifties as I prepared for a night out: always wear three pieces of women's clothing so the vice squad can't bust you for transvestism" (162).

12. In spite of Lorde's indictment of roles and her own refusal of either label, butch or femme, Davis and Kennedy write: "[Ki-Ki] didn't refer to an abandonment of role defined sex but rather to a shifting of sexual posture depending on one's bed partner. . . . It was grounded absolutely in role playing" (439).

## WORKS CITED

Alarcón, Norma. "The Theoretical Subject(s) of *This Bridge Called My Back* and Anglo-American Feminism." *Making Face, Making Soul. Haciendo Caras*. Ed. Gloria Anzaldúa. San Francisco: Aunt Lute Foundation Books, 1990. 356-369.

Bordo, Susan. "Feminism, Postmodernism, and Gender-Scepticism." *Feminism/Postmodernism*. Ed. Linda J. Nicholson. New York: Routledge, 1990. 133-156.

Butler, Judith. *Gender Trouble: Feminism and the Subversion of Identity*. New York: Routledge, 1990.

Combahee River Collective. "A Black Feminist Statement." *This Bridge Called My Back: Writings by Radical Women of Color*. Ed. Cherríe Moraga and Gloria Anzaldúa. New York: Kitchen Table: Women of Color Press, 1983. 210-218.

Davis, Madeline, and Elizabeth Lapovsky Kennedy. "Oral History and the Study of Sexuality in the Lesbian Community: Buffalo, New York, 1940-1960." *Hidden from History: Re-claiming the Gay and Lesbian Past*. Ed. Martin Bauml Duberman, Martha Vicinus, & George Chauncey, Jr. New York: NAL Books, 1989. 426-440.

de Lauretis, Teresa. "Sexual Indifference and Lesbian Representation." *Theatre Journal*, Spring 1988: 155-177.

Faderman, Lillian. *Surpassing the Love of Men: Romantic Friendship and Love between Women from the Renaissance to the Present.* New York: William Morrow, 1981.

King, Katie. "Audre Lorde's Lacquered Layerings: The Lesbian Bar as a Site of Literary Production." *Cultural Studies*, Vol. 2 (1988): 321-342.

Lorde, Audre. *Zami: A New Spelling of My Name.* Freedom, CA: The Crossing Press, 1982.

Martin, Biddy. "Lesbian Identity and Autobiographical Difference(s)." *Life/Lines: Theorizing Women's Autobiography.* Ed. Bella Brodzki and Celeste Schenck. Ithaca: Cornell University Press, 1988. 77-103.

Nestle, Joan. *A Restricted Country.* Ithaca: Firebrand Books, 1987.

Pratt, Minnie Bruce. "Identity: Skin Blood Heart." *Yours in Struggle: Three Feminist Perspectives on Anti-Semitism and Racism.* By Elly Bulkin, Minnie Bruce Pratt, and Barbara Smith. Brooklyn, New York: Long Haul Press, 1984. 11-63.

Raynaud, Claudine. "'A Nutmeg Nestled Inside its Covering of Mace': Audre Lorde's *Zami.*" *Life/Lines: Theorizing Women's Autobiography.* Ed. Bella Brodzki and Celeste Schenck. Ithaca: Cornell University Press, 1988. 221-242.

Rich, Adrienne. "Notes toward a Politics of Location." *Blood, Bread, and Poetry: Selected Prose, 1979-1985.* New York: W.W. Norton & Co., 1986. 210-231.

Thompson, Sharon. "'Drastic Entertainments': Teenage Mothers' Signifying Narratives." *Uncertain Terms: Negotiating Gender in American Culture.* Ed. Faye Ginsburg and Anna Lowenhaupt Tsing. Boston: Beacon Press, 1990. 269-281.

Wittig, Monique. "The Mark of Gender." *The Poetics of Gender.* Ed. Nancy K. Miller. New York: Columbia University Press, 1986. 63-73.

Zita, Jacquelyn N. "Lesbian Body Journeys: Desire Making Difference." *Lesbian Philosophies and Cultures.* Ed. Jeffner Allen. New York: State University of New York Press, 1990. 327-246.

# *Fierce Love* and Fierce Response: Intervening in the Cultural Politics of Race, Sexuality, and AIDS

David Román, PhD

The University of Pennsylvania

**SUMMARY.** In their performances of *Fierce Love*, the Pomo Afro Homos (Postmodern African American Homosexuals) enact some of the experiences of black gay men. Through performance, the trio intervenes in the prevailing mythologies around black and gay identities, but especially black gay identities, in the age of AIDS. This essay begins by examining two dominant productions in recent U.S. culture that display and proliferate anxieties about black gay bodies: John Guare's play *Six Degrees of Separation* and Magic Johnson's unsettling HIV disclosure. The Pomo Afro Homos address the phenomenon of containing black gay sexuality by insisting that the theatre and its inherent role in offering representations be seen as a viable site for contestation for black gay men.

At the beginning of their collaborative performance, *Fierce Love*, Pomo Afro Homos fill the stage with a cappella/gospel harmonies:

---

Correspondence may be addressed to the author at: Department of English, University of Pennsylvania, Philadelphia, PA 19107.

[Haworth co-indexing note]: "*Fierce Love* and Fierce Response: Intervening in the Cultural Politics of Race, Sexuality, and AIDS." Román, David. Co-published simultaneously in the *Journal of Homosexuality* (The Haworth Press, Inc.) Vol. 26, No. 2/3, 1993, pp. 195-219; and *Critical Essays: Gay and Lesbian Writers of Color* (ed: Emmanuel S. Nelson) The Haworth Press, Inc., 1993, pp. 195-219. Multiple copies of this article/chapter may be purchased from The Haworth Document Delivery Center [1-800-3-HAWORTH; 9:00 a.m. - 5:00 p.m. (EST)].

... these are some of our stories

our passions and fears

our victories and tears

drink them like water

savor them like wine

spread them like fire

We are

an endangered species

But our stories must be told . . .[1]

The opening song, which frames the performance, immediately invokes the heterogeneity of black gay experience(s) which *Fierce Love* will bring to life. Brian Freeman, Eric Gupton, and Djola Bernard Branner, the three performers who together are the Pomo Afro Homos (postmodern, African American homosexuals) begin *Fierce Love* by demanding the recognition of multiple black gay male subject positions. The Pomos enact what Kobena Mercer, writing on marginalized or minoritized situations, has explained as speaking *from* the specificity of experiences of marginality rather than speaking *for* the entire community from which they come (204, emphasis in original). Pomo Afro Homos at once provide a forum for some of the experiences of black gay men while reminding audiences of all colors that the juncture of black and gay, as novelist Steven Corbin explains, need not be read only as "a major two-point score on the shit list of oppression" (78). Rather, as the Pomos demonstrate, being black and gay calls for a cultural politics that recognizes and intervenes in the dominant social inscriptions around race and sexuality. The double bind of black homophobia and queer racism can exhaust the psychic resources necessary to counter such systemic oppression. With this in mind, it becomes easy to champion the Pomo Afro Homos for simply taking the risk of asserting black gay identities in such a visible venue as the theatre. However, as I hope to demonstrate, the Pomo Afro Homos go much further than simply staging and celebrating difference. *Fierce Love* must be read as a direct intervention in the prevailing mythologies around both black and gay identities, but especially black gay identities, and as a critical practice intervening in the historically situated popular discourses on race and sexuality in contemporary U.S. culture. That these same discourses contribute to an AIDS ideology rendering black gay men invisible suggests all the more the urgency of the messages within *Fierce Love*.

In order to establish my argument for *Fierce Love* as a necessary intervention, I'll begin by calling into question some of the dominant productions in recent U.S. culture that display and proliferate anxieties about black gay bodies. Specifically, I will discuss John Guare's enormously successful play *Six Degrees of Separation* (1990) and Magic Johnson's unsettling HIV disclosure (1991). *Six Degrees of Separation*, I'll argue, not only depicts the racist fears and anxieties of white heterosexuals and gays but, in light of its success with critics and audiences, perpetuates certain racialized sexual discourses. The Magic Johnson incident demonstrates both the racist discourse of white America associating blackness with AIDS and the rampant homophobia prevalent among U.S. blacks. In both cases, I am interested in both the production and reception of these two seemingly incongruent occasions and how these two moments reveal current cultural fantasies constructed to contain black gay sexuality. Pomo Afro Homos address this phenomenon by insisting that the theatre and its inherent role in offering representations be seen as a viable and necessary site for contestation. In this sense, Pomo Afro Homos join other gay men of color who have found theatre and performance a viable means of intervening in the cultural politics of race, sexuality, and AIDS (see Román, "Teatro").

## SIX DEGREES OF SEPARATION
### *AND THE SPECTACLE OF EXPERIENCE:*
### *BLACK GAY MEN AND THE EXPERIENCE*
### *OF INVISIBILITY*

By the end of John Guare's celebrated comedy, *Six Degrees of Separation*, Ouisa Kittredge, the white Upper-Eastside affluent liberal heroine of the play, is faced with what for her seems an impossible dilemma. Guare's play details the interruption of the lives of

Ouisa and her husband Flan by a black gay man, identified only as Paul, who arrives at their doorstep one evening claiming to be the son of Sidney Poitier and a Harvard classmate of their children. Claiming to have been mugged outside their Fifth Avenue apartment, Paul succeeds in winning the confidences of the couple so much so that he's invited to spend the night. In the morning, he'll join his father who is directing the film version of *Cats* and who is scheduled to arrive the next day to begin auditions. For Ouisa, charmed by Paul's stories of their children and his supposed father, Paul's arrival offers her an opportunity to connect emotionally with another human being: "I just loved the kid so much. I wanted to reach out to him" (31).

While much of the tone of the play in these early scenes can be categorized as comic, and Ouisa as the central voice of irony, once Paul's scheme is revealed Ouisa moves from comic disengagement to tragic identification. Everyone, she's read somewhere, is "separated by only six other people. Six degrees of separation . . . But to find the right six people" (81). For Ouisa this concept holds the key to, as well as the "torture" of, intimacy: that despite differences, there is a fundamental humanity shared by all people. Once aware that she's been duped, Ouisa still wants to hold on to the "experience" of Paul, the revitalization that the black gay man has provided for her through his attentive and demonstrative interest in her life. Moreover, Paul's humanity must be available to her on some level even if he is neither the son of Sidney Poitier nor her children's classmate.

By the end of the play, Paul is arrested by the police. Ouisa, not knowing Paul's true identity, now has no idea how to help him. "Why does it mean so much to you?" her husband asks (116). Transformed by her experience with Paul, Ouisa now questions the security of her liberal politics and identity. Her own epiphanic rhetorical question–"How do we *keep* the experience?"–follows her own insistence upon not turning Paul into an anecdote "to dine out on" (117). The play ends with Ouisa's own enigmatic and unarticulated scene of transformation. She imagines Paul once more, this time describing the two-sided Kandinsky painting that hangs in the Kittredge home: "The Kandinsky. It's painted on two sides. [He glows for a moment and is gone. She considers. She smiles. The

Kandinsky begins its slow revolve]" (120). The painting becomes the emblem of the play's leitmotif that "there are two sides to every story" (65) and announces Ouisa's own reconnection with her imagination. The conclusion offers Ouisa's epiphany as a model for its audience, or as Frank Rich writes, "a transcendent theatrical experience that is itself a lasting vision of the humane new world of which Mr. Guare and his New Yorkers so hungrily dream" (Rich, Review). Rich is not alone in his appraisal of the play. Most of the play's reviews in the popular press offer similar readings and champion Guare for writing a play that captures what is described as the mood and moral dilemma of an era in U.S. urban relations.[2]

If critics (and presumably audiences) are drawn to Ouisa's situation and revel in her resolute determination to "keep the experience," it seems logical if not necessary to interrogate the role that Paul–Guare's phantasmatic construction displaced onto his character, Ouisa–plays in the drama and determine how Paul's race and sexuality figure in for Ouisa and her audiences' own self-imaginings. Race is immediately and obviously marked in the play by the actors who perform the roles and further established by the textual narrative that insists on maintaining whiteness and blackness as two opposing defining social categories. In the earliest scenes, audiences are introduced to white characters and actors who set up these differences. The story addressed to the audience by Ouisa and Flan begins a series of enactments of the events leading up to Paul's arrival in their home. The Kittredges are entertaining one of Flan's prospective clients, Geoffrey, a wealthy white British South African who can help finance Flan's private art dealings. South African politics and race relations become the litmus test for white liberal policies and affinities, as the Kittredges delicately, and quite humorously, maneuver around Geoffrey's obvious pomposity–"One needs to stay [in South Africa] to educate the black workers and we'll know we've been successful when they kill us" (10)–in order to secure the two million dollars Flan needs to close a deal. But if Geoffrey's views of South Africa proved a challenge for the Kittredges, Paul's immediate arrival at their door puts into motion the vexed history of U.S. race relations for the white liberal politics they have been espousing all evening. Paul's seductive narrative detailing the class privileges available to him as the son of Sidney

Poitier ("I don't feel American. I don't even feel Black," 30) puts Ouisa and Flan at ease, and charms Geoffrey (Ouisa: "Even Geoffrey was touched," 25) so much so that he not only offers Flan the money, but leaves New York with the idea for a Black American Film Festival in South Africa.

Only when Ouisa discovers Paul the next morning receiving oral sex from a white male hustler is the goodwill of the previous evening retracted. The spectacle of sexuality *and* race–specifically of a black gay man–is too much for her, as she throws Paul out of their apartment. The Kittredges soon discover that they have not been the only ones who have hosted Paul. The rest of the play consists of the Kittredges–along with the other conned white liberal socialites–attempting to reconcile their seduction by Paul's rhetoric with their own unimaginative lives, although it is Ouisa who is most concerned with understanding these events. At first, she can only come up with the glib comment that "it seems the common thread linking us all is an overwhelming need to be in the movie of *Cats*" (68), but as she continues to unpack the events of the Paul incident she discovers that his presence has initiated a series of questions about herself, questions about her identity that can no longer be left unanswered. The black gay man thus becomes the vehicle for Ouisa to reevaluate her own beliefs and sense of self.

John Clum argues that the scene of frontal nudity dramatically stages the Kittredges' "feared unknown–a gay black stranger, an alien who brings into the Kittredge house and sexless marriage a threatening alien sexuality" (19). Clum's reading, however, focuses on how the naked male body of the white hustler represents "not male sexuality, but gay sexuality" (21). Clum continues: "In the world of Guare's play, blackness provokes a mixture of liberal guilt and uncertainty, but gayness provokes chaos" (22). While I agree with Clum's overall reading, I want to focus more specifically on the intertwining of race and sexual politics that eludes Clum in these quotes. Gayness alone is not what "provokes chaos" but, more to the point, Paul–as a black gay man–embodies the chaos in the play. That Paul is the only non-white character in the play further facilitates such a reading. This chaos is construed at one point or another by all the characters in the play. He is described as "this fucking black kid crack addict," "a black fraud," continually associated with drugs, urban crime, and AIDS (Ouisa to Paul: "Are you suicidal? Do you have AIDS? Are you infected?"). He is fetishized as a sexual object by Ouisa who enjoys watching him; by Trent Conway, the young white who teaches Paul the argot of "rich people" in exchange for Paul's body; and by Rick, the young aspiring actor from Utah, who, after his sexual encounter with Paul, commits suicide by jumping off a building. It is Paul and not the white hustler whose sexuality is never clear, who becomes the site of white liberal anxieties. *Six Degrees* demonstrates that being both black and gay only heightens the suspicions of the white heterosexual characters who interpret black and gayness as doubly duplicitous and inherently associated with AIDS. Yet, in light of these various incidents Paul is still always cast as an "experience": one that must be contained within the racialized sexual discourse of white liberalism.

While his race and sexuality are staged as a spectacle of difference, if not chaos, Paul, who is represented in *Six Degrees of Separation* as the ultimate transgression, is contained in precisely the anecdotal narratives that Ouisa sets out to avoid. Only Rick, who moved to New York with his girlfriend, shares the same profundity that Ouisa experienced with Paul. After a night of rented tuxedos and dancing at the Rainbow Room, Paul fucks Rick during a carriage ride through Central Park. Rick addresses this experience directly to the audience in the same manner that Ouisa conveys her stories: "It was the greatest night I ever had and before we got home he kissed me on the mouth and he vanished" (91). The direct audience address circumvents the inevitable filtering of narrative events via anecdote or gossip. Rick's sexuality is never an issue in the play for anyone other than himself ("I didn't come here to be *this*," 91), although admittedly, his suicide immediately told as an anecdote in the next scene curtails any threat his homosexual activities may pose and provides a clichéd closure to his character. Indeed, all the white men who have sex with Paul–the hustler, Trent Conway, and Rick–are conveniently led off stage after their encounters with Paul, further indicating that it is black gay sexuality and not white gay men that poses the problem for Guare's white characters. The fact that all of Paul's sexual relations are with white men further fuels the crisis in *Six Degrees*. Black gay sexuality is constructed in the play as duplicitous, aggressive, and uncontainable, rendering white men passive, penetrable, and as Clum suggests, "unmanned" (22).

Such a racialized sexual discourse eludes mainstream critics. The focus of the popular press centers on Ouisa and Stockard Channing's brilliant performance in the central role. Ouisa's journey is universalized not only by the production, but by critics who see in Ouisa the spiritual awakening necessary to resolve the effects of a postmodern politics of doubt and despair. Once again, Frank Rich–in a second review of the play published in the *New York Times* only two weeks after his first–leads the critical acclaim:

> What finally allows *Six Degrees of Separation* to become a touching, beautiful, sensitive work is that Mr. Guare doesn't waste time assigning blame for all the separations that turn a city's people into what Holden Caulfield called phonies. Instead the playwright points the way–by the lustrous examples of Ouisa's redemptive spiritual journey to authenticity and his own elevated art–to a transcendent alternative to the inhuman urban collage. This play invades an audience's soul by forcing it to confront the same urgent question asked of its New Yorkers. If we didn't come here to be this, then who do we intend to be? ("Guidebook")

Rich's notion that *Six Degrees* speaks to a specific New York milieu suggests that the play targets the specific issues of a certain constituency–mainly a white politically liberal elite. The venue of the performance, first at the smaller Newhouse Theatre and then the Vivian Beaumont (both at New York's Lincoln Center), would support this idea.

The performance venue, the mainstream review process–in particular at the *New York Times*–along with the issues and characters of the play, all contribute to the interests of a specific audience that is construed as both normative and universal by the very operations of the theatre industry. Audiences entering the theatre are asked to identify with Ouisa and share her interpretation of Paul. And since Ouisa participates with all of Guare's white characters in the racialized sexual discourse that they use to construct Paul, there is little room for audiences to question the assumptions that the play and the production offer as truths. Paul can only be defined as a spectacle of difference recast as an experience for liberal whites. As Guare's creation and Ouisa's fantasy, Paul has no identity other than the one imagined by Guare and his white characters. The ultimate irony brought forth by this process is that Paul could well be the son of Sidney Poitier, at least from the perspective of Paul's description of his supposed father: "My father, being an actor, has no real identity. . . He has no life–he has no memory–only the scripts producers send him in the mail through his agents. That's his past" (31). *Six Degrees of Separation* inadvertently stages how white privilege can erase black agency; blacks are actors who are given social scripts produced and imagined by others. Paul's identity, like Sidney Poitier's, is never known; instead, Paul remains to the end an experience for Ouisa offered by Guare to his audiences and, not surprisingly, ends up becoming the talk of the town.

*Six Degrees of Separation* is based in part on the true life story of David Hampton, a young black bisexual man who in the early 1980s posed as the son of Sidney Poitier to get inside elite and trendy New York establishments, and later into the homes of prominent New Yorkers, only to be arrested in 1983 and made to serve 21 months in prison.[3] The leap from Hampton's biography to Paul's case in Guare's play further demonstrates how black experience is translated into anecdote albeit under the rubric of art. Guare's play is inspired by the events of Hampton's life to the extent that Hampton felt he was entitled to a share of its profits. Hampton sued Guare, claiming that his personality deserved the same protection as patents, copyrights, or trademarks, only to have his case dismissed by the New York Supreme Court in May 1992.[4] The processing of David Hampton's experiences, reinterpreted by Guare in his construction of Paul and then presented to his central character Ouisa to offer back to audiences at Lincoln Center, sets up a series of transactions that tellingly reveal the limited discourses available within liberalism for discussing race and sexuality.[5] "There are two sides to every story," the play insists, but by offering only the one-sided perspective of white liberalism, *Six Degrees of Separation* obscures the actual experience of Paul. He remains the catalyst for whiteness to retain–at whatever cost–its centrality.

If *Six Degrees* demonstrated the limited discourses available to discuss black gay sexuality in the popular culture, Magic Johnson's announcement on November 7, 1991, of testing positive for HIV demonstrated that the way AIDS is addressed in relation to race and sexuality is also wanting. Despite the fact that black heterosexuals joined white gays and straights in the national forum on AIDS that followed Johnson's press conference, not all sides of the story were made available in the popular press. Gay men of color, especially black gay men, were denied the opportunity to voice how Johnson's announcement may help–or hinder–the battle waged against AIDS by gay men of color on a daily basis. Instead, what was played out in the weeks immediately following Johnson's announcement exhibited the insidious conflation invoked in the concept of "African AIDS" which erroneously associates blackness and AIDS, as well as sensationalist speculations of Johnson's "real" source of transmission.[6]

Magic Johnson's high profile since his disclosure has occasioned an unprecedented number of articles, editorials, radio shows, and TV discussions on AIDS, in particular (and not a moment too soon), on AIDS and communities of color. Johnson, singlehandedly with his announcement, returned AIDS to the international spotlight, so much so that even George Bush was forced to admit that he needed to improve his AIDS record. Leaders in communities of color were also forced to state their efforts to secure AIDS services, including health care and education, and cornered to go on the record for future implementations.[7] And yet the media frenzy surrounding Johnson's disclosure barely touched upon AIDS and gay and bisexual men of color. Johnson's own assurance on the Arsenio Hall Show that same week that he was "far from being a homosexual" was met with cheers of heterosexist, if not homophobic, complicity.[8] Six months later, Magic Johnson clarified his statement explaining that he wanted "everybody to know that [HIV] wasn't just a gay disease."[9] The interview, a cover story in the gay and lesbian publication *The Advocate*, was held "to start a dialogue with the gay and lesbian community" (36).

At the time of Magic Johnson's announcement, forty-four percent of all black men with AIDS cited unprotected sex with men as the source of contraction; moreover, twenty-three percent of all gay men with AIDS at this time were African Americans. And yet, as

Charles Stewart claims, black gay and bisexual men are "one of the largest and most invisible groups affected by the AIDS epidemic" (13). Stewart, a contributing editor of *BLK*, a black lesbian and gay periodical based in Los Angeles that has consistently reported on black gay and bisexual men and AIDS, further explains how it is that, despite these disturbing figures, gay and bisexual black men are the least targeted for assistance by either the government or non-profit agencies, pre- or post-infection. White gay community institutions, including AIDS service organizations, are often segregated, leaving black gays and bisexuals on the margins of inclusion. In order to counter the neglect by many white gay male AIDS organizations, AIDS agencies and councils addressing the specific concerns and needs of various people of color began appearing in the mid-1980s. Only one week before Magic Johnson's announcement, for example, the National Minority AIDS Council met in Los Angeles for its Annual Skills Building Conference. Over 600 people working to fight AIDS networked and exchanged information and strategies. Moreover, earlier that same month, the HIV and People of Color Conference held in Seattle brought hundreds of people of color together to form coalitions of support and power. Among the issues discussed in Los Angeles and in Seattle, and at like conferences across the country, is what has been awkwardly defined by HIV professionals as "non-gay identified men who have sex with men." Such men, who refuse to identify as gay or bisexual for whatever reasons, are perceived as posing a severe threat for the spread of AIDS. Mark Haile, however, explains that

> there is a construction of sexuality far more elaborate than mere 'straight' or 'gay,' especially in the black community. When coupled with the racism that is the history of this nation, that affects every aspect of life, the end result is a field of sexual identities for black lesbian and gay men that is identical to neither the white lesbian and gay community in America, nor the framework of sexual orientation as has been studied on the African continent. (23)

Rather than dismissing this sexual continuum as a readily available grid for the denial of homosexuality, Haile insists that communities of color should begin to recognize sexual variance within a more inclusive system than the current hetero/homo binarism. While non-gay identified men who have sex with other men need to have their communities understand and support the complexity of their sexual identifications, Haile makes sure to insist that Black gay and bisexual men should receive similar support. In other words, what is at issue is not the potential denial of non-gay identified men who have sex with men but rather the denial of out black and bisexual gays and lesbians by the larger African American community. It is precisely the systemic denial of black gay identity that contributes to the double bind of invisibility, what Michael Broder describes as the "twofold invisibility that black gay people face in this society, the invisibility of color, and the invisibility of sexuality" (7). If racism within the white gay community ostracizes black gays, homophobia in the black community only contributes to this black gay invisibility.

Many black gay and lesbian intellectuals and activists have been fighting this homophobia within the African American community and have written extensively on the subject. Ron Simmons, for instance, speculates that homophobia in the African American community is "not so much a fear of homosexuals but a fear that homosexuality will become pervasive in the community. Thus a homophobic person can accept a homosexual as an individual friend or family member, yet not accept homosexuality" (211). Barbara Smith offers a similar point and claims that the real issue is how "out" the individual is: "If you're a lesbian, you can have as many women as you want. If you're a gay man, you can have all the men you want. But just don't say anything about it or make it political" (see Gomez and Smith). Marlon Riggs, on the other hand, sees less tolerance:

> What lies at the heart, I believe, of black America's pervasive cultural homophobia is the desperate need for a convenient Other *within* the community, yet not truly *of* the community, an Other to which blame for the chronic identity crisis afflicting the black male psyche can be readily displaced... ("Black Macho" 254)

Riggs is concerned with the recent proliferation of derogatory and inflammatory representations of black gay men in the culture produced by heterosexual blacks. He cites examples from film, television, and popular music that display the fad for "negro faggotry." Such blatant disregard for the lives of black gay men, Riggs relates, demonstrates that "negro faggotry is the rage! Black gay men are not" (254). It has been up to black gay artists, like Riggs, to counter such stereotypes with self-made representations from the African American gay community. The same holds true for issues around AIDS and black gay men. In fact, it is essential to recognize this rage for "negro faggotry" within the context of black gay male invisibility in order to fully recognize the intervention efforts by black gay cultural activists. U.S. popular culture from *In Living Color* to *Six Degrees of Separation* intensifies the need for the assertion of black gay and bisexual identities, especially if the fight against AIDS is to succeed. Black gay cultural activists insist that the fight against AIDS and black gay invisibility must be fought on all fronts, including the theatre.

## FIERCE LOVE *AND* FIERCE RESPONSE: *POMO AFRO HOMOS* *AND THE QUESTION OF RECEPTION*

"There hasn't been anything like this in American theatre," Pomo Afro Homo Eric Gupton explains (qtd. in Miller, 13). Gupton is discussing *Fierce Love*, one of the few black gay collaborations in the history of U.S. theatre to openly and unabashedly present the issues of black gay men on stage. *Fierce Love* grew out of fellow Pomo Brian Freeman's interest "in developing an evening of safe sex stories" (23). When Freeman, Gupton, and Branner first met to discuss the project, they realized that they had a full evening of performance material that encompassed many facets of black gay life. *Fierce Love* premiered in January 1991 at Josie's Cabaret in San Francisco's Castro district, played in alternative performance spaces in Seattle, Chicago, and Los Angeles, and by the end of the year was performed at New York's Public Theater.

*Fierce Love* is composed of thirteen sections or stories from black gay life. Each story stands on its own as a fully realized presentation of black gay experience and may include all three performers or any one or two. The performance is formally designed to facilitate travel and adaptability. There is no set to speak of, props are minimal, and lighting and music cues are manageable enough to accommodate different performance venues. Part of this stripped-down-to-the-basics type theatre is undoubtedly due to limited finances; however the effect, like much current performance art, places the emphasis on narrative and the focus on the performers' bodies. But unlike solo performance, where voice and movement can be used to signal a shift in characterization and thus display the performer's versatility, the Pomos are able to manipulate this form more readily by staging any combination of their three bodies and voices. While the Pomos too display versatility, they inevitably destabilize any essentialized reading of their bodies since they cannot be reduced to any one notion of "African American Homosexual"; the postmodern, or pomo, is located in this freeplay of identity and performance. While the Pomos insist on being heard as black gay men, they offer no set reading of a black gay male identity. Spectators, regardless of race or sexual orientation, are forced to consider what it means to be black and gay. The Pomos perform multiple black gay identities; they continually shift the tone of the performance, disturbing an audience's expectations both formally and thematically.

After the short a capella prologue announcing the multiplicity of black gay male possibilities, the first item on the Pomo agenda is to zap Blaine and Antoine, the snap queens/movie critics of television's Emmy award winning black comedy series *In Living Color*, perhaps the most widely circulating images of black gay men in contemporary U.S. popular culture. A member of ACT-BLACK, a revolutionary organization of Pomo Afro Homos, storms the set of "Men on Mens" and threatens to out the two supposedly straight TV actors who have dropped the pretense of reviewing films and now "just look at mens." ACT-BLACK demands "an end to mainstream misappropriation of Negro Faggotry" and sends the snap happy pair into a fit of despair. Caught off guard, Blaine and Antoine respond, "Look Eldridge, we did politics in college . . . Hated it!" but they find themselves in no position to deny ACT-BLACK's complaint. The activist–as a supposed member of the Pomo Afro Homos, the militant black gay visibility group–mouths the concerns of Pomo Afro Homos, the black gay male performance trio. Black gay men, these Pomos show, will no longer allow the uninformed pilferage of black gay codes by heterosexual performers for the amusement of their equally ignorant heterosexual audiences. The fine art of the snap[10] is specific to the context of black gay lives and anyone who fails to recognize this context will be 'read' accordingly. The Pomos stage their own performance mission in this short comic scene; like the ACT-BLACK activist, their fellow Pomo Afro Homo, the performing Pomos will hold those accountable who either perpetuate black gay invisibility or participate in the cultural neglect of black gays.[11]

Once Blaine and Antoine are zapped offstage, the Pomos are able to present a series of alternative images which offer more insight into the actual experiences of black gay men. Ten vastly different scenes follow, each varying in tone, style, and point of view. Moreover, the Pomos are not afraid to stage the problematic and disturbing issues that many audience members would perhaps rather not see. "I Don't Want to Hear It!" the scene that immediately follows "Men on Mens," dramatically changes tone and stands to remind its viewers that the Pomos aren't simply on stage to replace Blaine and Antoine for the sake of audience amusement. To upset such expectations, *Fierce Love* next presents a serious and discomforting point of view of a non-gay identified man who has sex with other men. In "I Don't Want To Hear It!" Brian Freeman plays a working-class black who rides the audience for its assumption that he is gay:

> Gay? What is that, huh? Do I look like somebody's Gay to you? Yea, I like to catch a little taste of the other side now and then. That don't make me nobody's punk.

This scene could easily have been delivered as a critique of internalized homophobia and a bitter rebuttal to men who, while married and straight-appearing, continue to have sex with other men. Freeman's performance, however, simultaneously poses both a serious critique and an empathetic response to this man's situation. What, if anything, we are asked to consider, can the Castro gay community offer this working-class black man? Will the support from the predominantly white gay community match the understanding he receives from the African American community? At one point, the man actually confides his disgust for black gay men. Such black on black hate is sent up later in *Fierce Love* when we meet Peaches, Popcorn, and Pepper, three "effeminate black gay men" who, after years of suffering abuses as P.B.U.s ("poor, black, and ugly"), form in defiance the Just Us Club.

The Just Us Club, with its elaborate rituals and entitlements, shows how P.B.U.s counter the elitist tendencies of many gay men of color–"that's all them Bryant Gumbel lookin boys," explains Pepper–who frown on black queens not necessarily interested in, or economically privileged to, middle-class ideals. Rejected by whites for being black, the P.B.U.'s find little support from other black gays. Once again, the Pomos offer wicked humor that cuts both ways. At first, Pepper, Popcorn, and Peaches seem ridiculous in their affectations and nasty "dishing"; the three performers play this scene for laughs but the humor quickly turns when the P.B.U.'s lay down the law and refuse to be the last invites to the party. Since no one else will have them, they'll join forces to survive their neglected position in the underclass. In an act of solidarity, the P.B.U.s tighten their bonds–"tighter than Oprah's weave"–and form a club all their own. In other words, we are warned, don't go calling the Just Us Club for advice or a late night date, these girls are busy. By the end of the story, the Pomos have restored the dignity of the Just Us Club to the extent that when Pepper, Popcorn, and Peaches reclaim vogueing for all the "nellie sissies" and dance themselves off the stage, the *audience* is left with that empty feeling of exclusion.

In each of these scenes, and throughout *Fierce Love* the Pomos continually subvert the expectations of their audiences. Spectators are at once invited to share in the exploration of black gay life and then reminded that those who are not black and gay are more likely misunderstanding much of the performance. This insistence on positioning the audience "simultaneously inside and outside the comprehension of their performance" (Robinson) works to code *Fierce Love* in such a way that it always remains clear that these are stories by and about, and especially for, black gay men. "Just because the show is written for a specific community doesn't mean that other people are excluded. If they don't get certain jokes, they can ask," Brian Freeman explains in *The Advocate* (qtd. in Perry, 86).

While the Pomos perform *Fierce Love* for all audiences, spectators who don't share the experience of being black and gay are asked to think through their identification with, and self-positioning around the performance. One scene, "Sad Young Man," especially points to this process. In "Sad Young Man," a young black man tells of his experience growing up gay in a "Model Negro Family" residing in Roxbury, Massachusetts. Finding comfort in the records of Johnny Mathis and the words of the Rev. Dr. Martin Luther King, Jr., the young man grows to celebrate his identity despite the lack of support from both black heterosexuals and white gays. Freeman, who performs this monologue, continually punctuates his narrative with direct confrontations to the audience. "It's a black thing, you wouldn't understand," he matter-of-factly states.[12] Audience members who are not black and gay are brought into the story by the moving pseudo-autobiographical narrative of growing up gay in a black household, but Freeman has much more in mind than simply soliciting pity for his subject. "Sad Young Man," like Paul's narrative in *Six Degrees of Separation*, pulls liberal heartstrings but goes further in holding its audience complicit in such well-meaning politics. Nonblacks have much to learn about black culture and need to abolish their tokenistic practices of inclusion. Heterosexual blacks, on the other hand, have much to learn about homosexuality. The "Model Negro Family"–advocating civil rights for blacks–will need to come to terms with its many gay sons and daughters and fight for their rights as well. Freeman pulls the spectator into the narrative in effect to implicate spectatorial complicity in racism and homophobia. Black gays and lesbians, who presumably "get it," remain the ideal audience in this scene. Other gays and lesbians of color, who also must confront these paradigmatic structures of oppression, are led to consider the specificity of their own experiences. And yet, as this scene suggests, there remains a certain ambivalence regarding the place of non-white and non-black gays within this black/white and gay/straight polarization throughout *Fierce Love*. Viewing *Fierce Love* as a Latino gay man, for example, I shifted throughout the performance from direct identification to implicit incrimination. Realizing, of course, that the stories in *Fierce Love* are specific to the experiences of black gay men, I still was left wondering what position the performers held on affinities

with other non-black gays and lesbians of color. There are no specific moments in the performance that directly address black lesbians and/or other non-black gays and lesbians of color. Instead, the
Pomos seem to indicate that the spectatorial process–for all audiences–involves precisely this dynamic of self-positionality. *Fierce
Love* forces viewers to locate their own positionality with the material staged. Not all black gay men, for instance, will choose to
identify with–or be included within–the representations available in
the performance.

Another scene that foregrounds audience positionality is more
risky in that it focuses on sex. In Eric Gupton's solo scene, "Good
Hands," the performer delivers a powerful erotic fantasy of two
black men getting off in the back room of a predominantly white
gay club. But first, Gupton observes the many forms of racism
directed at him by a parade of white men, all of whom signal to him
that he should "take his black ass home." But then–this is after all a
fantasy–a beautiful black man walks into the backroom and the two
black men proceed to get busy. Gupton's slow and sexy delivery
first details the man's body and then provides a scene-by-scene
account of their erotic play. The stranger's "good hands" bring
them both to orgasm, at once eroticizing sex between two men of
color and the safe sexual play they practice. This in and of itself is
enough to bring many of its spectators to the edge of their seats but
Gupton catches his breath and prepares us for the monologue's final
*coup de théâtre*. The stranger explains to him what is equally true
for many audiences of *Fierce Love*:

> You know the white boys get real nervous when they see the two
> of us in the same room together, some of the brothers do too, but
> I like you.

The stranger then offers a hot and safe sex scenario which ends the
scene. The stranger in the backroom is nothing less than yet another
Pomo Afro Homo–a black gay man who cares about his brothers,
eroticizes men of color, and recognizes the necessity of AIDS
awareness and practice. Like "Hot Horny and Healthy"–AIDS activist Phil Wilson's safe sex workshops for gay men of color–Gupton's "Good Hands" educates audiences in safer sexual practices,

eroticizes sex between men of color, and extends unexploitative representations of black gay sexuality.

Of all the scenes of *Fierce Love*, "Good Hands" usually solicits the most participatory response from the audience. Shouts like "go ahead, Eric" or "save me some of that loving" move the monologue from the limits of the stage to the lively exchange between performer and spectator, blurring the boundaries between the two. Such a shared sexual fantasy points to the power of the theatre to inform its audiences of both the pleasures and the dangers coinciding in the age of AIDS. That most of these shouts come from gay men of color only reinforces the power of the representation so seldom available in the theatre. After all, the triumph in this scene comes from Eric's incredible encounter with a man of color in a predominantly racist environment.

Oddly, many whites sometimes respond by applauding the gay men of color in the audience who are engaging the performance. In this regard, the spectacle on the stage is expanded to include gay men of color in the audience who are participating in the shared fantasy. The risk here, as in *Six Degrees*, is that the realities of gay men of color may be experienced by some whites as anecdotal fodder. Liberal whites, in this sense, get double for their money: an entertaining performance and an equally entertaining side show from the gay men of color in the audience. And yet it seems that this risk of appropriation is worth taking since the gay men of color–regardless of white voyeurism–have shared in a powerful transaction of support. Eric, the performing pomo, has bonded with a sexy pomoafrohomo in the backroom of a gay club, and gay men of color in the audience have bonded with Eric, a sexy pomoafrohomo, in the spotlight of a darkened stage.

In a later scene, Djola Bernard Branner presents the other side of the AIDS reality. "Silently Into the Night" recounts the frightening ordeal of a black man coping with the death of his friend Aman. The by now familiar devastation of AIDS is bypassed to focus on the maddening funeral service taken over by the homophobic relatives who arrive to discredit the dead. The preacher–"Six foot one and every inch a Christian as Aman was queer. If you knew Aman you know that was some serious faith"–annihilates the gay friends with his gay-bashing rhetoric. Aman's friends learn that ritual mourning takes many forms; they leave the family service defeated. Recognizing that Aman's relatives were mourning his gayness and not his death, the friends organize another memorial service, one that honors Aman's life and celebrates the community of gays and lesbians who knew and loved him.

*Fierce Love* ends with a Utopian vision brought on by a disillusioned black queer nationalist and the good advice of James Baldwin. In "Toward A Black Queer Rhythm Nation," a young black gay activist humorously journeys through urban gay life in search of a cause. Feeling oppressed by Queer Nation, he finds himself at old clone night at the Stud. At the bar, he hears the musical refrain of the opening prologue to *Fierce Love*'s "We Are." The voices signal the arrival of another black gay man—"we'd seen each other before but never spoke"—who hears the same voices calling. Together, they leave and head off to the Box, a funk and soul club frequented by San Francisco's queers of color. But on this night it has "snowed"; the club, the white boys, the DJ, and the music are all "tired." Once again they hear the melody of "We Are" and notice the only other black gay man on the dance floor. Suddenly, their world is transformed from the tired predictability of the "monochromatic crowd" into a glorious fantasy sequence of black gay visibility:

> BERNARD: I looked up at the DJ booth and saw Sylvester push that white girl out of the way.
> ERIC: Willi Smith and Patrick Kelly were up on stage, modeling the fiercest drag I'd ever seen.
> KID: And James Baldwin was behind the bar, pouring free drinks for himself and everybody else. . . James says, "My dear young boy, You are a Black Queer growing up in America. I think you've hit the jackpot! Work it my dear. Work It!"

Inspired by the lives of black gay men who have died of AIDS and Baldwin's insight, the three men leave the club together not for a *ménage à trois* but for a "totally transgressive" act—sharing their various experiences through conversation.

Much of the power of this scene is in its evocation of a black gay male history signaled by Sylvester, Kelly, Smith, and Baldwin. That three of these men died of AIDS at the height of their careers further suggests that the younger generation, represented by Kid, holds the responsibility for remembering their names and contributions. For black gay men in the audience (and others) not familiar with Willi Smith's pioneering achievements in men's fashion, the Pomos insist that they learn.[13] The Pomos recirculate the names of the dead to remind the living of the legacy of black gay male achievement. By putting the lives of black gay men in a historical context–in particular, the effects of AIDS–the Pomos offer their black gay spectators an unprecedented opportunity in the theatre to respond to the magical refrain of the "we are" prologue and join them in the process of performing all their lives. The fantasy of returning the dead to speak to the living is usurped only by the final powerful image of black gay men who are alive today speaking amongst themselves. Such fierce love is what the Pomos are all about.[14]

While *Fierce Love* has been nearly unanimously praised in reviews in gay and lesbian publications, alternative newspapers, and the straight establishment press–all who eagerly dub the show a "must see"–it has been virtually ignored by the black press. Moreover, the Pomo Afro Homos were turned down by the 1991 National Black Theatre Festival in North Carolina, further limiting the larger African American community's opportunities to view their show. "I think the struggle for us in the next decade is coming out at home," Brian Freeman admits (qtd. in Jamison, 102). Before any change in black gay invisibility is to be realized at "home," black heterosexuals need to hear the difficult questions that the Pomos ask in their performances.

The challenge is still there for white gay audiences as well. There is always the possibility that white gays and lesbians and well-meaning straight audiences will fall into the "Ouisa syndrome"–recasting the experiences of black gay men in order to placate their own liberal political views. Like Ouisa in *Six Degrees*, audiences might respond in the old imperialistic enterprise of cultural tourism or tokenist inclusionary politics. The challenge for white spectators remains to forego Ouisa's self-obsessing indulgence, where the encounter with difference is perceived as an "experience": a spectacle consumed at the expense, however well intended, of the black gay man. Such a racialized sexual discourse, commodifying and reinterpreting black gay sexuality, is at the heart of Guare's play and, more pertinently, of much of the discourse around AIDS and people of color. In *Six Degrees of Separation*, the phantasmatic circulation of this racialized sexual discourse which passed from Guare to Ouisa to Lincoln Center audiences rendered Paul's case nothing more than an anecdote of the lived experiences of David Hampton. In AIDS discourse around issues of people of color, as the Magic Johnson incident revealed, blackness and homosexuality are set against each other, obliterating the experiences of those living at the intersection of each. Gay men of color who have died of AIDS, who are living with AIDS, and who are struggling to survive amidst AIDS, have long engaged in a fight against this reality. When the Pomos claim that "we are an endangered species but our stories must be told" they are not simply asking to be included within a multicultural paradigm of canonicity. Instead, the Pomos are using the theatre as a means to initiate communication and debate; "we need to be able to argue with the white gay community, amongst ourselves and with the larger society," insists Freeman (qtd. in Barbe, 14).

Recent events have demonstrated how direct interventions in the arts against these prevelant mythologies have found themselves recontextualized to serve the agenda of the growing fundamentalist right. In the early months of 1992, Marlon Riggs became the latest target of the New Right extremists when his award-winning film, *Tongues Untied*, was used in an anti-National Endowment for the Arts ad produced by columnist Pat Buchanan in his campaign for the U.S. presidency. In an editorial in the *New York Times*, Riggs blames the Buchanan campaign for scapegoating and maligning gays and lesbians of color. In the mudslinging match between Buchanan and Bush, Riggs writes, "gay and lesbian Americans, particularly, those of color, have again become the mud" ("Meet"). Given such a climate predisposed to attack visible gay and lesbian artists of color, cultural critics championing such works need to reconsider the ways in which these works are discussed. In this sense, I join Kobena Mercer who has called for a critical discourse that historicizes the social forces that produce racial and sexual rhetorics of marginality.[15] It is out of this context that the work of the Pomo Afro Homos begins to reach its deeper significance. The Pomos enter into this political arena via the theatre to intervene against the growing denial of the lives of black gay men whose points of view are seen in contemporary U.S. culture as simultaneously obscene and invisible: the paradoxical spectacle propounded by popular discourse, enabling the unnecessary AIDS-related deaths of countless gays of color.[16]

## NOTES

1. *Fierce Love: Stories from Black Gay Life*, Brian Freeman with additional material by Eric Gupton and Bernard Branner, unpublished manuscript. All subsequent quotes are drawn from the unpublished manuscript. Thanks to Brian Freeman for sharing the performance script with me. I base my analysis of *Fierce Love* on this text and the various performances I attended in San Francisco, Santa Monica, and Seattle between March 1991 and January 1992.

2. See for instance: Jack Kroll, *Newsweek*, June 25, 1990; John Beaufort, *Christian Science Monitor*, June 26, 1990; David Patrick Stearns, *USA Today*, June 19, 1990; Melanie Kirkpatrick, *Wall Street Journal*, June 25, 1990; and David Richards, *Washington Post*, July 12, 1990.

3. See, for example, Alex Witchel, "The Life of Fakery and Delusion in John Guare's 'Six Degrees,'" *New York Times*, June 21, 1990, C17; Alex Witchel, "Impersonator Wants to Portray Still Others, This Time, Onstage," *New York Times*, July 31, 1990; and Joyce Walder's profile of David Hampton in *People*, March 18, 1991, pp. 99-100.

4. Imprisoned first in the New York state prison system and then later as Paul in the New York City theatre, David Hampton announced after seeing *Six Degrees* that he would pursue, like Sidney Poitier, a career in acting.

5. Moreover, it points to the limited roles for black men in plays written and produced by whites. Both James McDaniel and Courtney Vance, two of the most esteemed actors in the United States, played the role of Paul during the New York run. In London, where the play opened at the Royal Court Theatre in June 1992, Paul was played by the very talented Adrian Lester. I base my analysis on performances I viewed in New York and London with Vance and Lester cast as Paul.

6. On the concept of "African AIDS" as opposed to AIDS in Africa see Cindy Patton and Simon Watney.

7. See, for example, Clarence Page, pp. 15-18, and a follow-up discussion in Lindsey Grusen, "Black Politicians Discover AIDS," *New York Times*, March 9, 1992.

8. There is a horrible double irony in this limited scheme; on the one hand, when asserting a heterosexual identity, AIDS is disassociated from gay men and the usual media conflation of AIDS and homosexuality, yet on the other hand, Magic is immediately reconfigured in racial terms and the conflation of Africa and AIDS. Within this binary system Magic must fall into one of these misconceptions. Most problematic, those who are of African descent and homosexual are either rendered invisible, or if seen at all must be rendered as obscene.

9. *Advocate*, April 21, 1992. Some gay and lesbian activists have complained that the cover photo of Johnson obscures the full masthead which reads "The National Gay and Lesbian Newsmagazine."

10. For a detailed education on the art of the snap see *Tongues Untied* by Marlon Riggs, 1990.

11. If heterosexual blacks are shown to misappropriate the snap, white gay men are exposed for coopting the symbols of African American history. In "Red Bandanas" the Pomos angrily reclaim the red bandanas whose currency in gay male circles as a sexual code undermines its legacy and significance for African Americans. When worn in the right hip pocket, the red bandana means "fuck me" but the Pomos wear the red bandana around the neck which means that "I am remembering my granddad who owned it before I did."

12. This scene is also one of the funniest in performance. Freeman's repetition of the phrase points out the degrees of limitations of various non-black gay male spectators' subject positions through humor.

13. Willi Smith, who revolutionized the commercial fashion industry with his Willi Wear line–"I don't design clothes for the Queen but for the people who wave at her as she passes by"–was 39 when he died of AIDS in April 1987; Patrick Kelly, yet another exceptional fashion designer, died of AIDS in January 1990; and Sylvester, the grand diva of disco for well over ten years, died of AIDS in 1988.

14. *Fierce* is black slang for *fabulous*.

15. See Kobena Mercer, and also Alisa Solomon's insightful essay, "Art Attack: What do Plato and Pat Buchanan Have in Common?" *American Theatre* 9 (1992): 19-24.

16. Thanks to Yvonne Yarbro-Bejarano, Brian Freeman, Karen Shimakawa, Dorinne Kondo, and Douglas Swenson. This essay was written in the summer of 1992 with support from the University of Washington Graduate School Research Fund.

## WORKS CITED

Beebe, Barbara. "Pomo Afro Homos: Brian Freeman Talks About *Dark Fruit* and the State of the Black Gay Community." *B & G* 3.3 (1992): 11-14.

Broder, Michael. "High Risk, Low Priority: Society Turns a Double Blind Eye on AIDS in the Black Community." *BLK* 3.7 (1991): 7-14.

Clum, John. *Acting Gay: Male Homosexuality in Modern Drama.* New York: Columbia UP, 1992.

Corbin, Steven. "The Fire Baptism." *Frontiers*, June 19, 1992: 78.

Freeman, Brian; with additional material written by Eric Gupton and Djola Bernard Branner. *Fierce Love: Stories From Black Gay Life.* Copyright 1990. Unpublished manuscript.

Freeman, Brian. "Pomo Afro Homos Presents *Fierce Love*." *Out/Look* 14 (1991): 58-62.

Gomez, Jewelle, and Smith, Barbara. "Taking the Home Out of Homophobia: Black Lesbians Look in Their Own Backyards." *Out/Look* 8 (1990): 32-37.

Guare, John. *Six Degrees of Separation.* New York: Vintage Books, 1990.

Haile, Mark. "'It can happen to anybody. Even me, Magic Johnson.'" *BLK* 3.9 (1991): 20-25.

Jamison, Laura. "Queer Like Me." *Village Voice,* October 8, 1991: 101-102.

Johnson, Earvin. "Magic." Interview by Roger Brigham. *Advocate,* April 21, 1992: 34-39.

Mercer, Kobena. "Skin Head Sex Thing: Racial Difference and the Homoerotic Imaginary." *How Do I Look? Queer Film and Video.* Ed. Bad-Object Choices. Seattle: Bay Press, 1991.

Miller, Alan. E. "Young, Gifted, and Fierce." *BLK* 3.8 (1991): 9-13.

Page, Clarence. "Deathly Silence: Black Leaders and AIDS." *New Republic,* December 2, 1991: 15-18.

Patton, Cindy. *Inventing AIDS.* New York: Routledge, 1991.

Perry, David. "Black, Fierce, and Funny: New Performance Group Crafts Stories of Black Gay Life." *Advocate,* July 2, 1991: 86-87.

Rich, Frank. "A Guidebook to the Soul of a City in Confusion." *New York Times,* July 1, 1990: C1,7.

_____ . Review of John Guare's *Six Degrees of Separation. New York Times,* June 15, 1990: C1.

Riggs, Marlon. "Black Macho Revisited: Reflections of a Snap Queen." *Brother to Brother: New Writings by Black Gay Men.* Ed. Essex Hemphill. Boston: Alyson Publications, 1991.

_____ . "Meet the New Willie Horton." *New York Times,* March 6, 1992: A19.

Robinson, Amy. Review of Pomo Afro Homos' *Fierce Love. Theatre Journal* 44 (1992): 225-227.

Román, David. "Teatro Viva! Latino Performance, Sexuality, and the Politics of AIDS in Los Angeles." *Lesbian and Gay Issues in Hispanic Literature.* Ed. Emilie Bergmann and Paul Julian Smith. New York and London: Oxford UP, forthcoming.

Simmons, Ron. "Some Thoughts on the Challenges Facing Black Intellectuals." *Brother to Brother: New Writings by Black Gay Men.* Ed. Essex Hemphill. Boston: Alyson Publications: 1991.

Stewart, Charles. "Double Jeopardy: Black, Gay, (and invisible)." *New Republic,* December 2, 1991: 13-15.

Watney, Simon. "Missionary Positions: AIDS, 'Africa,' and Race." *Differences* 1.1 (1989): 83-100.

# A Visitation of Difference:
# Randall Kenan and Black Queer Theory

Robert McRuer, PhD (cand.)

*University of Illinois at Urbana-Champaign*

**SUMMARY.** This essay is a consideration of the position of "region" in queer theory, particularly black queer theory. Although only minimal analysis has been directed at black gay cultural production, most attention given to black gay cultural production has focussed predominantly on urban areas/communities re-presented in films such as *Tongues Untied* and *Paris Is Burning*. This paper employs Randall Kenan's novel *A Visitation of Spirits*, which focusses on a black gay youth growing up in the rural African-American community of Tims Creek, North Carolina, to consider what cultural work is done when queer desire turns up in such an apparently unlikely and inhospitable place. Examining how region plays a role in the construction of centers and margins, this article argues against always shuffling queer desire "safely" off to the big city, and considers what transformative cultural work can be done on the "margins" of the queer world.

"[I]n Randall Kenan's book you get a brilliant tormented homosexual, Horace, who commits suicide," Henry Louis Gates, Jr.,

Correspondence may be addressed to the author at: 208 English, 608 S. Wright St., Urbana, IL 61801.

[Haworth co-indexing entry note]: "A Visitation of Difference: Randall Kenan and Black Queer Theory." McRuer, Robert. Co-published simultaneously in the *Journal of Homosexuality* (The Haworth Press, Inc.) Vol. 26, No. 2/3, 1993, pp. 221-232; and *Critical Essays: Gay and Lesbian Writers of Color* (ed: Emmanuel S. Nelson) The Haworth Press, Inc., 1993, pp. 221-232. Multiple copies of this article/chapter may be purchased from The Haworth Document Delivery Center [1-800-3-HAWORTH; 9:00 a.m. - 5:00 p.m. (EST)].

explains in a recent interview in *Callaloo*. Gates praises Kenan's novel *A Visitation of Spirits*, but he is nonetheless cautious: "[Although the suicide] is just a way of registering some pretty tragic facts of history . . . I want Randall Kenan to, as it were, take Horace to the big city in his next novel" (454). The migration to "the big city" is a recurrent image in contemporary gay and lesbian literature, and I certainly don't want to hold Gates individually responsible for a casual prescription made in the context of an interview. Indeed, at this point, with so little written on contemporary black gay literature, the very fact that a prominent non-gay academic expresses familiarity with *A Visitation of Spirits* and other lesbian and gay works is significant and encouraging. Nonetheless, although my critique of Gates' prescription is by no means meant as a dismissal or a de-authorization of his ideas, I do want to take his comments as a point of departure for my own thoughts on Kenan's text, for I find the need to shuffle characters like Horace off to "the big city" symptomatic of a regional elision in queer theory generally. What Gates elides in his suggestion to Kenan is the fact that taking Horace *to* anywhere also entails taking him *from* somewhere; in this case, the unmentioned "somewhere" is the fictional Fundamentalist Christian, rural African-American community of Tims Creek, North Carolina. Not the most conducive atmosphere for the expression of queer desire, certainly. But as liberal gay and lesbian thought likes to remind us, "we are everywhere," and rather than conceding that "everywhere" *actually* means New York and San Francisco, I'm interested in what (perhaps more radical) cultural work can be done when that "everywhere" includes such an apparently marginal and inhospitable place.

*A Visitation of Spirits* is organized around two days in the life of the Cross family of Tims Creek, North Carolina: December 8, 1985, and April 29-30, 1984. The text moves back and forth between these two days, and each section heading further specifies the exact placement of events in time: e.g., "December 8, 1985; 8:45 A.M. . . . April 30, 1984; 1:15 A.M." (3, 66). This temporal precision gives each section of the novel the appearance of measurable, scientific "fact"; the events of *A Visitation of Spirits*, however, belie any easy distinction between "fact" and "fiction." Dissatisfied with his life, Horace Cross attempts to use a magic spell to transform himself into a bird. When the transformation fails, "spirits" and "demons" reveal themselves to Horace in order to lead him on a whirlwind, neo-Dickensian journey through his own life. Past, present, and future blur together as freely as "fact" and "fantasy" as Horace's journey progresses. Even Horace himself is confused as to whether what he is seeing is "real" or not. One of the demons attempts to explain: "Ghosts? Yeah, you might call them ghosts. Ghosts of the past. The presence of the present. The very stuff of which the future is made. This is the effluvium of souls that surround men daily" (73). The echoes here, of course, are of the humanistic, transformative experience of Ebenezer Scrooge; Horace, however, is not in a position to experience the same sort of happy ending in *A Visitation of Spirits*. In contrast to the rich and English gentleman of Dickens' tale, Horace, after observing the constraint and confusion that he has endured throughout his young life, does not undergo some humanistic "redemption," but instead, commits suicide. In the end, it is not Horace, the individual, but the position and the place in which he finds himself, which are in need of transformation.

Before examining the possible transformation of Tims Creek, North Carolina, though, I want to center my discussion by introducing Marcos Becquer's analysis of snapping and vogueing, the black gay discursive practices employed in Marlon Riggs' critically-acclaimed film *Tongues Untied*. "Vogueing," developed by black and Latino gay men in New York City, is a form of dance in which dancers imitate and implicitly critique "high-fashion" styles and poses, such as those depicted in *Vogue* magazine. "Snapping" is a gesture of pride and defiance used to "read," punctuate, or invalidate another's discourse. Since both discursive practices "emerge both from within and against the cultural and historical discourses operating around them" (8), Becquer is able to argue in "Snap!thology and Other Discursive Practices in *Tongues Untied*" that "*Tongues Untied* can confront and condemn the regime of sameness which alienates black gays from the black community, the white gay community, and discourse/representation in general" (14). Becquer's analysis thus foregrounds "difference" while nonetheless arguing for the connective, political importance of a revised, subverted, and subversive idea of "sameness," which he argues is "always already a part of difference as well as vice versa" (15).

Becquer's theory is particularly relevant when discussing the tremendous outpouring of urban and secular black gay cultural production represented in films such as *Tongues Untied* and *Paris Is Burning*. His examination of snapping as a discursive practice, for example, concludes that "the sequence on 'Snap!thology' [in *Tongues Untied*] depicts the snap precisely in its ability to overcome the discursive mechanisms which position black gays beneath both black heterosexuals and white gays" (9). Black gays are positioned here apart from and yet a part of, on the one hand, white gays, and on the other, black heterosexuals, and "the very binarism of sameness/difference" (15) is deconstructed. That is, snapping (and later in Becquer's article, vogueing) works as an empowering and signifying difference for black gays, but this signifying difference nonetheless forges connections with the groups it critiques. With this revised idea of "sameness" in mind, Becquer concludes, "*Tongues Untied* is not a separatist film" (15).

Becquer's analysis is grounded in what he calls "the new politics of identity" (7). He writes, "[B]y understanding identity as a construction the new politics of identity offers the hope of deconstructing the binarism of otherness which marks discursive alienation and domination by acknowledging that the other is always already a part of ourselves and vice-versa" (7). Yet although putting "sameness" back into "difference" forges connections and hence undermines, as Becquer argues, black homophobia and white gay racism, this theoretical move should not overshadow the simultaneous need to challenge continuously the "regime of sameness," even as that regime is reproduced *inside* the cultural category "black gay." For despite Becquer's best efforts, his article concludes with the inscription of a fairly monolithic, snapping and vogueing "black gay identity," singular (16). Although he begins the article decrying "the essentialism inherent in notions of *the* black subject or *the* gay sensibility" (7), Becquer himself subtly moves from plurality to singularity in his discussion of black gay identities: *Tongues Untied* is, at the beginning, "a condensed version of black gay (collective) experiences" (8), but has become, by the end, a celebration of "the emergence of a black gay difference that is unique" (15).

Of course, the failure to pluralize "identity" or "difference" as he approaches the end of his argument is a relatively minor short-coming in an otherwise brilliant analysis. Becquer's deconstructive moves are, after all, crucial, since they are made on behalf of "black gays" in the face of what are indeed hegemonic white gay or black heterosexual communities. I don't want to invalidate Becquer's argument; I simply want to suggest, following Ed Cohen, that "no matter how sensitively we go about it, 'identity politics' has great difficulty in affirming difference(s)" (76). Becquer's article, with its critique of white gay and black heterosexual hegemony, recognizes the difficulty of affirming difference, but it simultaneously works to affirm the "sameness" that is always already present within "difference." Cohen argues, however, with a nod to Diana Fuss, that "identity politics is predicated on denying the difference that is already there in 'the same'" (76). This predication ensures that *difference* is what is denied or repressed even when identity politics is based on sophisticated poststructuralist attempts such as Becquer's to move beyond the sameness/difference binarism.

Still, I want to extend rather than disarm Becquer's critique. By pushing his analysis further, I hope to create a space in which to consider black gay cultural production (and perhaps queer cultural production generally) *outside* an urban, secular arena. It was no accident that I used Becquer's analysis to "center" my own. Until now, perhaps inescapably, queer theory has predominantly "centered" on urban areas. John D'Emilio and Estelle B. Freedman explain that it was, initially, in American cities that a gay subculture flourished in the middle of the twentieth century (288). But this urban queer "center" might be productively understood as part of a complex array of "centers" and "margins," since both concepts, as Michael Bérubé argues, should be understood relationally (308-309). This would mean, of course, that while black gays are undeniably marginal to black heterosexuals and both heterosexual and gay whites, and hence, strategically positioned to disrupt and decenter heterosexual and white hegemony, centering our own theoretical energy on urban black gays will always produce other margins. And if, following Bérubé, "the contemporary de- or a-scription of 'margins' be taken . . . as a means for locating and empowering writers to do various kinds of cultural work" (308), then we might consider, before placing Kenan's Horace "safely" (or more "appropriately") in an urban, and presumably more "central," environment, just what black queer desire is doing in, or does to, rural North Carolina. Essex Hemphill's words, with their subtle threat/promise that black gays will transform *whatever* community they are in, seem appropriate to me here: "I ask you brother: Does your mama *really* know about you? Does she *really* know what I am? . . . I hope so, because *I am* coming home" (42).

Near the end of *A Visitation of Spirits*, Horace's voice is presented directly for the first time in a section called "Horace Thomas Cross: Confessions" (245-251). Almost every sentence of this section in which Horace meditates upon his own home and life in Tims Creek begins with the phrase "I remember": "I remember the first time I saw Granddaddy kill a chicken. I remember it, dirty-white and squawking, and Granddaddy putting it down on a stump" (245). Other vignettes are employed to supplement this depiction of life in rural North Carolina as Horace's "confessions" continue. It quickly becomes clear, however, that despite the hardships Horace has endured, this rural setting is not simply the site of "backwardness" or "repression"; like other communities in which black gay men find themselves, Tims Creek, North Carolina, is a site of struggle and possible transformation. Horace's own queer desire emerges both from within and against the Christian community around him:

> I remember the first picture I saw of a naked man. I remember feeling ashamed. It made me hard. . . . I remember church and praying. I remember revival meetings and the testifying of women who began to cry before the congregation and ended their plea of hardships and sorrow and faithfulness to the Lord with the request for those who knew the word of prayer to pray much for me. . . . Then I remember the day I realized that I was probably not going to go home to heaven, cause the rules were too hard for me to keep. . . . I remember me. (248, 251)

Immediately before this final sentence, Horace asserts "I was too weak" (251). And yet, his "I remember me," with its placement in a paragraph of its own at the very end of his confessions, overrides such an assertion of "weakness." The sentence "I remember me" solidifies the confessions that have preceded it as ineradicable parts of Horace's identity; despite his difference(s), the community of Tims Creek, North Carolina, has shaped Horace's identity, and his staunch refusal to relinquish the various parts of this identity suggests forcefully that it is the community, and not Horace, which is in need of transformation. Along these lines, Gates suggests, "One thing that a good deal of contemporary fiction that deals realistically with gay themes achieves, which I think is very important, is to desentimentalize the notion of 'community' as an unadulterated good" (454). And yet, although this seems to me precisely what Kenan does with the story of Horace in *A Visitation of Spirits*, Gates is uncomfortable enough with Horace's suicide to envision *another* community for Horace in "the big city." I'm concerned, however, that locating Horace where, presumably, a "black gay identity" is more developed and secure, not only reinstates the "regime of sameness" that Becquer condemns, but also discounts Kenan's own critique of that regime. Horace's "difference" from the heterosexual and Christian black community around him certainly desentimentalizes that community, but *A Visitation of Spirits* goes further than a simple validation or celebration of "difference." Kenan is aware of and engages the problems inherent in the opposition between sameness and difference. And because this engagement takes place in, of all places, Tims Creek, North Carolina, Kenan is able to take his engagement with that volatile binarism in a different direction from Becquer, suggesting more forcefully that "difference" is irreducible *in spite of* and *in the presence of* "sameness." As Gayatri Chakravorty Spivak writes, "Whatever . . . the advisability of attempting to 'identify' (with) the other as subject in order to know her, knowledge is made possible and is sustained by irreducible difference, not identity" (254).

Let me be more precise. *A Visitation of Spirits* is a veritable treatise on the unstable opposition between sameness and difference. Horace Cross, as a black gay teenager, always finds himself at the intersection of contradictory identities: in his own family, he is "black," but not "gay"; at the community theater where he works, he is openly "gay," while his "blackness" is rendered invisible, particularly by the production itself, which is about the history of the Cross family (the *white* Cross family) in North Carolina; with his "alternative" and white high school friends, he is neither

"black" nor "gay." Only with Gideon, another black, gay character, does Horace find a "niche," where he should "fit" exactly. But,
although their relationship is consummated, Horace and Gideon do
not embrace a "black gay identity" together, an identity with which
they subvert and expose the contradictions of the various communities of which they are constituents. Perhaps it is because Gideon is
comfortable with his sexual identity, and Horace is not. Perhaps it is
because Horace is tormented by religious questions and fears, and
Gideon is not. Whatever the reason, Horace is not Gideon, and
Gideon is not Horace. Eve Sedgwick's first axiom in *Epistemology
of the Closet* comes to mind here: "Under the rule that privileges
the most obvious: *People are different from each other*" (22). Sedgwick writes,

> A tiny number of inconceivably coarse axes of categorization
> have been painstakingly inscribed in current critical and politi-
> cal thought: gender, race, class, nationality, sexual orientation
> are pretty much the available distinctions. . . . But the sister or
> brother, the best friend, the classmate, the parent, the child, the
> lover, the ex-: our families, loves, and enmities alike, not to
> mention the strange relations of our work, play, and activism,
> prove that even people who share all or most of our own posi-
> tionings along these crude axes may still be different enough
> from us, and from each other, to seem like all but a different
> species. (22)

Becquer need not, I think, be situated in opposition to Sedgwick
here; Sedgwick's axiom does not, after all, eradicate the political,
connective importance of "sameness." With deference to Becquer,
sameness is still always already a part of difference, and vice versa.
But in *A Visitation of Spirits*, this is precisely what Horace is not in
a position to recognize. In none of the complex identificatory locations in which Horace finds himself is he able to be comfortable
with "sameness," let alone use some subverted/subversive idea of
"sameness" to forge alliances with groups he nonetheless wishes to
critique. The workings of power in each of the communities of
which Horace is a part ensure that none of these communities are
comfortable with "difference" in spite of and in the presence of
"sameness," and this compulsion to be "the same," even as that

compulsion is reproduced within the cultural category "black gay," invalidates any of Horace's attempts to come to terms with his own circulation around the binarism of sameness/difference. "You black, ain't you?" Horace's aunt asks him (186). One of Horace's lovers from the theater taunts him, "Faggot. . . . What's the matter? Don't like to be called what you are?" (225). Even Gideon, in the heat of an argument, says to Horace, "But remember, black boy, you heard it here first: You're a faggot, Horace. . . . At least I know what I am" (164). In each of these confrontations, it's not that the labels are wholly inappropriate for Horace, it's just that every question of identity in *A Visitation of Spirits* needs to be followed by a "yes, but. . . ." Judith Butler's comments are particularly relevant to Horace's situation here: "The prospect of *being* anything . . . seems to be more than a simple injunction to become who or what I already am" (13).

In this context, Horace's suicide can be seen as an apt re-presentation of the violence involved in the attempt "[t]o alienate conclusively, *definitionally*, from anyone on any theoretical ground the authority to describe and name their own sexual desire" (Sedgwick 26), or indeed, any component of their own identity. That *A Visitation of Spirits* appeared in the same year (1989) that right-wing religious and political leaders attempted to suppress the findings of the Report of the Secretary [of Health and Human Services'] Task Force on Youth Suicide, which claimed that gay teenagers account for thirty percent of all teenage suicides (cf. Ruta 12-14), only underscores the urgency of re-presenting the compulsion toward sameness *as* violence. Horace's suicide is detailed in stark, scientific (and hence, "real") prose, and is juxtaposed to the "fantastic" events in this postmodern, magic realist text. The "realness" of the suicide moves the theoretical opposition "Is it Real?"/"Is it Fantasy?" to a more urgent level, and this violent conclusion to Horace's confusing circulation around categories of sameness and difference should emphasize the irreducibility of "difference" for black queer theory, and indeed, for queer theory in general.

Immediately after the suicide in *A Visitation of Spirits*, the question of what queer desire (and its violent extermination) is doing in and to rural North Carolina is foregrounded. As the novel concludes, the narration shifts to second person in a nostalgic section called "Requiem for Tobacco":

> You remember, though perhaps you don't, that once upon a time men harvested tobacco by hand. There was a time when folk were bound together in a community, as one, and helped one person this day and that day another, and another the next, to see that everyone got his tobacco crop in the barn each week, and that it was fired and cured and taken to a packhouse to be graded and eventually sent to market. But this was once upon a time. (254)

The section continues, lamenting the tragic loss of this idyllic way of life. And yet, this section is already and inescapably in dialogue with the suicide that immediately precedes it; because of this dialogue, the "time when folk were bound together in a community, as one," is exposed even as it is being constructed. The mythical, pastoral wholeness of this "community" is ripped apart as surely as "[t]he bullet did break the skin of his forehead, pierce the cranium, slice through the cortex and cerebellum, irreparably bruising the cerebrum and medulla oblongata, and emerge from the back of the skull, all with a wet and lightning crack. This did happen" (253). Bakhtin reminds us that "sexuality is almost always incorporated into the idyll only in sublimated form" (226). Kenan's juxtaposition here of idyll and suicide foregrounds the murderous consequences of such a sublimation. In the end, Horace's taboo desire transforms this community on the margins of the queer world. Kenan's shift to second-person narration further emphasizes this transformation: although "you remember" what this community was like, you should not, after *A Visitation of Spirits*, be able to consider this or any community without a queer sense that something is amiss.

"The task of queer social theory," Michael Warner argues, "must be to confront the default heteronormativity of modern culture with its worst nightmare, a queer planet" (16). Of course, such a queer planet will ultimately infiltrate more places than New York and San Francisco. Indeed, the term "queer" should suggest that this desire will continue to turn up and transform even the most apparently "inappropriate" places. To Gates' credit, he provides a hearty endorsement on the back cover of *Let the Dead Bury Their Dead and Other Stories*, Kenan's most recent work. In this collection, not surprisingly, Kenan does not hustle Horace off to New York City. There is still too much cultural work to be done in Tims Creek, North Carolina, where (as elsewhere) "[n]othing like talk of crimes against nature gets people all riled up and speculating and conjecturing and postulating . . ." (19). Although no one in *Let the Dead Bury Their Dead* is reducible to cultural categories such as "black," "gay," or "black gay," queer desire (in its many different manifestations or "visitations") permeates the collection. Michael Bérubé, writing about Melvin Tolson, describes Tolson as "an African-American literary version of the maroon, the escaped slave living on the frontier, imperialism's margin, raiding the nearest plantation periodically for supplies and planning the long-term offensive in the meantime" (145). Kenan, likewise, explains in one story from *Let the Dead Bury Their Dead* that the town of Tims Creek was founded by "the Former Maroon Society" (271), a community of ex-slaves who lived on the "margins" but constantly worked to pilfer and disrupt the hegemonic white "center." Like these fictional forebears, Kenan is engaging and disruptive precisely in his own refusal to capitulate to already-delimited notions of what is "central" and what is "marginal."

## WORKS CITED

Bakhtin, Mikhail M. *The Dialogic Imagination.* Trans. Caryl Emerson and Michael Holquist. Ed. Michael Holquist. Austin: U of Texas P, 1981.

Becquer, Marcos. "Snap!thology and Other Discursive Practices in *Tongues Untied.*" *Wide Angle* 13.2 (April 1991): 6-17.

Bérubé, Michael. *Marginal Forces/Cultural Centers: Tolson, Pynchon and the Politics of the Canon.* Ithaca and London: Cornell UP, 1992.

Butler, Judith. "Imitation and Gender Insubordination." Fuss 13-31.

Cohen, Ed. "Who Are 'We'? Gay 'Identity' as Political (E)motion (A) Theoretical Rumination." Fuss 71-92.

D'Emilio, John, and Estelle B. Freedman. *Intimate Matters: A History of Sexuality in America.* New York: Harper and Row, 1988.

Fuss, Diana, ed. *Inside/Out: Lesbian Theories, Gay Theories.* New York and London: Routledge, 1991.

Gates, Henry Louis, Jr. Interview. By Charles H. Rowell. *Callaloo* 14.2 (Spring 1991): 444-463.

Hemphill, Essex. *Ceremonies*. New York: Penguin-Plume, 1992.

Kenan, Randall. *Let the Dead Bury Their Dead and Other Stories*. New York: Harcourt, 1992.

_____ . *A Visitation of Spirits*. New York: Anchor-Doubleday, 1989.

Ruta, Suzanne. "On why gay teenagers are committing suicide." *Wigwag* (March 1990): 12-14.

Sedgwick, Eve Kosofsky. *Epistemology of the Closet*. Berkeley: U of California P, 1990.

Spivak, Gayatri Chakravorty. *In Other Worlds: Essays in Cultural Politics*. New York and London: Routledge, 1988.

Warner, Michael. "Introduction: Fear of a Queer Planet." *Social Text* 9.4 (Fall 1991): 5-17.

# Notes on Contributors

Marylynne DIGGS is a doctoral candidate in English at the University of Oregon at Eugene. She is currently completing a dissertation titled "Sexual Science, Resistance, and the Discourse of Identity: Re-presenting Homosexuality in American Literature."

Alice Y. HOM is a PhD graduate student in the History Department at Claremont Graduate School. She has published articles in *Amerasia Journal*, *Phoenix Rising*, and *Contemporary Lesbian Writers of the United States*.

Cheryl KADER, a doctoral candidate in English at the University of Wisconsin at Milwaukee, is currently completing a dissertation on feminist critical theory. She is Assistant Professor of Women's Studies at Beloit College.

AnnLouise KEATING, Assistant Professor of English and Women Studies at Eastern New Mexico University, is working on a book-length study that investigates issues of (self-)representation and subjecthood in the works of Anzaldúa, Allen, and Lorde.

Ming-Yuen S. MA was born in Buffalo, New York, and grew up in Hong Kong. Recipient of an undergraduate degree in art history from Columbia University, he is now a graduate student at the California Institute of the Arts.

Martin F. MANALANSAN IV is a doctoral candidate in anthropology at the University of Rochester. He is completing a dissertation titled "Ethnicity, Sexuality, and AIDS: 'Gay' Filipino/Filipino-Americans in New York City."

Robert McRUER is a doctoral candidate in English at the University of Illinois campus at Urbana-Champaign. He is writing a dissertation on gay/lesbian literature of the 1980s.

Ricardo L. ORTIZ received his doctorate in English from the University of California at Los Angeles in 1992. He is Assistant Professor at San Jose State University, where his teaching and research interests include eighteenth-century British literature, critical theory, and gay and lesbian studies.

Alden REIMONENQ, recipient of a doctorate in English from Purdue University, is Associate Professor at Saint Mary's College of California. He is currently at work on a bio-critical volume on Countee Cullen.

David ROMÁN holds a doctorate in comparative literature from the University of Wisconsin at Madison. He is Assistant Professor of English at the University of Pennsylvania, where he is completing a book-length study of the theatre of AIDS. His articles have appeared in a number of journals and books.

Lou ROSENBERG is a doctoral candidate at the Claremont Graduate School. She is writing a dissertation titled "Delight and Construct: Theatrical Self-Reflexivity in the Early and Postmodern Periods."

Shelton WALDREP is a doctoral candidate in English at Duke University and Coordinator for the *Lesbian and Gay Studies Newsletter,* a publication of the Gay and Lesbian Caucus for the Modern Language Association.

Gregory WOODS was born in Egypt, grew up in Ghana, and currently teaches in the Department of English and Communication Studies at Nottingham Trent University, England. He is the author of *Articulate Flesh: Male Homo-Eroticism in Modern Poetry* (1987) and of a volume of poems, *We Have the Melon* (1992).

# Index

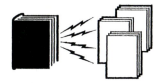

# Haworth
# DOCUMENT DELIVERY
## SERVICE
### and Local Photocopying Royalty Payment Form

This new service provides (a) a single-article order form for any article from a Haworth journal and (b) a convenient royalty payment form for local photocopying (not applicable to photocopies intended for resale).

- *Time Saving:* No running around from library to library to find a specific article.
- *Cost Effective:* All costs are kept down to a minimum.
- *Fast Delivery:* Choose from several options, including same-day FAX.
- *No Copyright Hassles:* You will be supplied by the original publisher.
- *Easy Payment:* Choose from several easy payment methods.

*Open Accounts Welcome for . . .*
- Library Interlibrary Loan Departments
- Library Network/Consortia Wishing to Provide Single-Article Services
- Indexing/Abstracting Services with Single Article Provision Services
- Document Provision Brokers and Freelance Information Service Providers

### MAIL or *FAX* THIS ENTIRE ORDER FORM TO:

Attn: **Marianne Arnold**
Haworth Document Delivery Service
The Haworth Press, Inc.
10 Alice Street
Binghamton, NY 13904-1580

or FAX: (607) 722-1424
or CALL: 1-800-3-HAWORTH
(1-800-342-9678; 9am-5pm EST)

PLEASE SEND ME PHOTOCOPIES OF THE FOLLOWING SINGLE ARTICLES:
1) Journal Title: _____
   Vol/Issue/Year: _____ Starting & Ending Pages: _____
   Article Title: _____

2) Journal Title: _____
   Vol/Issue/Year: _____ Starting & Ending Pages: _____
   Article Title: _____

3) Journal Title: _____
   Vol/Issue/Year: _____ Starting & Ending Pages: _____
   Article Title: _____

4) Journal Title: _____
   Vol/Issue/Year: _____ Starting & Ending Pages: _____
   Article Title: _____

**(See other side for Costs and Payment Information)**

*COSTS:* Please figure your cost to order quality copies of an article.

1. Set-up charge per article: $8.00
    ($8.00 × number of separate articles) _____

2. Photocopying charge for each article:

    1-10 pages: $1.00 _____

    11-19 pages: $3.00 _____

    20-29 pages: $5.00 _____

    30+ pages: $2.00/10 pages _____

3. Flexicover (optional): $2.00/article _____

4. Postage & Handling: US: $1.00 for the first article/

    $.50 each additional article _____

    Federal Express: $25.00 _____

    Outside US: $2.00 for first article/

    $.50 each additional article _____

5. Same-day FAX service: $.35 per page _____

6. Local Photocopying Royalty Payment: should you wish to copy the article yourself. Not intended for photocopies made for resale. $1.50 per article per copy
(i.e. 10 articles x $1.50 each = $15.00) _____

GRAND TOTAL: _____

*METHOD OF PAYMENT:* (please check one)

❑ Check enclosed  ❑ Please ship and bill. PO # _____

(sorry we can ship and bill to bookstores only! All others must pre-pay)

❑ Charge to my credit card: ❑ Visa; ❑ MasterCard; ❑ American Express;

Account Number:_____ Expiration date:_____

Signature: X_____ Name: _____

Institution: _____ Address: _____

City: _____ State: _____ Zip:_____

Phone Number: _____ FAX Number: _____

## MAIL or *FAX* THIS ENTIRE ORDER FORM TO:

Attn: **Marianne Arnold**
Haworth Document Delivery Service
The Haworth Press, Inc.
10 Alice Street
Binghamton, NY 13904-1580

or FAX: (607) 722-1424
or CALL: 1-800-3-HAWORTH
(1-800-342-9678; 9am-5pm EST)